I0725505

TESTIMONIALS

Enthusiastic Reader
Sherry Frazier, Book Publicist
I lived in London during the height of IRA activity. I never understood the Irish perspective until I read Stephen Archer's novels. The rich characters and the war they fought from the soul of ancestors for the future of their Ireland will remain in my heart forever.

ARC Book Review of *Fortunes: The Irish Clabs Book Six*
Dan Horwood
I just finished book six, and I enjoyed it very much. It's not like me to spend all day reading a book, but that's what happened to my last two days. I found that I couldn't put it down. And now I'm anxious to get into book seven. Please make it available as soon as possible.

Historical Fiction Company
Review of Revolution: *The Irish Clans, Book Five*
Complete review in the back testimonials section.
Mr. Archer does a remarkable job at offering us well-rounded, passionate characters in extraordinary circumstances. This book is alive with action and lush detail, giving the reader an Irish history lesson wrapped in an intense and captivating story. This is drama to the ultimate level. It has it all—history, adventure, intrigue, war, passion, love, escape, betrayal, sorrow, pain—all the elements which connect us all as humans. This engrossing book is a voice speaking from the past and linking history to the possibilities of myths and the promises of the future.

The Irish Clans

This is an epic story immersed in the tumultuous Irish revolutionary period of 1915 through 1923, while the world is embroiled in the Great War and its aftermath. The once mighty McCarthy and O'Donnell Clans, overthrown in ancient times, are not extinct. They are linked on two continents by a medieval pact entwining military history and religious mythology. Divine intervention plays a pivotal role in unearthing the secrets of the Clans' treasure and heroic exploits. The patriotism and passion of Celtic heritage lies at the heart of this intriguing story.

A tragedy at sea sets in motion the search for life's true treasures, both in 1915 Ireland, when the funeral of Fenian Rossa fans the flames of revolution, and in America, where the clans begin a journey toward their destiny in *Searchers*, the first book of the series.
Published March 2016

The mysteries of an ancient Clans Pact deepen beneath the horrors of WWI as Irish Rebels march toward revolution in *Entente*, the second book in the series.
Published May 2017

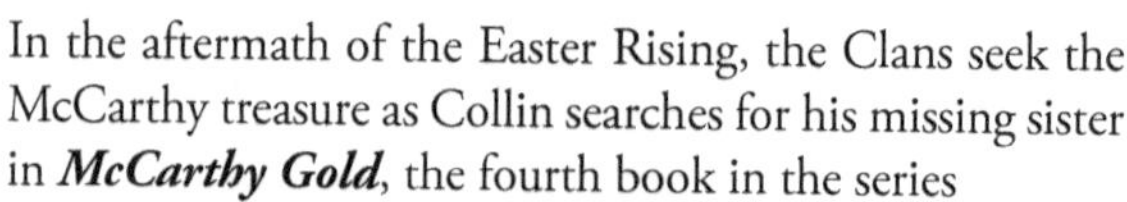

Irish Republican martyrs rise against overpowering British forces to spark the revolution in the 1916 Easter Rising, while the Clans search for unity and treasure to honor the Clans Pact of their ancestors in *Rising* the third book in the series.
Published January 2019

In the aftermath of the Easter Rising, the Clans seek the McCarthy treasure as Collin searches for his missing sister in *McCarthy Gold*, the fourth book in the series
Published January 2020

While fighting for Irish freedom, the McCarthys suffer brutal consequences of the merciless British oppression in the early years of the War of Independence in ***Revolution***, the fifth book in the series
Published March 2022

The mysteries of the O'Donnell Clan are explored in ***Fortunes***, the sixth book in the series, set in the last year of the Irish Revolution's War of Independence upheaval, leading to the Anglo-Irish Treaty of 1921.
Published September 2023

Future Books in the Series

The Clans, fractured at the start of the Irish Civil War in 1922, follow the ancient clues in an attempt to recover the O'Donnell Treasure they have lost, in ***Asunder***, the seventh book in the series.

The Clans, while supporting the Irish Civil War in 1922-1923, seek to unravel and unearth an ancient religious mystery that has confounded civilization for centuries in ***Revelation***, the eighth and final book in the series.

Fortunes

The Irish Clans

Book Six in the Series

Stephen Finlay Archer

Manzanita Writers Press
San Andreas, California

Fortunes: The Irish Clans
Book Six in the Series

Copyright © 2023 by Stephen Finlay Archer
All rights reserved.No part of this book may be reproduced, scanned, or distributed in any printed or electronic form without permission. Please do not participate in or encourage piracy of copyrighted materials in violation of the author's rights. Purchase only authorized editions. For information, contact Manzanita Writers Press.

ISBN 978-1-952314-05-6
Library of Congress Control Number: 2023910589

Publisher: Manzanita Writers Press
    manzapress.com
    manzanitawp@gmail.com
    PO Box 215, San Andreas, CA 95249

Cover Design: Lilia Lalova
Book Layout Design: Joyce Dedini-Runnells
Fortunes Book Six cover credits:
    Front cover: *Customs House in Flames,* Painting by Norman Teeling
    Back cover: *Flooren's Journal* by Stephen Archer
        The Penitential Beds, Painting by Sir. John Lavery
Searchers: Book One - Front cover:
    The Sinking of the Lusitania, Painting Courtesy of the Everett Collection
Entente: Book Two - Front cover:
    Canadians at Ypres, The Belgian Front 1915, Painting by William Barnes Wollen,
    Courtesy of the Princess Patricia's Canadian Light Infantry Museum
Rising: Book Three - Front cover:
    Montage of the Irish Easter Rising 1916, Painting by Norman Teeling
McCarthy Gold: Book Four - Front cover:
    The Money Diggers, Painting by John Quidor, Courtesy of the Brooklyn Museum
Revolution: Book Five - Front cover:
    Roadside Ambush, Painting by Martin McGrinder
Fortunes Book Six - Front cover:
    Front cover: *Customs House in Flames,* Painting by Norman Teeling
Asunder: Book Seven - Front cover:
    Montage of the Irish Civil War, Painting by Norman Teeling
Revelation: Book Eight - Front cover:
    Iona Abbey, Painting by Reverend John Butterfield
Author photo: Kathy Archer

This is a work of fiction. Any resemblance of my fictional characters to real persons, living or dead, is purely coincidental. The depiction of historical persons in these novels is not coincidental, and to the best of my knowledge, is accurate to events and their character in life. Some historical aspects may be augmented or adjusted for dramatic purposes.

INSPIRATION

"He was an Irish patriot, true and fearless."

Quote from Winston Churchill,
about Michael Collins, once his implacable enemy

DEDICATION

I dedicate this novel to the men and women who fought for freedom from the British in the Irish War of Independence 1919–1921. Leaders Michael Collins, militarily, and Eamon de Valera, politically, caused unrest in Ireland with their Gaelic guerrilla warfare tactics. As a result, England requested a cease-fire in July 1921.

Michael Collins and Arthur Griffith, the founder of Sinn Féin and one of the fathers of the Irish Free State, knew that the British would never give up their economic stronghold in Ireland. Foreign Secretary Winston Churchill threatened annihilation if the Irish did not accept British retention of Northern Ireland.

So, the Anglo-Irish Treaty in December 1921 was signed, separating Northern Ireland and creating the new Free State, which was to become the Republic of Ireland.

De Valera and about half of the freedom Republicans rejected this compromise thereby setting off a Civil War in Ireland from 1922–1923.

CONTENTS

Contents

Chapter One
Epistle

Sunday, November 28, 1920
Temple Residence Ruins, Dublin

As the waters bubbled up into a hellhole beneath the plowed-under Temple house, the putrid air was running out. Tadgh clutched a trembling Morgan to him, burying her head against his breast so she wouldn't see the end. Her arms wrapped around his waist and her terror augmented his dread. He could hardly breathe.

Tadgh fought back his guilt over dragging his loving wife into this deadly adventure. He could not have known that an underground dam would collapse, causing the long-buried branch of the River Liffey to drown out their lives. With the storm raging above them in Dublin for days, he should not have risked their lives.

His eyes darted back and forth in the gloom, a fading flicker barely emanating from their dying lantern. Their crushed-rubble underground tomb was what remained of the Temple residence demolished into the ground centuries before to make room for new buildings above. The immovable debris was only three feet above them where they crouched and only two feet high at a chimney twenty feet ahead of them.

Tadgh still sought a way out of their predicament as his thoughts raced, the way a dying man's life flashes before his eyes at the instant of mortality. They had just found marvelous and intriguing artifacts in the buried Temple, and mysteriously, a Jonathan Swift secret study. In their hurry to avoid the rising waters, they had stuffed these precious documents into the box on Swift's desk. Morgan had brought it with them as they fought their way up through the surging waterfall that now completely flooded the underground sanctuary below them. Did the papers contain clues to the whereabouts of Morgan's family treasure that they sought, or would the contents reveal other secrets that could be even more valuable? They would never know. They had no time to read the documents, even if they could somehow see them in the darkness. Perhaps after they were dead and the waters receded, when Jack and Deirdre would come and retrieve their bodies, some vestiges of these clues would remain intact, and Morgan's brother Collin could continue the search on behalf of the clans.

And then there was Deirdre's bodyguard and cook, Derek, an enigma. Why had he brought a gun on this hunt, and what were the two of them cooking up? What secrets did they harbor?

Tadgh agonized about what would become of his brother Aidan, and the freedom fighter Michael Collins. What would happen to the rest of the Republican warriors in their fight to the death for Irish independence in his beloved Ireland? Perhaps in the afterlife, he would find out. It pained him that he would not be able to battle for Ireland's freedom from heaven, if indeed that was where he was bound.

A rat scurried out from behind the bedpost and headed for the chimney, its beady eyes glowing in the failing light. Tadgh stopped and watched it wriggle off to the left of the chimney rubble, vanishing from sight. The creature did not reappear.

Tadgh gently unwrapped Morgan from his body, kissed her forehead, and said, "Wait here, *aroon*."

Morgan reached out, crying, "Don't leave me."

Derek slid sideways and took Morgan's hand. "What is it, Tadgh?"

"I don't know. Maybe nothing. Take care of Morgan. I'll be right back." Grabbing the ancient cutlass they'd found in Temple's iron chest, Tadgh crept forward on his knees toward the chimney. When he reached a mangle bed frame, he twisted himself through the obstacle. Cutlass in hand, he crawled forward on his belly.

With the house debris scraping his shoulders and his way blocked ahead, he called out, "Get ready to pull me out, Derek."

Tadgh squinted in the dim lantern light. The floor slanted upwards to where it was attached to the chimney. The vertical space of the crypt ahead of him was barely eighteen inches. Beside the chimney rubble, he saw a low section of wall that looked like dirt debris. A rat's head poked out from a hole in the wall and then disappeared. That hole had to lead somewhere. "Block the light, Derek."

Instead of hooding the fading lantern, Derek turned it down, but it extinguished, plunging the space into total blackness.

Morgan screamed, "Tadgh!"

Tadgh yelled, "Derek! Are you deaf? I said turn it down, not off!"

"Sorry, Tadgh. It's low on kerosene."

"Damn, lad." Tadgh thought he could see a faint light where the rat had been. "Morgan, I'll be right back."

Could their luck have changed? Maybe he was hallucinating. At the end of his reach, he repeatedly thrust the rusted weapon into the dirt near the spot targeted. He hit what seemed like rock debris and worked at clearing it until his arm ached. Then a breakthrough—the cutlass sank into the dirt to the hilt. He continued plunging, pushing the soil ahead, carving out a small opening. Tadgh smelled moist air blowing in from the other side. A dim light gleamed. What was on the other side.

He turned his head to call out. "Derek, I'm stuck. Turn the lantern back on and pull me back. I've found a way through."

Derek found Tadgh's ankles in the darkness and pulled him, careful to allow him to snake back through the bed frame.

Morgan gave a whoop. Removing the lantern chimney and feeling for the wick in the dark, she tried to restart the lantern. The heads of the matches she had in her pocket felt damp. The first match head broke off when she struck it on a dry beam just above her head. "The lantern won't light. I've got two matches left," she cried. She put them in the only place she knew was dry and warm, high up between her waist shirt and bosom, and rubbed them down.

Derek held the lantern, ensuring the wick was dry, and Morgan struck the next match on a nearby piece of metal she found. It fizzled and died without lighting. When she struck the last match, she cupped it and blew on it as it sparked. Its wood caught fire, and Derek quickly put the lantern wick to it before it could go out. It caught, and they were bathed in a faint glow.

Tadgh embraced Morgan and urged her to keep the lantern lit. He noticed the floor was awash with incoming water. It would soon flood the hole he'd made. "Help me move the bed frame, Derek."

First, they had to remove some debris. That took several minutes of shuffling on their knees. Even then, they could only force the bed frame a foot out of the way.

Tadgh pushed himself forward, his head now closer to the small opening. It took time thrusting with the cutlass and finally pushing with his hands to widen the two-foot-deep hole to crawl-space size.

"We should be able to squeeze through this hole," Tadgh said as he shimmied back through the tangled debris. He found it was easier this time.

Morgan peered at the narrow opening. Seeing the difficulty Tadgh was having, the image of the little boy trapped in the *Lusitania* stairs and who subsequently died on the boat deck flooded her mind. She cried, "I can't go through that."

We've got to go now, aroon," Tadgh urged. "I will crawl backward, and you can come after me face first. We will hold hands, and I will pull you through. You are smaller than I am. I know you can fit."

"*No, Tadgh! I can't!* It's like the *Lusitania* below decks."

"Forget the past. I promise I will get you through this. Just close your eyes and think of me holding you."

Tadgh tugged at Derek's collar and whispered, "Push her forward if she stalls." The cook nodded.

"Here we go now, lass." Tadgh held firmly to Morgan's hands, pulling her towards the chimney. She resisted briefly, then acquiesced.

His shirt caught on debris above him as he scrambled backward, and his feet hit the bedpost. This was harder to navigate while he was holding onto Morgan. He couldn't let go. "You need to let me come toward you a little, Morgan."

Morgan's voice quavered, "Are you trapped, Tadgh?"

"No, aroon." Tadgh pushed her arms back and wriggled forward, pushing his chest down, which cleared the snag. His shirtfront was wet. Slipping sideways to miss the bed frame, he resumed pulling her with him and said, "Let's keep going."

His feet found the hole he had opened, and he pushed back, crablike, elbows down. He was surprised that his legs started to drop as his knees passed the opening. How deep was the floor of the new sanctuary? He would have to drop down a distance.

We're almost there now, my love. I want you to suck in your tummy and hold your breath for a few seconds."

Focusing on holding Morgan's arms, he crawled backward. When his waist cleared the hole, he slid out, losing his grip on Morgan, and fell back several feet to the ground.

Morgan was terrified. "Tadgh! Help me! I'm stuck."

Tadgh reached up towards the opening and grasped her arms. "I've got you." He pulled her forward, and Morgan slid out, causing both to tumble and lie there, panting.

Tadgh held her. "Good girl. You made it."

The metal box appeared at the opening. Tadgh heard Derek's voice. "Take this before its contents get wet." Tadgh jumped up and grasped the edge of the box.

A minute later, they all stood in another underground tunnel about six feet high. With timber beam supports overhead, it ran perpendicular to the direction they'd been crawling. Tadgh could see a bare light bulb hanging from one of the beams a considerable distance away. Moisture had seeped through the tunnel walls making the dirt floor spongy but not muddy. It would be flooded soon enough.

"What is this place?" Derek asked.

Tadgh knew what it was—Michael's escape tunnel. He thought the rebels hadn't used it yet. Someone's been busy digging tunnels under Dublin's streets," Tadgh answered. I'm very familiar with the concept from my recent stay in one of the city's finest institutions. We're just damned lucky that they put one on this spot."

Morgan murmured weakly, "Divine intervention, I'd say, more than luck. Which direction, now?"

Seeing his wife shaking, Tadgh put his arm around her. "This way." Leading her farther to the right, he had a good idea where it would end up.

The tunnel took a left turn. Farther on, they came to the end of the tunnel where a wooden set of stairs went up to a landing and a locked door. Tadgh pounded on the door with his fist.

No response. He waited, ear against the wood, then banged at it again. Nothing.

Then he heard the sound of a gun cocking on the other side of the door and a voice saying, "Who goes there?"

It was a familiar voice. Tadgh responded, "Just a long-lost school chum, Mick, and fellow wanderers." As he had suspected, the tunnel led them right back to Michael Collins' intelligence control center bunker, right beneath Number Three Crow Street.

The door flew open. Michael Collins lowered his revolver. "How in God's name did you get in here, Tadgh McCarthy? I didn't tell you about this escape tunnel. And with your fine wife, too. You look like the mouse that the cat dragged in. Come on in."

Morgan smiled despite her wretched condition. "You have no idea how apt your analogy is, Michael. I am the mouse, and Tadgh, the cat. But he dragged me out, not in."

Collins stroked his chin, looking perplexed.

Tadgh stuck the cutlass into the wood floor. "Me and me maties just stopped by on a whim, Mick," he grinned. "A long story as to how we got in here, so it is."

Michael looked at his watch. "I've got time."

"I'll fill you in later, Mick. Right now, we need to find our friends. I'm sure they're worried."

Derek stepped forward and extended a hand. "Michael Collins, sir. I am honored to meet you. We applaud your commitment to free our country."

Michael looked at Tadgh, who nodded at him as if to say the man passed muster, and he shook the cook's hand. "You never saw me here, understood?"

Derek nodded. "Understood, Sir."

Michael turned to Tadgh. "You seem fit now. I need you to go home. You'll find a surprise there."

"What surprise?"

"Ask Aidan."

The adventurers had been gone six hours. Jack came up from the stairs into the pantry, looking stricken. "They could not have survived, Deirdre. The storage room and lower stairs are flooded. The entire subterranean tunnel of the Liffey is filled to overflowing, and the water is less than ten feet below us now."

Deirdre had never seen this much rain fall in such a short period and feared the worst. To calm Jack down, she told him, "Maybe they found another way out. All that water must go somewhere. Back into the Liffey downstream or all the way to Irishtown Bay."

"If you'd seen the torrent when the tunnel was just half-full, you'd know that no one could have survived being dragged downstream. And the water was near freezing," she shivered. "I shouldn't have let them go on that wild goose chase, Jack."

"Believe me. You can't stop Tadgh and Morgan when their minds are made up."

"I could have and should have, Jack."

"Morgan was brave to go on this dangerous search after being trapped by water on our dying *Lusitania*. She must have been terrified in the end." He shuddered and started to sob. "I loved her, you know."

Deirdre gripped him by the shoulders and held him to her to stop his shaking. "We both did." Her mind was racing. Being an ex-prize fighter, Derek would have found a safe place to survive if anyone could. But she had never been without his physical and emotional support. Morgan and Tadgh were friends she would hate to lose, and they had interesting information about the Temple history, but maybe this was God's way of protecting the Faith.

Jack tried to compose himself. "We've got to go and search for them when the water recedes, Deirdre. They'll need us."

Deirdre didn't look forward to that gruesome task but said, "Of course we will." She needed to know what had become of Derek.

Deirdre led Jack by the hand. "Come away now. Given the rain outside, it'll be at least a day before we can start any search. Let's go up to the residence, and I'll fix you supper. You must be exhausted." There was no more need for pretext if the Templar threat from the McCarthys was gone. And her attraction to Jack was something to reckon with. He made her heart flutter, that was certain. Morgan would no longer be a rival.

The Gilroy Grocery on the southwest corner of Temple Bar and Fownes Street, just a block south of the main surface River Liffey branch, faced east. Its residence was the second floor above the grocery store, with the kitchen windows looking out on Fownes. The wood-paneled parlor was a fair size with a wood-burning fireplace on the south outside wall. A dining area separated it from the kitchen. The four bedrooms facing Temple bar and the back alley were small and had been dingy when Deirdre moved in. Jack had helped put on a fresh coat of paint.

During the quick egg-on-toast dinner that Deirdre served on the large, wooden kitchen table, she plied Jack with liquor to calm his angst. They were into their fourth commiseration glasses of Jameson when a knocking on the locked door jarred them from their stupor. Deirdre, irritated, lurched downstairs to tell whoever was stupid enough to be out in this storm to bugger off. She saw the vision of a disheveled woman peering in on the other side of the rain-soaked window in the door.

Jack yelled down the stairs, "Who is it?"

"Someone who looks like Morgan out there. But it can't be. It must be the drink, Jack."

Jack came bounding down the stairs. More pounding on the door and then a pleading voice on the other side.

"Let us in, for God's sake, Deirdre. Haven't we had enough water for one day?"

Deirdre flung open the door. "It's Morgan!—all three of you!"

Jack reached the door in a flash, grabbing and hugging Morgan back from the dead. Caught in the moment and blurred with drink, he cried out, "I thought I had lost you forever."

Tadgh stepped forward to separate them and held Jack at arms-length. "Get hold of yourself, man. We're all right."

Deirdre embraced Derek. She had been keeping her composure for Jack's sake, and now the floodgates burst.

"There, there, lass," Derek cooed as he wiped tears from her cheeks. "You knew I'd find my way back, didn't you?"

Deirdre shook her head. "Oh, Derek, we were sure—"

Derek cut her off before she might blurt out their true relationship and pulled her back. "Let's get out of this rain."

Morgan held Tadgh's hand as he strode into the grocery with the tin box under his arm, the cutlass still hanging from his belt.

Tadgh tried to lighten the mood. "I see you've gotten ahead of us in the drinking department. Bartender, line them up for me and me mateys."

Deirdre led them upstairs to the kitchen. She broke out three more glasses and filled them with Jameson as she said, "You all look like muddy ragamuffins. We're relieved to see you."

"Not as relieved as we are to be alive, Deirdre," Morgan said, sipping her drink. Derek and Tadgh downed theirs in one swallow.

Jack blurted out, "I was sure that you had all been swept downstream and drowned. What happened?"

"We almost did drown, Jack." Morgan's eyes darkened. She recounted the harrowing tale and her last words with Jack in the tunnel.

During this explanation, Deirdre handed them towels, saying, "You'll all need baths before you catch your death."

Tadgh said, "We're past that point now, lass, to be sure."

Morgan described the water rising into their underground tomb.

"My God, Morgan! You must have been in such distress." Jack edged closer to her.

Sitting beside Morgan, Tadgh hugged her to him, saying, "We all were."

Jack got up from the table and faced Tadgh, his lips pursed and eyes narrowing. "You knew Morgan's background, Tadgh. How could you lead her into such a deadly situation? You should have gotten her out of there before the water level rose that high."

Tadgh stared him down but knew he was right. "I got carried away with our search."

Morgan put her hand on Jack's arm. "We didn't know that an underground obstruction would break."

Remembering Morgan's entreaties to turn back before that happened, Tadgh was heartened by his wife's support. *That's my girl.*

Deirdre deflected them from their argument by reaching forward for the rusted, breadbox-sized iron casket that Tadgh had left on the kitchen table. She clutched it to her bosom. "You found the chest."

Tadgh was happy enough with the diversion. "Amazingly enough, we did. Morgan thinks it was Divine intervention again. What you're holding is a smaller version that we found on Temple's desk."

Deirdre looked at the box quizzically. "Where's the chest then?"

Morgan pointed at Tadgh and Derek. "It took both these men to drag the main chest out from behind the bookcase and the last bullet in Derek's gun to open it."

Tadgh let that last comment go without questioning it, yet he noted the eye contact between Deirdre and her cook.

Morgan continued. "We removed its important contents before the water deluged the study. It was too big and heavy to bring with us."

Derek added, "There's no point in going back for it when the water recedes, Dee. Whatever else was in it, as well as all the books in the bookcases in the study, will have been destroyed by the water."

Deirdre commented, "Maybe God *did* intervene. By the sounds of it, you needed something beyond yourselves to fight your way out of that hell."

Tadgh chuckled. "Yes, we did, Deirdre, in the form of a little furry creature who happened by at just the right time."

Deirdre looked puzzled.

Morgan offered an explanation. "A rat saved our lives. What was left of our light glinted off his eyes in the dark. He scampered through a tiny opening in the debris, and Tadgh saw it."

Deirdre looked astonished.

Derek poured himself more liquor and said, "It's true, Dee. We'd all have drowned or been asphyxiated if Tadgh hadn't seen and pursued that little rodent."

Deirdre looked at Tadgh with new appreciation before saying, "All God's creatures, as they say."

Morgan took a sip of the liquor. "Like I said, Divine intervention by one of God's rats."

Tadgh reached forward. "Shall we see what we found in the chest? I'm sure that we're all dying to know."

Morgan looked up into his amber eyes. "And we almost did just that to get it, Tadgh."

"Aye, lass."

Tadgh pried the lid partway open and stopped. "Deirdre. You may know this. Why would Jonathan Swift be in the Temple study?"

Deirdre's eyebrows lifted. She looked at Derek before answering. "That is news to me. And quite curious. All I know is that Swift traveled to England after graduating from college in Ireland and became the secretary to Sir William Temple before the elder statesman died in 1699."

Tadgh pulled the Swift memoir of Sir William Temple out of the tin box. "How can that be? You said that Sir William Temple died mysteriously in 1627. Jonathan Swift wrote this in 1699."

Deirdre peered at the dog-eared and faded manuscript. "That was Sir William's *grandfather* of the same name, Provost of Trinity College. He was born in 1555 and died in 1627. Swift was the secretary for Sir William Temple, his grandson, the First and Last Baronet Temple of Sheen. *That* particular Sir William was born in 1628 in Dublin."

"Then what about this handwritten note scrawled on the cover?"

Deirdre took the document and read, "'All that is good and amiable in mankind has died with you, dear Father.' I have no idea, Tadgh."

"You can see here that this note was signed by Jonathan Swift." Tadgh frowned at her. He suspected suppressed information on her part.

"I told you, I don't know, Tadgh. Perhaps the term *Father* refers to our Christian Lord. Swift was Dean of St. Patrick's Cathedral here in Dublin."

Morgan retrieved the manuscript from Deirdre, spreading it flat on the table before saying, "That's what I thought, Dee." Then she turned to her husband, pulling the box toward her and removing the oilskin. "Stop interrogating her, Tadgh. I want to know what this contains."

Tadgh took the ancient bundle, laid it on the table, and cut the binding with the tip of the cutlass.

Deirdre eyed the blade. "Where did that beauty come from, by the way?"

"It was in the main chest."

"Was it, now." She took the rusted weapon and ran her hand along its blade. "Still sharp after all these years." She examined the hilt and pommel. "Moroccan, wouldn't you say? How curious."

"It's certainly ancient, Dee," Derek piped up.

The grocery owner laid the cutlass on the kitchen table and turned to the oilskin. The deteriorating cover fell apart in pieces as she did so. Her mouth dropped open. "What have we here?" The bundle contained a leather-bound octavo-sized book approximately six by nine inches. "Looks well-worn, as if someone pawed over this tome again and again." She touched the book in awe.

Morgan peered over Deirdre's shoulder. "What's written on its cover?"

Deirdre turned it over. She hesitated, started to rise, wanting to leave with the book in hand, but sat back down in her chair. It was inevitable that the McCarthys would learn about Temple's covert religious connections. She needed to make sure they didn't find out that she and Derek were the last ones left, charged with protecting the Faith. She read, "Diary of the Irish Knights Templar," then shot a look at Derek, which Tadgh missed.

Morgan peered at the document. "Fascinating and quite puzzling. Read what it says."

Deirdre read the first three pages silently.

Finally, Morgan put her hand on the diary, so Deirdre had to stop reading. "What does it say?"

"Now, this is quite interesting." Deirdre looked up. "In the first section, Provost Sir William Temple describes his history. I presume it was written by himself, being all in the same hand. He states that he was secretary to the 2nd Earl of Essex, Robert Devereux, during the Anglo-Spanish war of 1596 that the Earl led successfully for the crown." She peered back down at the page, lips moving without utterance, while she perused the written words. Then she spoke, "Two of Devereux's military leaders in that war were George Carew, who became the President of Munster in southern Ireland in 1600, and Sir Henry Docwra, who became governor of Derry in the north after the defeat of the Clans at the Battle of Kinsale in January 1602. He says that Devereux was a covert Knight Templar, and he convinced his three subordinates to 'join the quest' as he puts it here."

Morgan tried to take hold of the book herself, but Deirdre wouldn't let go. "What quest would that be, Deirdre?"

"I'm coming to that, Morgan," Deirdre admonished. "In addition to the mission of conquering the Clans given by Queen Bess to Devereux in 1599, he had a plan to learn the secrets that the fleeing Knights Templar had inserted in the *Book of Ballymote* [3] in the late 1300s. According to this journal, Devereux was in communication with Scottish King James VI, who had heard rumors to that effect, passed on supposedly from Templars who had successfully reached Scotland via the western Ireland route."

Morgan's eyes widened with this revelation. "The words in the note I found were 'Fleeing Knights Templar.'"

"So it would seem. And here's a strange reference to that book you were examining."

Derek was staying silent, but Tadgh asked, "What secrets?"

"I don't know." Deirdre read on, then looked up. "Sir William tells us more about this. Queen Bess had Devereux beheaded in 1601 for attempting a coup against herself on behalf of King James. Sir William was in peril of a similar fate until he gained favor with the new King after Elizabeth's death. He took up the quest, making it his mission to acquire the *Book of Ballymote* and discover its secrets. But first, he had to gain the position of 4th Provost of Trinity College here in Dublin to accomplish that goal." Deirdre tapped the page with her finger. "There is a section here where he lists all the Irish lands he acquired after returning to Ireland in 1609."

"He sought wealth above all else, then? Is that what you are reading?" Morgan reached out again. "Let me see for myself."

Holding the diary fast, Deirdre hesitated but offered, "Come sit beside me, and we can read together."

Derek had been sitting quietly on the edge of his seat. "We should eat something, Dee."

"I have some Irish stew still on the stove. Could you fetch it and bring bread?" She didn't take the hint about stopping, her eyes riveted to the page. Derek gave her a sour look but got up from his chair to comply. She continued reading the text, then stopped to explain. "There is a notation here that Docwra remained in Ireland. Temple continued corresponding with him to acquire the book. Let's see, now—" She read several more lines to herself.

Morgan had been following along and chimed in, "Sir William recounts here that his fellow Knight Templar, Docwra, tried to be conciliatory with the remaining Irish in part to gain the book first from Rory and then Niall Garve O'Donnell, who desperately wanted to be the Earl of Tyrconnell. Then, in September 1607, Rory O'Donnell and Hugh O'Neill led the Flight of the Earls from Ulster headed for Spain, but a storm drove them to France. Niall's wife went with them. After that happened, the King saw no need to negotiate with the remaining clan members. There was a revolt in Derry in 1608 involving Niall and his son. They were arrested, implicated, then sent to the Tower of London for life. Docwra returned to England in disgrace since his policies had failed."

Tadgh got up and tried to read over Morgan's shoulder. "But what about the book?"

"Just be patient." Deirdre gingerly turned the ancient page and pointed at a paragraph. "It says here that Sir William Temple found the *Book of Ballymote* that had been hidden in a Derry cobbler's shop by Niall before he was captured. Docwra threatened the death of Niall's son Neachtain to force him to divulge its whereabouts."

"Temple *did* have it in 1610, then?" Morgan pressed.

"That's what is written here."

Derek set out stew in bowls and soda bread on the table for the three of them and went to the bar for more Jameson. "I like this place, Dee. There's always plenty of good food downstairs." He sat at the table, took a spoonful of soup and a swig of his drink, and stared at his boss over the rim of the glass. Tadgh thought he was trying to get her to stop reading. So, he picked up one of the documents from the table and handed it to Deirdre. "We found this in the chest. Odd, isn't it?"

Deirdre saw the inscription and glanced away before commenting, "After you mentioned the book to me, I looked it up. My references say that he had a scribe at Trinity make a copy of part of the book. This could be that section."

"But why the section with the migration of the Jewish nation into Europe?" Tadgh touched the page, pointing. "That's the same section where Morgan found the tiny note."

"I have no idea, Tadgh." Deirdre resumed scanning the diary.

Derek finally spoke up. "We've had an exhausting day, Dee. We should stop for tonight."

Jack ignored that suggestion. "Who are your references, by the way?"

Deirdre was too engrossed to stop but answered her suitor. "It was presented in the Annals of the Four Masters. They were written in the 1630s, I believe."

Turning the page, Morgan found a yellowed vellum sheet tucked in against the spine. "Wait a minute. Here's something titled *Copy of Missive provided by our ally, Niall Garve O'Donnell, November 3, 1601.* It's related to our quest."

Deirdre asked, "Is that a signature?"

Morgan squinted at the ancient scrawl. "It is signed by none other than Henry Docwra."

Tadgh perked up. "That was before the Battle of Kinsale."

"That's right. Let's see, now." Morgan read passage aloud.

Conversation overheard between Red Hugh and Rory at Ballymote Castle October 30, 1601. 4000 foot and 3000 horse O'Donnell troops heading south to meet with Spanish at Kinsale, Hugh O'Neill to follow. Red Hugh has a box containing a copy of an ancient epistle from St. Columba received by the O'Domhnaill Clan Chieftain before the saint left Ireland in 561. Original is where they hid the O'Donnell treasure. I will try to find it.

Tadgh sat bolt upright. Morgan put her hand on his arm, staring at him.

"Does that ring a bell for you, Tadgh?"

"It does. The idea that there was a family treasure. I wonder if it was monetary or just sentimental items."

"That is *your* ancestral family, isn't it, Morgan?"

"Yes. This note is quite old, and Niall was such a liar, I'm told. If there was some treasure, it is likely long gone."

Tadgh added, "It's unusual that Niall O'Donnell would offer information about a family treasure to the English."

Deirdre wanted to keep the conversation going. "Remember that he was trying to curry favor with them by betraying his own Clan to become chieftain. Listen, there's more."

> *Red said that this epistle talks of a gospel given to St. Patrick by God at the time he showed him the entrance to hell, which the saints were warned to protect.*

Derek choked on his Jameson and started coughing.

"You all right?" Deirdre asked her cook.

"Just a subterranean croup. Nothing to worry about, but it is getting late."

Deirdre looked at her watch. "Yes, it is, but let's get through O'Donnell's letter, shall we? He wrote more about it."

Deirdre continued to read.

> *Red Hugh became a Knights Hospitaller when he acquired Ballymote Castle. He believes it is the O'Donnell Clan's destiny to protect the epistle and, therefore the gospel. In case they are killed in battle, Red Hugh will have his ally Brian MacSweeney get a copy of the epistle to the Grand Master, Fra Alof de Wignacort of the Knights of Malta, head of the Knights Hospitaller. Red Hugh charged Rory to unearth the original epistle and take it to the Grand Master himself if Brian is unsuccessful and Red is incapacitated. This epistle may be crucial for Britain's success in Ireland.* [5]

Morgan downed the rest of her Jameson in one gulp. "This diary is full of strange, revealing history. I am more interested in the mystery of the gospel."

Deirdre closed the diary. "That's enough reading for now. I suggest that you all stay at my place tonight. You must be exhausted, and it's still not fit for man nor beast outside."

Tadgh put the documents back in the tin box and reached for the diary.

Deirdre tucked it inside her blouse. "I'll keep the diary until tomorrow, and we can resume examining it then."

Tadgh stared at her, wanting to object, but then relented as Morgan coaxed him toward the second bedroom. Derek headed to a cot in the downstairs office.

Jack and Deirdre were left to tidy up.

"You did a fine job helping me today, Jack. Without you, I would have lost all my storables. And bravo for helping your colleagues in their time of need."

"I am relieved that they made it out alive. Especially Morgan." His eyes started watering. "With what she went through being trapped on the *Lusitania* . . ." He shook his head, tears in his eyes. "How agonizing it must have been, threatened by the rising water and trapped in the tunnel today. I hope she won't have nightmares."

Deirdre went to Jack and held him close, saying, "I know you love her, Jack, but you've got to let her go. I know you were there on the *Lusitania* with her and felt the same panic as the ship went down. So, what happened today affects you all the more."

She took the dishtowel and dried Jack's eyes. Then she held his head in her hands, gazing into his eyes. "Now she's safe with her husband, Jack, and we're here together. Let's say we go to my bedroom to rest."

Jack, with a nervous laugh, answered, "To *your* bedroom? And where in the world will *I* sleep? You only have one bed in there."

"Why, with me, silly."

Chapter Two
Irish Templars

Late Sunday, November 28, 1920
Deirdre's Bedroom, Temple Bar Pub, Dublin

"*I*t looks as if the rain is stopping," Jack mused.

"Come away from the window and into bed," Deirdre urged. "I won't bite you."

Jack didn't move, his back to her.

"Is there someone else?" she whispered. "Is that why you're afraid of me?"

Jack thought about that. With Morgan married to Tadgh, there was no chance for him there. "It's not fear. But I need you to know I was injured when the *Lusitania* sank." He turned to her. "I haven't been quite myself since." The drizzle on the windowpane held his interest again.

"Morgan told me all about it." Her voice softened. "You were very brave then, Jack. Still are. Come to bed." She sat up, illuminated in the lamplight, naked as a robin from the waist up.

Jack blurted out, "But Deirdre, we hardly even know each other." He stayed at the window as if guarding an assigned post and toyed with the lace curtain.

"I respect you, Jack. You're a fine upstanding young man, unlike many of the rabble around here these days. Morgan and Tadgh trust you, and that's good enough for me. Now, do I need to get out of bed and chase you down?" She laughed and moved the covers aside, revealing sensuous thighs.

Jack held up his hands as if surrendering. He approached her side of the four-poster bed and sat on the edge, looking away from her. "I don't want to disappoint you."

Deirdre took his hand and stroked it gently. Then she stared into his fretful eyes. "Being a pub owner and bartender may seem like a very social profession, but I am very lonely. When I kissed you earlier, there was a jolt of electricity. Did you feel it, too?"

"I . . . I did."

"Touch me, Jack." Deirdre guided his hand to her breast.

He pushed gently against her cushioned bosom, his fingers spreading to caress her. Her skin felt soft and supple. "It's been a long time." He could feel the heat below and the pulsing.

"Our friends almost died today. Life is too short. Why don't you join me?" She pressed her cheek against his hand and closed her eyes.

"I want to." But Morgan's face reared up, and he was awash in guilt. *Was he betraying her? What craziness.*

"Then come." Her eyes were beguiling as soft lashes fringed shining orbs.

Jack got up, turned down the light, removed his clothes in the dark, and crawled into bed on the opposite side from Deirdre, face down, trying to keep himself in check.

"Come close to me, Jack."

When Jack didn't move, Deirdre slipped over to him and lay her body alongside his, gently touching his shoulders, back, and buttocks, teasing him. "Roll over, darling."

Jack turned on his side to face Deirdre, curled his arms around her, and gently drew her against him. The scent of her musky body made his heart pound. He could hardly breathe.

Deirdre reached down and found what she was looking for, quite large for the size of this man. But then, she wasn't surprised. He had large hands.

"I can see you like me, Jack."

"Ah, love, you are beautiful, but . . ." His voice grew husky.

"Sure, but you love Morgan. You said it yourself earlier." Her voice turned husky, sad, almost.

Jack pulled away from her under the covers. "Ever since I met Morgan on the *Lusitania*, she drew me in. She was so selfless with all our lives at stake. So heroic. Her image guided me through my rehabilitation after the sinking. You can understand that, can't you?"

Deirdre stretched her arm and clutched his hand. "It must be hard to be the third person in a love triangle, especially when the other two are happily married. You can pine away forever, and the only person to lose out on a romantic life will be you, Jack. It doesn't have to be that way. I can offer you a better kind of love." She pulled him in tight. "Let yourself go, Jack. I need you."

"I know you're right, Deirdre. You excite me, that's certain, but I feel guilty right now."

"If I kiss you like this?" Deirdre covered his mouth with her own. And he didn't fight her. But something stopped him, and he pulled away. "Delicious, but not tonight, lass."

Disappointed, Deirdre let him go. Her ego was crushed. She hadn't slept with a man in over a year and hadn't been rejected this way before, especially at this arousal stage. She liked Jack and needed to find a way to get past his unrequited love. Then she felt the pang of guilt herself when a thought flashed into her head—it would have been better if Morgan had died in the flood. *Lord, I don't want to think like that.*

"All right, Jack. I've only one bed, so we'll have to make do. You can stay here, or there's the chesterfield in the parlor. I won't ask you again tonight, love, but we'll have to see about that longing in your loins in due course. I must say you are a right healthy lad."

"I'll stay."

Deirdre saw that Jack couldn't hold back a smile despite his inner turmoil.

The next morning, Tadgh awoke refreshed. He could see the sun shining in through the northeastern window of the corner bedroom, its rays illuminating the dust motes in the air until its warmth fell on his beloved's raven locks. Morgan was nestled against his right side, curled up like a cat. Even her breathing sounded like purring. When she opened her eyes, he was gazing into motionless green globes.

She sat up and tousled her hair. "What are you thinking, *mavourneen?*"

"How fortunate I am to have you in my life, and how lucky we are to be here, alive, this fine morning."

"I am the blessed one, Tadgh." She pushed closer, leaned over, and kissed him gently.

"I wonder how many of your cat lives you've used up, *aroon.*"

"Not as many as you, Tadgh. But we've got plenty left, I hope. Can we stay here a bit longer?"

"At least until we understand what is in that strange diary."

"I wish we didn't have to go home, Tadgh, to the war. I think you've done enough for the cause. Let Michael and the others throw their lives away."

Tadgh shook his head. "My country needs me. I'm still an able-bodied soldier." Seeing the troubled look in Morgan's eyes, he offered, "I've several lives left, don't ya know."

"But you'd be dead if I hadn't risked my life and Aidan's life to save you. I need you more."

Tadgh was tired of the same old arguments from Morgan. She understood his needs but continued to impose her Florence Nightingale beliefs on him. "I promise I will survive, lass."

"That's a hollow promise."

Tadgh had to change the direction of the conversation. "I still don't trust Deirdre."

Morgan frowned.

Tadgh was glad she didn't criticize him for that belief as she rubbed the sleep from her eyes. He mused, "All that Knights Templar information. [4] Doesn't it seem to you that the *Book of Ballymote* has turned out to be more important than just providing clues to the O'Donnell treasure?"

"Strange and exciting. What do you think?"

Tadgh was distracted by the vision of her, with a bosom round and full. "This is what I think. Perfect." He cradled her breasts.

"There you go, like a cat with catnip," Morgan laughed, arching her back and pressing her nipples into his hands.

He knew she was teasing him and didn't want his arousal to end up a disappointment this morning. He pulled his hands back. "Later then."

"Perhaps, if you behave." Her eyes twinkled.

"Let's get dressed and go to breakfast, Morgan. You are too tempting."

Morgan swung her long legs out over the edge of the mattress and found her slippers on the floor. "What about my question?"

Tadgh brought Morgan her robe from the bedstead and wrapped it around her. "Obviously, more is buried here than your ancestors' valuables, but that's not our concern. Was Sir William Temple searching for O'Donnell treasure? There was the part in that traitor Niall's note to Governor Docwra, but that was only an oblique reference when he wrote about the epistle from St. Columba."

"Maybe if we could find the epistle, we could find the treasure, Tadgh."

"Supposedly, they were buried together."

A faraway look appeared on Morgan's face before she spoke. "But Red Hugh commanded his brother Rory to unearth the original epistle and take it to the Hospitaller Grand Master, whoever he was, if Red was incapacitated. We know Red died the next year in Spain while negotiating for further Spanish support."

"Poisoned by Carew's spy." Tadgh nodded slowly. "It starts to make sense."

"What do you mean, mavourneen?"

"Think about it." Tadgh padded to the window in his underwear, felt the sun warm him briefly, and gazed outside. Then he turned to face her, waiting for it to register.

Morgan clicked her fingers. "Of course! Carew was Devereux's man and a Templar, to boot. The spy killed Red for the epistle since Docwra had already told him what Niall O'Donnell had written. Temple was in on it because he had been Devereux's secretary up until his execution." She went to him, laying a hand on his shoulder, and looked at the world beyond the window. Temple Bar was bustling once more despite the threat of ongoing military skirmishes. All that water had drained back into the Liffey a block away or evaporated with the sun's heat on the glistening cobblestones.

Tadgh kissed her on the cheek. "Completely different outside today. I wonder what's flowing under us now."

Morgan returned the kiss, lingering, then felt a chill. "I don't want to think about that ever again. It's not our concern anymore."

"Aye."

Morgan turned away from the window. "I wonder if Red was also on his way to Malta to confirm the Grand Master received the epistle from his compatriot. Brian MacSweeney, was it?"

"Deirdre said your ancestor was killed in Spain, so I doubt it. I wonder whether Rory dug up the original epistle and took it to the Grand Master after the Flight of the Earls in 1607 as Red had requested."

Morgan pulled the robe closely around her. "That would surely depend on whether the copy had gotten through."

Tadgh scratched his stubbly beard. "Perhaps. I wonder what happened to Rory. Carew and Docwra knew from Naill's letter that he was charged with conveying the original epistle."

Morgan sat down at the mirrored dresser and combed out her hair. She had gone to bed with it wet from their bath together, and now it was unruly. "Maybe that's one of the reasons for the Flight of the Earls to Continental Europe. And maybe he was killed like his brother, and the British got the epistle."

Tadgh took her comb and started to stroke her black locks, carefully holding the hair above the knots so it wouldn't hurt. "That can't be, Morgan. Temple wouldn't have been looking for the epistle years later if they'd found it, would he? He was part of their Templar group, after all. We must look into Rory's demise."

Tadgh paused, looking at the bone comb for a moment. "You know what this reminds me of, lass?" He continued stroking her hair, now devoid of tangles.

Her eyes were closed. "Of course, I do, mavourneen. It was when you first brought me home to Creagh, when I was almost dead, not knowing who I was. You were kind and understanding then, my love." She clutched his hand, stopping his ministrations. "This is the same comb you used four years ago. That's when I started to fall in love with you."

Tadgh eased her out of the chair, opened her robe, and pulled her up against his chest. "You made me love you, aroon, for which I'm eternally grateful. Let's go back to bed now. Finish what we started."

Morgan held him briefly and then pushed him away. "Later, lover. I'm hungry."

Tadgh reached out again. "Ah, not like my hunger." He ached for her.

"Wasn't last night enough for you?" she teased.

Tadgh's amber eyes flashed. "Never enough of you."

Morgan stood back, the day pressing on her despite his temptations. "Later, love."

Tadgh looked for the discarded clothing they had peeled off the night before and thrown to the floor. The soiled garments would need to be washed before they could be worn again. Nowhere to be found. They were gone. And then he spotted something on the dresser. He found the clothing washed and neatly folded on the dresser by the closed door. Pointing, he said, "Morgan, you didn't—"

"It wasn't me, Tadgh. We were busy all night long, remember? Must have been that woman you don't trust, taking them up after we fell asleep."

Tadgh retrieved Morgan's bandeau brassiere. "Here, let me help you with this contraption." She let her robe fall. He brushed his arm across her breasts as he handed it over, checking whether her nipples were still swollen from his lovemaking the previous night.

"Really, Tadgh. You've a one-track mind." She batted his hand away and slipped the garment over her head. "Get yourself dressed."

"It seems a shame to bundle all that beauty up so soon, aroon."

Morgan laughed, picked up her shirtwaist from the bureau, and slipped it on. "Do you think that the epistle got delivered by MacSweeney?"

Resigned to the reality of Morgan's mood, Tadgh reluctantly handed over her pressed trousers. "We'll never know, will we, and communications might have been so poor after the Battle at Kinsale that Rory wouldn't have known either."

Morgan pulled the trousers on and buttoned the waistband. "We don't know what happened to MacSweeney."

"No, aroon, we don't. We will just have to find the O'Donnell treasure and see whether the original epistle is still buried there."

"But what if that document is the key to finding the treasure?"

"I doubt that. It was written over a thousand years before the treasure was buried."

"But *an Cathach* was ancient, and look how important the document was for finding your McCarthy gold."

"Touché, lass," Tadgh conceded, pulling on his pants. "We clearly don't have all the pieces to this puzzle, that's certain."

"We've got to find out what or where *PP* is. William Temple seemed to know where it was from his scribbles in the book."

"I need to look at that diary myself, Morgan. And you only saw part of it."

"I trust Deirdre. She was my bridesmaid, after all. Remember how she protected us from Boyle?"

Tadgh wanted to tread lightly on his wife's feelings, but there was something odd about Deirdre's inquisitive probing, her seeming knowledge beyond what she had shared with them all. Those looks that passed between her and Derek. Why was the man carrying a revolver? "Deirdre might inadvertently gloss over some important information, not knowing what we know about the O'Donnell treasure," he said. Tadgh donned his shirt, ran his hands through his hair, and opened the door to go to breakfast. "After you, my love."

Jack looked unusually chipper at Deirdre's kitchen table when Morgan and Tadgh appeared. His newfound sweetheart was singing "The Rose of Tralee" as she fried bacon on the stove.

Morgan took in the scene. "How did you sleep, Jack?"

Jack looked up sheepishly from *The Irish Times*. "Soundly, for the first time in ages."

Morgan winked at Deirdre, who smiled back, confirming what she was thinking. *Good. He found companionship.* Although she did feel a twinge for some reason. "So did we, after a wonderful bath."

"I see that the sun is shining. No more rain, I hope. What's the condition of the grocery, Jack?"

"Derek reports the water is receding in the storage room, Tadgh. We should be able to open the store later in the day after cleaning up the mess. The streets are still wet but no longer inundated. It says here in the paper this morning that the storm has caused over a million pounds in damage. It was the worst three-day storm in recorded history other than the flood of 1802. The trams aren't yet running, and the schools and many businesses are closed for at least today."

Morgan situated herself beside her husband at the table. "Then we are all fortunate, aren't we, Jack?"

Jack smiled at Deirdre, who giggled and waved a spatula at him. "*I* certainly am, Morgan."

"I can see that." She directed her gaze to Deirdre. "Did you read any more of the diary?"

"No, I was quite tired, and ah, preoccupied."

"Can we resume taking a look at it after breakfast?"

Deirdre shoveled bacon and eggs onto the serving tray and brought them to the table. "Of course, Morgan. I'm as curious as you are. Now let's eat up."

Deirdre assigned Derek to wash the dishes after their full Irish breakfast meal, while Jack went to check on the storage room and tunnel condition. Deirdre retrieved the diary from her bedroom and returned to the McCarthys in the kitchen to examine the document.

As they sat at the table, she began, "Where were we? Oh yes. The missive from Niall O'Donnell, an ancestor of yours, Morgan."

Morgan wondered why Deirdre had made that statement. Just because she had the same last name? Did Deirdre know about the Clans Pact? How could she? "He was no ancestor of mine. Collin and I come from Red Hugh's side of the clan, to my knowledge."

Deirdre opened the diary to the page after the O'Donnell note. "Let's see. Notations from Docwra to Temple in 1608, recorded by William, about the epistle. He—Docwra—says that their other Knights Templar colleague in Ireland in 1601, George Carew, was notified of Niall's note and sought to find the epistle. William says he was informed that Wilmot in the south thought he found Thomas Fitzmaurice and killed him in December 1601, on Carew's orders, without finding the epistle. Sir William later states that Fitzmaurice was found alive. MacSweeney's men were mostly rounded up near Listowel, but McSweeney was never found. Carew assumed their leader was a diversion and that Red Hugh kept the copy. When Red Hugh survived the Battle of Kinsale and headed to Spain to convince King Phillip III to supply more troops, Carew sent a spy named Blake to kill him after first acquiring the epistle. The spy succeeded with the first assignment in 1602 by poisoning him, but not the second." She looked up from interpreting.

Tadgh twirled his mustache. Their assessment earlier in the bedroom was verified by William Temple himself. "It would seem that our Irish history was driven by this epistle, wouldn't it, Deirdre?"

"To some extent, I agree. William goes on." She traced the following several lines with her finger while her lips moved silently. She said, "Listen to this. Attempts to gain the epistle from Rory O'Donnell after the Battle of Kinsale failed. He professed ignorance. Docwra convinced the King to make Rory 1st Earl of Tyrconnell in 1603 to get him to divulge the secret hiding location, which upset Cousin Niall. When Governor Docwra's negotiation strategy to appease the remaining Clan Chieftains failed, King James I recalled him. Rory and Hugh O'Neill, realizing they would be arrested, chose instead to flee to Spanish-controlled Flanders and then on to Rome. Also, it says here Docwra reported that a spy was sent after Rory to acquire the epistle before he could deliver it to the Grand Master on Malta. Rory was intercepted at the Roman port of Ostia before he could board a boat. He fell ill and returned to Rome where he died in 1608. The official cause of death was listed as malaria, but Docwra reported he was poisoned like his brother. Unfortunately, the epistle was not recovered."

Tadgh squeezed Morgan's hand under the table. "All this happened before Temple returned to Ireland in 1609, don't ye know."

"That's right, but remember, Temple was Devereux's secretary and was, it would seem, a Knights Templar who was likely the scribe for this covert organization." Deirdre got up, relit the stove, and put the kettle on for tea. "We really must repaint this kitchen. I don't like this faded pea-soup color."

Morgan moved her chair to look at the diary herself. "This is a treasure trove of information about my family history, buried for almost two centuries. Amazingly, almost right under your pub and grocery, Deirdre."

"My *former* pub, you mean." The kettle was boiling. She poured the water into her favorite pot. Extracting two silk tea bags, she tossed them in the pot, then secured the lid and applied the cozy. Deirdre worried the diary would expose more of the subject of her own quest, a challenge that lay fallow until yesterday when this astonishing diary of her ancestor had appeared. Morgan and Tadgh had accomplished that. If she wanted these Adventurers, as they referred to themselves, to help her find the relic, then they would have to be informed. She wished Derek would return with his revolver at hand.

She poured the steeped tea into three mugs, set them on a tray with milk and sugar, and brought this to the table.

The women scanned the pages that described where William had acquired land and more about his futile examination of the *Book of Ballymote* after he obtained it.

Morgan looked up at Tadgh. "He certainly became a hard-nosed landowner, as well as one who performed his duties that improved the administrative functions of Trinity College."

Deirdre turned to a particular page. "Listen to this. It is in the senior William's hand."

> *Having failed to acquire the epistle from the O'Donnells, I decided to contact the Hospitaller Grand Master, Fra Alof de Wignacort, to determine if he had received it from one of them. I introduced myself as one of two remaining Knights Hospitaller in Ireland, which of course I am not.*

Morgan realized all of this was not illuminating where PP was located. She kept listening in vain for another reference to a search for the O'Donnell treasure. According to the documents, Sir William Temple seemed fixated on this epistle, whatever it contained. She stayed put, looking over Deirdre's shoulder, glued to the pages being read and turned.

Deirdre leafed on and found what she was looking for. Before speaking, she added milk and two sugar lumps to her cup and stirred. "Here it is. William reports in February 1611 that he had not received a reply from the Grand Master and concluded that the Hospitallers had not received the document. His language is quite acerbic at this point." She took a sip from her cup.

"Acerbic?" Tadgh quipped. "Hardly the language of a pub owner."

"I'm not a pub owner. I'm a grocer, and a well-read one to boot."

"Then what does the word mean?"

"Sharp, bitter. Kind of like you, Tadgh."

That barb didn't go unnoticed by Morgan. She was about to comment when she was startled by something she was reading. Pointing at a page near the end of the diary, she exclaimed, "Look at this, Deirdre. It reads that Sir William Temple was murdered!"

Deirdre swiveled back around and peered intently at the text.

That revelation got Tadgh's attention. He stood up from the table and came around to see for himself. "By whom?"

"There's an entry on January 15, 1627. It is written and signed in an agitated scrawl by Martha Temple, William's wife. I can hardly understand it. She writes, 'Saint Brigid. William is dying. His heart is failing from the fight.'"

Tadgh peered down to read the words on the page. "What fight?"

Deirdre fumbled with the pages and finally found the next entry. "Oh, my goodness. Here it is. Later that day, Martha writes an extensive account of it—"

William was visited by an Arab professing to be a Dutch Knight's Hospitaller from Malta named Flooren. We entertained him in the basement study. Strangely, he was looking for the St. Columba epistle. William asked him why the Grand Master had not responded to his inquiry years earlier, and the soldier said that he had finally been sent in response to that request. When William asked him the name of the current Grand Master, he gave the wrong answer. William refused him and ordered him out of our house.

The warrior got violent and grabbed me, pulling a cutlass out of his garments, holding it to my throat. I was powerless. He demanded information about the epistle. To save my life, William gave him a small casket containing a copy of the original note from Niall O'Donnell that he kept on his desk. Unfortunately, it also contained our copy of Sir Owain's journey. I could feel blood trickling down my neck.

Seeing the shape of the cutlass, William yelled out 'Barbary Pirate' [6] which angered the warrior. That distracted the devil for a moment, and William lunged and took the pistol from the Arab's waistband. The cutlass clanged to the ground as they fought over the gun. I picked up the sword but didn't know how to use it. When it looked like the devil would overpower William and shoot him, I rushed at him and stabbed him in the leg with his own weapon.

I could see that William was in trouble, gasping for air. The pirate attacked me and threw me sideways into the wall. The last thing I remember is our John bounding down the stairs. When I woke up, John was holding my head. The warrior and the small box were gone, and my poor William was dying of a heart attack.

Morgan could see that her bridesmaid was choking up at the news. She patted her hostess's hand. "Deirdre, are you all right? What a dreadful calamity. Have another sip of your tea. It will calm you."

Deirdre's head was spinning. *To think that this diary, which explained so much, had been right under her and her father's feet all this time. This would rekindle her search for God's holy treasure.* "It is just such a shock.

Poor Mrs. Temple. No wonder William had a heart attack, being seventy-one at the time." Her eyes misted over.

Tadgh was more pragmatic. "At least that explains the cutlass. That weapon saved our lives, even if it wasn't used as intended. John, I presume her son, must have run the pirate off before he could regain his weapon." He peered at the entry again. "What's that note about? The mentioning of Sir Owain's journey?"

Morgan answered. "Like my vision at Temple House?"

"I have no idea, aroon. It's very confusing. Why did Temple have that document?" *Deirdre seems disturbed by this revelation. Why?*

"What vision?" Deirdre asked.

Morgan explained her nocturnal ghostly visit from armored Sir Owain on horseback and Charlotte's explanation that he only appears to those in anguish just before their needs are met.

Deirdre, squinting and rubbing the tears from her eyes, appeared confused.

Morgan took a sip of her tea and read on since Deirdre was still recovering from the shock. "There's another entry the next day. Martha has regained her wits, I think, and has decided to tell the authorities her husband died of a heart attack without mentioning the pirate nor anything about the epistle. She said she needed to protect the secretive nature of the Knights Templar."

Tadgh picked up the diary and waved it in the air. "It appears that the Temples, in the end, were the remaining Knights Templar left in Ireland."

Morgan grabbed his arm. "Put the diary back down before you damage it."

Tadgh set it on the table and sat beside his wife, the document now in front of him.

Morgan commented, "We can't be certain of that. But the only references we can see here are to them—Devereux, Carew, and Docwra. We've come to the end of the entries in this diary."

Tadgh leafed through the remaining blank pages. "Hold it. You're wrong. I see more writing farther back, in a different hand."

"Not Martha's writing?" Morgan raised her eyebrows.

"Decidedly a more masculine script." Tadgh fingered the page at the entry in question. "See here."

Deirdre perked up. "What does it say?"

"The first entry is February 28, 1667. Here is a passage."

When it looked as if John was deathly ill from syphilis, I invited his family to stay at TR during his illness. Had to, as John and I are the last Knights Templar left in Ireland. William came home from Surrey last week. Today I learned from Gwen, our upstairs maid, that he has been with John's wife, Abigail. I've turned him out, the philanderer. Such a stain on the Temple name.

Tadgh pored over the rough text, "John who? The son, Temple?"

Morgan pointed to the word on the page. "No. The entry is signed by John Temple. Look here. There's another entry in the same hand."

May 2, 1667. My dear friend Jonathan Swift died today. Abigail overwrought. She confessed that she is pregnant but not with John's child. William's. Damn him. I will fix things.

Deirdre dried her eyes and came over to sit on the other side of Tadgh. She peered down at the page as Morgan read silently. Finally, Deirdre said, "There are more entries by John Temple. Abigail gave birth to a son she named Jonathan on November 30th while still residing at the Temple Residence. The following June, he was turned over to his uncle Godwin Swift to be raised."

Tadgh stroked his mustache. "Why?"

Morgan consulted the pages. "John Temple writes that Abigail moved to Surrey, England, to be near the father, William, who was married. To avoid disclosure of his son's indiscretion, John arranged for the baby to be brought up by his uncle, a lawyer in Dublin who was a friend."

The two women looked at each other, flabbergasted, then reached for their teacups. Tadgh had let his grow cold on the other side of the table.

Finally, Morgan closed the diary and patted the cover, saying, "This is all truly unbelievable. Secrets hidden and protected for more than two centuries."

Deirdre wished she had read on further in the diary the night before. Perhaps she could have removed the evidence somehow. These two friends would have to be dealt with if they continued their investigation. As her father had schooled her before his death at the hands of the Association, she must follow the quest of her ancestors now that this startling knowledge had come to light.

"It goes with the bits that are historically known," Tadgh said. "I repeat. To think that much of the monumental historical conflict here in Ireland was because of a sacred epistle."

Morgan pointed at the cover. "Now I can see why they wrote this in a diary named for Irish Knights Templar."

Tadgh was looking at Deirdre, who seemed overcome with emotion, as he said, "Do you think that Jonathan Swift was a Knights Templar, along with his father, Sir William Temple, the statesman?"

"Does John Temple refer to the search for the epistle?"

"No, Tadgh, just his parents. I don't see any mention of it in John's writing."

Morgan had reopened the diary and was flipping through the last blank pages. "But look here, there's a final entry in another more flourishing hand. It is dated October 10, 1739."

Tadgh stroked his mustache again. "Wait. Are you sure? Wasn't that the date we found on the seal to the basement study, aroon?"

"That's right. Now, can you guess who wrote this entry?"

"Aha! Would it be Jonathan Swift, the satirist, and illegitimate Temple offspring?"

"Smart lad. Listen to this—"

> *Before my mind goes completely, I am writing this note. My attempts to find the epistle have been futile. I sense that all is lost. I have heard one of the Templar myths of the travels to our land by the sainted one. Without the epistle and thus the gospel, I cannot confirm or deny. What I have presumed, I have recorded satirically in my book of travels. Only our Lord God will divulge in the fullness of time. There are villains about. I am sealing this hidden Templar study against them.*

Tadgh jumped up and strode to the stove to stoke the fire. He turned, poker in hand. "That explains why the study was sealed. Bloody hell! If only we left it that way until after the flood. There must have been books in that library that could tell more of this story."

Deirdre seemed to perk up and offered levity. "It's all water over the dam. We've got what we've got, and it appears to be substantial. Thank you, Morgan, for suggesting this adventure."

Morgan spoke up. "This diary also explains why the younger Swift's note on the Temple memoirs referred to his father, William. And why he went to England to be his secretary in the last years of William's life."

"True, Morgan. But what did he mean when he wrote, 'What I have presumed, I have satirically recorded in my book of travels'?" Tadgh pointed to that sentence. Then he looked up from the document and asked the women, "*What* book of travels?"

Morgan remembered. "Wasn't there a manuscript of one of his novels in the chest?"

Tadgh went to the bedroom and brought back the tin box. Rummaging through it, he pulled out the hand-scripted tome. "Here. 'Travels into Several Remote Nations of the World. In Four Parts' by Jonathan Swift. "

Deirdre seemed lost in thought. "Satire . . . book of travels . . ." She suddenly put two and two together. "Of course! *Gulliver's Travels!* The satire about Queen Anne and others."

Morgan picked up the ancient manuscript. "Right you are, Deirdre. Very famous and inflammatory in Swift's time."

Morgan ran her fingers over the cover of the tome. "I heard it was the only way to criticize the government in those days without getting your head chopped off." She started leafing through the document. "He must have had a reason for locking this manuscript up in the chest and hiding it behind the bookcase. This is an original handwritten manuscript, likely worth a fortune."

Tadgh took back the document and opened it to the first page. "Hello—what's this?" He pointed to the page.

"What is it, mavourneen?"

"An annotated table of contents, with four stories of different lands."

Deirdre leaned forward for a closer look. She opened her mouth to speak but thought the better of it. *Let them figure this out for me.*

"I've read about them."

"Have you now, Morgan."

"At the orphanage. They gave us some books to read to the other children to keep us all quiet. There was a dog-eared copy of this book, which I read to Lucy and the others."

"You remember now?"

"It's all coming back to me. I remember a land of big people and one of the little people."

"Then, can you explain these little drawings beside the titles of the stories in this table of contents, Morgan?"

She looked at the manuscript. "Let's see. Gulliver was first shipwrecked on the island of little people called Lilliput, where he was tied up on orders from the king. He became a confidant but fell out of favor. He escaped by boat when he refused to lead the Lilliputians in war against their neighbor nation."

"What is the hand-drawn figure beside the title 'Lilliput,' aroon?"

"I don't know exactly, but it looks like a peaked building of some sort, with the words *Beit Hamikdash* underneath."

Deirdre squinted at the crude sketch. "What does that mean, Morgan?"

"I have no idea, but it is likely Hebrew because I remember reading that Swift was obsessed with the language. He called the near humans in the fourth voyage *yahus*, which I believe is a Hebrew word."

Tadgh covered the page with his broad hand. "All right. But how about the second voyage, Morgan?"

"If I remember, Gulliver went to Brobdingnag, a land of giants. He became a possession of the queen. He fell out with the King over weapons of war from other countries that could be used to invade his country. He escaped when he was carried off by a bird."

"You're right again, my love," said Tadgh, moving his hand aside. "This drawing looks like the pyramids of Egypt, doesn't it?"

"What's that word below?" Deirdre asked.

Morgan turned the document to the light. "*Tanis*, I think. It's smeared."

"That's a city in ancient Egypt, isn't it, Morgan?"

"I don't know." Morgan consulted the manuscript. "Voyage number three took Gulliver to several countries, first a desolate, rocky island, and then, a country called Laputa where science, mathematics, and astronomy were paramount, especially if they didn't have practical application. Along the way, he goes to Glubbdubdrib, where he visits a mythical magician's dwelling and discusses history with the ghosts of historical figures."

"The drawing for this voyage also looks like the pyramids, doesn't it?"

"No, Tadgh. I've seen this distinctive shape before but can't place it right now. The word below it is *nãvi*."

Tadgh addressed Deirdre with narrowed eyes. "How curious, don't you think?"

He noticed her squirm in her seat as she answered, "Yes, very, Tadgh." *What was she keeping from them?*

Morgan returned to the table of contents. "The last voyage was to Houynnhnms, I think. Hard to say, *Houynnhnms*. The wise creatures were horses, and humans were base animals called *yahus*. Gulliver associated with the intelligent animals, but he looked like the yahus. The drawing, here, is of a pointed rock on a hill, and the word scrawled below it is *Torah*."

Tadgh pointed at the sketch. "It looks like Lil Fail on the Hill of Tara."

Deirdre crowded in to look for herself, remembering her father's death near that very spot. "This is all probably just meaningless doodling."

"I'm not so sure," Tadgh said, lifting the manuscript carefully to examine the sketch. "The handwriting of the manuscript and the words with the drawings seem to match. I would guess this was the original manuscript for the novel and that Swift inserted these drawings and words for a purpose."

"I agree with Tadgh, Deirdre," Morgan added. "He went to a lot of trouble to bury this with the diary in a safe place."

Deirdre took the document from Tadgh and leafed through it. "I can't find any more marginal notations. I still think this may mean nothing at all. Still, it is curious."

Tadgh tried to take the manuscript from Deirdre to put it back into the box, but she wouldn't let go.

"We should keep all these documents here in my residence for safekeeping. That was our agreement, Tadgh."

"I did agree to that." He got up and handed the box to the grocery owner. "You will keep them safe, won't you, lass?" He had his suspicions.

Deirdre gathered the documents into the box. "Of course, my friends."

Tadgh picked up the cutlass and made a fencer's lunge. "I'll just take this as a souvenir of our latest escapades."

"You're welcome to it, Tadgh. Fancy yourself a Barbary Corsair, do you?" Deirdre chuckled, then looked at her watch. "My, my. I wonder if the boys have the store ready to open."

They met Jack down in the storage area. "The water has receded now, well below the level of the tunnel we dug," he reported.

"But it's still too wet in here to move the storables back down," Deirdre said, bending down and pinching some of the moist soil with her fingers. "It may take a month for it to dry out."

"Perhaps we should return to the basement study to examine more of the books, then?" Tadgh suggested.

Morgan shook her head. "I am not going back there, Tadgh. Besides, if that basement stronghold kept the water out for over a hundred years, then it will be keeping all that water inside now. All the books will have been destroyed, as Derek said."

"I'm going up to see how Derek is doing with the store," Deirdre said. She started up the stairs. "Coming, Jack?"

Tadgh gripped Jack's arm and shook his head slightly.

"Give me a minute. I'll be up shortly," Jack said to her.

Tadgh waited for Deirdre to be out of earshot. "I am disappointed William Temple presumably knew where PP was located, but with all the startling revelations in his diary, there was no mention of it. His note in the *Book of Ballymote* was encouraging. But unfortunately, despite all the risks we took, the whereabouts of the O'Donnell treasure still eludes us."

"At least we're all still alive, mavourneen."

Jack looked confused. "You're losing me."

Tadgh said, "We'll fill you in later, Jack. Right now, we have to decide what to do, and Mick has ordered me home."

As much as Morgan hated the war, she was curious about the condition of her home. "Let's go today. If we must. We're still at risk here in Dublin."

Jack stepped away from Tadgh's grasp, rubbing his arm. "I'll stay here for now. Deirdre needs me to get this grocery back on its feet. Perhaps I can be helpful in further study of whatever this diary of yours unearthed."

"A wise choice," Morgan smiled.

Tadgh looked Jack in the eyes. "Remember, no word of our search for Morgan's family treasure to Deirdre."

"Right you are, Tadgh."

"You'd better get these stairs repaired, or someone's going to get hurt, Jack," Morgan said.

Tadgh turned to her. "Mick said that Aidan has a surprise for me, I'm told. Do you know anything about it?"

"You'll have to ask Aidan about that, my love." Morgan knew Tom Barry was bivouacking his 3rd West Cork flying column in the control center of their home at Creagh. Aidan was a member of the unit that had been leading guerrilla attacks on RIC barracks and other targets of late. As far as she knew, their home had not been compromised. She was dead set against Tadgh getting back into the fight, but her voice didn't count.

Having settled their near-term plans, they headed back up into the grocery.

The Irish Times had been dropped off for Monday, November 29. The front-page headline blared:

Kilmichael Ambush. IRA kills 17 elite RIC Auxiliaries trying to surrender!

Tadgh picked up the paper and scanned the report. "*Jaysus.* That's Cork West. It says here that three IRA members were killed, including McCarthy."

Morgan's green eyes riveted on her husband's, filling with tears. "Poor Aidan!"

Chapter Three
Dillon's Cross

Tuesday, November 30, 1920
Creagh, Ireland

*I*t was three hundred and nineteen years to the day after Red Hugh O'Donnell venerated the Holy rood at Holy Cross on his way to Kinsale. It had been three years, seven months, and sixteen days since Tadgh last saw his home as he steered the Kerry into his driveway at Creagh on the banks of the Ilen River.

After the news about Kilmichael, Morgan had told him about the housing for the flying column and involvement of Aidan. Michael Collins had details of the ambush but could not confirm whether Aidan was one of the three rebels who had died in the attack.

Kerry's 670 cc sv V twin engine was smoking when he brought the motorbike to a halt in front of two mud-splattered lorries. Tadgh noted the bullet holes in the vehicles.

Usually accustomed to the bumpy ride, Morgan rubbed her backside when she stepped out of the Watsonian wickerwork sidecar.

Hearing the familiar full-throated rumble of the bike, Aiden saw an all-too-familiar face rush out of the house, and Aidan threw his arms around his brother.

"Thank God, you're safe," Tadgh cried as Morgan limped over to join the hug. "We heard about McCarthy's death, Aiden. We thought the worst."

"Cousin Michael McCarthy was killed, Brother. I was there. We fought to a great victory, so we did. To make them pay for bloody Sunday at Croke."

Tadgh remembered a remote cousin by that name who lived in Dunmanway, northeast of Skibbereen. He cringed as he remembered the last time he saw him at his own murdered parents' funeral.

"Tom Barry is here, Tadgh, with a part of the flying column. We're finally using our control center. Tom stood out in the road to flag the bastards down at Kilmichael and blew up the first lorry with a Mills bomb. What a bloody marvelous leader. Come inside and meet him."

Tadgh was thankful Aidan was alive, but he was more than a bit jealous that he now had a new hero.

Before they could reach the house, wiry Tom Barry came striding out in a black trench coat with a broad smile under a shock of black hair. "This must be the famous Tadgh McCarthy, eh, Aidan?"

He shook Tadgh's hand vigorously. Tadgh instantly liked this energetic twenty-two-year-old.

"Infamous, more likely. Let me introduce my wife, Morgan. She's the famous one in our family."

"That's what I heard from Tomas before he was arrested. You both have been leaders of our movement. And how you broke Tadgh out of gaol, Morgan! Legend, my lass, legend!"

Morgan was not impressed. The front yard was all chewed up by the vehicles. Frowning, she responded, "We do our part, Mr. Barry."

"Call me Tom, my dear. Thank you both for the use of your home. Pivotal to our success."

"How many are here, Tom?"

"Eighteen, Tadgh—Michael, Jim, and Pat are gone, brave souls. And presently twenty now that you're home. We have eighty more housed in various safe houses. I hope we have not ruined your kitchen, Morgan. Molly is a good cook, though."

"Not Molly MacIntyre, surely."

"Yes, that's right, lass."

"I met her in Dublin with my Cumann na mBan work, looking after the families of the fallen."

Morgan led the men into the parlor through the stout oak front door. From there, through the kitchen doorway, she could see her IRA sister as she stood near the hundred-year-old Stanley stove. Suddenly Morgan felt violated. *My stove. My house.* As her eyes adjusted to the dark room, she saw soldiers in various states of dress lounging on the parlor chesterfield and chairs. Their boots were filthy, and the ashes from their cigarettes were all over the hemp rug. The smell was rank. The men hadn't showered in days.

She turned to the nearest man and shook her fist. "Besides a lack of manners, don't you men have any common sense?" Pointing to the ash on the rugs, she added, "You could set this house on fire!"

When the man didn't move, she yelled, "*This is my—house!*"

Tom's eyes narrowed at this attack on his men, but he kept his tongue.

Tadgh saw Morgan's plight and stepped between her and the men. "What's your name, lad?"

The object of Morgan's ire sat up at Tadgh's question. "What's it to you?"

"I'm the owner of this house, and I'll ask you to respect it, *and* its mistress, so I will! Stand to attention and tell me your name."

The slovenly soldier stood up and looked at his leader. "Do I have to take orders from this bloke, Tom? We've just come from a hell of a fight."

Tom glared at the assembled group. It was Tadgh's house, but this was war. The men were dog-tired and shell-shocked. He didn't need this further annoyance from Morgan, but he couldn't let discipline slip. In the owners' absence, they had been treating this safe house like a transient hovel. "You men. Stand to attention!"

They all jumped up, hands by their sides.

"You will obey Morgan here when you are in this house. Is that understood?"

The men nodded wearily.

"Now, Willy, answer Tadgh's question. And show respect. This man was a leader during the Rising. He suffered for years in the Joy and almost died on hunger strike until this woman and our comrade Aidan broke him free, at great risk to their lives."

The recalcitrant soldier gave his name and where he was from. It turned out Tadgh knew his father.

Morgan looked at the commander. "Thank you, Mr. Barry." She turned to the soldier and pointed. "Willy, you see that broom over there beside the fireplace?"

"Y-yes, Ma'am."

"It won't sweep itself. I suggest you clean this rug as well. And the rest of you men—there are ashtrays on the sideboard. Please use them in the future."

Aidan piped up. "Now that the owners are home, I suggest, sir, that we spend most of our time downstairs in the control center when we're here."

The men groaned, but Tom took the suggestion to heart. "Good idea, Aidan. Let's leave our hosts to their own parlor and kitchen."

The soldiers filed out except for Willy, who started sweeping. Molly popped her head in from the kitchen. "Am I to feed them all downstairs from now on?"

Tom spoke to her softly. "Aye, lass. It's for the best."

Morgan's eyes popped. "Well, well, Molly?"

Molly turned. "Morgan! Is that you?"

Morgan came to the doorway and hugged her former compatriot. "I trust you're taking good care of *my* kitchen."

"It's a large group of men to feed, as you can plainly see. You came from Dublin? How are Constance and the good doctor Kathleen Lynn these days?"

Morgan had no idea but quipped, "Oh, the countess is her normal feisty self, don't ya know. Can I help you with the meal?"

Molly answered, "Much obliged." The two women stepped back into the homey kitchen together.

"How'd you end up here?" Morgan stirred the stew Molly had prepared.

"One of the men assigned to Mr. Barry. Charlie's a friend of mine if you know what I mean." Molly cut up some vegetables on the wooden cutting board.

Morgan could only imagine what had been going on in one of her two bedrooms. "My home smells like a pigsty."

"I know, but I couldn't stop them. They've had it rough." Her knife made short shrift of the rugged slough of potatoes and gnarled carrots.

"I'm back, and that's going to change." Morgan knocked the wooden spoon against the side of the pot and firmly set it on the counter.

In the next hour, down in the control room, Tadgh heard reports about Tom's leadership from the men. Jim Kearney said, "Any man who would stand on the road before an oncoming enemy, men would die for him." As Dan Canty, another of the Volunteers told him, "Tom's a tradesman, and soldiering is his trade. Our leader can take boys and make soldiers of them."

Tom came in from checking the condition of the beaten-up vehicles. Tadgh seized the opportunity to find out his background. Tom flicked his cigarette into an ashtray and sat on one of the cots. "I enlisted as a volunteer at the age of seventeen to fight the Kaiser," he said.

"In the trenches?"

"No, as a gunner in the Mesopotamia Expeditionary Force under General Townsend." Tom offered a smoke.

"Thanks. I don't smoke, never have." In truth, he had no desire after seeing his parents murdered and their family home torched. "I read that you were pushed back, weren't you?"

"Aye, a nasty business, Tadgh." Tom lit up again. "The 30,000 of us beleaguered troops, one and all, had to withdraw to Kut el Amara. We couldn't break the Turkish-German ring."

"Must have been a harrowing experience."

Tom nodded somberly. "I survived only to be wounded later on the borders of Asiatic Russia."

"Then you returned home?"

He shook his head in the negative. "I went on to fight in Egypt, Jaffa, Jerusalem, Italy, and France until the war ended." He ticked off each of the countries on his fingers as he named them.

"If you fought for England, Tom, why are you now fighting against them?"

"Believe it or not, I fought for Ireland as part of the British Isles. But after witnessing the atrocities the British forces committed here in Ireland, let's say it has motivated me to put my military expertise to work for the Republicans."

"Good lad." Tadgh decided not to tell Tom about his own involvement with the unsuccessful German support for Ireland back before the Rising. "Morgan and I fought in the Belgian trenches near Ostend."

"Invaluable experience, wasn't it, Tadgh. Then you'll be my deputy officer in charge. That's sorted."

"I'd like that, Tom, but I want to treat my brother Aidan as an equal."

"Fair enough."

Tom graciously gave up the master bedroom to the returning owners and bivouacked in the basement control center with the men. Molly continued to stay in the spare upstairs bedroom, and the two women got along famously. Morgan noticed that she had an odd habit of taking an afternoon walk through the woods alone, probably craving solitude from this murdering insanity. But she seemed to take longer than a regular walk would take. With daily duties pressing, that was an unusual diversion. Morgan shrugged it off.

Tadgh was delighted to be home again and in the thick of the fight. At least Tom's Volunteers were using the ninety rifles he had brought to his safe house before the fire consumed the rest of the shipment. For now, thoughts of his recent harrowing trials slipped from his mind. He had questioned his wife about Molly, who seemed shifty to him. Morgan told him she only had a passing acquaintance with the young woman but was happy to have feminine companionship in these harrowing days.

The mood of the flying column had brightened considerably after their Kilmichael attack on the bloody elite C Company RIC Auxiliaries outside Macroom. They had dealt the bastards a mortal blow for the first time since the Auxies had arrived in July when they started pillaging and burning pockets of rebel resistance in West Cork. Those damned ex-World War British paramilitary soldiers that Churchill had sent over to support the RIC. But the tide was turning in favor of the freedom fighters.

While Tadgh re-engaged with the flying column, Morgan turned her attention to plans for Collin's arrival back in Ireland. His newspaper had assigned him to come to Dublin as a senior foreign correspondent since the War of Independence [2] had intensified after Bloody Sunday.

Aidan drove her to Skibbereen, where she telegraphed Jack in Dublin to understand the arrangements. He checked and a day later confirmed by return communication that Collin would arrive at the Cunard dock in Queenstown on December 10. Jack told her that he planned on picking Collin up and arranging a car for him to drive to Dublin for his assignment with *The Irish Times.*

Morgan asked Tadgh if she could go to Queenstown to meet them and brief Collin on what they had learned during their buried Temple residence adventure.

Tom Barry concurred with the plan for Tadgh to take her if he would check out the military climate in Cork City itself. There were rumors that the Auxiliaries might be planning a reprisal for the Kilmichael defeat.

In the late morning of Friday, the 10th, Tadgh and Morgan climbed onto the Kerry for their trip to Queenstown. Clouds to the west were harbingers of a storm on the way as a bitter wind whipped off the Ilen River.

Dressed warmly with a woolen scarf protecting her shapely neck, Morgan nervously picked at the exposed wicker edge of the sidecar.

She checked her watch for the tenth time that morning. "What are you waiting for, Tadgh? Let's get going. Collin's arriving about five o'clock. We need to be on the dock when his ship arrives. It's been four years, you know."

Tadgh knew how long it had been since he last saw his brother-in-law. Most of the time, he had been in the bloody Joy. "Aidan said he would come out to see us off."

As if the mention of his name summoned him, Aidan strode out of the house with a frown shaping his countenance. "Don't let your enthusiasm blind the risks of exposure, you two. Come back in one piece."

"Surely you mean two pieces, Brother," Morgan said as she reached out and kissed him on the cheek.

"I think you are more at risk here than we will be." Tadgh gunned the engine.

"Off with ye, then," Aidan said, "but remember that the bastards in Cork are madder than ever."

"Right you are," Tadgh yelled back just before he spurred the Kerry out onto Baltimore Road.

♣ ♣ ♣ ♣

"There's Jack," Morgan said as they arrived on the Cunard dock around two o'clock.

Jack marched over and announced, "The *Aquitania* will be here in about two hours. They just radioed that they passed the Fastnet light."

Tadgh pointed at the office. "What's your status, Jack?"

"I'm getting settled with Deirdre at the grocery."

Morgan smiled and winked. "I'm sure you are, dear boy."

Jack turned crimson. "But that's not what you meant, was it, Tadgh."

This was the first time the McCarthys had been back where the tragic fire had taken place, where Jack's employee had turned against them and ruined everything. What a lack of judgment Jack had shown, resulting in the loss of crucial arms for the revolution and the punishing incarceration of his compatriot. It was the kind of mistake that would haunt the man for the rest of his days. He knew it, and they could see his hard regret etched into the lines of his face.

"Here, there's a new manager. I'm not fired, just replaced and on leave for now. Management finally decided I won't be charged for abetting a traitor. I can still have access to arrange transportation at sea and on land, thankfully."

"I'm sorry this happened."

Jack turned his head away to avoid Tadgh's stare. "Not your fault, Tadgh. I trusted the wrong longshoreman, and you paid the price. I'm the one who is sorry."

"It seems we both are."

Jack looked back at them. "At least the new manager has no idea who you are. That's one less thing to worry over."

Tadgh left Morgan to wait with Jack for Collin's arrival while he ventured alone into Cork City. The disguise he had chosen this time was that of a longshoreman with a stringy beard and dark glasses. He carried a hook in his belt and had borrowed Aidan's Webley since his Luger had melted in the warehouse fire that destroyed his imported arms from America.

Tom had told him to contact Sean O'Hegarty, the militant IRB member who assumed control as OC of Cork #1 brigade after the demise of both Mac Curtain and then Cork Mayor Terence MacSwiney.

On his way there, Tadgh circled past the RIC barracks on South Terrace, off Sullivan's Quay. Several RIC constables, dressed oddly in army khaki pants and dark green RIC tunics, caps, and belts, assembled outside on the street, many arguing with their counterparts.

True to Tom's word, Tadgh found O'Hegarty living in Mac Curtain's old home in Blackpool on the north side.

"Glad to meet you, McCarthy. Your brother is a credit to our movement."

Tadgh could see that this man brooked no interference. The front entrance was barred, and he had a well-heeled but menacing pit bull terrier named Connolly. *Good.*

The OC cautioned, "There's been a development today because of Kilmichael. You'll need to be careful. Cork, Tipperary, Limerick, and Kerry are now under martial law with curfews. Anyone with a weapon of any kind or out after ten o'clock will be shot on sight."

Tadgh decided he had been foolish to be riding past the RIC office. He'd have to be more careful, mainly where Morgan was concerned. "What's the mood in the city, Sean?"

"I expect an eruption from the Auxiliaries because of Kilmichael. But we're continuing to hound them, keeping them off balance."

"I saw a dozen RIC goons down on South Terrace wearing British army trousers. Angry-looking curs."

"That's them," O'Hegarty affirmed. "We call 'em Black and Tans. Lloyd George turns a blind eye to their burning and pillaging. Bastards all."

Tadgh thought that over for a few moments. "Would it be better to take a more defensive posture now? Cork is still basically a Protestant city."

"I disagree. Tell Tom to keep fighting with all his might. Hit and run. That's what Collins wants. And Tadgh, this is important. Do not carry a gun. We don't do that anymore in case we are stopped. We keep them in safe hidden places like our homes until and unless we are on a mission. Afterward, we stash them back out of sight. Understood?"

"Yes, sir."

Tadgh, ready with information for Barry, arrived back in Queenstown just after the Cunard liner docked. Authorities were questioning disembarking passengers. Morgan and Jack were waiting at the foot of the gang-way when Tadgh joined them. Having a bit of time, he filled them in on what he had learned from Sean. "Mark my words, Morgan. There's going to be hell to pay in Cork City very soon. Our men are pushing the Auxil-iaries to the breaking point."

Morgan scowled. "That's not good, Tadgh. We had better be headed back to Creagh before that happens."

"We will be, I can assure you, love." He didn't feel sure at all.

Morgan was not convinced. She saw that look in his eyes. She would have admonished him further, but she spied Collin at the top of the gangway, suitcase in hand. He looked more mature somehow, more like a businessman. Maybe it had something to do with the grey suit he wore or the swagger in his step. She waved wildly. He caught sight of her and waved back as he descended. After weaving his way past slower passengers, he strode onto the dock toward his relatives.

Dropping his valise, he swept Morgan up into his arms, tears running down his face, a smile ear-to-ear. "I am so happy to see you, Sis." Letting her back down, he reached out and shook the men's hands vigorously. "You, too, Tadgh, and Jack. It's been a long time."

Morgan beamed.

Tadgh clapped him on the shoulder. "You look fit, Collin."

"So do you, given what's happened."

Tadgh took Morgan's hand. "All because of this fine lass who rescued me and takes good care of me, that's certain."

"You've cleared customs on the ship, I presume. Let's go to my flat. I have a company sedan," Jack announced curtly.

Morgan sensed Jack was not at all pleased with all the backslapping. Maybe it was regret.

Collin said, "Thanks, Jack, for getting me across the pond on time."

"Just doing my job, my old job, that is."

Jack's rooms near the docks in Queenstown were spartan, typical for a bachelor, with a small parlor that also served as a dining area, an adjoining kitchenette, two small bedrooms, and a shower-equipped bathroom. The ambiance was a drab off-white. He had prepared supper, and they sat down to beef brisket and turnips.

After swallowing her first few bites, Morgan began, "We've much to tell you, Collin."

"About the war?"

"No. About what happened to the guns, Tadgh's incarceration, and his departure from captivity, among other things." Morgan left out the risks she and Aidan had taken to free Tadgh.

"Tomorrow, we'll take you to see where the guns were destroyed," Tadgh proposed. "They've left it there for us rebels as a monument to the futility of gun-running."

Jack stopped mopping up the gravy with his piece of bread and stared blankly ahead for several moments, then stared down at his plate, mumbling regrets. "Tadgh, I am so sorry. After all your efforts. The loss of your treasure. Your terrible ordeal in prison." His head stayed down, not meeting anyone's eyes.

Tadgh took a swig of stout and wiped his mustache. "Can't be helped now, Jack, can it. I played a part in that fiasco at the warehouse. Even more important to find the O'Donnell treasure, now, don't ya know. That's ahead for us."

Morgan grasped her brother's hand across the table. "We've learned more about our birthright."

Collin was torn. He realized how important his family treasure had become to supporting the revolution, and he was intrigued to know what they had uncovered. But he was mindful of his promise to Kathy not to search for it. His curiosity got the better of him. He cupped his right ear and leaned forward. "Go ahead. I'm listening."

The three Adventurers, as they called themselves over the years, proceeded to tell their compatriot all about their visit to Professor Lawlor, the minute Temple annotation in the *Book of Ballymote*, and all that went on during the flood under Temple Bar.

"Jaysus! I'm glad I didn't know about that when it was going on. I'd have agonized about all of you."

"We were worried, Collin," Morgan said. "It wasn't because of the war."

"That's why Kathy made me promise not to search for our treasure. She still relives the nightmare, with that evil policeman Boyle embedded in her dreams. But she's not here. You can at least illuminate me about what you've found out."

Tadgh gave a terse summary for both Collin and Jack.

Collin, ever the newspaper reporter, made it even simpler. "From what you've said, it appears William Temple searched for some element of chivalrous lore because of his Knights Templar association, but you didn't find out anything to help us determine what the letters PP mean in Tadgh's locket."

"Only that Temple referenced FP or PP in the note he scribbled in the *Book of Ballymote*."

Collin stared at his compatriots. "But your review of that book, which we expected to carry some clue, came up with nothing except for that one item."

Tadgh finished off the last morsel of brisket before answering. "Not necessarily. There are quite a few areas of interest. Just nothing pops out at the beginning or end of any section at this point."

"I find the part about the Barbary Corsair strange and fascinating at the same time." Collin worked on the last of his brisket.

"I know, Brother, we found it quite bizarre ourselves," Morgan said. "As far as history tells us, those pirates only invaded Ireland once, and that was down in Baltimore in 1631, a full four years after the reported attack on the Temples in Dublin. And that was a customary raid for slaves."

"If the pirate wasn't after the O'Donnell treasure, then what *was* he seeking?" Collin asked.

"The same thing that William Temple, Docwra, Carew, and then Jonathan Swift looked for—St. Columba's Epistle."

"I see, Tadgh. You say that Deirdre shows some interest in the whereabouts of our treasure?" Collin looked intently at his brother-in-law. "Is that just general curiosity?"

"No. I think there's more there than meets the eye. With her and her cook."

Morgan shook her head. "I don't agree with Tadgh. She claims an interest in all things Temple because of his affiliation with her former pub. That's all."

Collin's ears pricked up. "*Former?*"

Morgan relayed the unfortunate circumstances surrounding the total loss of her family business. "But she owns a grocery now on the next street."

"My, my. You people certainly have been busy, haven't you."

"One for all and all for one," Tadgh recited. "You're one of us, and we're back together now. You remember the Clans Pact you made with me, don't you?"

Collin frowned. "Of course, but I'm here as a war correspondent first."

"Don't tell me that you're not tempted, Brother," Morgan teased.

"Of course, I am. Temple went to a lot of trouble to build a secret underground study to protect his Templar interests. He was at least aware of PP, it would seem."

Tadgh saw a spark of renewed interest. "Aye, Collin, that's certain."

Collin grunted. "Kathy forbade me to seek the treasure with you because of her perception of the risks. Clearly, what you have just gone through would confirm her opinion."

"A historic freak storm at just the wrong moment almost did us in. Not a villain like Boyle."

"I understand, Tadgh, but Kathy won't see it that way. I have three children as well as my wife to think of." Collin took a photograph from his wallet, smiled, and passed it around. "As you can see, Liam is four, Claire is three, and little Shaina is one. They're all rambunctious, so they are. Kathy sends her best, by the way."

Morgan saw the sparkle in her brother's eyes when he spoke of his family. "Do you miss them, Collin?"

"Aye, truly. They are my joy in life. I hated to leave them. Shaina has our Ma's eyes, don't ya know, Sis."

Morgan felt the pangs of inadequacy to see the lovely family that her brother had nurtured. If only Tadgh would give up his warring ways, they could try for a baby again. She kissed the picture, smiled, and handed it back, saying, "You have beautiful children, Collin, and Kathy looks radiant." Remembering her sister-in-law's state of mind in 1916, she asked, "You're here with her blessing, then?"

"If I stick to reporting the war."

"Oh, and you think that's safe, do you?" Tadgh snickered, "Come back to Creagh with us, and you'll see for yourself."

"I know you need treasure to buy arms, and I agree it should be used for the Cause if indeed it could be found. I will be covering the war from Dublin while you are fighting it in Cork West. I can research anything you need using my newspaper connections, including going back to meet with Professor Lawlor if that would help."

"Perhaps," Morgan said. "We found out that Deirdre knows of Lawlor."

"Does she, now. Odd for a store owner to take an interest in historical literature." Collin narrowed his gaze at his sister. "Don't you think?"

Morgan's eyes dropped to her plate as she played with her fork, moving bits of food around. "We have no idea, Collin. I've told you I trust her."

Jack said, "We do," offering Collin a bottle of B&C stout.

Tadgh downed his remaining beer in one swallow. "Jack does more than trust her, right lad?"

Their host turned his back as if to get more stout from the sideboard as they all noticed his face turning red.

"I can see it is true," Collin said, glancing at his sister as he pulled the cork and took a swig.

She smiled. "They're an item. Jack is managing her store."

Tadgh took a bottle of stout from Jack and popped it open. "We'll leave it at that, then. I am going to be very busy with the war, as you put it. You, Morgan, and Jack, here, can continue to figure out and communicate about the treasure."

"All right, Tadgh. I can be reached through the offices of Mr. Healy, the publisher at *The Irish Times,* or at the Shelbourne. We will have to work out a code for the treasure matters."

Tadgh took Collin aside later and taught him the one Mick Collins had given him.

Before they all went to bed, Tadgh said, "If I'm right, there will be a very newsworthy event in the next couple of days in Cork City, especially now that the counties have been put under martial law."

Morgan pressed him gently on the arm. "We need to get away from this violence, mavourneen."

"In good time, my love. Tom wanted me to scout out the mood of the city. Oh, and Collin, perhaps you can stay here for a few days before going to Dublin. It might be worth your while drumming up some first-hand news if you catch my drift."

"Your hunch or a known fact?"

"A calibrated guess," Tadgh said with a smile.

Collin frowned. "I am supposed to report to Mr. Healy as soon as possible. My paper expects hard coverage."

"I can guarantee there will be some hard news generated here in the next few days."

"You said a couple of days, Tadgh, so I'll give you two days."

"Fine, you can accompany me to Cork City tomorrow morning."

"I'll have to contact both papers."

"I can arrange that," Jack offered, gathering up the dishes.

"All right, then." Tadgh beamed. "That's sorted."

Morgan stepped between them and got right in Tadgh's face, her green eyes blazing. "Not so fast, my love. Our purpose was to meet with Collin and inform him of our progress, not put him in harm's way."

Tadgh put his arm around her waist and pulled her in. "We've done that. Now I am just trying to steer your brother toward a developing war news story to help him justify his trip here. Plus, I am being Tom's eyes and ears."

Collin sought out his sister's eyes. "It would help me, Sis, if Tadgh's right."

"You men. Trying to get yourselves killed. Promise me that you'll stay out of the fight if it occurs, mavourneen."

"It is just a scouting trip. I will promise to make sure Collin and I are safe."

Morgan pushed back against Tadgh's grip, her eyes fierce. "I'll come with you, then. Where you go, I go. We can take Jack's car, can't we, Jack?"

"If I go with you, yes," Jack announced.

Collin shook his head. "I think you should stay here, Sis."

For once, Tadgh agreed with his brother-in-law.

"Not on your life, boys." Morgan stood there, hands on hips, a formidable wall.

Collin grimaced. "I didn't like the way you put that, Morgan." But he secretly liked her spunk.

She turned on her heel to help Jack clean up the kitchen. "It's settled then. We're all going."

Tadgh knew better than to cross her. She'd saved his life more than once already.

The next day, before they left Queenstown, with it being a sunny but cold Saturday, they took Collin to see what had happened to the arms they had risked everything to procure. He wanted photos of it for an article in his paper. The burned-out warehouse was a few blocks away. The molten metal blobs, fused gunstocks, and barrels were all that remained of the seven boxcars of munitions they had bought in America using the McCarthy Gold treasure. Jack hung back, the guilt for his part in the debacle too much to bear.

Collin kicked at the nearest clump of metal and groaned. "After all that trouble to acquire these arms using your incredible treasure, this is all that's left." He met Tadgh's eyes with his own. "I am profoundly sorry." It didn't sound any better than it had yesterday.

"*You're* sorry? I kicked myself all those years in the Joy for not whipping that stealing bastard before the warehouse caught fire."

Morgan looked back outside the burnt hulk of the warehouse and waved her arm. "Jack. You come in here. It wasn't any of you boys' fault. What's done is done. Let's drop it now. We've another treasure to hunt and find."

As they left, Collin thought of the Toronto waterfront warehouse nine years earlier, where his life changed in an instant. He remembered his decision to free his mentor Sam just before the arsonist burnt it down. An uncontrollable shiver ran down his spine. If Sam hadn't carried him out in the nick of time, he'd have died a fiery death just like these guns. Kathy wasn't the only O'Donnell with nightmares.

The four Adventurers drove to Cork City. Collin hoped the *Cork Examiner's* editor, George Crosbie, would be in his office. John Healy had recommended he contact his counterpart. Jack pulled up at their offices at Ninety-Five Patrick Street, Blackpool, noticing the police guard at the entrance.

Tadgh and Morgan ducked down in the car before they could be seen. Collin leaned over toward Jack. "Best I go in alone. Give me thirty minutes." Collin jumped out while Jack watched him go.

He relayed that the guard was demanding that Collin provide identification, all the while staring at their car, a hand on his holstered revolver. "All right, he's satisfied now, and Collin is entering the building."

Tadgh peered over the sill of the car window. Seeing the guard's disinterest, he asked Jack to drive them by the RIC barracks on the other side of the Lee River. Jack questioned his judgment but obliged.

Cruising by, Tadgh grew concerned and commented, "That's strange. The blighters are nowhere to be seen."

Morgan nudged him. "What does that mean?"

"It's not a good sign, Morgan."

"We should go home, then."

"We will, soon." Tadgh wasn't going to miss this opportunity to hit back at the enemy. "Head back to pick up Collin, Jack."

Collin had found the balding George Crosbie, dressed in a black three-piece suit and hard at work on a Saturday in his smoke-filled mahogany-paneled office. When Collin was ushered in by a secretary and introduced, the editor stood up from his papers and came around his desk.

Extending a meaty paw, he shook Collin's hand vigorously, saying, "I am here this afternoon because we expect trouble. The IRA will resist martial law. The Auxiliaries are looking for a fight after Kilmichael. The city is a powder keg, son, and you'd be wise to leave."

"Best time for a reporter to be here, sir, that's certain. Mr. Healy suggested I check in with you upon arriving from Canada."

"How is the old buzzard?"

"Fine, I assume, sir. I haven't been up to Dublin yet." He stared at Crosbie. "By the way, I was questioned by the police guard at the entrance."

"We've had threats since we generally support the Crown."

"IRA?"

"Precisely, my boy."

"Any idea where this trouble will erupt?"

"No. The attacks and reprisals are sporadic but deadly."

Collin took the seat Crosbie offered. "Do you personally support a united and free Ireland, sir?"

Crosbie's eyes narrowed. "That's an odd question, lad. I just told you the *Examiner* is unionist."

Collin grinned. "That's what Mr. Healy likes about me. I ask questions that probe. Some of your mayors have a different conviction, I understand. I'm just trying to ascertain whether the mood of the city is changing. Off the record, of course."

Crosbie blew out a thick cloud of smoke. "Harrumph. Mac Curtain and MacSwiney, the both of them, I grant you, were honorable men for their cause. I understand their passion for freedom, I do. But the British will never allow their business enterprises in the north to break away. Fact of life, son." Crosbie stubbed out his cigar with a flourish. "Other papers like the *Southern Star* and *The Cork Free Press* have been suppressed. Been that way ever since General Maxwell assigned Lord Decies to stamp out revolutionary journalism after the Rising. Defense of the Realm Act and whatnot."

Collin tapped his fingers on the publisher's desk in front of him. "It has been my experience, and I saw it personally in Dublin after the Rising, that severe oversight, if I can use that term, serves to antagonize, rather than subdue the population. That goes for attempts to muzzle the press, I might add, sir."

"That remains to be seen, son, but current actions support your view. Being an objective newspaperman, I leave it at that."

"Fair enough, Mr. Crosbie. I plan to stay here for the next few days to see what develops."

"In that foolhardy case, I want you to work with my political reporter."

Crosbie made a call, and a bespectacled young man came running.

"Alan Ellis, meet Canadian reporter Mr. Collin O'Donnell. Show him our city and the most vulnerable areas."

"Certainly, boss." Ellis offered his hand, and Collin shook it. Alan said, "I plan to be out by City Hall until curfew this evening at ten o'clock.

You can join me. But we'd best be careful. Now there is martial law, about a thousand RIC and Auxiliaries came down out of Victoria Barracks and took over the city last night. Brawlers, they are. There's going to be trouble soon enough."

"Don't take any unnecessary chances, Alan," warned Crosbie.

"No, sir. We won't."

Crosbie nodded and with a "Good luck," turned his back, dismissing them, and walked to his desk.

On their way to the front entrance, Alan told Collin he needed to go to his desk and make a telephone call to his wife first. They agreed to meet at the curb.

Jack's vehicle drew up to the curb when Collin emerged from the newspaper office. The police guard watched closely as Collin jumped in the back seat, almost crushing the hunched-over Morgan and Tadgh.

Morgan said, "Drive around the corner, Jack, and stop out of sight."

Once away from the *Examiner*, Collin explained the plan.

Morgan glared at the men. "Haven't you done enough, Tadgh? You almost died. Let that reporter take the risks. He'll give us a report in the morning."

"We've been through this, aroon. I feel fit enough. There's a war on. My commander gave me an assignment."

"You, too, Collin," scolded Morgan. "You've shown us your loving wife and three small children at home. Why risk your life tonight needlessly when an Irish reporter can get the information for you?"

Collin thought about that momentarily. Then his newspaper correspondent instincts took over. "My boss sent me across the ocean to give firsthand accounts and analysis of this war. How can I do that if I don't see it for myself?"

"Honestly, I've said it before, you men and your war. If I can't change your minds, then I'm going with you."

"You'll do nothing of the kind, my love," Tadgh said. "Especially tonight. Probably nothing will happen, anyway. You'll go with Jack."

Collin piped up. "For once, I agree with Tadgh, Morgan. Go with Jack."

Morgan threw up her hands. "Where?"

Jack thought for a minute, a chance to be alone with Morgan. He scribbled the address Number One Brian Dillon Road, intersection Old Youghal Road on a piece of paper and handed it to Tadgh. "I contacted

George Finstead, one of the Cunard managers, before leaving Queenstown. He lives in the city with his wife and young daughter. They offered to put us all up for the night if necessary. Morgan and I will go there in case you need us. You boys can come to us on the tram before the ten o'clock curfew."

Tadgh looked at the paper. "That's near Dillon Cross, right? I've been in a pub there."

"Right at it."

Morgan shook her finger at her husband, then hissed, "You listen to me, Tadgh McCarthy! I didn't go to all the trouble of liberating you from the Joy just to have you get yourself and Collin arrested or killed. Be at Jack's friend's house by ten. Promise me!"

Tadgh kissed her solidly on the mouth. "I'll bring us back safe and sound after we find out what's going to happen, by dawn at least."

Morgan pulled him by the collar, looking him square in the eye. "Ten o'clock curfew!"

Before Morgan could argue further with the hard-headed men, Collin said, "Best drive back to the *Examiner's* entrance, Jack. Alan should be there by now."

Ellis was pacing the pavement when they arrived. He hopped into the back seat and was surprised to find it occupied. Jack drove off down Patrick Street and stopped.

Collin said, "We're getting out here, Alan," and he and Tadgh jumped out onto the curb. Ellis followed, and Collin introduced Tadgh as Duffy since he wasn't sure of Allan's political allegiances.

After Morgan joined Jack in the front seat, he turned the automobile around and headed back up Patrick Street to safety.

The three men turned left down Princes Street, walking toward Lee River.

IRA Captain Seán O'Donoghue received intelligence of two lorries of Auxiliaries planning on leaving Victoria Barracks just before eight that night, heading for the city down Old Youghal Road. He expected intelligence officer Captain James Kelly, a suspected British spy, would be on board. He and five of his men positioned themselves between Dillon's Cross and Harrington Square, planning an ambush to kill all the British in the convoy. One brave rebel, Michael Kenny, stood across the road dressed like an off-duty British officer to flag them down. The others would then throw bombs into the British lorries from behind a four-foot wall along the route.

They implemented their plan like clockwork, including rifle volleys into the two lorries, each carrying thirteen Auxiliaries. They set their escape in motion, through O'Callaghan's Field, down to Gouldings Glen.

The rebels wounded thirteen Auxiliaries, and one Temporary Cadet, Chapman, subsequently died in the encounter. Bystanders later said that the Auxiliaries avoided a worse slaughter by taking immediate refuge in neighboring O'Sullivan's pub, dragging their wounded with them.

Jack's manager's home was located within a hundred yards of the attack. He heard the explosions and rushed out just in time to see the Auxiliaries pour into the pub, with the one bombed and bullet-ridden lorry sitting derelict and the other still idling in the roadway.

Jack realized this was still an active war zone as bullets whizzed by him, and he turned to escape.

One of the Auxiliaries ran back out to drive the still-serviceable second lorry back to the barracks for help and saw Jack attempting to flee the scene.

"Come on back, Jack! There's nothing you can do!" Morgan yelled in his direction from the front door near Old Youghal Road. "There's no telling what they'll do now!"

He heeded her advice and ran to the safety of the home where George's family cowered in the parlor. "It'll be all right, George, they're not headed this way," consoled Jack through gulps of air.

Morgan saw Jack wince, probably from the pain in his back, as she comforted the wife and young daughter.

When an hour passed without reprisal, Morgan thought she could relax a little. "Tadgh and Collin should be back soon." She sat back in a comfortable chair, but her respite was short-lived. She heard a pounding at the door, followed by a shout, "Open up! This is the police!"

Jack opened the door a crack.

A man shouted on the other side. "That's him. The one I saw on the road after the attack."

Auxiliaries pushed the door open wide and commandeered all occupants of the home, dragging them out onto Old Youghal Street. They took particular delight in threatening Jack with their bayonets, and Morgan prayed they didn't pierce through his clothing. She looked around and saw the occupants of six other houses being herded toward them.

"The bombs came from here!" the Auxiliary in charge bellowed and then directed his shouts to the people in the neighborhood. "We're burning your hovels to the ground!"

Morgan's yell that this was not true was ignored. The Auxies were out for blood.

"My God! No!" George's wife screamed with her fists clenched up against her chest.

Auxiliaries shattered the windows of the family's home with rifle butts. Other men in uniform carried out whatever valuables they could. When they finished, one of them threw an incendiary bomb through the front door, and it exploded.

George's wife flung herself at the man, wailing. The two of them clutched their terrified daughter.

Flames swiftly engulfed the house. The scene repeated itself along Old Youghal with home after home until fire billowed from the whole row in one gigantic inferno. All the while, Auxiliaries aimed their rifles at the residents, holding them all hostage.

The Auxiliary who had singled out Jack marched up to him once more. He hit Jack across the face with the butt of his rifle, drawing blood from Jack's mouth. "You were part of this plot!" the Auxie screamed.

Jack cried out and collapsed to his knees. He scrabbled in his pocket for his Cunard identification. He held out the bit of printed pasteboard, now spattered with his blood, hoping for some understanding and comprehension. It was futile. The attackers were crazed with revenge. He pleaded with them, "I heard a loud noise. I only rushed outside to see what it was and if anyone needed help and—"

The Auxie cut him off. "Shut your bloody gob!"

The commanding officer strode up. He plucked the bloodied card from Jack's hand, sneered at it momentarily, then threw it away. "Stand this man up, strip him naked, and make him sing 'God Save the King' until I tell him to stop."

Two Auxiliaries yanked Jack to his feet. One held him at gunpoint while the other wrestled off his coat and ripped open his shirt, the buttons popping away. Then he undid the belt on Jack's trousers.

The violation inflamed Jack. He wanted, in the most awful way possible, to kick the Auxiliary in the most sensitive bits. Let the bloody coward have a taste of his own medicine! But that would have gained Jack nothing except another rifle butt across the face or a bullet in the head.

The Auxiliary pried off Jack's shoes and pulled his pants down. Moments later, Jack stood unclothed in the freezing December night air, vainly trying to cover his privates. Morgan wanted to give him her coat but thought better of it. Up until now, she had not been recognized. George's wife covered her young daughter's eyes.

"Sing, you bastard!" the Auxiliary yelled.

Jack started singing raggedly—

> *God save our gracious King;*
> *Long live our noble King;*
> *God save the King!*
> *Send him victorious,*
> *Happy and glorious,*
> *Long to reign over us:*
> *God save the King!*

At least the fires offered a semblance of warmth. Time slowed for Jack, forced into continuous singing. The song had three verses, but Jack knew only the first one, the one he sang over and over until his voice gave out and turned into a croak.

Despite his predicament, or perhaps because of his strength to stoically endure it, Morgan thought he was wonderful.

Waves of back spasms from his prior *Lusitania* injuries, enhanced by the cold air, rolled over him. He sank to his knees on the pavement. From across the street, the officer yelled, "That's enough! I've word the bastards came from Blackpool. We're done here. Let's head downtown."

With that, the Auxiliaries rushed off down Old Youghal Road, leaving the citizens homeless. None were dead, but now they were out after curfew and subject to being shot on sight.

Jack's nose oozed blood, and his lip swelled. He could feel with his tongue that the blow from the rifle butt had knocked out a tooth, and he was shaking from the cold. Morgan helped him to his feet, noticing him wince.

"Old injuries, Jack?" she asked, and he nodded, his face turned away.

While Jack retrieved his scattered clothes and began to put them on, Morgan saw that he had a muscular physique and marveled at it. Perhaps the marvelous rippling effect resulted from working on his body through arduous therapy during recovery from the back injury. No wonder Deirdre was interested.

Morgan tore a strip from the bottom of her blouse. Finding a nearby patch of snow that wasn't yet dirty, she wet the cloth. Turning Jack's face toward her, she said, "Hold still. I'm going to clean you up best I can."

Jack's eyes lit up. "Aye, lass. Much appreciated."

As she worked on his face, she watched his eyes change to hard flint. She touched his injuries, and she saw him try not to flinch, his jaw tight. Once he was dressed, she saw him shake off his pain to thank her again, and with a squeeze of her hand, he took charge, a manager still.

The other families scattered, looking for refuge, except for the Finsteads. Even with his voice gravelly and worn, Jack's concern for all the others shone through. "Come with me. We must get off the street. Curfew."

Morgan saw that George's family couldn't stop staring at the smoldering ruin of their home. Moving between them and their blackened abode, she gently put her arm around the man's wife and said, "I know this is terrible, but it could get worse for you if we don't get out of sight. Fortunately, our automobile is parked farther up Brian Dillon Road. It's probably undamaged. We can take you to a safe place. Jack, help me lead them there."

Jack swept their daughter up in his arms and headed for the car at a jog. As he expected, that jarred the Finstead adults back to reality, and they set out after Jack and their daughter on the run.

"Get in, everyone, hurry," Jack urged when they reached the safety of the car.

Jack saw the manager hesitate. He'd just seen his home go up in flames. "Where can we go?" pleaded a stunned George.

"You will stay in my flat in Queenstown until we can figure out what to do. I won't be needing it."

"We couldn't."

"Do you have an alternative?"

"No. We've lost everything."

"Then come with me."

Morgan placed the daughter in the back seat, and the parents climbed in beside her.

Jack eased himself into the driver's seat, but Morgan closed the back door and stood transfixed.

Jack leaned out his window and said, "Let's go, lass."

"I am staying right here until the boys return."

"You'll do nothing of the sort, my dear. There'll be more convoys of Auxiliaries coming past here from Victoria Barracks, I can assure you."

"I'm staying. My husband should be right along since it is after curfew."

"I heard him say they would be back by dawn, not curfew, Morgan." Jack could see that there was no place to hide in the aftermath of the burnings, and it would be dangerous for her to remain there.

"Get in. We'll wait a few minutes, and then we'll go, with or without them. After I drop you off at my flat, I'll come back for the boys if they aren't here in ten minutes."

Morgan shot him a stern look but toyed with the passenger door and finally hopped in. "We'll decide after we wait."

Jack's limit on the waiting period expired. Behind them on Youghal, another loaded Auxiliaries Lorry rumbled by, heading into the city without stopping. He fired up the sedan and drove east, carefully avoiding the roads around Victoria Barracks.

"I'm not happy leaving the boys like this," Morgan snapped. She clasped her hands, twisting them in her lap.

"You don't have to like it, girl. I helped save you on the *Lusitania,* and I'm not going to lose you now." Jack realized he sounded in charge; he was happy he finally said it.

Usually in command of any situation, Morgan was impressed by Jack's strength so soon after his humiliation. Thinking back on his body so painfully revealed, she realized she liked this strong man who could stand up to and wasn't hell-bent on killing his enemies. A man who might live long enough to have a family. It wasn't right to have these thoughts—not fair to Tadgh. But where was her husband now? It was after curfew. Jack had been there to protect her while Tadgh was off, God knows where, likely risking his life again. What did Jack mean about not losing her now? What about Deirdre? It felt good to be wanted by a man who would take punishment to minimize risk to his loved ones. She had a momentary thought for herself, thinking about what *she* wanted for a change. She scolded herself for having such sinful thoughts and drummed them out of her head, or so she thought.

Jack, for his part, kicked himself for not seizing the opportunity to kiss the love of his life to show his appreciation for her kindness in his hour of need.

Chapter Four
The Burning

Saturday, December 11, 1920
Downtown Cork City, Ireland

*T*adgh and the two reporters sat waiting in Clancy's Bar on Princes Street. The barkeep announced that the last round would be at nine o'clock so that patrons could head home before curfew. Twice that evening, the Black and Tans visited the establishment and swept the room for persons of interest. Tadgh retired to the loo both times and avoided detection.

After the pub shut its doors, the three made their way north to St. Patrick Street in the shadows of the buildings, away from the streetlights. A little after ten, they saw a small group of Auxiliaries with tam o'shanter caps weaving down the main shopping street, apparently in a drunken state and cursing all the while. Moments later, the men threw incendiary bombs into the Grant and Company building, with explosions igniting fires that quickly spread to the roof. Collin slipped out of hiding with his No. 2 folding Autographic Brownie camera—just long enough to get an unmistakable silhouette of the perpetrators against the backdrop of flames.

Minutes later, the Fire Brigade raced up, and the Superintendent jumped down from the pumper to survey the damage. His men followed, setting up the hoses before he announced, "Never mind that, boys. This building's gone. There's more trouble to the east."

Before the man could climb back up, Alan darted out and grasped his arm.

"Alan Ellis of the *Cork Examiner*. What's going on?"

"Huston, here. Auxiliaries were attacked earlier near Victoria Barracks. About fifty of them then headed out on a rampage. I think they want to burn the city. We're going to be overwhelmed here shortly, I'm afraid."

"Where? Near the barracks?"

"Dillon's Cross, lad. I'm sending a pumper. There are houses burning!"

With that, Huston was up and gone down St. Patrick Street, bells clanging.

Collin heard the exchange. "Duffy. That's where our folks went!"

Tadgh shouted, "How far to Dillon's Cross, Alan?"

"About a mile and a half."

"Show us."

In the shadows, the three rushed east on St. Patrick's Street toward the bridge. They hadn't covered more than a third of a mile when they came upon a horrific sight. The eastern sky was lit up like day. Where the Munster Arcade and Cash's Department store had recently stood, a massive conflagration now threatened the surrounding businesses. Huston's pumper gushed water on the blaze.

Battling Auxiliaries tried to bayonet the hoses, sabotaging the firefighting efforts.

Tadgh thought of aiding the firemen but realized it would be suicidal. Skirting the melee and heading northeast, he said, "C'mon, lads. They're mad arsonists. They won't give us any mind."

Allan hung back, aghast. He couldn't believe what was happening to his city. Tadgh had to pull him along.

Collin kept snapping pictures of the fires at various businesses until they crossed Patrick's Bridge. Everywhere he looked, he was painfully reminded of his own harrowing warehouse fire experience in his youth. He hoped the fires and streetlights would give enough illumination to expose the film. The focus could also be off, given how shaky his hands were from the memory of that deadly night so long ago. They stopped long enough for Collin to reload another spool of film in the No. 2.

They reached Dillon's Cross a little after eleven o'clock. Houses smoldered with frequent flareups. What was left of them, anyway. Collin took pictures of the ruins and the burnt-out Auxiliary lorry, which had been dragged to the side of Old Youghal Road. He felt a tug on his coat sleeve, turned, and saw Tadgh pointing. One disoriented man still wandered on Old Youghal Road.

Tadgh, Collin, and Alan approached him slowly with their hands visible to show they meant him no harm. Collin then asked the man, "Where's Number One, Brian Dillon Park? Can you tell us?"

The man lifted his soot-stained face. He looked to be middle-aged, with red-rimmed and bloodshot eyes. And not from drinking, Collin grimly surmised. The stranger seemed dazed, but who wouldn't be?

"Number One, Brian . . . ?" the man repeated blankly. "Oh . . . Finstead? George Finstead's house?" His voice cracked. "Why, it's gone. It's gone, it is! Like mine." The man pointed to the corner house reduced to smoking rubble. Then he dissolved into tears. His shoulders heaved.

Collin scanned the street without seeing Morgan. He put his arm around the unfortunate man for support. With as soothing a voice as he could muster, Collin said, "We're friends of George. Where is he? Do you know where he went?"

The man dragged a sleeve across his face and composed himself with great effort. "Gone. Along with his whole family. Oh! And there was another man with them. And a woman. I remember. The Auxies burned the house. They stripped one poor man naked in the street, they did."

Collin's fears grew. "Who took them?"

"No one. They left in the man's automobile after the goons left."

Tadgh chimed in. "When?"

"Dunno. Maybe an hour ago."

Collin took the man's hand. "Thank you, sir. It's not safe here. Wait a minute, and we will help you."

Tadgh and Collin walked down the street, a block away from the cloud of smoke, where they could speak privately. The newspaperman turned to his brother-in-law. "Where would they go?"

Tadgh answered immediately. "Jack's a smart lad. He'd have taken them out of harm's way. Queenstown, maybe?"

Collin clenched his fists. "Here we thought we were sending them to safety, and they ended up in grave danger."

Tadgh threw up his hands. "The best-laid schemes o' mice an' men gang aft a-gley, as they say."

Collin swept his arm out towards the burnt-out hulks. "Robert Burns aside, I fail to see the levity here with these schemes of mice and men. My sister was right."

"In war, sometimes humor is all that keeps us sane, Collin."

"All right. What should we do now, Tadgh?"

"At least one of us should stay here. Jack will come back for us, that's certain."

Ellis had taken Collin's cue and was organizing neighbors on the next street over to take in the displaced man when Tadgh and Collin found him.

Tadgh asked, "What happened to all the families whose houses were torched, I wonder?"

Alan told them that neighbors had temporarily taken in most.

Collin pulled Alan aside, asking, "What's your plan?"

"I'm going back downtown as soon as I get this sorted."

The Canadian newspaperman turned to Tadgh. "If my sister and Jack are safe, I'm going with him for the story."

Tadgh knew Morgan would disapprove of him letting Collin go back into that war zone unescorted. Besides, Tom was expecting a full report. "Then I'm going with you." Jack and Morgan would just have to wait.

The three of them returned to Patrick's Bridge over the north channel of the Lee River. By then, it seemed that the whole downtown section of the city was ablaze.

Alan surveyed the devastating scene. "Sweet Brigid. The Auxiliaries have gone berserk. There'll be hell to pay for this. You can bet your life on that."

Collin busied himself taking pictures.

Tadgh and the two reporters caught up with Superintendent Huston. He and his firemen were pinned down by sniper fire at the river just north of the City Hall. From their vantage point just north of Clontarf Bridge across the south channel of the Lee, Tadgh could see officers carrying petrol cans into the government building from East Albert Quay.

Alan was livid. His city was being ravaged. "Those bastards intend to torch City Hall. Why destroy their own buildings? It doesn't make sense. They are obviously out of control."

Collin pointed his camera at the fire brigade, hoping to get this on record. "Aye. How can we stop them, Duffy?"

Tadgh rubbed his mustache and said, "We can't, but maybe we can assist the firemen."

"How?"

"By taking out the sniper. Wait here with Alan. I'll be back."

Collin held a hand out to hold his brother-in-law back from any reckless action. Too late. Tadgh was already gone.

The fire pumper was just across the river from the hall, on the north side of the Lee. Sniper fire erupted from high in the City Hall. *Where?* Tadgh raced west on Lapp's Quay on the north side of the river. He scanned the building's façade until he reached Parnell Bridge. *There!* He could see the flash of rifle fire coming from the third story, the sniper's barrel exposed.

The effective range of his Webley was fifty yards. From the north shore, he was at least a hundred yards away. Shooting would only invite return fire. This job would need to be done up-close and quietly.

Tadgh crossed Parnell Bridge. He entered City Hall from the west side, away from the activity on the quay. Animated voices sounded on the ground floor to his east. Worse, he smelled petrol while bounding up the stairs two at a time to the third floor.

In the north hallway, he removed his belt. Then he heard an intoxicated voice from below. "We're set here, Jocko. Time to go."

The office door nearest Tadgh flew open. The sniper rushed into the hallway. Tadgh was on him in a flash. The marksman whipped around and got a shot off. Tadgh had dropped to the floor and then rolled to the right. The bullet missed his head by inches.

The sniper aimed again. Tadgh pounced, whipping his belt around the gunman's neck. He spun him around, tightening the noose with his knee in Jocko's back. A gurgling sound, a crack of the neck, and it was over.

Tadgh felt the explosion rock the east side of the building. It took him less than a minute to strip off the corpse's clothes and don them himself. This would be an excellent disguise for later. He took the sniper's Ross Mk III rifle and headed for the west stairwell.

The smoke from the ensuing fire was choking him when he reached the ground floor. He rushed out the west doorway and headed away from the growing inferno toward Parnell Bridge. As Tadgh approached his comrades on the north side of Clontarf Bridge, he saw them being prodded by two Auxiliaries.

Seeing a familiar uniform with sniper stripes, one yelled, "Hey! You're not Jocko."

Tadgh's Webley rang out, and the Auxie fell at Alan's feet, blood oozing out of the hole in his forehead. The other officer raised his revolver to shoot. Tadgh wheeled and pulled the trigger, but his weapon jammed. Collin instinctively gave the soldier a roundhouse punch, knocking the man off balance. His shot went wide. Tadgh lunged. His knife caught the man just under the Adam's apple, and the silent fellow died as he fell in a heap at Collin's feet.

Alan was petrified. Collin jumped forward and clapped Tadgh on the back in awe of his brother-in-law's military prowess. He took pictures of the fallen Auxiliaries.

"We'd better move from here," Tadgh said, pulling Alan away from the scene of his attack toward the firefighters.

The city fire raged. Tadgh's action went unnoticed by the mob. To the south of the bridge, with the sniper fire stopped, Huston got to work. By the time Tadgh and the reporters reached the fire brigade, the crazed Auxiliaries had moved on to incinerate the nearby Carnegie Library.

One firefighter brandished a pickaxe at Tadgh. Collin stepped in between, flashing his reporter's credentials. "Hold! He is not an Auxiliary. He's disguised to get rid of the sniper shooting at you." The firemen backed off.

Tadgh would have liked to change disguises, but his longshoreman's togs had likely been burned up in the City Hall inferno.

Huston was deploying his men. Tadgh thought they had no chance of saving the historic building. The arsonists knew what they were doing.

"We have reinforcements that arrived two hours ago from Dublin," the superintendent told them when they got him aside. "But the city's ruined. I've counted over fifty businesses destroyed, and I'd guess another two hundred buildings damaged so far. Latimer and his Auxiliaries will pay for this disaster."

Alan explained that Lieutenant Colonel Owen Latimer was the K Company Auxiliaries' commander stationed out of Victoria Barracks.

Tadgh checked his watch. "I think we've seen enough. We've got to get back now."

Collin stowed his No. 2 camera in his knapsack and nodded his head.

Ellis said, "I'm going to stay and report to the *Enterprise* in the morning. It's been quite a night."

The newspapermen shook hands and wished each other Godspeed. Collin closed the loop. "Thanks, Alan. I'll check with you later."

Tadgh and Collin found Jack and Morgan at Dillon's Cross at six in the morning. Jack was distributing supplies from the Cunard office to the displaced victims taking refuge in neighbors' homes. Morgan was caring for three children burned in the attack with a medical kit she had brought from Queenstown.

"Thank God you are both all right," Morgan cried out when they found her. She gave both a fierce hug, Tadgh first. "I wanted to come after you, but Jack refused."

"Since when do you take orders from *any* man, aroon?"

"Don't you be starting in on me, Tadgh McCarthy. We heard the whole town is on fire."

"It is," Tadgh confirmed. "But I'm glad you are both safe. We got wind that you were burned out of the home here, and Jack almost killed."

"It was a bit embarrassing at the time." Jack fingered his collar. "Morgan was a rock."

"Were you, lass? How, may I ask?"

"She kept the angry homeowners from doing anything rash. Probably saved my life."

Tadgh knew Jack must have been in danger. "I'm sorry we missed all the fun."

"Don't you kid about that, Tadgh. Jack was stripped naked and forced to sing the British anthem until he collapsed."

"I wouldn't have done it, lass," Tadgh said, shaking his head.

"Try refusing with a rifle pointed at your heart, Tadgh," Morgan snorted, her hands on her hips.

Collin came over, waved his camera, and interrupted, "All right, you two. I think I'd better get to Dublin with these photographs. I've got a bit of a scoop here, I think."

"And we've got seven families with out homes anymore," Jack retorted.

"Well said, Jack. At least your heart's in the right place." Morgan's eyes burned, angry with their banter.

Tadgh noticed Morgan's change in behavior towards him. He had had enough of the praise for Jack. "All right, lass. I promised we'd come back safe, and here we are."

Morgan thought better of responding to this callous remark in mixed company. She'd have loved to blow off steam by saying, "Fine lot of good that did us!" but what was she furious about? She'd handled worse than the Auxies, even back at the orphanage. She didn't need Tadgh and his bloody war. But she had to clean up the messes his bloody war caused. Turning to her *Lusitania* savior, she found a calming face and said, "Let's go, Jack, and make sure those poor families are housed and fed."

"Would you like help, aroon?" Tadgh offered.

Taking Jack's hand and pulling, Morgan looked over her shoulder and answered, "No need. We've got this handled. You boys had a rough night, I can see. Why don't you take a rest in the car?"

Tadgh was miffed but let her go as he and Collin headed out onto Old Youghal Road to examine the bullet-ridden lorry, now discarded in the ditch.

He kicked the dirt. "Morgan usually gets my humor, Collin. It helps me relieve the stress of the war. We've come through scrapes together, don't ya know."

Collin placed his hand on Tadgh's shoulder before looking him in the eye. "I'd be careful there, Brother. She loves *you* dearly but *not* your war, that's certain."

They arrived at Jack's home two hours later, where the Finstead family fretted. The sun had just come up. Under happier circumstances, it might have looked like a lovely Sunday in Queenstown. But behind them, in the western distance, they could all see the smoke blotting out the city skyline.

The morning's *Cork Examiner* reported that police dogs sniffed out the scent of escaping IRA ambushers O'Donoghue and Mahony using a cap left behind by an escaping member of the flying column. They tracked them to the home of two IRA members on Dublin Hill. The Delaney brothers, uninvolved in the raid itself, were roused out of their beds by the furious officers at two in the morning and shot dead.

The new manager was explaining that Cunard would put George and his family up in one of the cottages lining the banks of the bay when Tadgh rolled the Kerry out from behind the house.

"We're leaving now, Jack."

"I'll go back to the grocery after I drive Collin to Dublin. I'm available if you need me."

Morgan knew damned well it wasn't the grocery Jack was most interested in. She hoped that Tadgh didn't notice her flushed face as an unexpected tinge of jealousy seized her mind. Then, to erase it, she gave Tadgh a sensuous kiss on the mouth. The heart flutter was still there with her man.

"What was that for?" Tadgh asked, pulling her in.

"Because I love you, you rapscallion, despite your death wish."

Chapter Five
Barbary Pirates

Sunday, December 19, 1920
Shelbourne Hotel, Dublin, Ireland

lthough there were no more achievements like Kilmichael, the 3rd West Cork Flying Column continued to escalate its attacks on the local RIC establishment. Sitting at breakfast that morning in the Shelbourne's Bar and Lounge, Collin read that train service in the area, halted after engineers refused to provide service to the Black and Tans, was restarted with scab labor. But the British establishment infrastructure was clearly rattled.

Leading up to Christmas, Collin was firmly ensconced in Dublin and working closely with his former colleague and, as it happened, Kathy's cousin, Maureen O'Sullivan. His report on the burning of Cork made headlines in Dublin and Toronto. One of his photographs of Tadgh's dispatch of the two Auxiliaries would have made excellent copy, but it would also have incriminated his brother-in-law. Instead, Collin used his photo of the Auxies' attack on Huston's fire brigade outside the Munster Arcade. Before the papers hit the streets in Toronto, he telegraphed Sam and Kathy to let them know he was all right and that he had kept a safe distance from the melee. It was true for that one photograph, at least. No sense in worrying the missus.

Mr. Robertson, the publisher of the *Toronto Evening Telegram,* and *The Irish Times* owner, Mr. Healy, both appeared quite happy with his work. While all that was going on politically and militarily, Collin couldn't break away to visit his sister.

On December 20th, Healy summoned both Collin and Maureen to his office. Peering out from behind his ornate mahogany desk, he asked them, "What do you two know about this potential Government of Ireland Act that His Majesty's parliament is planning to pass?"

"I heard from *Tely* sources that de Valera raked in a lot of money on his America tour," Collin said. "He's back now, isn't he?"

Maureen consulted her notes. "Back and feisty, I understand. Got the Castle's attention, to be sure. My sources in London say it's put a bee in parliament's bonnet."

The publisher tapped the ash of his cigar in his lead glass ashtray. "That all aligns with my information. They're going to try to pass a fourth Home Rule Bill splitting Ireland in two, the northeastern six counties and the other twenty-six counties. In this way, two Irish parliaments would still be part of the United Kingdom, with the Lord Lieutenant of Ireland presiding over both."

"To appease de Valera?" Collin ventured.

"Not bloody likely, O'Donnell. It will only anger him, I'm sure. Lloyd George is in a tough bind. The conservative unionist members of parliament will support this bill while the liberal nationalist members will be dead set against it."

"Then why propose it?" Maureen paused from her hen-scratching.

Collin's face lit up. "To show them who's boss."

Healy puffed furiously, and cigar smoke engulfed his animated face. "Precisely, my boy! I want you two to get me this story when it breaks."

Three days later, Collin wrote his article for the *Tely*. The Government of Ireland Act was passed into law. Just as Healy had predicted, de Valera, head of the southern Sinn Fein party, vociferously opposed its implementation, as did the rebels fighting for independence.

While Morgan grew increasingly isolated at Creagh, Tadgh and Aidan fought for liberty side by side as members of the flying column, and the house ran like a military camp. Hell, it *was* a military camp. Volunteers still came and went with muddy boots as if traipsing through a barnyard. The column had relegated the two women to support tasks. Even Molly had become an overworked mess cook, and the kitchen showed increasing signs of wear. Christmas came and went with only a passing nod. The men had no time for such frivolity.

Morgan remembered that even in the ghoulish Belgian trenches, the fighting stopped on Christmas. She and Tadgh had talked about their altercation the night of the Cork burning, but nothing had been resolved. The war and killing took precedence over their marriage. If Tadgh hadn't been hell-bent on killing every British soldier during the Rising, his time in the Joy had now hardened him to that level of merciless hatred. As she lay in bed alone night after night, with her husband and brother-in-law gone on some dangerous mission, Morgan longed for those early days in this room, where Tadgh ministered to her in her need, where the two of them gently fell in love. This sanctuary was her only solitude.

In the mornings, she would awaken, wondering if her husband and Aidan were missing in action or worse—dead. Then the triage cycle for the wounded and sweeping up the debris would start again. Tom had his own medic. Morgan was only brought in when he couldn't handle the workload himself after a particularly bloody mission.

Once Tadgh asked her why she seemed depressed, but she shrugged it off without answering. She saw no point. He was in a different world, one that had grown ever more morbid and revengeful.

On January 24, 1921, the Roman Catholic Archbishop of Tuam, Thomas Gilmartin, printed a letter stating that IRA volunteers who took part in ambushes "have broken the truce of God, they have incurred the guilt of murder." This notice of ex-communication resulted in an attack on the newspaper that published this rebuke.

Finally, one evening in late January, Tom reported that Peader O'Donnell had been named the OC of a Donegal Flying Column. It came as a shock to the McCarthys, given his pacifist attitude during the Rising. Morgan snapped. She immediately wired Collin with the news and asked him to find out if she could come and stay at the grocery. She decided to resume the O'Donnell treasure hunt without Tadgh. This helped to snap her out of her doldrums.

The next morning, Morgan met Tadgh at their bedroom door. "I'm unhappy here, Tadgh. I am not in agreement with you about this fight, like before. I can't contribute to or influence your actions. And I can't prevent our house from being ruined by your comrades. I want to go to Dublin and stay with Deirdre and Jack for a month. That way, I can be near Collin before he goes home. We can work on finding my family's treasure to help your cause. I can support Constance and the Cumann na mBan that way, perhaps."

Tadgh led her inside and closed the door. "I can't deal with that today, Morgan. I need your help here."

He wasn't listening. "Oh no, you don't, Tadgh. Admit it. You hardly notice my existence these days."

"I had a harrowing experience last night."

"Really. Only last night? You are gone most nights with the men."

"We were conducting an ambush at Dripsey, but the bastards were waiting for us. Two of our men were murdered, ten captured."

"Aidan?"

"He's all right. Just shaken. The dead were his friends."

"Next time, it will be you two."

"It gets worse, Morgan. We found out the informer was a sixty-year-old woman, Mrs. Lindsay. Tom has ordered me to detain her and her chauffeur. If the Auxies execute our men, I am ordered to execute her in cold blood."

Morgan was horrified. "You can't do that, Tadgh, surely."

"Those are my orders."

Morgan's thoughts went dark. Tadgh would not have accepted that order before he was incarcerated. Not for a private citizen, a *woman*. He had changed, just like the rest of them, ruled by the primitive law of an eye for an eye.

Morgan was upset, her eyes dark and accusing, mouth set in a grim line. "You've changed, Tadgh, just like your bloodthirsty compatriots and the damned Auxiliaries. All you seek is revenge, not resolution. I need to get out of here now! Think about how I feel about all this, for once, and put yourself in my position."

"I know, I know. You save lives, and rightly so. I'll think about your request."

With that, Tadgh rolled over on the bed with his fatigues still on and fell asleep, still dirty.

He didn't hear Morgan say, "I'm not your subordinate. It's not a request!"

Collin wrote back that Deirdre would be happy for the company. Morgan was formulating a plan of her own.

Cork was fast becoming the most violent county in the war. On February 15, Morgan heard that thirteen of the finest 3rd Flying Column volunteers, led by Charlie Hurley from Creagh, attacked the Upton Inishannon train on its way to Bandon. The men talked about it. They didn't realize fifty Essex regiment soldiers were on board, intermingled with the civilian passengers. When the IRA men started firing as the train slowed in Upton Station, all hell broke loose. Two attackers were killed, plus one was mortally injured. Several civilians were killed and more wounded. Three of them were even detained as suspect IRA accomplices. The British sustained injuries but no casualties. That was unfortunate, according to Tadgh.

Tom Barry held a council meeting that evening. "The risks are multiplying the more successful we become with our raids. We dare not let up, my lads."

For the first time, Tadgh was worried. The British would find their safe house sooner or later. He was relieved when, miraculously, the nine men, with two more injured from the Upton raid, limped back to Creagh.

That night Tadgh agreed to let Morgan go to Dublin. Aidan would take her on the Kerry and return on the 19th. He was uneasy about it but shrugged it off.

His decision was inconsequential. She had already packed a bag.

On Friday, February 18, the column had a day off in the rain to rest. Morgan cornered Tadgh in the bedroom the evening before she left. "I want to talk to you about my family's treasure. Remember how important it is to find it and arm the revolution?"

"Yes, I remember. But the war here is more urgent. My men are counting on me."

"More urgent than finding the wealth that can fuel this revolution of yours?"

"Ours, Morgan. Ours. The treasure will have to wait."

Morgan moved to the bureau covering up the entrance to Tadgh's secret office. "I've had a lot of time to think about it."

"And?"

"Where's that cutlass?"

"In my hidden room."

"Show me."

Tadgh opened the small door and wiggled into the secret room. "Come on in, lass, if you're not too claustrophobic. I remember what you said when you were in here before."

Morgan squeezed in and stood up. "I endured the flooded ruins of the Temple Residence. I can survive in here."

She looked around at the long, skinny windowless chamber. It was about four feet wide and ran the full twenty-foot length of the bedroom. The end and side walls were rough stonework all the way up to the twelve-foot-high, roughly hewn wood ceiling. On the far end, she noticed a ladder mounted to it with a trap door above it in the old-beamed ceiling. The original built-in roll-top desk spanned the entire width of the room on the opposite end by the door. Tadgh had long since removed the castle drawings from the wall and replaced them with photos of the various

Gaelic relics they connected with the search.

Morgan looked back at the desk. "Remember what you said when you first showed me this room five years ago?"

"Not offhand, aroon."

"I asked you, 'Do you have any idea who may have lived here?' and you answered, 'Maybe it was a left-over Barbary pirate's ghost,' and then you let out a mournful wail for effect."

"Yes, I guess that's what I said because of the strange, carved initials on the desk and symbols on the stair banister."

The cutlass lay on the desk with the rolltop open.

Morgan picked up the weapon and examined it. "Speaking of carved initials, did you see the initials at the base of the blade here?"

Tadgh looked where she showed him. Inside the fancy scroll etching, now showing streaks of rust, he could barely make out three letters. "FJH, I think. There's a space between the second and third letter." He opened the center drawer of the desk and took out his glass. "There's a smaller letter in between. It's a 'y,' I think. Initials of the owner, perhaps."

"That wicked thing is quite heavy. I wonder how they could have swung through the yardarms of their ships with this beast in their teeth."

Tadgh waved the weapon back and forth in that confined space and clamped it in his teeth.

"You're impossible, Tadgh. Don't you dare put that rusty thing in your mouth!"

Tadgh laid it back down on the desk. "You used to think I was gallant."

"Not if you're killing old women." Morgan didn't want to be dragged down into another morbid discussion about the merits of the war. She asked, "When do you think this house was built?"

"I don't really know. Long ago, to be sure."

Morgan turned and slipped out of the room. "Come with me."

She led him out into the garden, now a muddy mess from all the lorries coming and going. "Ugh! Look what they've done to my roses. And the vegetable garden!" She pointed to the weeds in the ruts.

"Is this what you wanted to show me? We'll replace them after we've won the war."

"You mean *if*."

"No, I mean *when*, Morgan."

"Either way, that is not what I brought you here to see. Look over there on the corner of the foundation of the house. I noticed this when I was trying to garden."

On a cornerstone just above the foundation facing the street in the gathering dusk, Tadgh saw one of the many old bullet chips most likely caused by a sundry attack over the ages. "It's just a nick in the rock."

"Look closer."

Tadgh bent over. "Hello! What's this? There's a date etched into the stone, so there is." He squinted. "Looks like the numbers one, six, three, and the last number partly obliterated by a bullet ding. It's either a one or a seven. I never saw that before."

"And when did the Barbary pirates attack Baltimore?"

"June 1631, I think. What does this have to do with the O'Donnell treasure?"

"Come back inside. You'll see." Once they were back in Tadgh's secret room, Morgan said, "Do you see it now?"

Tadgh pulled on the hair of his mustache. "What?"

"The connection between this house and the cutlass."

"Nonsense, girl," he scoffed.

Morgan shook her head. "I don't think so, Tadgh. The pirate was sent to question William Temple about St Columba's Epistle, with Temple being one of the few, if not only, Knights Templar remaining in Ireland in 1627. Think about it! An epistle given to my ancestors in the sixth century. That sounds exciting. Maybe the epistle holds a clue to the location of PP."

"I don't have time for this, Morgan. I've another mission to plan."

"Take time, Tadgh. For me. For what's important to me!"

"Oh, all right. For a minute. That note from your traitor ancestor said an original was buried with the O'Donnell treasure. How can it provide a clue to finding the treasure?"

"Don't you think it strange that there are only two times in the history of Ireland where Barbary pirates came ashore in Ireland?"

"As far as we know."

"Yes, and now it might be possible that this house, built in 1631 or 1637, had a pirate owner or occupant, at least."

"I was teasing when I said it, Morgan."

"But you also told me you bought this house because it was mysterious. Did you think it held secrets?"

"The secret room, yes, but it was after you found the carvings in the banister that I kidded you about the pirates."

"I think you were dead right, Tadgh, and we are destined to discover the truth together."

Tadgh threw up his hands. "That would be too much of a coincidence, lass."

"Would it, though? The Barbary pirates attacked Ireland at Baltimore, a mere four miles from here down the Ilen River, and only once."

He stared at the Moorish cutlass on the open rolltop desk for a minute before turning to face her. "Huh. I see what you mean. They attacked in 1631, and this house was built in 1631 or 1637. I'll bet it was 1631." Tadgh picked up the cutlass again and whistled. "But that would be four years after William Temple was attacked in Dublin."

"I still think that there's a connection here. In fact, I can feel it, Tadgh. Do you remember what happened when I touched the building for the first time?"

"You said there was a feeling of history, a powerful force of déjà vu."

Morgan took the cutlass from him. "I still feel it when I touch the stone with the date, but it's strongest here, in this odd little room, when I hold this weapon."

"I think you're just overwrought, Morgan. What are you saying, then?"

"There could be clues left here by a Barbary pirate."

"But where? I know every nook and cranny of this old house. I suggest you ask Collin to research the attack on Baltimore before we start tearing this house apart."

"Fair enough, mavourneen. Now come to bed."

Tadgh sensed Morgan's thoughts shifting. He knew that glow in her sultry green eyes. "I see that look, aroon. And though it makes my heart burn on fire with the thought of you, we can't have another pregnancy right now."

Morgan stripped off her shirtwaist and unbound her breasts. "That's *just* what we need, my love. But don't worry. I am not fertile at the moment. This will just be practice."

Tadgh checked his watch, then gave his wife a peck on the cheek. "I'm late for that meeting. Tom will be angry. I'll come right back when it's over."

What about me? Morgan recoiled from him and yanked her clothing back on, saying, "Don't bother." She wasn't sure if Tadgh had heard her as he turned and left the room.

Two hours later, he returned to find her sound asleep, curled up in a ball. He didn't notice that she had been crying, the pillow wet with her sadness.

The trip to Dublin was uneventful and less painful than usual for a seven-hour ride in a wicker sidecar. Morgan saw that Aidan handled the Kerry less aggressively than his brother. During the trip, they mostly remained silent, both with their thoughts, until they were at the outskirts of the city.

With the wind in her face, Morgan was elated at having escaped from the captivity of her own home, if it was still her home. She was looking forward to being with her friends in a saner Dublin, despite the damned war.

For the first time in weeks, she laughed and threw her arms in the air. "Don't you feel it, Aidan?"

Her brother-in-law turned his eyes from the road long enough to ask, "Feel what, Sis?"

"The wonderful feeling of freedom, like after we broke Tadgh out of the Joy."

"Aye, that was grand, it was. But freedom will only really come when we've banished Britain from Ireland. I can't wait to get back to Creagh. I wonder what mission I am missing this morning."

Morgan frowned and slapped his arm to get his attention. "You are on a very important mission to get me safely to the grocery without either of us being arrested or killed."

Aidan nodded his head and downshifted into a blind, wooded curve. There ahead, not far enough to evade, was a British lorry broken down at the side of the road. The driver had his head under the hood, and a corpulent officer stood over him.

"Hold on, Morgan. I'm going to drive by them. I might need to speed up."

Morgan adjusted her gray wig that the wind had shifted. They were disguised as an older rural couple heading into Dublin for supplies.

The officer saw them coming and stepped into the roadway with one hand up, and the other with a revolver pointed at them. Aidan hesitated. Should he gun the Kerry and race past them? The bastard could open fire. Presumably, the blighters couldn't pursue. Or should he stop and bluff his way through? There might be other troops in the area. "Let me do the talking, Morgan."

He pulled up beside the lorry and stopped. In his best rural County Kildare accent, he asked, "Need a hand, Officer?"

"O'course I need a bleedin' hand. Who are you people, and where are you going?"

"We're the Smitthins from outside Newbridge, headed to the market in Rathcoole, Sir."

Aidan dreaded the next question, 'Show me your papers,' because there hadn't been time to forge any. He had his hand on the throttle. But the question never came.

Instead, the meaty officer lifted Morgan forcefully out of the sidecar, ordering Aidan, "You're going to take me to the Castle. I'm late for a meeting. You can come back for your woman after that."

Aidan shut off the motor, flipped the kickstand, jumped off the motorcycle, and came around to confront the officer. His muscular driver, who looked to be a mean Limey, poked his head out from under the boot. Per standard practice, Aidan had not brought a gun, but he had a knife hidden in his boot. He gauged his chances of neutralizing both of them. Morgan could get hurt, be recognized, or both. Their disguises were suspect.

"My wife is frail. Let me take a look." He brushed past the driver and stuck his head down into the engine compartment. "Try to start it for me, young sir."

Aidan saw Morgan step out of the way, but she appeared poised to jump back into the sidecar if he motioned to do so. The officer was examining the controls. He looked like he might steal the Kerry and drive off on it himself.

To Aidan's amazement, the driver obeyed him. The engine coughed and then died. Aidan said, "We see this on the farm all the time. What's your petrol status?"

"Half full."

"Then it's your fuel valve." He'd seen the symptom on one of Barry's vehicles. He hoped to hell he was right. If not, he'd fight his way out.

"Switch off the ignition!" he yelled as he picked up a spanner from the fender that looked the correct size. A few minutes later, he disconnected the line to the valve and was thankful to see gunk in the intake.

"Hand me that rag," he snapped at the officer as he glanced down at the cloth on the front bumper behind him. He loved ordering this goon about almost as much as he would enjoy dispatching the bastard. But Tadgh would kill him if he let Morgan be injured or captured.

The officer shouted, "Damn you. Get it yourself."

It was out of reach, and Aidan was holding the line up to prevent the petrol from draining out.

He had a good angle on them now. He could rip out the distributor cap, overpower the officer, and the driver was still in the lorry. *Oh, I'd love to do it!*

Morgan saw him deliberating and hobbled to the bumper, picking up the rag. "Here, Husband. Don't anger the nice officer. Is it the same issue we had with the tractor on the farm?"

Aidan used the rag to wipe out the intake and sealed the line back up. He said, "Mother, get back in our sidecar."

"Start her up again," he shouted to the driver. The engine coughed and died again.

"Again!" This time the engine caught and ran.

Aidan closed the bonnet, wiped his hands on the rag, and handed the dirty cloth and spanner to the officer, making sure the gunk got all over his hand. "Anything else?"

The officer didn't even thank him as he got into the passenger seat of the lorry.

Aidan taunted him. "Can you give us an escort into the city, Sir?"

The Britisher growled, "Get that piece of junk out of our way."

Aidan was happy to oblige, and the lorry lumbered ahead.

After a mile, Aidan said, "See, Sis. I can use kid gloves on the enemy."

"But you wanted to kill them, didn't you, Aidan."

"But I didn't, did I."

Morgan had to admit it. "I'm impressed. Maybe there's hope for you yet."

A little farther along, Morgan announced, "I hate all this killing, Aidan. I see what it's doing to you and Tadgh."

"What do you mean, Sis?"

"Tadgh has changed since he was in the Joy. Inevitable, I guess. He's hardened in his obsession with killing the enemy."

"You're right. We've all changed. Nobody likes to harm another human being, but it must be done for the sake of our country. The damned British are killing us."

"That's your viewpoint, and a good one, Aidan. But the British have their perspective because of our actions. I don't condone what they did in Cork, for instance, but we ambushed them to set it off."

"They have brutalized us for centuries, Morgan. We have to stop them."

Morgan had to yell over the noise of the motor as Aidan gunned it up a hill. "But look at the Great War. Over seventeen million men and women died. And for what? The countries' borders mostly didn't change. The world lost a generation of young men, some childish and egotistical leaders flexed their muscles, and the arms companies got rich. You should have seen the carnage, Brother."

"Great War or not, the British still treat us like vermin."

Morgan shifted to where she could see Aidan's eyes. "And we act like mice, hiding in our holes and darting out to steal crumbs of food."

"But Michael's guerrilla tactics are working, don't ya see?"

"I see that our lives have been irreparably damaged, Aidan. Keep it up, and we'll all be killed."

"For the good of Ireland, Morgan. The martyrs of the Rising are all dead. We're still alive and fighting for freedom. That's something. We can't let them down."

"You and your brother are grand men, lad, caught up in a never-ending nightmare." Morgan saw she couldn't convince either of the McCarthy men that saving lives was infinitely better than taking them. And she had been reduced to being a nursemaid, not even allowed to take charge of triage in her own home.

"You're the best, Sis. You saved me, you know."

"Temporarily, it would seem."

Aidan pulled the Kerry to the side of the Dublin Road and stopped. Consulting his map, he turned to Morgan and announced over the idling Abingdon engine, "I'm going to take the back roads from here on out to avoid any British checkpoints they might have set up because of martial law. It might get a wee bit bumpy from here on out."

Morgan noticed Aidan's cheeky, wry grin as he took off up a dirt side road, enveloping them in a spinning cloud of dust.

Aidan dropped Morgan at the tradesman's entrance to the grocery and then headed for the Temple Bar pub. To a great extent, Morgan spoke the truth. He realized her moral compass guided them all. But he could never let Tadgh, Tom, and his compatriots down.

It had been a long time since he had seen his old girlfriend, waitress Aileen. He had wondered all this time what had become of her. He soon found out.

Aileen giggled upon seeing Aidan. She had an extra jiggle to her now somewhat older wares. "Hello there, my fine lad. Can I be of service?"

She seemed so superficial now that he had known Morgan and had found real love with his darling Marjorie. He missed seeing his schoolteacher love these days because of the war. Too dangerous for her. "It's good to see you too, Aileen. I just dropped in to say hello, then I'll be going."

"Some pints then, love?"

"Just one, lass. I'm driving, and there's the devil about."

"Honestly. Aidan. You're no fun anymore."

"You're the second one to tell me that today, Aileen. Now off with ya."

Morgan found Jack helping Derek in the store. "I see they have you domesticated now, my lad."

Jack liked how she said it, especially the word *my*. "Just waiting for your return, luv. Deirdre will be happy that you're here." He reached out, took her hand, and held it firm.

Morgan gave him a peck on the cheek. "I'll be staying a month, give or take, if that's all right." Glancing down, she added, "You can let go of my hand now."

Jack quickly drew his arm in and responded sheepishly, "That's what you wrote in your telegram. You can have the spare room."

Morgan's eyes twinkled, and she laughed. "You're not using it then, Jack?"

"I'm happy here, Morgan." It was a rhetorical question that he chose to ignore. Deirdre was a loving soul, but here before him was the unattainable love of his life.

"I can see that. Deirdre must be feeding you well. Good for you in all this madness."

"Life goes on in the big city, lass."

"Have you seen Collin recently?"

"He comes to Temple Bar some evenings for supper, often with his colleague Maureen, I think he calls her. You know who she is. The reporter from *The Times,* your sister-in-law's cousin."

"Yes, I remember hearing about her. Fetching girl, Kathy told me."

"Aye, she is. Collin should be over here soon. Now let me get the boxes of lettuce from storage so Derek doesn't give me the dickens. You'll find Deirdre upstairs in the residence. She's working on the bills, I think."

Jack couldn't get over how good Morgan looked despite the worry lines now etched on her face. It must be tough out there with all those dying Volunteers. But she'd survived the horrors of the Great War travesty. She seemed genuinely happy to see him, uplifted even. But he was with Deirdre now, and Morgan was married, albeit to a killing machine. And he loved his beautiful shopkeeper and their lovemaking, didn't he?

"See you later then, Jack."

"I'll pine away while you're gone, Morgan." Jack knew that was true now that she was back. His heart was wonderfully full here with Deirdre while Morgan was gone. But he was thrown into a hopeless, emotional quandary when she was near.

Before Aidan left for Creagh, he came back to the grocery. Morgan hugged him fiercely. "Your job is to save yourself and look after Tadgh. Can I count on you to do that, Brother?"

"I promise."

"All right. Be off now before curfew. Godspeed."

Collin popped into the residence at seven in the evening without Maureen and was delighted to see his sister.

Morgan flew to his arms and hugged him fiercely. "You're a sight for sore eyes, Brother. Just what I needed." Her eyes misted over.

Collin held her tight for a minute and noticed her trembling. It wasn't normal for her to be this emotional. "I can see that, Sis. Are you all right?"

"Better now." Morgan let go and wiped her eyes with a hanky.

Collin took the handkerchief and dabbed her cheek. "Can we have supper together, for once?"

"Love to. Here in the residence would be good."

They sat and ate the stew that Derek brought, and they each drank a B&C for old times' sake in the closed-off dining area. Jack, Derek, and Deirdre left them alone so they could visit privately while they ate their meals in the kitchen.

"How are you doing here in Dublin, Collin?"

"The war consumes my time and thoughts, and my readers in Canada seem to love my reports. I was headed home soon, but Mr. Robertson wants me to stay on until we see if this Home Rule law will resolve the conflict."

"That could take years, Collin. What about Kathy and the children?"

"I missed Christmas with them, and that pained me, but they understand."

"Do they, Collin? Are you sure?"

"I think so. I got a lovely telegram on Christmas Eve."

"What did it say?"

"'—Merry Christmas,' of course, silly."

"What else?"

"Let me think. 'Hurry home soon.' I remember that. Also, 'We all miss you terribly during this dreadful war.'"

"Is that all?"

"Just about."

"What do you mean by just?"

Collin hesitated. "She ended with 'Remember your promise.'"

Morgan put down her fork, looked up, and stared at her brother. "When you arrived off the boat, you said, 'Kind of promised.' Did you, or didn't you make a promise?"

Collin looked away from her piercing emerald eyes. "I . . . I don't know what I said exactly, Morgan. The important thing is to stay out of danger, isn't it? That's what I thought I was agreeing to, for Kathy's sake."

"I think the important thing is to keep your promises, Brother. You've been in risky scrapes just covering the war. Why, at the Cork burning—"

"I didn't burden Kathy with the gory details. She would just worry."

"Don't you think that she's worrying all the same?"

Collin knew she would be. He could imagine her pacing in the Finlays' parlor. "I just prefer to keep our communications light, Sis."

Morgan clasped her brother's hands across the table. "Look at me. She's your life partner. Take it from me. Don't keep any secrets from Kathy. And don't stay away too long, Collin. This is not your war, and you have a lovely wife and family, so Tadgh tells me."

"Now who's talking about convincing someone to go to Canada, lass?"

Morgan winked her eye. "Touché." She realized that he was never going to give up trying to get her to go there.

Collin savored a mouthful of Deirdre's apple pie. "Speaking of Tadgh, how is the McCarthy Ri?"

Morgan thought for a moment. "He's consumed by the war."

Collin took her hand from his shoulder and held it fast. "What's wrong? Something important, I suspect."

"It's Tadgh and the whole flying column war. I'm not his priority these days. At least he seems sure of himself again. The spark has gone out of our relationship ever since the Joy. I have an overwhelming sense of dread."

"But you still love each other, right?"

"We had a big fight the night before I left, Collin. I told him how I feel."

"This war will end, Morgan, perhaps sooner than you think."

"What then, brother? Tadgh needs Brits to kill, and I'm afraid he's dragging Aidan into the same compulsive lifestyle."

Collin saw an opening—Canada—but he knew she wouldn't leave Tadgh, no matter how bad his obsessions got. He needed to get her out of her melancholy. She needed to get back to nursing or some other self-fulfilling endeavor. He checked on Jack and Deirdre, who had gone down to the grocery, before returning to Morgan. He suggested they go to her bedroom in private. Once there with the door closed, he asked, "What's new on the non-violent O'Donnell treasure front?"

Morgan perked up. "I have a task for you if you're able. I know what you promised Kathy, but I need to tell you something important. I think there is a connection between our house in Creagh and the Barbary pirates that attacked Baltimore back in 1631, and maybe the pirate that killed Mr. Temple. Maybe you could share the news with Kathy."

"Maybe." Collin thought for a moment. "Your assertion seems far-fetched, but I will look into the attack in Baltimore for you. I am well versed in the resources of Trinity College and the newspaper archives here in Dublin now. What about the RIA? Do you think Professor Lawlor could help?"

"Perhaps, but he's more interested in Gaelic relics, not pirate lore."

Without any warning, the bedroom door squeaked on its hinges.

"What are you two O'Donnells cooking up? Anything you can share?" The two O'Donnell heads whipped up—and saw Deirdre standing in the open doorway.

Collin instantly felt like saying, "Haven't you heard of knocking first?" But he tamped down his anger and kept his mouth shut. This was, after all, her house. He flashed a look of alarm at Morgan, but he saw no concern in her facial features.

He thought it strange that Deirdre seemed to show up at just the wrong moment, but he kept his mouth shut. Something odd about that woman. Morgan seemed enamored with her bridesmaid. He would have to talk to Tadgh about it when he saw him next.

"Thanks for looking in on us, Deirdre. We're just catching up. I was trying to convince my brother to go home to his wife and children and leave us alone."

"Wise advice, Morgan. For us all. Have you seen Jack?"

"I thought he was with you."

"That is where he should be, but now that *you're* here, he seems distracted, not himself."

Collin sensed friction and said, "I'd best be going. Thanks for dinner, Deirdre. I'll see you tomorrow evening, Sis."

"Bye, Brother." Morgan turned to Deirdre. "I am quite tired from my trip and would like to get settled in here for the night."

"You know where the towels are in the hall closet. I'll leave you to it, then, and get back to Jack." Deirdre left, closing the door firmly behind her.

The next evening, Collin and Morgan headed for supper at the pub. They chose the private back snug. During their meal, Collin gave his siter a full report in hushed tones. "I researched the attack. It was carried out by the famous corsair, Jan Janszoon van Haarlem, a former Dutch captain of the Salé Rovers, also known as Murad Reis the Younger. Murad's force was led to the village by a man called Hackett, the captain of a fishing boat Reis had captured at Grindavík, Iceland, in exchange for his freedom. Apparently, the Protestant English had occupied Baltimore. Hackett, a Roman Catholic, wanted revenge. The traitor was left behind by the pirates and was subsequently hanged from the clifftop outside the village for his conspiracy. This was the only recorded act of slave piracy conducted by the Barbary pirates in Ireland."

Morgan took a sip of her brew and flipped the curls from her eyes. "Don't you think it odd that the only attack, ever, was just four miles from our home in Creagh?"

"Possibly. But the fact is that this Hackett led them to Baltimore. Sounds like the location wasn't predetermined by the pirates."

"All right, but once there, then maybe they left a corsair behind."

Collin consulted his notes. "Maybe. Murad captured one hundred and eight prisoners who became slaves in Morocco. He took the English Protestants but left the Irish Catholics behind. Only three made it back to Ireland, buying their freedom. I also found out the remaining settlers in Baltimore vacated the town, most moving to Skibbereen and beyond. Baltimore was virtually deserted for generations."

"A pirate could have disguised himself and built our home at Creagh that year."

"Or it might have been one of the displaced settlers."

"Who just happened to carve the skull and crossbones into our banister?"

"A traumatized Irish settler who couldn't get the skull and crossbones out of his head?"

"With the initials of Jacques de Molay, the last Knights Templar Grand Master?"

Collin took a swig of his stout and swallowed before answering. "Point well taken, Sis. I found out more about this Jan Janszoon fellow. Quite an interesting chap." Collin stuck his fork into his beef and kidney pie to release steam and help the meal cool. "He was a Dutch pirate who turned Turk after being captured by the Moorish state in 1618. He began serving as a Barbary pirate, one of the most famous of the 17th-century 'Salé

Rovers.' Together with other corsairs, he helped establish the independent Republic of Salé at the city of that name, serving as the first President and Grand Admiral."

Morgan stared at her brother, her tankard at her lips. "It must have been a fascinating era."

"There's more. In 1627 Janszoon captured the island of Lundy in the Bristol Channel and held it for five years, using it as a base for raiding expeditions. Didn't you say that the Barbary pirate attacked William and Martha Temple in 1627?"

"Yes, and the sacking of Baltimore was in 1631, four years later. Interesting." Morgan dipped her bread in the pie sauce and took a bite.

Collin consulted his notes again. "The Salé Rovers were constantly at war with the Knights Hospitallers then operating out of the island of Malta in the Mediterranean. In 1635, near the Tunisian coast, Murat Reis was outnumbered and surprised by a sudden attack. He and many of his men were captured by the Knights of Malta. He was imprisoned in the island's notorious dark dungeons. He was then mistreated, tortured, and suffered ill health. In 1640 he barely escaped after a massive Corsair attack that was carefully planned by the Dey of Tunis to rescue his fellow sailors and Corsairs."

While Collin was talking, Morgan was trying to connect the dots. What was she missing? Something he had said. "Like I was saying, Jan Janszoon van Haarlem was a very wealthy and influential man."

Morgan slammed her tankard down on the table, spilling the contents. *"That's it!"*

Startled patrons looked their way.

Collin pulled her to him, turned to the other patrons, and announced, "Forgive us. My younger sister is drunk." Then he kissed her forehead.

The other customers resumed their meals and conversations. Drunkenness was a common acceptable occurrence in this establishment.

Collin asked Morgan in subdued tones, "What's *it*?"

"Jan Janszoon van Haarlem. JJvH."

"What does that mean? His initials?"

"I forgot to tell you, Brother. There were initials on the cutlass we found in Temple's iron chest. FJyH. It wasn't a *y*. It's a *v*. I have a feeling of déjà vu, but I can't figure out where it's connected, and to what. I'll bet the cutlass belonged to a pirate named F Janszoon van Haarlem, a relative of the Murat Reis. I'm even more convinced one of Janszoon's men built our house. I'm guessing they occupied Creagh as a base within Ireland after they sacked Baltimore. Just like occupying Lundy during this period."

"Why would they do that, Morgan?"

"In order to find St. Columba's Epistle after they couldn't get it from the Temples, the last Templars. They stayed there until at least 1632 when they left Lundy."

"But how would they have found out about the epistle in the first place, Morgan? You said that this pirate demanded it from William Temple."

"That's still a mystery, Collin."

"If they were after the epistle, and I doubt it, I wonder if they found it?"

"I doubt that very much because Jonathan Swift was still searching for it in the 1700s."

A pang of nagging guilt hit Collin as he was caught up in the treasure adventure once again. "That doesn't mean the pirates didn't find it in the 1600s if they kept it secret. One way or the other, how does this get us any closer to finding our ancestor's treasure?"

"Niall's note says that Red Hugh buried the epistle with the treasure. I think, Collin, if we find one, we will find the other."

"That means if the pirates found the epistle, then the treasure is long gone to the coffers of the Salé Rovers."

"Do you always look at the glass half empty, Brother?"

"Funny you should say that. You sound like Kathy. I thought I had broken that habit when I found you."

"I'm going to search our Creagh house thoroughly when I get home," Morgan said in hushed tones.

"I can check the records for any published large influx of wealth into the Salé Rovers' coffers in 1632."

"You do that, Brother."

With that said, they finished their meal in silence. Collin headed for the Shelbourne, and Morgan went back to the grocery.

The Irish Times hit the streets at six on Monday morning, the 21st. Deirdre knocked and burst into Morgan's bedroom with tea and the paper, waking her up.

Wiping the sleep from her eyes to see, Morgan groaned, "What's so urgent, girl?"

Deirdre gently laid the paper face down on the bed beside her, then put the teacup down on the nightstand. "Here, let me help you sit up."

Deirdre fluffed the pillow behind her when Morgan sat up in the bed.

The grocery owner handed her the tea. "Have a sip first. Careful, it's hot."

Morgan warmed her hands on the cup and took a sip of the sweet tea. "What is happening, Deirdre? Is the war over?" Then she saw the pained look on her host's face.

"I'm truly sorry, Morgan. You'd better read the page four national news."

Morgan swept the tangled ringlets from her face and set the teacup back down. She picked up the paper, opened it, and tried to focus on the newsprint.

"Oh no!" She jumped out of bed, knocking over the teacup and spilling the hot liquid down her nightdress. She held the stained garment away from her chest but otherwise took little notice. An agonized expression came over Morgan's face as she imagined the worst. "I've got to get home."

Chapter Six
Clonmult

Monday, February 21, 1921
Dublin, Ireland

Morgan read the article aloud and did not believe it.

Clonmult Ambush. IRA Casualties - Reverse Kilmichael.

Irish Republic Army (IRA) volunteers occupying a farmhouse in Clonmult, County Cork, were surrounded by a force of the British Army, Royal Irish Constabulary, and Auxiliaries last evening. The IRA members feigned surrender after the thatched roof of their dwelling was set ablaze. Some of them exited the home, but the others restarted shooting. In the action that followed, twelve IRA volunteers were killed, eight captured, five of whom were wounded.

The 4th battalion of the IRA First Cork Brigade was led by Captain O'Connell and was aided by two members of the 3rd West Cork battalion. Both were extracted from the burning building, one seriously wounded. Names of three the IRA men taken into custody were O'Sullivan, Moore, and Higgins. The other captives have not been identified.

Jack rushed into Morgan's bedroom. "What's happened? Michael Collins is downstairs looking for you."

He saw the ashen look on her face and tears streaming down her cheeks.

Oh, Jack. I don't know yet. Tell him to come up to Deirdre's parlor, please."

She threw on the clothes she had worn the night before and ran in to meet Michael.

The IRA Leader was pacing the room as she entered; he stopped and turned toward her. "You have heard?"

Morgan trembled. "Tadgh?"

Collins crossed to her and held her shoulders. "I'm afraid so, lass. We don't have intelligence from inside Cork Gaol. I can't tell you his condition yet."

"When will you know for sure? How did it happen? Clonmult is east of Cork City, isn't it?"

Michael helped her down onto the chesterfield and sat beside her, holding her hand. "They were short of rifles in 1st battalion. Tadgh and another member of Tom's column took them a few of the ones your husband brought back from America—bad timing. We now know we have a traitor named Dan Shields in our midst. He led the bastards to the farmhouse near Clonmult. The Auxies and the RIC overwhelmed the farmhouse. Tadgh and the other man from Tom's column fought bravely but were captured."

Morgan could hardly get the next question out. "Is Tadgh one of the ones who was wounded?"

"Aye, I'm afraid so. He's better off than the dead. Seven were mowed down by the Auxies after they had surrendered. We're trying to get an informant inside the prison walls."

Morgan stood up ramrod straight near Michael's face. "Don't bother getting your informant *in!* What are you going to do about getting my husband *out?* I need to go home."

"We're already working on it, Morgan. You won't have to break him out this time. But I must tell you that Cork is a hotbed of tit-for-tat retribution just now. It is helping our Cause internationally. The burning last month shows just how volatile the situation has become."

"I need to go home," she repeated.

"I've already arranged transportation and security for you and your companions to your safe home or to Cork City, whichever you desire. But Morgan, I will caution you. Make no mistake, the British are still searching for you."

"I'll see how Tom Barry and Aidan can help us get Tadgh out." Then Morgan broke down, pounding on the man's chest. "You damn men and your war. You're all responsible. Hasn't Tadgh been through enough?"

Michael let her vent against his shoulder until her wrath was expended. Tadgh had been a school chum, and he had served the Cause with great distinction, including several years in the Joy almost dying on a hunger strike. But many good men were valiantly fighting and losing their lives to the Limeys. This carnage couldn't be helped. It was hard to comfort all who were grieving. He was here because Morgan was special.

My God, she had broken her husband out of the Joy with her brilliant initiative and guts. "Morgan, we are doing everything humanly possible to get Tadgh out, believe me. You know where to find me when you get organized for your trip." With that, he was gone, as if he had never been there at all.

Jack and Deirdre overheard the conversation from the residence kitchen and came in as Michael left.

Morgan said, "I'll call Collin. He will know what to do."

Jack thought, *Hell, I know what to do. Collin is just the brother from Canada.* But instead, he said, "All right. I will call him for you. He should be awake at the Shelbourne by now."

Before he could act, Collin came bounding up the stairs, out of breath. "I saw the newspaper this morning, Sis. Was Tadgh involved?"

Morgan fell into his arms, sobbing. "Oh, Collin! Thank God you're here! It's Tadgh again. He's in jail and wounded."

By suppertime, Collin had their plan organized. He convinced both Healy and Robertson he should go to County Cork. He used a recent attack on Skibbereen by the rebels and the escalation of the conflict throughout Cork and Kerry as a justification. Jack wanted to stay close to Morgan, so he offered to go. They decided to take Jack's truck and handle their own security. Morgan was too angry to accept any of Michael Collins' pity.

The following morning, Deirdre took Jack aside before they left. "I am worried about Morgan. At some point, even the strongest spirits must break. She's close to that point. Make sure her brother takes good care of her."

"I'll make sure of it, darling." Jack was torn. His love for this grocery owner grew every day, and he truly believed that she loved him. But Morgan needed him now, and he wanted to be the one she turned to.

"Good. Keep me informed of everything, my love, and come back to me as soon as you're able."

Holding her firmly, Jack pulled her close to him. "You've given me a wonderful new life to lead, Deirdre."

Deirdre kissed him fiercely on the lips. "Remember, keep me informed."

Morgan, Collin, and Jack arrived at Creagh in Jack's sedan mid-afternoon. The 3rd West Cork Flying Column was operating as though nothing had happened. Aidan was out on a mission with Tom Barry.

Molly met them at the door. "Tadgh's in trouble." That was enough to set both women to crying.

Collin intervened, "Do you know his status, lass?"

"Oh, Molly. Let me introduce my brother Collin and my friend Jack. They are both to be trusted."

"Pleased to meet you," she acknowledged them perfunctorily. Then she turned her attention back to Morgan. "We don't know what is happening to Tadgh yet. Aidan has been trying to find out. You'll need to talk to Tom when he gets back."

To keep her mind off her troubles, Morgan set up temporary sleeping accommodations for her two companions in the parlor. She dreaded going up to the bedroom alone.

The Flying Column returned just after dark. Morgan heard the men say they had felled trees and set explosions to block the roads around Skibbereen. She knew that this, and the disruption of the mail service, were two of the main daily tasks they accomplished when not on an ambush or attack on RIC barracks.

Barry seemed startled to see strangers in the safe house. He drew a Webley he had taken off a dead Auxiliary. "Morgan! Who are these men?"

"Hold on, Tom! This is my brother Collin, and our friend Jack, both sympathetic to our Cause. They both aided Tadgh in bringing the guns you are now using into Ireland."

Collin pushed the muzzle of Tom's gun down. "For full disclosure, I am a Canadian reporter from *The Toronto Evening Telegraph*. I'm here to write about your Cause, not harm it. Surely, foreign support must be an important factor toward your success, true?"

Barry acknowledged that value.

Morgan pleaded, "Tell us what you know about Tadgh."

Tom reiterated to Morgan what Michael said about trying to get an informant within Cork Jail. But he had no concrete plan to achieve that goal.

Morgan faced the commander and prodded his tunic with her pointed finger. "That's not acceptable to me. I guess I will have to break him out of prison again myself with Aidan."

Tom gently pushed her hand aside. "I'm sorry, but I can't let you do that, lass. If you get caught, and they force you to tell them where we are, you will endanger our operation."

"I know my Tadgh won't talk, and I know I wouldn't. How sure are you that your other captured man won't divulge that information?"

"I trust my men. I hand-picked them all. And besides, we assassinate any traitors in our midst. They all know *that*." Tom stared directly at Collin as he said it.

Morgan's eyes burned a hole right through him. "You can order Aidan, I presume, but you can't order me."

Tom stood squarely facing her, hands on hips. "Don't cross me, woman."

"Don't you dare threaten me in my own house, or I'll turn you out!"

"It's not your house anymore. It belongs to the IRA."

Morgan picked up the broom by the stove and brandished it in the leader's direction. "Get out of my house *now*, you, you ingrate!"

Tom was about to rip the broom from her hands when Aidan came through the door just as Collin was starting to intervene. He held up his hand to stop him. "What's going on here, sir?"

"We're having a squabble about who is in charge."

Aidan stepped forward and gently took the broom from Morgan's hands. Then he held her to him. "I may take military orders from you, sir, but I warn you not to lay a hand on my sister. This is her home, and you are a guest in it. Is that clear?"

Collin stepped back. Aidan was doing a fine job.

The leader was taken aback by this insubordination but realized he needed the safe haven and the support of Aidan. He let down his guard. "I realize you are all upset by the capture of our two men by the British. We are doing all we can to try to get them released. Please be patient." He questioned Molly about the evening meal and turned on his heel to join his men downstairs in the control center.

Morgan and her three comrades met in the parlor. Molly had brought them Irish stew before the other men were fed.

Aidan was ashen. "It is all my fault, Morgan. I was slated to deliver the rifles to them, but I didn't get back from Dublin in time. Tadgh insisted on taking my place."

It suddenly struck Morgan that the guns Tadgh had used his treasure to buy had been his downfall. Tragically ironic.

Collin saw his sister's eyes glisten, a frown forming, and put his arm around her, drawing her in.

Morgan squeezed Collin's hand and composed herself.. "You know Tadgh's mind won't change once he decides on a path. What do you know of his wound?"

"I'll tell you straight. All I know comes from Captain O'Connell from 1st Battalion. He escaped from the farmhouse to get reinforcements after the roof caught fire and was forced to stay in the nearby trees for a few minutes. The enemy had circled the building. He said the volunteers who surrendered when the roof of the building caught fire were all lined up and shot by the British, who then opened up on the house itself. Tadgh and Frank McPhee trapped inside eventually surrendered. Tadgh was shot in the leg and couldn't stand when they carted him away."

Collin was sitting on the chesterfield beside Morgan, holding her up. She sagged and started crying.

"They didn't kill him, Sis. They could have. That's a good sign, isn't it?"

Collin clenched his fist and shook it in Aidan's direction. "We can't just stand by and do nothing. Jack and I don't take orders from your commander."

Aidan glared at Collin. "What's your plan, then? A frontal attack by two civilians? That would be suicidal. We must rely on Tom and Michael. They are the military geniuses."

"Genii," Collin corrected. That reminded him of when Kathy used to correct his grammar all the time.

"Whatever you say, Collin. Don't you think I would be the first one to infiltrate the jail if I thought I would have a chance?"

Even in her state, Morgan was shocked. Only three months earlier, Aidan wanted to storm the Joy to get Tadgh out. Now he was totally under the spell of the damned rebel leaders.

Collin threw up his hands. "I don't know. I suggest we all get some sleep. Let me mull over the problem."

Five frightful days passed without anyone producing a plan that had a chance of succeeding. Barry talked only of how to find and assassinate the spy, Dan Shields. Morgan's and Aidan's desperation grew. Finally, on Sunday the 27th, a week after the ambush, Michael sent word by courier. An inside informant had been found. He had parents in Dublin that Michael was using as pressure points to convince their son to find out Tadgh's status. Michael was formulating a plan.

"How long do we have to wait? I can try my nursing trick again. It worked in Dublin, and they may not have heard of that scheme in Cork."

Aidan threw up his hands. "I think they will have all of our history in a dossier, Sis. We wouldn't be able to use that ruse again. And besides, the Spanish flu epidemic has passed."

"I don't care. It's like last time. Promises and no action. I'm going to try something on Tuesday if Michael still doesn't have a plan by then."

That day, the flying column stood down due to heavy rain. Collin suggested the four of them find more clues to the O'Donnell treasure in the house to pass the excruciating hours. Morgan had already briefed Aidan on the status of the investigation. The men were shocked when she showed them Tadgh's hidden genealogy room off their bedroom. By the light of a candle on the desk, she explained her theory of the potential Barbary pirate association with the house. Collin was skeptical, and Jack feigned interest. This represented one subject where he could get closer to her than her brother.

Going out to the landing, Morgan said, "Look at the railing going downstairs. Maybe the cutlass initials are carved there? I know that *FJvH* looked familiar, and we found Jacques de Molay's initials there."

They examined the railing with its many carved symbols and initials without success and returned to the secret room.

"I remember there were initials carved into this desk, but I can't remember what or where they were." They looked on its surface and inside its drawer but missed the *FJvH* because it was obscured by a blob of wax that had dripped off the candle base.

Finally, Jack asked, "What's the purpose of that ladder on the narrow-end rock wall of this tiny room?"

Looking up, Morgan said, "I don't know. Tadgh never talked about it."

The flat ceiling was a good twelve feet above the old wood floor.

Collin climbed the ladder to the ceiling. "There is a hatch of some sort here." He pushed up on it, but it wouldn't budge. Then he noticed the hardware. He called down. "There's the edge of two rusted hinges visible here at the rock wall and a small finger-pull latch ring opposite, buried in the hatch wood. I'll try to pull on it. Maybe I can pry it loose. Looks as if it hasn't been used in ages, though."

The wood around the latch ring had swollen over time, so he took out his bone-handled Imperial jackknife, flipped it open, and started digging at it to get his finger through the metal circle. When he finally did, it wouldn't budge. "This thing's rusted shut."

Having descended back down the ladder to the others, he said, "There must have been an attic up there in the past, I guess. Otherwise, why would there be a ladder here? Those cross beams go through to the main bedroom, and the ceiling looks as old as the house." Sounding doubtful of the whole idea, he added, "I think your idea that a Barbary pirate lived here is highly unlikely, Sis. Wishful thinking."

Morgan had to agree that although there was concrete proof of the connection between Temple's assailant and the leader of the Baltimore attack, they could find no similar evidence that those hit-and-run attackers occupied the home.

This diversion, while they waited, did lighten their mood temporarily. Morgan went to her lonely bed, thinking about how to prove this was a pirate's home. Then the agony of imagining Tadgh in a cold cell, potentially dying of a wound she could not fix, swept over her again.

Monday morning, the grim reality of the situation set in once more. Morgan made plans to stay at Jack's house with George's family in Queenstown and to find a way to get to Tadgh, starting on March 1st. Jack was only too happy to cooperate.

Her plans crashed to a halt when one of the volunteers returned with a copy of the *Skibbereen Eagle*. Seven members of the IRA held at Cork Gaol had been executed that morning. No one heard of any trials for the guilty men. Officials released a few names, but others were withheld for security purposes until next of kin could be notified. Tadgh's name was not among those identified.

Morgan confronted Tom Barry shoving the paper in his face. "See what your inaction has done. Seven volunteers dead, and it's on your head."

"We don't know yet whether our men were executed today. Most were from 1st Battalion."

"They were all IRA, weren't they?" Morgan snorted.

"Ya . . . I will go to Cork and talk to the informant this evening."

"I will go with you."

"You will do no such thing, Mrs. McCarthy." Tom turned to Aidan, who had accompanied her for support, and ordered, "Aidan, please control your sister-in-law."

"Then I will go with you, sir."

Tom eyed his subordinate and Tadgh's wife. "That adds risk, but I can see that you are both adamant about it. All right, Aidan. We leave in an hour."

Morgan couldn't eat any supper despite Collin and Jack's efforts to get her to take some sustenance. She kept pacing the parlor until Tom and Aidan returned. When they came through the doorway, Jack saw Aidan's grim face and moved to Morgan's side.

"Well?" Morgan demanded.

Tom bowed his head as he spoke clearly, "There's no use sugar-coating the news, lass. Our informant didn't know the men and couldn't confirm all the names, but one of our two 3rd Battalion men was executed this morning."

Morgan broke down in tears, and Collin rushed to her assistance.

Aidan spoke up. "It could have been Frank, Sir, our other West Cork volunteer."

"I'm afraid not. McPhee has no next of kin, but O'Connell said he wasn't injured. Our informant was a cook and server. His information came from what he overheard from the guards. They had said they had heard that one of the executed men had been from 3rd Cork West. He had previous civil grievances leveled against him, *and* he had a serious leg injury. Like with Connolly after the Rising, they had to prop him up to shoot him." He shook his head and looked down. "Mrs. McCarthy, I am deeply sorry."

Morgan sagged against Collin. "They couldn't notify the next of kin, so they're withholding the name, is that it? Oh God, no! Then it's true! Tadgh's dead!"

"I'm afraid so."

Stunned, Morgan sank to the ground, her head in her hands. The ocean rushed into her brain, washing Tadgh's face up to her in waves. She reached out to him, floating on the flotsam, but he pulled away, agony in his eyes. They drifted apart.

Sobs wracked her body and stopped, almost as if a powerful force inside her took control and steered her back to the present. *Heavenly Father, why?* She agonized and then blamed herself. Had she been more insistent, more stubborn with Tadgh, maybe he would have listened to her and not gone.

She rose, took a deep breath, and fixed her eye on Tom. Now defiant, she spat out, "I don't care what happens to me, Tom. I'm going to bring

Tadgh's body back."

"Not a good idea. They will not release Tadgh to you, and you will be imprisoned or worse."

Morgan remembered what Collin had told her about the awful fate of the Easter Rising martyrs. Shot and their bodies dumped in quick lime. She blanched, tears streaming, and sought comfort with her brother, who embraced her and held her shaking frame.

Aidan stepped in front of his superior and brandished his fist. "Damn you, Tom. I agree with Morgan. This tragedy is on your head. You let Tadgh take those rifles without checking how secure the farmhouse would be. Then you did nothing for more than a week. And now *this!* My brother is *dead!* If that isn't leadership incompetence, then so help me, I don't know what is! I am going to report you to Michael Collins."

Fortunately, his words in the parlor were not heard by the other Volunteers, or else Aidan would have been brought up on charges of insubordination. Tom Barry realized this condemnation was the understandable anguish of a brother and wife and let it pass. "That is your prerogative. Meanwhile, we have a war to wage."

Collin had been observing this confrontation while holding Morgan in his arms. He was afraid she was going to collapse. "Can you at least try to confirm from your informant that Tadgh was executed, sir?"

'If we can get another informant, yes. I didn't want to mention it for fear of upsetting Mrs. McCarthy further, but earlier this evening, our man was followed when he came to meet us. While he was giving me his report, he was shot in the back. We barely escaped with our lives."

Collin turned to Aidan, who nodded concurrence with his boss's terrible news.

Barry continued. "They'll be vigilant, looking for spies after this."

Morgan screamed at Barry. "Send a priest in, for God's sake! They must let him in to give last rites. And confirm who was executed."

"Not with the current state of affairs in Cork, Madam. We are completely shut out. Maybe when things cool off."

It was Aidan's turn to complain again. "You know that's not going to happen, Tom."

"Once again, Morgan and Aidan. I am truly sorry for your loss, but we are at war, and you must realize that Tadgh died valiantly serving his country. You should both be proud of him."

That said, the leader left them speechless in the parlor and exited to rejoin his men.

The worst had happened. Morgan, two relatives, and a friend were left in agony. Collin found Molly, and together they helped his distraught sister up to the bedroom. She kept muttering about the damned men and their war. Once he assured himself that she had cried herself to sleep, he left her and returned to the parlor where the other two men were in the process of getting drunk. Collin realized Jack initiated this action to help Aidan deal with his sorrow. Otherwise, Aidan might have gone after Tom physically and ended up in deep trouble with his rebel superiors.

There was no reasoning with them now. Collin sank into the corner chair and tried to make sense of the situation. He kept an eye on the other two to make sure Aidan didn't get violent. Finally, at about midnight, they dropped off in a drunken stupor.

Collin assessed the situation and debated with himself about how to proceed. There was no reason for Morgan to stay in this house with all its flying column actions and remembrances. This wasn't her fight. Likewise, there was no reason to go to Cork to try to claim the body. Dublin would just create more problems. With the war raging there, she would be constantly reminded. He realized that for the first time in his life, he had to take the lead for the family. The O'Donnell family. He hadn't been able to save Da or Ma. Now that Morgan was indeed in trouble, it was up to him to save her.

What would Sam do? He remembered his own experience with terrible grief when he believed Claire, renamed Morgan, had died on the *Lusitania*. They held a memorial service for her where all his and Kathy's friends came. *It really helped me then.*

The only solution he produced was to take Morgan and Aidan to her relatives in Dungloe, to Aunt Biddy and Peader. They could hold a service there for Tadgh even though they didn't have his body. That might ease her mind. Then he could finally convince her to come to Canada.

Once Collin came to this conclusion, he fell asleep in the chair.

He woke with a start five hours later. It was Tuesday, March 1st. Molly was banging pots in the kitchen at four in the morning in preparation for feeding the men. Aidan and Jack were still fast asleep on the floor, competing for the loudest snore.

Collin ached for his sister and Aidan, his stomach roiling. What if Kathy had died, murdered in cold blood, or, heaven forbid, one of his children? He would be devastated. His life would end with theirs. Suddenly, he missed them. He had only contacted them three times since he arrived in Ireland. He should have done more, a lot more.

He wondered about Morgan's state of mind. She was strong. Look how she had sprung her husband out of the Joy. But she'd been through so much, and now this disastrous news. Then there was Aidan's hot head, although he had shown remarkable restraint recently. Collin realized that he wasn't going back to Dublin anytime soon. Reporting on the war was essential but not as important as looking after his kin. But which kin held priority? His family in Canada was safe. He couldn't go home until these matters were resolved. He had to steel himself for the trials ahead. *I need Kathy's advice. I'll send her a telegram today.*

Collin eased himself from the chair. His lower back hurt like hell. He mounted the stairs to check on Morgan and found her bed empty. In fact, the bedroom was empty. He checked the bathroom, and she wasn't there, either. Then he remembered Tadgh's special room off the bedroom.

Collin bent over to investigate the cramped, windowless space. There, in the dim light of a candle, sat Morgan at the rolltop desk. She was fingering the ancient cutlass. Collin guessed she had come to Tadgh's special place to feel closer to him. The loss must be devastating.

"Morgan, dear, why don't you come back to bed? You need your rest."

"He's coming back to me. I can feel him mostly in this room. He'll be back today."

Collin came and knelt by her side. "I know that's what you want, Sis. That's what we all want, but he won't be coming back, I'm afraid. You need to accept that reality."

"No. You're wrong. He's not dead. He'd have found a way to escape. He must have. He'll be home soon."

Collin realized she wasn't ready to leave her home and accept Tadgh's death. He didn't suggest leaving for a memorial service yet.

Morgan broke down in tears. "My mind's confused. What would Tadgh want me to do? Fight the war? Find the treasure? Go with you? I don't know anymore. I can't just leave him here in trouble."

"He's not here anymore, darlin'. He's with the angels now, having given his all for the freedom of Ireland. Just like the Easter Rising martyrs. Think of him that way if you can."

"I ache so, Brother."

"I know exactly how you feel, Morgan. I was there when Ma died. Come with me now."

Collin guided her out into the bedroom, leading her back to bed.

"Lie down and get more sleep. I will be right here with you until you wake."

Morgan collapsed on the bed and held out her hand for support. Collin took her hand in his and sat on the side of the bed while she dozed off.

He had a lot of logistics spinning in his head. How long would it take for her to accept that Tadgh was gone? He couldn't stay away from Dublin forever. Moreover, Kathy expected him home. He missed her and the children. He'd need Jack's support. And then there was Peader. He was embroiled in his war up north. Could they have a safe reunion for such a memorial service? With these thoughts spinning, Collin lay down beside his sister and fell asleep.

Chapter Seven
Destruction

Tuesday, March 1, 1921
Creagh, Ireland

*J*ack awoke with a pounding headache and saw Collin coming out of the kitchen. He propped himself up against the chair, looked around with vacant eyes, and rubbed his forehead. "Where's Aidan?"

Collin pointed to the stairs at the back of the hallway. "The cook said he's already in the control center having breakfast with the Volunteers." Molly appeared in the doorway and handed them each a plate of bacon, eggs, and toast. "Rise and shine, boys. Take this and go join them."

The long staircase led down to an attached boathouse behind the home on the Ilen River. They emerged into a cavernous boat slip with thirty-foot-high doors at the back. And on the river, an enclosed boat dock, and the clandestine activities within. Jack recognized the thirty-five-foot-long hooker sailboat moored there. It looked exactly like the one he had seen Tadgh and Morgan sailing in long ago, off the Cunard pier, except that now it had a standard dirt-red lug sail.

They both looked confused. This old boathouse had all manner of nautical paraphernalia on the benches and walls around the slip, including the back wall adjacent to the house and set into the hillside. Lots of ancient and rusting fishing gear. But there was no control center, no men, no Aidan.

Collin wondered whether this could have been the hiding place for a Barbary pirate sailing vessel. He would have to have kept it out of sight after the Baltimore attack.

Then muffled voices came from behind the back wall. Collin knocked repeatedly, and miraculously, a section of wall covered with old pictures and tangled ropes cracked open.

Tom came to the hidden door. "Sorry, Lads. Can't let you in."

Collin spoke up. "We're here for Aidan, and Molly gave us food."

"I couldn't eat anything right now," Jack said, thrusting his plate forward.

Tom accepted the meal. "Wait here. I'll get him."

While they waited, Collin ate his meal while sitting on a nearby keg and explained his idea of a memorial service to Jack.

Jack liked the idea of the funeral but hated the thought of Morgan leaving to go to Canada. "It's too soon, surely, Collin."

"I know. We'll wait a few days. I must sell Aidan on the idea. Surely, I can convince Morgan."

"Is it wise to leave this home to the flying column unsupervised? They might tear it up."

"They're already doing a fine job of that, Jack."

Aidan came through the door, looking no better than Jack felt. "I want to go and get Tadgh."

"No. Aidan. He's gone."

"I know, Collin. But his body."

"He's gone, lad. They will have buried him themselves."

"We'll dig him up then. I must."

Collin wanted to put an end to this recovery talk. "I thought you would have heard. The British dumped the Easter Rising martyrs into a quick-lime pit. I suspect they are still using that barbaric process."

Aidan cringed.

Collin added, "I didn't want to mention that detail to Morgan, but she may have remembered what I told her years ago."

Aidan looked crestfallen. "Couldn't we wait and see if Michael or Tom can find another informer? Without either Tadgh's body or confirmation that Frank is still alive, I have real trouble accepting my brother's death."

Collin put his arm around the Volunteer's shoulders. "I know you wish Tadgh were still alive, Aidan, but I fear he is dead. I'm truly sorry, lad. I saw the hatred in Cork City the night of the burning. Tadgh was wanted for murdering RIC officers there. We can wait a while, but eventually, we must get Morgan out of this hellhole."

"This is her life now, too, Collin, much as you don't approve."

"She's a lifesaver, not a killer, Aidan. Her love for Tadgh and you has kept her here."

"I'm not sure that's true, Collin. Not now. I want to get the bastards and avenge Tadgh's death. I want to kill Dan Shields personally, with my own hands."

"I'll give you two weeks to confirm Tadgh's death. Then I'm going to take Morgan to our relatives in Dungloe."

"Fair enough, but only if she agrees to go. In any event, I won't be going."

Jack listened to the two men through the haze of his hangover, trying to put himself in Morgan's shoes. She must be devastated. He had to save her from all this mayhem and not lose her to her brother and Canada. Eventually, he wanted his job back at Cunard when this was all over. But how could that be? Morgan was wanted for murder. *As his sister!* He shouldn't be thinking this so soon after poor Tadgh had been murdered. And what about Deirdre? He honestly loved her, or was it her lovemaking that he lusted after, and not love, after all? There was much to be sorted out.

Back in Toronto, the snows of winter were dissipating on Sunday, March 13th, with just a flurry in the crisp morning air. Kathy was still ensconced at the Finlays' Number Ten Balsam residence. That morning, she helped prepare breakfast before church, with her five-year-old Liam and his two younger sisters, Claire, and Shaina, underfoot in the kitchen.

Collin's telegram lay on the kitchen table.

"Poor Morgan," Kathy lamented. "After all they have been through together, it is unbelievable that her Tadgh is dead, murdered."

"Who is Morgan, Mommy?" four-year-old Claire asked.

"Your namesake, dear."

"What's a namesake?"

"You were named after her. She's your auntie a long, long away across the ocean."

"How am I named like her? You call her Morgan, Mommy."

Sam chuckled and waited to see how Kathy would handle that question.

Kathy picked her daughter up out of her booster seat and gave her a hug. "It's a long story for when you're older, but she *used to* be named Claire."

Little black-haired Claire, with a ringlet down to her shoulders, looked confused when she sat back down but uncharacteristically stopped her questioning. Lil offered the seven children more pancakes and syrup while seven-year-old Dot reached over and cut up Claire's food for her.

"Thank you, Dot." Sam noticed this selfless act with pride. His youngest daughter was becoming a positive, helpful soul.

Dorothy beamed lovingly at her father. "Claire needed my help."

Lil said, "Now let her eat it herself, Dot. Finish, everyone, or we'll be late for church."

"Yes, Mommy."

As usual, Liam and Lil's boys Ernie and young Steve sat together on the side bench, wolfing down their pancakes saturated in Quebec maple syrup, oblivious to the conversations around them.

Sam realized that his kitchen table had become too cramped for the lot of them. With everything going on at school and with his art, he hoped Collin would return so he could take his family home, just a few blocks away from them. "Does Collin say when he may be coming back, Kathy?"

"Not in so many words. He's more interested in his sister's well-being and trying to convince her to move here to Canada."

Sam remembered talking to the University of Toronto Medical Department staff about accepting women to become doctors, specifically Morgan. Now women doctors and nurses staffed the prominent Toronto Women's College Hospital. "An opportunity for her becoming a doctor here should be Collin's ace up his sleeve to get his sister to move here to Toronto, now that poor Tadgh is dead."

"I hope you're right, Sam. I miss Morgan. Having them both here, safe and sound would be wonderful."

Sam was pleased to see that Kathy was more self-assured in her marriage than she had been the first time Collin left her to search for his sister in Ireland. And that wasn't saying much, given her state of mind five years ago. Sam reckoned that her three children had much to do with it now.

Kathy took a final gulp of her tea. "Excellent breakfast, Lil. Let me help wash up." She stood up and picked up her empty plate.

"Leave it, girl. We'll do the dishes when we come home."

Sam mused on that word, *home*. He didn't begrudge Kathy staying with them for a time, but this was not her home. Her and her brood, filling the house. The practice of Lil looking after the young ones while he and Kathy taught school had now expanded to the O'Donnells staying over most of the time. He loved them dearly, but couldn't they spend more time at their own lovely home a few blocks away while Collin was gone? How long had he been in Ireland this time? Three months? A man needs quality time with his own family.

Kathy returned from the kitchen and picked up two-year-old Shaina, who was still mucking around with her food instead of eating it. Sam noted that at least the child wasn't throwing it this time. "All right, children. Off you go. Let's get our hands washed before we go to church."

Liam and Claire scampered with the Finlay children upstairs out of earshot.

Lil popped her head in from the kitchen to make sure Sam was moving to get ready. He looked at Lil for support and found none. He decided it was time to say something. "Kathy, I think you need to stay in your own home. It could have problems in the winter without people warming the place. Collin will be home soon to help."

Kathy looked shocked, then finally said, "The children love playing together, and I like the company, dear."

Sam was one voice against two, or maybe nine. The tension of having seven children under one roof was wearing him down. Surely four were enough. His ticker was not happy. He could feel the missed beats, or rather, the heavy beats afterward. He put his hand over his heart. That didn't help.

Lil said, "I love you, too."

Kathy said. "I don't like to talk about it in front of the older children. I worry about Collin, you know, Sam. Several of the pictures he's sent back to the *Tely* show he was close to the fighting."

Sam lit his pipe and thought, *here we go again. Tadgh's death must have set her off.* "He's a smart lad, your husband. I'm sure he'll be fine." He had told her this a hundred times. How many more reassurances had he left? At some point, she had to accept reality.

"Can't you ask Mr. Robertson to have him reassigned home? Three months is a long time."

Sam wished he could, but he knew the answer he'd get. He had already used up what goodwill he had left from his former boss's boss years ago. And anyway, Irish Canadians across Canada were lauding Collin's stories. "I'm sure he'll be home soon. They say that the Home Rule Bill might settle the matter."

"I'm worried that he might go after the O'Donnell treasure, and you know what happened last time." Kathy was ready to launch into more of her fears, but she held back when it came to the treasure.

Lil was about to ask about missing details of what happened again when the children returned and closed the conversation.

After they were all squeezed into Sam's Ford for the short ride to St. Aidan's Church, Kathy said, "He promised he wouldn't, you know."

From the back seat, Lil peered at Kathy between the two children nestled on her lap. "Wouldn't what, dear?"

"Go searching for the damned treasure."

Norah blurted out from the back seat, "What treasure?"

Carefully holding Shaina, Kathy reached back from the front seat and tickled Norah under her chin, making her laugh. "Just a pipe dream, Norah."

Claire asked. "Unca Sam's pipe?"

Here we go again. Sam pulled up to St. Aidan's Church. He was exhausted. He decided that he really needed to get Lil to convince her best friend to stay at her own home.

Collin got the sense that Tom's and Michael's only consideration for the dead was to invoke retribution and not hope for resurrection. In the last two weeks, they had not acquired any new intelligence about events within Cork jail. Collin tried to use his influence with Mr. Healy and his paper to find out without success. He saw that even Aidan had now accepted Tadgh's death.

Morgan was happy that Jack was there with her at Creagh since Collin traveled back and forth to Dublin in Jack's sedan under journalist protection. Perhaps because of their shared tragedy on the *Lusitania*, Morgan accepted Jack's efforts to take her mind off Tadgh's death and the ongoing stress of war around them, but only for a few minutes at a time.

Tom had given Aidan the assignment to track down Shields to focus his anger. Until now, the traitor had eluded them.

When Aidan wasn't on a mission, he took Jack and Morgan out on the hooker. At least at sea, they could temporarily break free of the horror.

On these trips, Morgan's numbed mind cleared slightly. Her beloved husband was dead. She missed him but not his combative nature. She believed in his Cause but not the way it was being fought. Sean O'Casey was right about the pen vs. the sword. Michael Collins and Tom Barry be damned.

"A penny for your thoughts, lass," Jack asked, sitting next to her in the bow as they rounded the Fastnet light that morning.

When she didn't immediately answer, he reached over and pulled her shawl closer around her neck against the cool, northwest breeze. Aidan was in the stern, manning the tiller and trimming to keep the sails filled as they skimmed along in the three-foot swells.

She finally said, "I could have done better, Jack. Changed him. Helped him more."

"Nonsense, Morgan. You said it yourself. No one could change Tadgh once he set his mind to something, especially about driving the British out of Ireland. You did your best."

"Did I, Jack? Despite my creed of saving lives, I abetted three of his murders and even killed for him."

"To keep him alive, Morgan. You saved his life."

"For what? To be tied to a chair and executed like a dog and then thrown into a lime pit?"

She started crying again, and Jack put his arm around her. She went limp against him.

"It would have been better for me to have let him die peacefully in the Joy. He was almost dead, then, you know, and I restored him to life—for this?"

Jack locked his eyes on hers. "You mustn't let yourself think that way, Morgan. It will do no good. You always tried to get Tadgh to see the merit of saving lives, always." Morgan hung her head and went silent. Jack left her to her thoughts, content to have her beside him.

Minutes later, Morgan raised her head and said, "I'm worried about Aidan. He's got his brother's hatred for revenge. I couldn't stand to have them both dead."

"I know. It must be hard."

"I am still terribly confused—all the danger and death. In New York, at the orphanage and the mill, on the *Lusitania*, in the trenches, in the Rising, killing to get him out of jail, and now here. All I ever wanted to do was help people. It seems so overwhelming."

"That's natural. You've lost your companion, lover, and best friend—your whole world." He wanted to say, *but I'm here*. He held his tongue.

Morgan started to weep again, head in her hands. "We fought the night that I left to come to Dublin. Maybe if that wasn't on his mind, he would have escaped."

Jack gently pried her hands away from her face and held them, "This is not your fault, Morgan. Tadgh was a driven man and a ruthless soldier. I saw him in action in Cork. You heard Tom. They were greatly outnumbered at that farmhouse."

She pulled her hands away. "Still, I was off in Dublin. I deserted him when he needed me most."

"You couldn't have known what was to happen, and besides, you wouldn't have been allowed to accompany him on that mission anyway."

"But don't you see, Jack? We had always gone together. 'Where you go,

I go' was our motto. But not in this bloody war. And now he's gone." The tears flowed freely.

Jack was at a loss for what to say next. He would stay near and be a comfort for her. She needed time to sort out her feelings. He took out his large handkerchief and dabbed at her tears.

By March 14, upon Collin's return, the two weeks of waiting had ticked away. After supper, Collin found Morgan and Jack sitting in the parlor, sharing stories about their childhoods. He heard Jack ask her about her father's murder, their escapades and struggles in New York, and her abduction and resulting servitude at the orphanage in Rhode Island, and it all came back to him.

He stoked the fire in the blackened stone fireplace and saw his opportunity to broach the subject of his sister returning with him to Canada. He shared with her how he had held a service for her in Canada when he thought she had been presumed dead and how it had helped him deal with his mourning.

Morgan appeared to be thinking about his request to go to Dungloe for a similar memorial to honor Tadgh, as she was quiet, and her eyes had softened.

She turned to Jack. "What do you think of the idea, Jack?"

"It would help to ease some of your pain, my girl."

Collin took her hand.

"I'm not sure at this point, Brother."

Collin squeezed her hand and continued. "After the memorial, why not come to Canada with me and see your two nieces and nephew? There is no reason for you to stay in the middle of this bloody war any longer. In Canada, you can concentrate on saving lives in a safe, brand-new world. You'll love it there."

"What about the treasure?"

"We can try to find it before we go when we're up in Donegal. Perhaps Peader can help."

"But all the clues seem to be down here."

Collin had to agree with her. "We'll take all the documents with us. We will be able to think more clearly away from this strife. You'd support that for Morgan, wouldn't you, Jack?"

Jack hugged her. "It's a fine opportunity, that's certain, but there's a lot to think about here, too."

Collin eyed Jack with suspicion. He was not an ally at this juncture. Now was not the time to argue for and against.

Morgan looked up into Jack's eyes. "You've been a good friend in these troubled times. I'll do whatever you both suggest."

"I agree with Collin about the memorial service. We can discuss what happens after that, at another time."

Collin clenched his fists behind his back but said nothing. He needed Jack's support since the man seemed to have Morgan's confidence.

Morgan scanned their faces with sorrowful eyes. "All right, boys. I'll go if Aunt Biddy agrees to host the event and Aidan joins us." The downward curve of her mouth showed beleaguered resignation.

Collin encountered Aidan on the night of the 16th at the parlor table. "Time's up. I want us to go to Dungloe." He explained his idea for a memorial service and how it had helped him get over his sadness in the past.

"But your Claire, I mean Morgan, was alive, so maybe Tadgh—"

"We've been through that at least a half-dozen times, Aidan. Different circumstances."

"I know. I know. But I can't leave. I haven't found Shields, and it would be desertion."

"There'll be time enough to enact revenge in due course. Right now, it is crucial to gather with family and honor your brother's memory. Will you help us?"

Aidan jumped up from the kitchen table and pounded his fists on it, knocking plates and a tankard of stout on the floor. "No! The only way I can honor his memory is to find and kill Shields, then kill as many British bastards as I can with our flying column."

"You can come back to seek your revenge *after* this family healing time."

The grieving brother's face turned red. "*Your* family. Not mine."

Collin took him by the shoulders and shook him. "Think of your sister-in-law, all she has been through and done for you. We are one family now, and we need to celebrate Tadgh's life together. It is important for you to be there for Morgan at the service. She won't go without you."

Aidan shoved Collin aside and sat back down, head in his hands. While Molly scolded him and cleaned up the mess, he finally muttered, "I'll think about it."

Collin clapped him on the shoulder. "That's all I ask, Brother."

Collin went to Tom Barry. "Aidan is obsessed with finding and killing that traitor Shields. He still wants to go to Cork and claim Tadgh's body, and we both know that would not be good for your Cause."

"It's understandable. His brother."

"Yes, but he could jeopardize your operations. I need him to go with his sister-in-law to Donegal for a few weeks, my parents' home, to get their heads straight. Then he can return and be of better use to you, sir."

Barry nodded in agreement. "He's been distracted, I'll grant you that. Send the lad to me."

Later that evening, Aidan talked to his superior.

"Michael got your complaint about me."

"Did he, now, Tom."

"Our leader has great respect for your brother and you. We think you should take whatever time you need to deal with your loss. I can't have any mistakes made due to a lack of concentration. You will not be considered a deserter."

Aidan swallowed hard. "I want Shields, sir."

"That could take months."

"I'm not certain how long that would take, but I want to be the one to kill him."

"I understand, Aidan. Right now, I need you to stand down. That's an order."

"I'll talk to my sister-in-law, sir."

Tom put his hand on Aidan's shoulder as he turned to go. "Let me know what comes of it, lad."

Aidan decided to hold off a few more days.

On Friday, March 18, Barry assembled the Volunteers. "We're going to our second safe house in Ballymurphy in preparation for a raid to support No. 1 Brigade in Cork City itself on Sunday."

As Aidan was about to jump into the back of the lorry for the forty-mile drive with the Volunteers, Collin stopped him. "What about our trip to Dungloe?"

"I will likely go with you when I return from this mission."

"*If* you come back. Morgan needs your support before it's too late."

"My brigade needs me. Ireland needs me. Tom said I could go this last time before going with Morgan and you."

The lorries pulled out of the driveway, leaving Collin behind. He decided that they would go to Aunt Biddy's with or without Aidan when he returned.

The British commanders found out about Tom's plan and organized a major operation to capture the IRA column. During the day, the Auxiliaries mobilized more than thirteen hundred troops to converge on the farmhouse in Ballymurphy from several different directions. Four hundred British troops came from Cork, two hundred from Ballincollig, three hundred from Kinsale, and three hundred and fifty from Bandon. Later in the day, about one hundred and twenty Auxiliaries also left Macroom. The British mounted their sweep early the following morning. At nearby Crossbarry, a convoy of the troops descended from lorries and proceeded on foot or bicycle to catch the IRA unaware.

Only aware of the danger at the last minute, Tom Barry resolved that his men, one-hundred-and-four strong, with only forty rounds per man, would have to fight their way out of the encirclement. Barry observed that one of the British columns advancing towards Crossbarry was well ahead of the other British units. If his men could break through this British line, roughly the same strength as his force, they might escape.

Barry moved his men to ambush the British at Crossbarry crossroads, being in position by five-thirty in the morning. The first twelve British lorries came into view of the IRA at eight o'clock. They reached Crossbarry and, caught by surprise, were hit by a crossfire at very close range. Three British vehicles were destroyed by a mine planted by Aidan and his mates under the bridge, which detonated as they passed. The British took significant casualties, and many fled the scene. Barry's men collected the British arms and ammunition before setting fire to the lorries. Another British column of about two hundred attacked from the southwest then retreated after a stiff firefight. Two more British units converging on the area from the southeast tried to dislodge the IRA from their ambush position, but again, without success, and fled in disorder. Taking the chance to escape offered by his quick victory, Barry marched his men to safety while the British were disoriented. The action had lasted for under an hour, with ten British dead and several wounded. Barry's column was outnumbered ten to one but lost only three brave Volunteers, with three more injured.

When they arrived back at Creagh, Tom gathered his men for a debriefing. "You should all be proud, lads. This was one of the largest firefights of the War of Independence, and we won the day. This engagement will go a long way toward motivating the entire nation."

Aidan was so energized he insisted upon staying with the column, and Barry rescinded his order to stand down. Collin realized Morgan wouldn't go without him. The newspaperman took Jack aside on the 21st. "Morgan won't listen to me. Can't you convince her?"

"Give it more time, Collin. She's lost her husband, and Aidan is compensating by going in search of the traitor."

"I've run out of time, Jack. My paper will order me to go back to Dublin. They loved my story about the war status here in Cork West, including Crossbarry as a reporter living with a flying column without revealing our location. So now the *Tely* wants more reporting first-hand about the fight in the capital."

"Give me a week, Collin. I'll try to convince her and Aidan."

"Don't wait. I expect to be sent home to Canada shortly since I've been here for over three months. That was my commitment to my boss."

Dan Shields had been busy. Hidden in a copse of trees near the Crossbarry bridge, he had seen Barry and his flying column head for the hills of the Gurranereigh area. He followed them until they retrieved their lorries at the farmhouse. It took him six days to finally track down their safe house in Creagh and one more to get word back to British military headquarters in Cork City. Then he waited in Skibbereen for reinforcements. If only Aidan had looked closer to home.

Collin gave up on Jack, finally realizing the strength of the man's attraction to Morgan. He remembered the night of the burning in Cork City. *I thought he was sweet on Deirdre. Maybe I need her help. I shouldn't have mentioned Canada. He's not going to want to go there.*

He went to Tom again on the 27th. "I need to take Morgan to our relatives' home in Donegal, and I need your help, sir."

"Fine by me."

"She won't go unless Aidan comes with her."

"I already told Aidan he should take time off to deal with his loss. But he's too obsessed with finding Shields."

"Can you order him to go, then? Please."

"I rescinded that order once. He is a valuable asset."

Collin was ready for this response. "Let me remind you that Aidan's obsession could jeopardize your organization, Tom."

Tom had noticed Aidan's preoccupation at Crossbarry. He had to be reminded to set the charges. "All right. Consider it done. On the condition that we can continue to use this safe house, which was paid for by the IRB, by the way. Our other retreat has been compromised."

"Thank you. I'm sure that will be acceptable."

That afternoon Aidan found Morgan playing a chess game with Jack in the parlor. He hovered over them, watching. Finally, he said, "I've been ordered to stand down and take you to your relatives, Sis."

Morgan fiddled with her queen. "Is that the right thing to do?"

"Collin seems keen for you to see your Aunt Biddy."

"What do you think, Jack?"

"As I've said before, I agree, my dear. The newspapers report there are more British forces in this area every day. Soldiers, Auxiliaries, Black and Tans, over twelve thousand in Cork County. Under martial law, they are killing innocent citizens and burning out their homes at will."

Morgan captured one of Jack's rooks with her queen. "Just like Tadgh told us about the other times through the last three hundred years. They don't change, do they?"

"That's why we must defeat them, Morgan. Tom thinks I am too much of a fanatic now."

Morgan stood up to face her brother-in-law. It just slipped out. "Nonsense, Aidan. You are just trying to avenge Tadgh's murder." Morgan instantly regretted blurting that. How could she be a moral compass if she let her negative emotions rule her mouth?

Aidan smiled. "Aye, be careful, Sis. Your warmonger side is showing."

She couldn't help it. Seizing his coat collar, she hissed, "Just for one man, Aidan. Promise me you will make him pay for what he did to Tadgh."

Jack started to stand up, and Aidan waved him down. He stepped back and then took her hand, sitting her down. "I promise to find and kill Shields when I return. But first, I've been ordered to get you out of here to Dungloe."

Faced with the decision to leave her home, to leave all that reminded her of Tadgh, she snapped, "I've decided to stay and fight. Give me a gun. Then if I'm killed, I can be reunited with Tadgh."

Jack jumped up and went to her, laying his arm on her hunched shoulder. "That's nonsense, Morgan. Tadgh would have wanted you safe, wouldn't he?"

"As I told you a few days ago, it has always been 'I go where you go.'"

Aidan surprised Jack when he said, "No. You can't go there, Morgan. Tadgh would want you to find the O'Donnell treasure to fulfill the pact and support the revolution. You are a McCarthy Chieftain's queen. Remember that."

Morgan moaned. "I'm not thinking straight."

Collin overheard the conversation from the kitchen and came running. He was out of patience with this dithering. "We are going, all of us. Morgan is meant to save lives, not to take them. Aidan, get the boat ready."

"What? Today?"

"For high tide tomorrow morning. Provision her now. Jack, can you help Aidan, please?"

"Certainly. We'd better bring warm clothes, then."

Half an hour later, when Collin came up to check on her, Morgan was fretting in her bedroom, cradling her wedding picture that Collin had taken at Blarney Castle.

"I hate to leave our home, the only one I can remember."

"You can make a new home with Kathy and me in Toronto."

"But Jack—"

"Aren't Jack and Deirdre an item?"

"He's been such a dear man to me, too."

Collin realized that he was pushing too fast. "Let's go to Dungloe first. Then we can talk about the rest later."

The setting sun streamed in through the western window. At least it looked like the weather would be cheery for the voyage. After using the bathroom, Collin descended to the kitchen and convinced Molly to make a supper plate with black tea for his sister. Then he went to the parlor sideboard and poured himself a stiff drink of Jameson from a bottle the boys had almost drained.

An hour later, Jack appeared just as Morgan had disappeared to the bathroom before going to bed. "I just came up to make sure Morgan has packed her clothes for the trip, Collin. We're ready down in the boathouse."

"She told me what to pack. She's having a little difficulty with things this evening. I think we should get out of here as soon as possible."

"Aidan says we should be able to get to a friend's home near Tralee by sundown tomorrow, but only if we leave by nine. There will be a full moon to light the way if we're delayed."

Collin pulled Morgan's valise from under her bed and opened it. "What about the Volunteers, Jack?"

"They are preparing to go on a mission as if nothing happened. I couldn't do it, Collin. Killing, I mean." Jack took the folded clothes Morgan had laid out on the bed and started stacking them neatly in her valise.

"I guess you get hardened to the dangers and disasters during wartime. Horror begets horror, I'm afraid, Jack. They say it gets easier after a while, especially if the enemy has killed your compatriots and is trying to kill you."

"Not for me, Collin, I can assure you." Jack opened a drawer, saw her undergarments, and decided to leave them for Morgan to choose.

Collin said, "I hope you'll never be forced to find out for yourself."

"What am I going to do with my company sedan? I am responsible for it?" Jack picked up a pair of Morgan's shoes.

"Not those shoes. She wants the brown ones. We're better off at sea, Jack. You'll pick it up when we come back after the memorial."

Jack packed the shoes in. "All right. Her valise is packed, except for her unmentionables, that is. I'll take it down to the boat when she's finished."

In the morning, Morgan had difficulty leaving her bedroom for the trip. She walked out to the stairs with Collin and then came back and sat back on the edge of the bed, softly crying. The minimal sleep she had gotten reduced her anger to melancholy temporarily. Collin crossed to the back wall to push the bureau back over the low door to the secret office before leaving.

The first Mill's bomb came crashing through the eastern bedroom window facing the road. Collin dove for it and tossed it back out the window. It exploded outside, shattering the downstairs parlor window.

Collin heard shouts from below. Aidan rushed upstairs to the bedroom. "Anyone hurt?"

"We're all right. What's happening?"

"The Black and Tans have found us! Someone must have tipped them off. We're under attack!" Aidan saw the broken window.

Collin said, "One of those oval, black hand grenades came in there. I threw it back at them."

"Damn, you're lucky. They usually go off five seconds after you pull the pin and release the lever."

"What's happening downstairs, Aidan?"

"Tom is setting up to fight through the east windows. We don't know how many bastards are out there. He wants us to take Molly and get out by boat to the west. He'll hold them off. Says he owes us. C'mon, there's no time to lose! Jack's at the boat."

They heard gunfire from inside and outside of the house.

Morgan had been sitting there in a stupor. She jumped up and ducked into the private office. "I've got to save Tadgh's papers."

Collin headed in after her. "There's no time for that, Sis. We need to get out of the house now!"

At that instant, another Mills bomb exploded into the house somewhere above them.

Collin's voice cracked. "The roof will be on fire now. Hurry!"

Suddenly, the ceiling collapsed near the far wall, debris raining down.

He was shocked to find this little room bathed in a beam of light. Looking up, he saw that a section of the ceiling and roof above it had been blown out just beside the top of the ladder. There, on the floor in the spotlight, glaring up at them through empty sockets amongst the fallen ceiling debris, was a wizened skull with long white hair, the upper portion of a spine still attached.

Oblivious to that gruesome scene, Morgan was madly rifling through the drawers of the desk.

Aidan poked his head in. "Whatever you're doing, there's no time for it. C'mon!"

Morgan reached down beside the desk and pushed a locked box toward her brother-in-law. "Here, take this, Aidan. It's apart of what's left of the McCarthy jewels."

Collin was thankful that she had thought of that in her state. His salary would tide them over for the time being, but eventually, she would need to convert them to cash.

Collin had an idea. From a vantage point up at the roof level, he could take a moment to scout out the enemy's position and strength. He stepped past the debris and clambered up the ladder finding that it had initially been extended up through the ceiling into an attic. *Why was that ceiling hatch still locked tight?*

He was able to climb up through the gaping hole. He stepped off the top of the ladder beside the hatch onto the broken attic floor next to the spot. There in front of him, prone, with arms stretched out and still clutching an iron hook looped through the attic side of the hatch latch, was the skeletal remains of a large man, missing his head and neck. He must have been decapitated by a falling roof timber that pierced the ceiling. Despite the damage from the Mills bomb, it only took a moment to realize that this poor man had died holding the hatch shut.

From there, he could see out to his left across the roofline to the roadway three hundred feet away to the east. About a dozen police in black pants and khaki shirts were crouched in the ditch at the road. So far, the goons had not flanked the house toward the river as far as he could see. *Good.* One of the bastards was hidden among the trees closer to the home on the roadside. He was probably the one throwing the bombs.

Collin saw Jack's sedan shoot up several feet in the air from an explosion, presumably of its petrol tank, flames raging.

He turned to descend the ladder when the next bomb hit the roof at the front of the house. This one was incendiary. He stood back up and looked out. Most of the front of the roof was on fire. It wouldn't be long before the whole top floor would be engulfed. Better get out, fast!

As he turned, he glimpsed a metal clasp caught in the sunlight. On the attic floor in the crook of the skeleton's free arm, a small chest lay half-hidden in dust, embroidered in spider webs. The roof on the other side of the chest caved in, fire igniting the ceiling. The bones of the skeleton started to smolder. Collin reached down, picked the box out of antiquity, and then scrambled down the ladder.

Morgan was staring at the skull, her arms full of papers, including the old Douay-Rheims family Bible. Collin picked up the cutlass with his free hand and stuck it behind his pants belt. Then he put his hand on the small of Morgan's back and guided her out into the bedroom.

The bed and the drapes behind it were on fire, and smoke rapidly filled the top floor. The vision of the Toronto warehouse fire swept over him, and he was momentarily paralyzed. Aidan yelled out at them from the top of the stairs to hurry.

Collin came alive. "Quickly, Sis. Downstairs." He led her to the top of the stairs. He could see twenty Volunteers in the parlor firing at the enemy through the broken east windows. Molly was reloading their weapons while they kept shooting.

"Get Morgan and Molly out of here," Tom yelled from the mayhem. "We'll hold them off and escape down the riverbank to Skibbereen."

"I saw them from the roof," Collin yelled back. "There are about a dozen in the trees at the road, non-circling, and one closer blaggard throwing the bombs."

"Thanks. Get going!"

Aidan and Jack had already unfurled the lug sail, opened the boathouse doors, and started to inch the boat out into the current when Morgan, Collin, and Molly appeared on the boathouse stairs. The roof of the boathouse was already alight, and the smoke billowed. It didn't look possible that the house would be spared. Aidan ordered them to lie down behind the cabin after jumping on board. It took three minutes to get the hooker out into the river, during which time the gunfire didn't let up. They couldn't see what was happening because the fire and smoke obscured their view. By the same token, the English would not be able to see them either.

As they slipped out into the river, Aidan was at the helm. That's when he heard a cry from the woods downstream of the house.

"They're getting away!"

Aidan stared, shocked. For there, in the woods by the shore, he saw none other than Dan Shields calling and pointing toward the hooker. *He was the one that led the bastards to our safe house!*

"Grab the tiller, Jack," Aidan called out as he dove for the Enfield rifle he had laid on the seat beside him. "Hold her steady. It's that traitor, Shields."

The informant was still waving his arms and screaming to get the assault force's attention when Aidan's bullet entered the man's mouth and silenced him forever.

Morgan rushed over and hugged her brother-in-law. "Good shot, Aidan!"

"That was Shields. I'd know him anywhere. I promised I'd get him, Sis. I am glad it would be here and now."

After the hooker rounded the first bend in the river, two explosions in quick succession boomed and lit up the eastern sky.

Retaking the helm, Aidan spun around to look. "Sweet Saint Brigid! The whole magazine must have gone up. God in heaven!"

Jack spoke for all of them. "I hope those men got out."

Chapter Eight
Pilgrim's Path

Tuesday, March 29, 1921
Off the Skellig Islands, Celtic Sea, Ireland

After midnight, **Aidan** navigated past Skellig Michael, heading for Tralee Bay. Morgan sat quietly in the cockpit beside him while Aidan focused on steering to trim the sails.

Morgan looked at her brother-in-law, slightly shorter than Tadgh but otherwise a remarkable similarity. She spent much of the time thinking about her husband. She was mesmerized by the stars on this clear moonlit night, remembering their time together years ago when he taught her to steer the hooker toward Venus. They had been on their way to rendezvous with a freighter carrying the guns. That was the night she had plucked Tadgh from the sea, fiercely fighting to save his life, just as he had saved hers after the *Lusitania* had gone down. She switched her gaze outwards over the gunnels. The full moon looming near the western horizon cast a pearled reflection off the sea as they plowed northeast through the three-foot swells. His words, *where you go, I go, my love* resonated in her mind. Her thoughts took a dark turn. *I could easily dive into the sea, and I'd be with you soon enough. This same sea that was your master.*

She shifted to the port side of the boat and peered over the edge at the water below, so appealing. For a moment, she thought she was back floating on that piece of the *Lusitania's* lifeboat transom just before she was knocked out. From the depths, she wondered if she heard Tadgh's voice calling her. *What is he saying? Come to me, aroon?* She leaned out farther, the water mesmerizing. She gripped the gunnels, almost toppling out when the boat rolled to portside in the swell.

Morgan heard her husband's voice again. *Free Ireland? Protect Aidan? Save yourself?* She couldn't make it all out. *Wait. It isn't Tadgh at all. It's Byron calling my real name, Claire. How you must have suffered that terrible day when the Lusitania went down, my love.*

She remembered the nursery. The babies crying. *That's it. He's yelling to save the babies. I'll join you shortly, love.* Morgan's mind churned. She couldn't rescue Byron or the babies in their terrible hour of need. She read that all twenty-nine of them had perished, just like her own unborn child,

Tadgh's child. And her child. She'd let them all down, the babies. She hadn't been able to save the lovers in her life, either, not the man committed to saving lives, or her husband committed to taking them.

Suddenly the sea seemed menacing, roiling in front of her. Was it an illusion, or was the giant octopus from that nightmare at Temple House reaching out of the deep to grab her, to drag her down into the dark depths?

To his left, Aidan saw Morgan from the corner of his eye just as the boat rolled her way. She appeared to be going overboard. He let go of the tiller and lunged to catch her. The vessel lurched to port again, throwing her out, the sea trying to take her. Miraculously, he caught her around her waist and dragged her back onboard. The sails went slack as the boat lost its way, bobbing like a cork.

Jack and Collin had been nodding in a trance from the rocking motion, propped up against the cabin in the bow. They jumped when the boat floundered, Collin to the mast and Jack to the stern, leaving Molly still asleep.

"What's going on?" Jack cried, seeing the McCarthys sprawled on the port-side deck. He raced to grab the tiller, pushing it hard to port.

"Morgan almost fell overboard, Jack," Aidan said, wheezing from the exertion.

Morgan sat up and coughed. "They called to me from the water."

Aidan took the helm as the hooker righted itself into the wind.

Collin returned to the stern and lifted his sister onto the seat, ensuring she was away from the gunnels. "Who called to you?"

"Tadgh . . . or Byron. I'm not sure. They're both dead now, you know."

"Wasn't Byron the nurse from the *Lusitania*?"

"My first love. He's down there." She pointed overboard.

The men looked at each other, worried.

Jack pointed skyward. "No, Morgan, he's up there with Tadgh."

"I couldn't save any of them," she cried out.

Collin held his sister by the shoulders as the boat hit a rogue wave, then righted itself. "Who?"

"My men and their babies. Their faces are fading, you know. I can hardly see them anymore."

Collin was no psychologist, but he knew danger when he saw it. Morgan was in no condition to be left alone. This voyage had triggered bad memories. He sat down between Morgan and the gunnels. "I'll just stay here with you for a while, Sis. You just try to rest."

"I'll be all right."

"You listen to Collin, Morgan. We're here for you," Jack said.

Morgan slumped against her brother, emotionally spent, and Jack sat at her feet.

Around two in the morning, Aidan steered the hooker through the narrows into Barrow Bay just before the full moon set behind him. He was exhausted. During the twelve-hour trip, he contemplated his role in life. Tadgh, who he idolized and counted on for support, was gone. He was in charge now, and with it came the responsibility to comfort and care for Morgan. He wasn't sure he was prepared to help her the way she had helped him. They'd lost their home, and now he was the last McCarthy chieftain. He would be a deserter if he didn't return to the 3rd Cork West Flying Column in a month, assuming it still existed. It all seemed overwhelming. It made him ache for Marjorie, his schoolmarm sweetheart, and thoughts rushed in of a future family with her, with little Aidans waiting in the wings.

With the tide in, Aidan brought the boat smartly about and nestled it up against the wall at Barrow House. It had been their refuge after Boyle's henchman had shot him, and he had spent time healing there.

"I'm going to wake Maurice up," he told Collin. "Lash off the hooker and wait here."

McCarthy mounted the steps to the imposing manor house and rang the bell. Eventually, lights popped on, and a scruffy Maurice Collis opened the door.

"Well, as I live and breathe, it's Aidan." He clapped the younger McCarthy on the shoulder. "You and your brother have a strange way of appearing at the oddest moments. Come in, come in, lad."

"I've got Morgan, her brother, and friends with me, Maurice. We need your help."

"Of course, my boy. You are all welcome, to be sure. Is Tadgh not with you, then?"

Aidan's eyes clouded. "He's dead, Maurice. Executed not a week ago by the damned British at Cork jail. Morgan's devastated."

Maurice's mouth dropped open. "Aidan. I am deeply sorry. This infernal war is killing off our brave champions of freedom. Tadgh was a grand soldier, and you should be so proud."

"I am, Maurice. The bastards attacked and burned our home just yesterday. We barely escaped with our lives."

Maurice pulled Aidan in and gave him a fatherly hug. "You, Morgan, and your friends have a new home now, Aidan. At least temporarily. I'll get Martha up, and we'll get you all sorted."

"I'm sorry to put you out in the middle of the night."

"Nonsense lad. Be off with ya."

Minutes later, they were all sitting in the immense grand parlor with Martha fawning all over them. She took great care in making sure Morgan was comfortable. Maurice stoked the fire in the massive stone fireplace and pulled the chairs and chesterfield closer to its warmth.

Martha brought tea and Irish soda bread for everyone and laid it on the glass-topped driftwood table near the fire. Then she brought blankets. "As you know, Aidan and Morgan, we have seven bedrooms, most of which we never use. Our home is your home until you get settled."

Sitting beside Jack, holding her hand, Morgan managed a smile. "Thank you, Martha. We are much obliged."

The woman of the manor avoided talking about their loss for the moment. "You're welcome, I'm sure, Morgan."

They were all bedded down by four o'clock, Collin staying with Morgan. He sat in a chair beside her bed like a sentinel, and she lay there in silence. Sleep would not come until later to either of them.

Martha let them sleep until ten, then prepared a late breakfast. When they were all assembled in the kitchen with eggs and bacon on their plates, she announced, "Maurice has taken his fishing crew out for the day and will be back by five."

Aidan remembered his nifty Manx Noby trawler *Slanu III*, a finer fishing vessel than his Galway hooker. Since Pearse replaced the destroyed hooker with a new one that Aidan had brought to Tadgh five years earlier, he wondered if he was now the owner, or did the Irish Republican Brotherhood own it as well? He decided to claim it. The boat was their only home now.

Collin explained the plan to hold a memorial service for Tadgh at the O'Donnell home. He observed that Morgan ate slowly, seemingly lost in her thoughts.

After the meal, Collin noticed the wall telephone and asked to use it. Two minutes later, he was talking to Aunt Biddy in her tailor shop in Dungloe.

"To what do I owe the honor of a telephone call after all this time, nephew?"

"I've sad news, Aunt Biddy. Morgan's husband Tadgh is dead." He explained the circumstances.

"Damn, Limey bastards. Executed without a trial, you say."

"Aye, Auntie. Morgan's strong, but she's in shock." Collin explained his idea for a memorial.

"No body, either, you say."

"Likely buried in a pit in quick-lime like the Rising martyrs."

"How awful. Of course, we can have a service here. I'll arrange for the priest."

"Thank you, Auntie. Where's Peader now?"

"I fear for him, Collin. He's been named commander of a Donegal flying column operating between here and Derry. I wanted him to stand up to the British bullies, but only civil unrest."

"Times have changed, and now Tadgh is dead."

"Poor Morgan."

"Yes, and they burned down her home yesterday. We're with friends near Tralee."

"Sweet Brigid, no! Meenmore can be your home now, yours and Morgan's."

"Mine is in Canada, Biddy. Remember? With Kathy and the three children."

"She was pregnant, then, when she was here, was she?"

"Yes, Biddy. A girl. Claire. She's almost three now, and we've had another girl since. We call her Shaina."

"After your mother. That's a fine name. My, my. How time does fly, to be sure. When do you want to come here?"

"In a couple of days, by boat. Four of us, if that's all right."

Aunt Biddy went silent.

"You still there, Auntie?"

It took another minute for her to answer. "Yes, lad. Can you stay there in Tralee for a bit? The British have finally realized that we are fighting back up here. They've just moved over a thousand troops into Donegal, and they're raising a ruckus, so they are. Give it a couple of weeks for their damned sweep to go through."

Collin twirled the wall phone cord in his fingers. "Are they arresting people for no good reason and burning down houses?"

"That's right."

"Same bloody oppressive tactic they've been using for centuries, Auntie. Certainly. We can stay here in Fenit until you say we can come."

Collin reported the news to Morgan and the others. Morgan didn't seem to care one way or the other.

Mrs. Collis had overheard the conversation. "You're most welcome here. At least the police haven't been hounding us personally up until now. We'll have a fine supper. I've a lamb just slaughtered."

Collin piped up. "Thank you, Martha. We'll be out of your hair as soon as possible."

"We'll see about that, lad. There's a storm coming in off the Atlantic. They say there'll be snow."

"I need to get into Tralee to contact the Cumann na mBan," Molly announced. "I need to find out what happened to the flying column."

"That can be arranged when Maurice gets home," Mrs. Collis told her. "The old Hudson still runs, although it makes a hell of a racket these days."

"It always did," Aidan said.

Collin wondered about Molly. It would be reasonable for her to want to connect with the IRA network, but he had noted her comings and goings each day for her afternoon walks back at the Creagh residence. Where did she go? What did she do? And to whom, if anyone, did she talk?

Jack led Aidan down to the boat to take inventory of what they had brought, mostly to get the younger McCarthy's mind off the tragedy.

Aidan sized up the small quantity of clothes and supplies. "This is all we have left in this world, Jack."

"It reminds me of my own situation just after the *Lusitania* sank. Not only was I penniless, but I had a broken back to boot. At least you and Morgan have your health."

"At the moment, Jack. At the moment." He picked up two scattered sweaters in the tiny cabin, "What is this old box, then?"

"I dunno. Collin brought it on board just before we escaped."

Aidan and Jack brought the relic up to the house, looking for Collin, and ran into Morgan alone in the parlor, rocking by the fire on a two-seater.

"Where's Molly? Gone to Tralee?"

"She's out for a walk, I think, Jack. Says she needs her constitutional each day in the afternoon."

"Hey, Sis. Can you give this to Collin?"

She took the small chest from Aidan and started wiping it off with her sleeve. "Where did this come from?"

"Collin brought it."

At that moment, Collin strode into the room. He saw what Morgan was holding. "I almost forgot all about that little box. Found it in the attic when I went up to check the enemy's position. In all that commotion, I forgot to mention it. The rest of the skeleton was lying in the attic, right by the ceiling hatch. He was holding the trap shut with a hook from above. He seemed to be protecting that box with his other arm."

Morgan had been using spit and her handkerchief to clean the curved top of the leather-bound box. "Collin, look."

There, burned into the old leather, almost unreadable, were the letters *FJvH.*

She held it out. "The same initials as on the cutlass. I was right. I was right," she kept repeating.

"That enemy bomb that exposed the attic must have been Divine intervention."

"Why yes, Collin."

"Are you saying that my finding this relic and our missing Barbary pirate in the gloom and dust of the attic is not just a coincidence?"

"Absolutely, Brother. You're an important part of this adventure, to be sure."

Collin thought of the commitment he made to Kathy to focus on his war reporting and not risky fortune hunting. *Thank God she doesn't know how dangerous it had been during the Cork Burning, not to mention the Creagh firefight.* Though deadly, he had to admit that those altercations were thrilling, much like the boxing matches back in New York. He had been remiss in sending her regular news of his whereabouts and how safe he was. He should send her another telegram as soon as possible. At least the hidden family treasure was something Morgan could think about to get her mind off Tadgh. "I saw his little dust-encrusted box because the sun was shining in on it."

"From God, Collin. From God."

"Or from Tadgh looking down from on high," Jack added. He instantly regretted saying that because Morgan started to sniffle.

Jack sat down beside her and used his handkerchief to wipe away her tears. Then he lifted the small chest, examining its lock. The box was about ten inches by fourteen, with a curved top about eight inches off the base. The leather covered what seemed to be hardwood, and there were bands of metal along its edges and over the top.

Morgan took the ancient relic, turned it over, and fingered the clasp lock mechanism. "How odd. This is a small replica of the casket we found behind Temple's wall bookcase. Wait a minute. Martha Temple wrote in the diary that her husband gave the pirate a small chest to appease him."

The four of them tried to figure out how to open the relic. Collin went to the kitchen to search for a suitable implement without success. When he returned empty-handed, Aidan took out his Webley. "Morgan, put it down on the hearth and stand back. I'll shoot off the lock."

"That's what Tadgh did." Morgan caught herself, remembering, and started to cry again. Jack took the box and set it down.

Martha heard Morgan crying and rushed into the parlor. She saw Aidan with the gun in his hand. "Aidan!" She barked. "No shooting in this house. You know the rules!"

He sheepishly lowered the gun.

"We've talked about this before." Before returning to the kitchen, where she was fixing supper, she asked, "What are you trying to do?" Seeing the box and its lock, she shook her head. "Land sakes, you youngsters. No sense at all." She went to the kitchen and returned to them, wielding a pig sticker with a narrow yet strong blade.

"Give me that thing." She inserted the point in between the clasp and the lock's shackle. Using the handle of her rolling pin as a fulcrum, she jerked the knife up and out. The clasp ripped off the metal band with a loud snap. And then she handed the chest to Aidan.

"I bet you wouldn't know how to break a chicken's neck, neither." With that said, she strode back into the kitchen.

Collin took the box. The rusted hinges on the lid creaked as he forced it open. Peering in, he exclaimed, "Old Papers." He started sifting through them. His eyes widened. "Hang on, what's this?" He extracted an ancient vellum from the chest. "Look. It's the original of Niall O'Donnell's note." He handed it to Morgan.

She scanned it. "This confirms what Temple wrote in his diary. Flooren was the pirate who attacked William Temple and his wife in 1627."

"And that was his skeleton back at Creagh." Collin dug out another relic. "What do we have here?"

Morgan was perking up at the find. "This looks like an old notebook full of entries."

Jack looked down at the journal. "Did all those ancient men keep journals?"

"Seems so, Jack." Morgan nodded. "It was the custom in those days so they could recount the details later for historians. At least the ones who thought highly of themselves. Like Johnathan Swift with his father William Temple's life story."

"Read us an excerpt."

Morgan scanned the first page. "I'd love to, Jack, except I don't understand Arabic."

"All right, Sis. We'll need a translator whom we can trust." He handed her the box. "What else is in the chest?"

"Look at this. When Tadgh and I were at the RIA with Professor Lawlor—" Morgan caught herself, remembering, her lip quivering, with tears welling up in her eyes.

"It's all right, Morgan." Collin came over and put his arm around her. "What did you find?"

"It's a copy of the document that the professor mentioned when we talked about Sir Owain." She remembered the note in Temple's diary that said the pirate had taken their copy of Sir Owain's journey.

The men asked, in unison, "Who is Sir Owain?"

Aidan held out a crooked little finger. "What goes up the chimney?"

Collin linked with his pinky. "Smoke."

"What was that all about?" Jack wanted to know. "I am losing the thread of what is going on with hand signals and secret messages."

"It's an Irish custom," Morgan explained. "If two people say the same thing at the same time, then they have to do what Aidan and Collin just did to avoid bad luck."

"But who is Sir Owain?"

Morgan explained her experience at Temple House with the apparition of the medieval knight on his steed, signifying resolution of an emotional dilemma was at hand. Then she relayed the input she had received about the document describing his journeys from Professor Lawlor.

"And you believe this ghost story?"

"You found me the next day and resolved my amnesia, didn't you, Collin?"

"Only because I did a lot of reporter legwork to track you down."

"Then your appearance at Sean O'Casey's home when I was there was a result of careful reporter legwork, as you put it?"

"It was just a coincidence, Sis."

"Was it?"

"I didn't see Sir Owain there."

"He might have taken a different form, like Sean himself, Collin.

Don't you see? All this has been ordained."

Collin almost said, *including Tadgh's death,* but fortunately held his tongue. "We're off track, Sis. What is the document you have there?"

"It looks like a very long poem in Old English verse. The title, as written here and told us by the professor, is *Tractatus de Purgatorio Sancti Patricii* by Henricus of Sawtry, or Saltrey, if you want to spell it that way. If I remember what Lawlor told us, this poem recounts the tale of Sir Owain's penitential trials at a portal to Hell in Northern Ireland. He came from Europe by way of the western Ireland route. A branch of the Ballymote monastery existed on the very site of the Templar castle a hundred years before the knights built it in the early 13th century. Sir Owain was said to have stayed there in 1154, according to the Chronicles of Roger of Wendover. Temple House, where we stayed, was built beside the ruins of that castle, and Sir Owain appeared to me that night out of the mists of those stones."

Morgan looked down at the document again, then added, "The lady of Temple House, Charlotte Perceval confirmed that Sir Owain's spirit had been seen before, including to herself."

Jack looked mystified. "How do you remember all of this, Morgan?"

"Easy. I'm a reporter's sister, remember?" Leafing through the folios, she said, "The beginning of the poem is missing."

Collin's ears pricked up, and he came over to look. "Didn't the other relics have pages missing as clues?"

Morgan flipped back to the beginning. "Right. But this copy was inadvertently in this box that Temple gave the Barbary pirate in 1627, twenty-five years after Red Hugh had died."

"Temple could have found this clue that Red Hugh or Florence MacCarthaigh Reagh left hidden years before. Maybe even located where the O'Donnell treasure was hidden." Collin paused to think.

Jack chimed in. "We know that Temple didn't find the treasure, and therefore the epistle, or Swift wouldn't have been looking for it in the 1700s. We don't know if Rory removed the religious artifact and took it with him before the Flight of the Earls in 1607. Even if he did, he wouldn't have taken the treasure, would he?"

Collin held the *Tractatus* up. "Unlikely. Red would have told him it was to be left for the time of revolution."

Morgan added. "We don't even know if this document had any significance to the pirate. It was just in the box. What are the first words in the poem now, Collin?"

He chanted,

> *And lived in dedeli sinne.*
> *Seyn Patrike hadde rewthe*
> *Of hir misbileve and untrewthe,*
> *That thai weren inne.*

Jack looked over his shoulder at the words. "What in heaven's name does that even mean?"

Collin squinted at the page. "It may be meaningless. We need someone who can translate Old English and Arabic. When I go back to Dublin, I will contact the professor. He'll be able to help us."

As Collin started to put the documents back into the chest, Morgan noticed a ragged edge sticking out of the back of the pirate's journal. "What's that?"

Collin opened the ancient cover gently and said, "Look! There's a back pocket!"

Morgan reached down to extract a yellowed scrap of paper, then stopped. "Put the journal down on the table, Brother. I'm afraid this flimsy paper will disintegrate if I pull it out. It's sticking to the leather pouch."

Collin held the journal open on the parlor table for her while she pulled back the edge of the pouch to expose its contents. Then carefully, she pried the leather away from the paper until it slid out onto the table. The letters were crude, as if written in haste. And they were in Gaelic, a language none of them understood. Again, she thought of Tadgh, breathed deeply, and exhaled, eyes tearing up. Would there ever come a time when her painful loss would subside? Would it dull with time and disappear entirely, or would it always be this sharp, this pounding? And then a horrible thought struck her—would she one day forget him altogether? That she could not allow.

Morgan returned the journal to the chest and closed the lid, leaving the strange paper lying on the table. Then she went to one of Martha's bookcases flanking the fireplace, pulled out a suitable tome, and inserted the piece between its pages for safekeeping.

Later, after Maurice returned from the day's fishing, while Martha and Molly were doing the dishes after supper, Morgan asked him to come to the parlor and translate the document.

Their host read it to himself and then said, "Where did you get this, lass? It's very odd."

"We found it at home before we left. What does it say?"

"That's what is strange. It references my ancestor, Thomas."

"Read it out loud, please!"

Maurice moved closer to the Adventurers and summorized—

Grand Master Hospitaller. There is an ancient epistle of great importance to your cause from St. Columba, being sent to you for protection by Red Hugh O'Donnell via Thomas Fitzmaurice. Alas, I cannot fulfill this sacred order because we are being roundly defeated by the English here at Fenit. Search for it, my lord. Signed Brian MacSweeney in the year of our Lord, December 1601.

He rubbed his chin and stared at Morgan. "Does this make any sense to you?"

Collin shook his head. "I have no idea about any epistle, Maurice, but this scrap of paper is old and must have been quite important, I should think. It's very perplexing."

"You found it in your house?"

"In the attic, sir," Collin said, stepping in to close the book and tuck it under his arm.

"The message is even more strange than the document itself, lad. It rings true though, don't ye know."

Morgan's green eyes locked on their host's. "How so?"

"Red Hugh O'Donnell did send forces on his way south to liberate my ancestors."

Collin took Maurice aside. "Interesting, thank you, Sir. This is a riddle for another day, that's certain. Now, how about that brandy you offered me after supper, eh?"

Later that evening, in the privacy of Morgan's room, the Adventurers discussed the recent revelation. Collin was the first to speak. He absently fingered the heirloom locket around his neck. "This seems to be a clue to a different mystery unrelated to the search for the O'Donnell treasure. There is no reference to P.P."

"But the contents of this chest are consistent with William Temple's diary even though he didn't mention this scrawled note from MacSweeney," Morgan said, twirling her curls behind her ear.

Jack noticed that positive sign. She had not done that thing that showed she was perplexed since Tadgh had died.

"And how did it come into the possession of our Barbary pirate?" Morgan added.

"Good questions, indeed, but we can't go on a wild goose chase looking for a lost epistle in the middle of this war. Let's stay on track and go to Meenmore as we planned. We owe that to Tadgh," Collin said.

"What do you think, Jack?"

"I agree with your brother, Morgan. We need to honor poor Tadgh as we already planned."

Morgan looked up into Jack's face and smiled. "I know you both are right, but what would Tadgh have done?"

Aidan walked in just in time to hear the last exchange. "He would have gone after the O'Donnell treasure, Sis. For the Cause and because it is our destiny."

Jack saw that Aidan, in his brother's absence, was starting to take charge, and he supported the young man. "I agree with Aidan, Morgan. We should go to Meenmore for Tadgh's service and *then* try to find PP."

Collin was too intrigued to say no, despite his promise to Kathy.

Collin was on edge the following week at Barrow House while they waited for Aunt Biddy to call and tell them it was safe to come to Dungloe. He noticed that Jack was taking the opportunity to get closer to Morgan. Finally, when they hadn't heard from Auntie, Collin took the train to Dublin to report there and to Healy. He took the small box and its contents with him.

After Molly connected with the Cumann na mBan in Tralee, she returned to support Morgan despite Jack's insistence on leading that effort.

Aidan connected with the commander of the Tralee IRA battalion, John Joe Sheehy, at his field headquarters to see if he could find out what happened to Tom Barry's column. Following Michael Collin's lead, the small safe house was in plain sight on Caherslee Road, just east of Bonsecours Hospital.

"We know that Barry attacked the RIC barracks at Ballineen on March 31st. When did you say your house was torched, lad?"

"March 24th, Sir."

"Then at least some of them survived. They killed ten British mercenaries at Ballineen. We understand the 3rd West Cork Flying Column is on the run now because of the marauding sweeps by the enemy in the area."

Aidan realized that he would not likely be able to return to Barry's column. "I'll be here for a couple of weeks. How can I help you, Sir?"

The commander paused, and Aidan waited. "You can be of assistance. You're new to the area, so you can move about more easily than the rest of us. We're dealing with the same heavy-handed British retaliation tactics you encountered in Cork. Major Mackinnon, the Auxiliary leader, is a ruthless, vindictive bastard here in Tralee, indiscriminately killing militant and civilian men in cold blood in front of their families and setting their homes on fire."

He must be like Boyle, Aidan thought. *Pure evil.*

"This fellow Mackinnon has proved to be quite elusive and has escaped assassination." Sheehy showed Aidan a photograph of the man. "He's a tall, broad-shouldered Scot who walks with a confident swagger. Find out where he goes and when if you can. We have five Fianna boys who can help you, and O'Riordan, here, will have him executed."

Two days later, on April 4th, the Auxiliaries led by Major Mackinnon swept through Ardfert, apparently looking for rebels. They viciously attacked citizens and burned one of their houses. Fortunately, Barrow House escaped their ire.

That evening, Maurice slammed the door upon arriving home from his day of fishing on *Slanu III*. "Those damned military police killed my best jigger, Conor, today. Why can't our boys execute that bastard Mackinnon? He moves around a lot, but he is foolhardy as well."

Aidan brought the man a stout and sat him down in his easy chair by the fire. "What else do you know about him, Maurice?"

Maurice downed the ale in one gulp. "We call him the scourge of Tralee. He murdered two fine young men who thought they had found a haven at Mrs. Byrne's home last Christmas night. He stuffed their bodies in the outhouse before he burned down the home. The evil, brutality, and indignity shown by this devil knows no bounds. My mates tell me his one weakness is golf. He often plays at the Oakpark Golf Course, traveling with several of his goons."

Aidan got his host another brew. "I'll take care of this."

Aidan camped out with three of the younger boys at the golf links. Four days yielded nothing. Then, late in the morning of the fifth day, Aidan saw his prey for the first time. Mackinnon was an overbearing, arrogant ass, to be sure. Strutting about with his bodyguards. From a distance, it looked like he was a lousy golfer.

That night, he and O'Riordan scouted the course and hid a rifle at Kenny's Fort near the 3rd green. There was cover for a sniper in a nearby tree.

On Friday, the 15th, Aidan and the boys saw the Major checking in for a round of golf and sent one of the boys for O'Riordan. He brought their best marksman, Con Healy, and hid him in the tree before Mackinnon finished the first hole.

The bastard was purported to always wear body armor. Healy aimed for the head from a hundred yards, hitting the man twice before he slumped onto the third green.

The scourge of Tralee was dead, but revenge of the Auxiliaries under Brigadier-General Crozier was swift. They rolled into nearby Ballymacelligott in their Crossley tender armored vehicles that evening, where the Christmas murders had occurred, burning at least fifteen houses, including that of the parish priest. Then they raided the home of one of the Christmas night victims and killed his uncle.

Shops in Tralee closed immediately for the weekend but did not escape the blood lust of the Auxies. By Wednesday, they burned several shops, the railway station, and destroyed the printing presses of two newspapers in town. That was in retaliation because they refused to put a black mourning banner on their first pages following Mackinnon's funeral on the Tuesday. Aidan was there when *The Kerryman* was attacked and took the news back to Barrow House.

"It had to be done, lad," Maurice exclaimed, pounding his fist on the kitchen table hard enough to knock the salt and pepper shakers over.

Martha bent over and swept up the spilled salt, then tossed it over her left shoulder into the sink. "Really, Maurice. You'd better watch your blood pressure."

"That MacKinnon deserved what he got. These Auxies need to be stopped."

Aidan now knew Maurice would be true to the Cause, no matter what came to pass.

Collin returned from Dublin on Saturday with the ancient chest before the Tralee railway station was destroyed. He had convinced Robertson he should investigate the Tralee disturbances for the *Tely*. He told Morgan that Professor Lawlor had been unavailable for consultation.

When Aidan arrived back at the Collis home and reported on the turmoil in town, Collin decided Donegal could not be a worse risk than Tralee. He called Aunt Biddy and convinced her to let them all come immediately.

That Wednesday afternoon, Martha came into the parlor with tea and biscuits as Collin, Jack, and Morgan were planning their trip north to Dungloe. She asked them, "Did you ever figure out what was written on the documents in that old box?"

Morgan looked up from her notes and answered, "No, Martha. We're stumped since the documents are written in old English and Arabic."

Martha thought for a moment. "Why don't you take them to the cathedral ruins before you leave? It is a heritage site now, and they have historians who may be able to help you. They know all about Maurice's ancestor Thomas Fitzmaurice who established the Franciscan Friary in the 1200s, and Saint Brendan, who established his Celtic Christian monastery on the site in the sixth century. We're quite famous, you know. The cathedral was established in the twelfth century and was a great teaching center for all of Europe."

"We heard about that from Maurice." Morgan had an idea. "Have you ever heard about a knight named Sir Owain?"

"No, dear. Best talk to the historians about that."

"Could we borrow the Hudson to go talk to them?" Collin asked.

"Yes, of course. But do it tomorrow. They'll be closed up for today by now, I expect."

Maurice came in from Fenit, where his fishing boat was moored, having picked up Molly coming back from her walk. After dropping her in the kitchen to assist Martha with the evening meal, he met with his other guests in the parlor. "There's a storm brewing. I suggest you get Aidan to give you a hand and lash your hooker down more securely."

"Aye, captain." Jack rushed out to find Aidan.

Maurice tried to be chipper. "There you are, Morgan. What have you been up to?"

"Trying to figure out how to translate documents we found in this old chest." Morgan explained Martha's suggestion.

"Good idea. My wife's got a good head on her shoulders, bless her. If the weather's foul, I'll drive you there in the morning. I must share one thing I remember about our ancestor Thomas Fitzmaurice, from what my father told me. It might be pertinent."

"The one who established the Ardfert Friary in the thirteenth century?"

"No, lass. The 18th Lord of Kerry and Lixnaw, the ally that Hugh Red O'Donnell tried to liberate on his way to the Battle of Kinsale in 1601."

"Yes?"

"He survived Kinsale and lived under English rule until 1630."

Collin was interested. He closed his notebook and turned to Maurice. "What do you remember about him?"

"It's a strange story about an event in his life. Apparently, at Christmas in 1626, he was visited by an Arabic man who demanded to know the whereabouts of a religious document authored by our own St. Columba. When my ancestor said he knew nothing of the document, the man got violent. Thomas got into a sword fight with the man and drove him away in self-defense. They never found out where he came from. It's odd that you found documents written in Arabic in your home that may have come from the same era, isn't it?"

Morgan looked at Collin. "It could be the same man whose documents we have."

From the corner of his eye, Collin saw Molly slip into the far end of the parlor through the kitchen door. She started to pull plates from the corner cupboard, pausing the clattering while Morgan was talking.

Collin interrupted his sister with small talk until the cook left the room, then took her aside in his bedroom. "What do you know about Molly, Sis?"

"She supported Kathleen and me in Dublin when Tadgh was in jail."

"Did she seem very chummy with you?"

"We get along together. She is a hard worker."

Collin thought for a moment and tried a different tack. "When did you meet her?"

"She got reassigned to our chapter of the Cumann na mBan as soon as I was taken in by the good doctor. Why do you ask?"

"Did she go away for afternoon walks alone even back then?"

"Yes, I believe she did. Mostly without asking. Said it relieved the stress of war."

"I don't know about her, Morgan. I think she was trying to listen to part of our conversation just now when she came in for the plates. We should be careful of any loose talk around her, lass."

Morgan shook her head. "I think you are just an overly suspicious newspaperman, Collin. Anyway, I've got more important problems than worrying about her."

Collin's eyes narrowed. "All the same, I'm going to look into this woman's connections."

Morgan opened the door to the bedroom and stepped out into the hallway. "You do that if you must. I'm going to rest before dinner."

Collin could see the melancholy creeping over her facial features. Their recent horrific life-changing events seemed to erode her usual Florence Nightingale show of strength. She had always taken charge when Tadgh was alive, but now it wasn't clear to him if or when she would come through this ordeal.

"Would you like me to accompany you, Morgan?"

She turned from her brother and mumbled, "I need to be left alone."

An hour later, Morgan was awakened from a fitful nap when a flash of light pierced her closed eyelids, followed by an instantaneous clap of artillery thunder. She was back in St. Stephen's Green with the machine gun erupting, and searing pain coursed through her leg where the bullet had smashed through her flesh. *Where is Tadgh? Is he all right?*

She shot up in bed and opened her eyes only to realize she was in a rustic bedroom, dark and foreboding, its heavy drapes flapping in the storm. The window had blown open. She was sweating profusely. Suddenly the more abject horror of reality hit her. Tadgh was dead, shot while helplessly tied to a chair. He was gone, and she couldn't do a thing about it. She couldn't even bury his body. The agony of it all seared her heart and numbed her brain.

What would she do without him? Without his strength, his cunning, his love?

Then she remembered that their love had been strained at best since Tadgh was in prison for so long and throughout his terrible hunger strike. He hadn't been the same man afterward; he'd turned savage and vengeful. The war and those damned British soldiers did that to him. But she loved him more fiercely than ever since he had died. She had to accept that reality. Now there was just dear Aidan, who had gotten caught up in the killing. *For the sake of what?* Liberty.

And she was a hunted woman. She'd killed a guard to save Tadgh, a man who was just trying to do his job. She loathed herself now for doing it, entirely against her own beliefs.

What was she to do now? Collin wanted her to leave all this grief and danger and move to Canada, where he said she would be safe. But Toronto was where her Ma had been murdered on the waterfront by a rapist, the same rapist who later assaulted Kathy, the woman who would become

Collin's wife. Collin himself had killed that murderer in self-defense, protecting Kathy from harm. That place didn't sound much safer than here in war-torn Ireland.

But what about the possibility of becoming a doctor practicing at the Toronto Women's Hospital? Surely that would be the culmination of a lifetime of saving others, her calling. But if she left, then she would be abandoning Aidan and the Cause that he and brave Tadgh had fought to the death for. Just like she abandoned Tadgh during the week when Michael Collins and Tom Barry had said they would save him, when Tadgh was still alive. Damn them.

Her mind kept racing in circles with no resolution to her dilemma. The only thing she knew for certain was that she wanted to be dead and reunited with the love of her life. Yet she knew that was selfish since it would cause more grief for Collin and Aidan, not to mention Jack, who had been particularly kind all along. And suicide went against her beliefs—her love of God and her desire to preserve life.

What was she to do? Another thunderclap vibrated the windowpane. Morgan decided what she needed to do right now was to close and latch that window to stop the freezing rain from pouring into her room. Then she needed to wash her face and change her waist-shirt for dinner. By God, she could not break, no matter what life threw at her.

Chapter Nine
Association

Wednesday, April 20, 1921
Barrow Bay, Tralee, Ireland

Collin was pleased to see that Morgan appeared for supper in a much better mood. She seemed to be slipping in and out of fits of melancholy. After the lamb stew and bread pudding, while Molly helped Martha with the dishes, Morgan and three companions thanked their hosts and met in her room again. Collin observed that the intrigue about the Barbary pirate appeared to be lifting her spirits, except when she connected it to Tadgh.

"I know we decided to focus on PP. But do you think the pirate came to Fenit to interrogate Maurice's ancestor before meeting with Temple? That's the story he told me today."

Collin stepped back from the window to answer Morgan. "The timing is right. Now we know why. He had that scrawled note from MacSweeney."

Morgan twirled her black curls behind her ear. "Oddly, Maurice said that his ancestor told the Arab that he knew nothing about the epistle. Yet he was the recipient per Niall's letter. Maybe he lied."

"And why would Red Hugh send it to him anyway?" Jack asked.

Maurice told us that years ago. Thomas Fitzmaurice was a Knights Hospitaller, like his namesake who established the Friary. Niall's letter said Red Hugh was trying to get a copy of St. Columba's Epistle to their Grand Master, didn't it?"

"Yes, and now we have the original of that letter. Flooren was well informed." Jack cocked his head to one side. "But how would Barbary pirates be involved?"

They all agreed that they were missing crucial pieces of the puzzle.

Collin picked up the old English poem document and flipped through its pages. "I still think that searching for this epistle is not helping us find our O'Donnell treasure."

Morgan massaged her throbbing forehead. "I'm not so sure, Brother. I feel like we're missing something important, and it is right in front of us."

That night the lightning strikes stopped, but the wind howled, rattling the windowpanes as Morgan tried to get to sleep. In the wintry cold of the dark bedroom, the ache for her husband returned. She would go mad if she continued to let herself dwell on those images and thoughts. But she couldn't stop. It was excruciating. The worst she had ever felt. Worse than being trapped below decks on the *Lusitania,* thinking every breath would be her last.

Collin, Aidan, and Jack had been a great comfort, but they could not fix what ailed her. As a nurse, she realized she had to get control of her thoughts and body. Otherwise, she would get very sick, and that would only hurt those she loved who were still alive. But she couldn't let Tadgh slip away. It wasn't right, and none of it made sense. *Damn these warmongering men.* Pulling the covers around her head, she cried herself to sleep.

A cold rain, almost sleet, pelted down on the old Hudson as Maurice steered towards the Ardfert Cathedral ruins two miles from Barrow House on Thursday morning. Aidan and Jack had stayed behind to check on the hooker's condition and prepare for their voyage.

"I know one of the historians, name of Anthony Fuller. He will certainly be able to help you with old English translation."

The rain abated as they approached the stunning ruins, with its Romanesque west doorway, a magnificent 13th-century east window, and a spectacular row of nine lancets in the south wall.

"This must have been a magnificent cathedral in its day, Maurice," Collin remarked. "I can see how it could have attracted students far and wide."

"Together with my ancestor's Franciscan Priory, a half-mile away, they had an extensive library for its time in medieval Europe. The battlements were added in the 15th century, but unfortunately, they did not keep out the bloody British during the Confederate Wars in 1641. All we have left are the ruins."

Collin ran his fingers across one of the weathered effigies of ecclesiastical figures from the late 13th century that looked out from the wall beside the east window in the south transept. "See here, Morgan? Truly magnificent."

Tony Fuller was a mouse of a man with bristling whiskers. What he lacked in physical stature, he more than made up with his knowledge. His bright red bowtie stood in stark contrast to his well-worn brown suit on this dreary morning in this hallowed place.

"How may I help you folks today? A tour of the cathedral grounds?"

"No, sir. We found old documents and need them translated."

The historian's eyes brightened. "Old documents, you say?"

Morgan stepped forward, opened the old box, and pulled out the folios of the poem.

"Just a minute, m'lady. Let me see that chest."

Tony studied the outside of the vessel carefully, running his fingers along the metal edges. Then he licked his finger and rubbed the leather. "Interesting piece. Judging from the scrollwork on the metal bands, I'd say it is old English, likely 17th century. See the cinquefoil arches?"

Collin stepped forward and took the chest out of the scholar's hands. "That's very interesting, Sir, because one of the documents we need to have translated is in old English. The other is written in Arabic."

"Arabic, you say. We have an Oxford University student originally from Morocco. He has been here from Dublin the last two weeks to study our Ogham stone and other antiquities. He is following the ancient escape route of the Templars and educating us about his country. Did you know that the Murat Reis, Jan Janszoon von Haarlem, led an attack on our seaside town of Baltimore?"

"Yes, sir. We're aware of that." Collin said, turning to face Morgan. "Can you give us a minute, Mr. Fuller?"

"Certainly."

Collin took Morgan aside into the cloisters, careful to bring the chest with him.

"Don't you think it strange we found out a Barbary pirate came here to Fenit in the 1600s, and there is another Moroccan heritage student here, now? Didn't you say that there was a Moroccan student with Professor Lawlor at the RIA? What was his name?"

Morgan's eyes glazed over. "Let me think. Fazook, ah, no, Fazaar, that was it."

"I wonder if this is the same young man."

"I guess we will find out."

Collin spoke softly. "Why would such a student want to learn about Irish antiques, including the Ogham language? Maybe we should not show him the pirate's journal. We don't know what is in it."

"But how will we figure out what it says?"

"That will have to wait. Maybe Professor Lawlor could help. We can get Mr. Fuller to translate the poem."

"That is strange. I agree. Let's wait on the pirate's notebook."

They returned to where Tony and Maurice were discussing the establishment of the friary back in the 13th century.

"I sent for Abbad. He should be here momentarily."

The five-foot English student of Moroccan heritage sauntered in a few minutes later, notebook in hand. He wore horn-rimmed glasses on his hook-nosed face. After greeting the visitors, he said, "Understand you have a document needing translation that comes from my homeland."

Collin glanced at Morgan, who shook her head.

Studying the young man's facial features, Collin showed him the chest but didn't let him hold it. The student's face lit up.

"Does this chest contain the document you need to be translated?"

"Actually, no. The document needing interpreting is written in old English."

Tony looked confused.

"I may have misspoken earlier. The document is in old English." Collin pulled out the poem.

The student's eyes cast down. "In that case, I can't help you, I'm afraid."

"But I certainly can," Tony said enthusiastically. "Thank you for stopping by, Abbad. Sorry to have bothered your studies for nothing."

Collin saw that Abbad tried to see the letters inscribed into the chest. "That's no problem, sir. I am curious as to what was in that chest, though."

"No need to keep you, son." Collin closed the chest and put it under his arm. "We'll just work with Mr. Fuller here, thanks."

When Abbad made no motion to leave, Morgan said to him, "Can you show me the Ogham stone I've heard so much about?"

"Why yes, yes, I can. It's very old."

"Do say." Morgan took him by the arm and led him out of the room.

When they were gone, Tony started. "I thought you said—"

"I'm sorry, sir. I was wrong. I'd like for you to look at this ancient poem."

They walked to the historian's office. Collin handed him the well-worn set of folios. Tony read the verses to himself. "I know this story. It was published in the middle of the twelfth century and became quite popular with those who could read." He examined the folios. "This copy is quite old, you know. Could be worth a small fortune."

Morgan found them in the office several minutes later. She'd managed to extricate herself from Abbad.

Tony turned to her as she entered. He held up the document and said, "I was just telling your brother here that this is the story of Sir Owain when he made a pilgrimage to Patrick's Purgatory. The title is in Latin, though. *Tractatus de Purgatorio Sancti Patricii* by Henricus of Sawtry, or spelled Saltrey, translates to *Treatise on Saint Patrick's Purgatory* by Henricus of Sawtrey."

Morgan realized what she should have seen all along. Maybe it was the way that the scholar had said it. PP stood for Patrick's Purgatory! She thought Charlotte had said that Sir Owain took a pilgrimage to purgatory without mentioning Saint Patrick. Niall's note said a Gospel was given to St. Patrick at the time he showed him purgatory. *Why didn't I see this sooner? It must be a real place. Not just a myth. The story is not just a parable.*

She looked at Collin. That fact had dawned on him also. "Can you translate the first few lines for us, please?" Morgan asked.

"Certainly, my dear. Let's see, here goes—

> *And lived in deadly sin.*
> *Saint Patrick had pity*
> *Of their false belief and error*
> *That they were in.*"

"How about the rest of the poem, sir?" Collin urged.

Tony looked askance. "All twelve hundred lines?"

"Oh. Then, why don't we just read it together?"

The historian started in, describing much pertaining to the knight's time in purgatory, his awful trials and tribulations, and then finding salvation before returning to the earthly world. It all sounded gruesome. But where was this place Sir Owain visited?

At one point, Tony read the lines aloud.

> *When Saint Patrick from sleep he woke,*
> *Good signs he found and them took*
> *Of his dreaming.*
> *Book and staff he there found,*
> *And took them up in his hand*
> *And thanked Heaven's King.*

Collin thought, There's the reference to the Gospel from God.

It took three hours to wade through the whole poem. At the end of it, Morgan asked, "I think that this must just be a parable, isn't it?"

"No, no, lass. Patrick's Purgatory is the most important place of pilgrimage in Ireland. Famous nobles from all over Europe came from early times to do penance at this sacred shrine. To walk the circles, and, if worthy enough, to spend a frightful night in the pit."

"The pit?" Morgan weakly echoed.

"Yes. The pit on Station Island in Lough Derg where God showed and subjected Saint Patrick to purgatory." The historian went to his records and pulled out a file named Patrick's Purgatory. From it, he extracted a page and thrust it into Morgan's hand. "See here, lass."

Morgan and Collin studied the ancient map of Hibernia by Betelius, dated 1560. It showed the central feature of Patrick's Purgatory up north in the land of Tyrconnell more clearly than any city. "You can plainly see that the purgatory was one of the main features on maps at the time."

Then he showed them a map of Station Island drawn by Carve in 1651 that depicted its features, including the pit in question.

Collin pointed at the two maps. "Could I take photographs, sir?"

"Certainly, son. Let me put them under the lamp."

Map of Betelius Inverted Map of Ireland 1560 (Hibernia)
Featuring Patrick's Purgatory
(By Ferrando Bertelli – Early Lafreri School, Italy)

Map of Station Island, Lough Derg
Published in Carve's Lyra Hibernia, dated 1666
(But likely drawn before 1632)

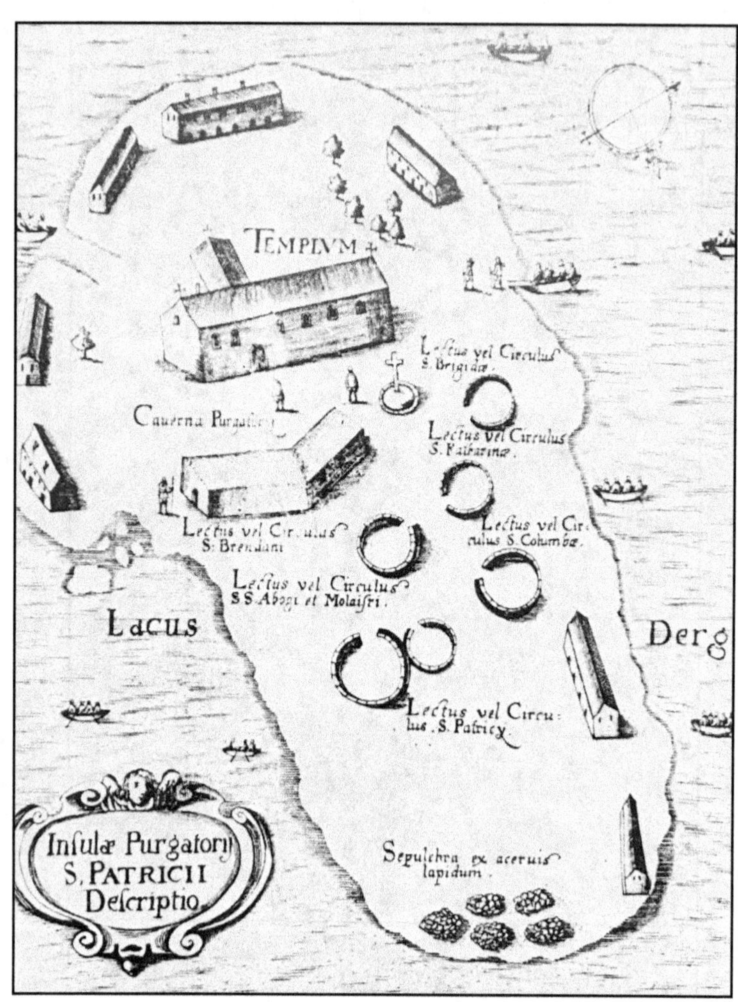

As Collin snapped the photographs with his No. 2, Morgan asked, "What else can you tell us about this purgatory, Mr. Fuller?"

One of the nuns poked her head into the historian's study and asked if anyone wanted tea. Fuller graciously accepted the offer for the three of them, and she left.

The historian consulted his notes. "There is much mythology there, lass. It is said after St. Patrick was shown it in the early 5th century by God, one of his disciples, St. Dabheog, took charge of the site and built a monastery on the adjacent Saints Island. Saints Columba and Brigid were also purported to have spent time at the purgatory."

"Saint Columba, you say?" Morgan asked. "I understand he was from our clan."

"But you said your name is McCarthy."

"Married name, sir, and proud of it. My maiden name is O'Donnell, from Donegal."

"I see. In that case, your clansman, a celibate monk is the most revered saint in our land, even beyond our own St. Brendon. I was taught that he had the wisdom of St. Patrick, so he did. Much mystery surrounds Colum Cille."

Collin's ears twitched. "Mystery?"

"Our Hospitallers were sworn to secrecy."

"About what?" Morgan asked.

Fuller chuckled. "If I knew, it wouldn't be a secret, now, would it, lass."

This sounds like the Book of Ballymote, Morgan thought. She had to press further. "Who says these things?"

"We know that the Templars fled through here and Ballymote to Scotland during the persecution in the 14th century. We presume they knew."

Morgan smiled. There was that connection, *Ballymote.*

Collin saw the conversation drifting away from their intended path. "Tell us more about Lough Derg, please."

"When early pilgrims would come for penitence, they would first go to the monastery on Saints Island for fifteen days of prayer and fasting. Then St. Dabheog's successors would decide if the sinner was worthy of visiting the pit on adjacent Station Island to stay the night. After their twenty-four hours' stay, if they lived to tell the tale, they would undergo another fifteen days of fasting and prayer before leaving for home along the ancient pilgrimage trail through Drogheda."

"This is not just myth, is it?" Morgan wanted to know.

"Not at all, lass. Of course, Irish records were sparse, to say the least, but this document you brought for me to translate is the earliest proof that Sir Owain did indeed go there and witness purgatory and heaven."

The nun reappeared with a plain white china service. "Sugar?"

Morgan said, "Yes, two lumps, please."

"It's the devil's concoction, don't ye know," Tony said. He took his tea black.

"What, tea?"

"No, lass. Sugar. It destroys the body, so it does."

"I like it anyway. What else is there to know about this purgatory place?"

"You seem very interested in St. Patrick's lair. Might I know why?"

"I found this old copy of Sir Owain's tale in the chest, and I am naturally curious."

"I see. What else is important? The monastery probably included religious recluses called anchorites. They lived in beehive cells, whose ruins are preserved in the penitential beds that can still be seen on Station Island. The penitent walk the circles around them, praying."

Collin couldn't see the point in wasting time with this historical drivel. He was anxious for them to be on their way to Dungloe, and the historian was droning on.

"Around 1130, the monastery was given to Augustinian Canons Regular by the authority of the cathedral in Armagh, under Saint Malachy. They rebuilt the monastery on Saints Island itself in the 15th century."

Morgan was fascinated and asked the historian to continue.

"After the Flight of the Earls in 1607, there were conflicts with the Franciscan friars at Donegal Abbey who wanted to change the pilgrimage route. There were altercations, but the history is vague in this time period when Britain was taking control."

Collin said, "I think it is time to go, Morgan."

Before he could take hold of his sister and usher her to the door, Mr. Fuller said, "One last thing. On October 25, 1632, because of hostilities, the British sealed off the pit and forbade any future overnight visits. There is no record of Canons Regular of St. Augustine at Lough Derg after that. But the now persecuted Franciscan friars, originally from the Donegal Monastery, turned up in the summer months to administer to the perseverant pilgrims."

Collin pricked up his ears. "1632, you say?"

"Yes. That date is certain. An altercation occurred on that date that caused the British to shut it down, and the pit has never been reopened."

Morgan got up from her seat, then stretched and yawned. "Thank you very much, Mr. Fuller, for helping us with our research about this poem. We should probably be going."

Now Collin wanted to stay. "Can you visit the monastery on Station Island today, sir?"

"Yes, lad. They offer a three-day penitence program. But you would have to contact them if you were interested. I've never been myself."

While all this was taking place, Maurice visited a Hospitaller friend in the village. When returning, he was led to Mr. Fuller's office. A hook-nosed, dark-skinned young man standing just outside the historian's closed door jumped back upon Maurice's approach and disappeared into the ruins.

When Maurice and his visitors arrived back at Barrow House, the rain had stopped. Martha announced that supper would be at six. "Have you seen Molly? She went for a walk an hour ago, and I need her to help me."

Morgan started to put her coat back on. "I'll go look for her."

"You'll do nothing of the sort," Collin said, insisting on taking her coat and putting it in the hall closet. "Come to the fire. She'll show up on her own."

He checked on the hooker and met up with Jack and Aidan, filling them in on what they found out.

While offering to help with the boat, Collin concluded, "The place of religious significance for Red Hugh was Patrick's Purgatory on his own lands."

"Where on the island—and how—would he have been able to hide his treasure there among the friars and pilgrims?" Aidan asked, cinching the final reefing knot on the lugsail.

"I don't know the answers to those questions. One step at a time. We're going to Donegal to pay our respects to Tadgh, first and foremost." In preparation for the voyage, Collin hid the pirate chest with its documents in the cabin under the bunk.

A hundred yards away, hidden in the woods, Molly was meeting with her partner as she had done daily since she arrived at Creagh and again here at Barrows Bay. Too far away to hear the conversation, they were watching the interaction of the people on the hooker.

"You're not going to leave them nor go to Tralee."

"I did your bidding, Abbad, once you found out I knew the woman. I got stationed at their house. I've been cooking for those grubby rebels, and I almost got killed for it. Isn't that enough? The family is going to Dungloe to visit relatives for a family wake. That's all."

"Silly woman," he hissed. "They are searching for the elusive epistle, and therefore, the gospel. I heard them talking to that dumb historian about Patrick's Purgatory. I am going to steal the chest that the O'Donnell had under his arm tonight. I think it was Flooren's, and it is legally mine. I will read my ancestor's document, which should gain us wisdom in our search for the prize. Then I will return the chest before dawn."

"Why would you give it back?"

"So, the infidels can continue their search, none the wiser. Once we've achieved our goal, I will pry it from O'Donnell's dead body. If my heavy-handed ancestor Flooren hadn't caused such a commotion in trying to search the pit in 1632, the British wouldn't have shut it down. But now we have a glorious opportunity."

"Why can't the Association do this?"

"Damn them, Molly! In 1899 our incompetent leaders dug in the wrong place, and a lot of good that did them. My father, and now I, have pretended to be loyal members to get their financial support. We don't share with them what we find, just useless morsels. My uncle Abd el Krim is in desperate need of the prize to free North Africa. Understood?"

"What about your brother Fazaar?"

"He too pretends to be Association. But he's with us."

"I don't see him here, helping."

"His assignment in Dublin supports the professor and aids in finding out what they know. He'll join us when we need him."

"Anyway, Abbad, they won't let me accompany them to Dungloe. I'm not family."

"Find a way, Molly. Our family is counting on you. We cannot fail. Now get you back to the house, woman."

Molly turned to go, and Abbad gripped her shoulder and squeezed hard.

"Be on the lookout for that grocer woman from Dublin; Deirdre's her name. She didn't fool me. She'll be snooping around before long, and she could interfere with our quest. My father took care of her father when he tried to stop the digging in '99. We're going to deal with her."

Abbad didn't tell his concubine he had already failed once in that task.

It neared suppertime. Fresh from her walk, Molly bumped into Collin, returning to the house.

"I've noticed Morgan's melancholy. It is to be expected, I'm sure. I would like to accompany you at least to Donegal to offer my assistance to her in her hour of need. Sometimes a woman needs another woman to share her problems. Would that be all right, Collin?"

Collin sized up Molly's countenance. Nothing he could detect. "That would be up to Morgan."

"All right. I will ask her."

"Did you find out what you needed with Mr. Fuller today, Morgan?" Martha asked as she was serving the turtle soup at supper.

"Yes, he helped us with the translation of a document in old English. We really appreciate your hospitality, but we need to go on to Donegal tomorrow, where we are expected."

"The weather should be favorable at sea," Maurice said, breaking off a piece of bread for his soup. "Can we help you with anything else?"

"Yes. Molly asked me if she could stay on with us until Donegal, but I decided she should go into Tralee tomorrow as she originally planned. Could you take her after we leave, please, Maurice?"

Molly scowled and said, "I wish you would reconsider, Morgan."

"We've taken you away from your duties longer than we should have. You'll be better off with the Cumann na mBan, and heaven knows their services are badly needed here in Tralee now, according to Aidan."

Maurice slurped his soup. "Certainly, lass. Consider it done."

They all turned in for the night earlier than usual. The tide would be favorable at eight in the morning. Collin could see the sadness settling in again now that the day's activities were completed. He suggested that he should sit up with Morgan overnight again. She was glad of the company and support.

After his sister had completed her ablutions and was tucked into bed, Collin settled on the corner chair with a woolen blanket around his legs. He could see faint wisps of his breath since the room had no fireplace. "A penny for your thoughts, Sis."

"I am trying to be positive, Collin. I am imagining you, Kathy, and your three children in happier days. They seem adorable from the picture you showed me."

Collin described his children in more detail, giving anecdotes about their charming behavior and leaving out the stresses that little ones impose on a family.

"You have a lovely family, don't you? You must miss them terribly."

"I do, but I know that Sam and Lil are taking good care of them."

"I liked Sam, Collin. That painting of his family was superb."

"He's a grand artist, Sis. They have four children now." Collin couldn't resist the opportunity. She had brought it up. "You'll meet them all when you come to Canada."

When this comment didn't cause a response, Collin asked, "You still awake?"

"Now's not the time, Brother."

With that said, their conversation ended. Morgan turned her face to the wall and appeared to drop off to sleep.

Collin couldn't sleep, worrying whether he could convince Morgan to come to Canada. He was anxious about the chest and the box containing Tadgh's documents she had saved before the fire. They were still in the boat cabin for the trip in the morning. Should he get them? Around midnight, the hair on the back of his neck stuck straight out. Collin pried himself out of the chair and went to the window overlooking the bay. He rubbed the nearly frozen condensation off a section of the pane to see. The moon was up, basking the front lawn and fountain in its glow, its light flowing out and over the glistening water of Barrow Bay beyond the moored hooker.

There, in the trees to the left, he saw a lone figure sneaking toward the shoreline.

Even with his cramped back, it took Collin under two minutes to put on his britches and shirt. He picked up the ancient cutlass from the top of the bureau. Another couple of minutes to exit the house. Where was he? That's when he saw the torchlight on the hooker, coming from inside the small cabin.

He crept to the edge of the trees, not fifty feet from the hooker, crouched down, listening. *Silence. Then a grunt of satisfaction.* Moments later, the slender man with a squirrel-hooked nose, the one introduced as Abbad by the historian, emerged from the cabin into the moonlight with the chest under one arm and a revolver in his other hand.

Collin was almost invisible. The rodent jumped over the gunnels and headed for the trees to Collin's right. His cocky movements led O'Donnell to believe that the thief thought he was getting away with the small chest.

Collin waited until the villain was passing him by, then he sprang up alongside and stripped the gun from his hand with one swish of the cutlass.

The robber looked down at the rusting cutlass, his knuckles bleeding. "What the—?" Abbad realized that his plan was foiled. Now he would have to kill O'Donnell and keep the chest.

"Give me the chest, and no one will be seriously hurt, lad."

"Not on your life." Still gripping the box, the rodent dove for his gun.

Collin stepped on his arm before he could reach it. "I would be worried about my life if I were you."

"This is the property of my ancestor Flooren, and you will not take it from me as long as I live."

The robber dropped the chest and whipped a knife from his boot. Collin sidestepped the slash at his calf muscle and lost his footing on the man's arm.

Abbad lunged and picked up his gun. He swung it up at Collin. *BLAM!* The first shot missed its mark as Collin jumped to his right. *BLAM!* The second bullet whizzed past him. Before his assailant could fire again, Collin threw the cutlass at him from a few feet away.

The blade pierced Abbad's shoulder. His face contorted in agony. The sword fell to the ground at his feet. His gun hand was useless. Abbad painfully tried to switch hands, but Collin's uppercut cracked his jaw. The revolver went flying. Abbad stumbled but remained standing.

In the moonlight, Collin could see the crazed look in Abbad's eyes as he debated what to do next.

"You will all pay for this infamy!" the robber yelled, just before he turned and ran into the woods.

Collin started to run after him when Morgan threw open the bedroom window and yelled out to him. "Collin! What's happening? Are you shot?"

He stopped. A sharp pain stung his cheek. He put a hand up to his face and pulled it away. He stared at his palm. *Blood.* That second shot must have grazed his face, yet he hadn't felt it. The fight, his fear, and a burst of adrenalin must have numbed the pain.

He yelled, "I'm all right, Morgan!"

"I need you, Collin."

Collin realized that his most urgent duty was to care for his sister's well-being. The robber wouldn't get far with that wound, and he'd be no further danger to them this night. Collin returned to collect the pirate chest, gun, and cutlass and headed to the house, kicking himself for his stupidity. He should never have let the relic out of his sight. Thank God the thief hadn't found the box with the McCarthy jewels, Tadgh's Bible, and other documents hidden in the cabin.

In the morning, at breakfast, Collin described the nocturnal altercation. "That man we saw at the cathedral yesterday tried to steal our belongings. He has a shoulder wound, and I hope to God I loosened a few of his teeth. At least the relics are safe." His cheek still stung where Morgan had cleaned and bandaged the wound.

Maurice snickered and chomped down on another rasher of bacon. "We always have excitement when you boys come to visit. I'll make some inquiries in the village. He would probably have sought medical assistance."

Collin considered staying another day to track the culprit down, but they were committed to leaving for Biddy's to organize the memorial service. Plus, now they had a location for their family's treasure. Beyond that, he still hadn't contacted Kathy, and he had an obligation to his newspaper to consider. "That would be much appreciated, Maurice. You can reach us through my auntie's tailor shop in Dungloe. I'll leave the telephone number."

Molly did her best to maintain an indifferent appearance during this alarming conversation, but her heart was pounding. Poor Abbad! How seriously was he wounded? Fortunately, now she was going to stay in the Tralee area. Hopefully, she could find and tend to the man she loved.

Noticing Molly's consternation by the pained expression on her face, Morgan asked her, "Are you feeling all right this morning?"

"I, ah, I'll be fine once I get on my way to Tralee after you leave."

"So shall we," Aidan said, getting up from the table and giving his second Mom a peck on the cheek. "Morgan and this woman saved my life, don't ye know."

"Go on with ya," Martha blushed, clearing the dishes.

"It's true, Molly, she did." Morgan kissed Aidan's forehead. At least the younger McCarthy was still alive. But not the one she loved as a soul mate.

They bid Maurice and Martha a fond farewell, thanking them profusely for their hospitality and support. The tide was in. They cast off for their voyage north at eight o'clock that Friday, April 22nd. In stark contrast to the storm a day before, the sun shone. Spring was in the air. They snaked through the narrow exit from Barrow's Bay past the Fitzmaurice castle ruins on their left, and the round tower ruins on the right, heading out into Tralee Bay. At least at sea, Aidan and Morgan felt alive again.

Map of Donegal Showing IRA Brigades, 1921

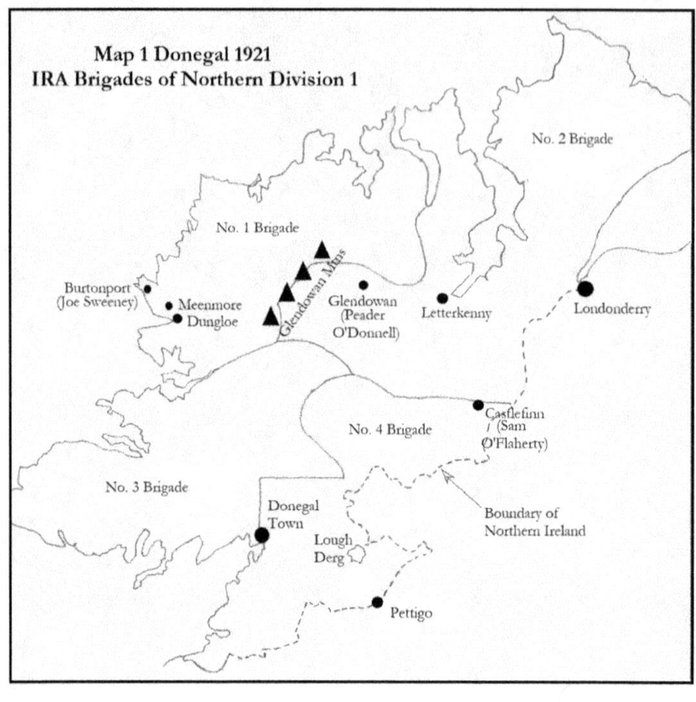

Chapter Ten
Ambush

Saturday, April 23, 1921
Dungloe, Donegal, Ireland

idan sailed the hooker toward Dungloe Harbour at sunset. They had come from the quaint seaside town of Westport after lunch, a place seemingly untouched by the war. The day had been sunny but cold, with a freshening breeze out of the southwest. Morgan remembered the trip five years ago, on this very boat, as if it were yesterday. Tadgh had pointed out the island of Arranmore where Peader was to teach school. Now Aidan manned that same tiller. She thought Aiden was almost the same age now as Tadgh had been when she was here last with him. Tadgh had always been Aidan's guardian, his rock. Morgan remembered the early days when he needed constant guidance when they had coaxed him out of his insecurities due to his parents' murders. He had matured. Surely now, with Tadgh gone, it was her role to care for Aidan, especially in this wretched war. Tadgh would have wanted her to look out for him and tend to any injuries that befell him.

While Morgan was watching Aidan work, expertly steering the boat, they sailed past the promontory fort on the south shore of the island. She recalled Tadgh explaining that this fortification went back to pre-Celtic times before St. Patrick, where they worshiped pagan deities. But that trip had been long ago, when Tadgh was alive and vibrant when they were in love. Now, darkness descended from the twilight sky and strangled her heart once more.

Aidan skippered the hooker into Dungloe Harbour and moored it against Quay Road. He cleared it with the harbormaster to berth his boat there. The Adventurers gathered their belongings and headed north through the town, about a mile and a half up Pole Road. Once they reached that charming white country home at Meenmore, Biddy welcomed them all as an integral part of her family. She had found friends and neighbors who might have known Morgan's parents and invited them to the memorial service planned for Sunday, the first of May.

Collin was happy to see that Morgan's demeanor improved with the bubbly personality of their aunt. The war had not dampened the woman's spirits. She offered to take care of her niece's needs at this critical time in her life. Her children had flown the nest with her second oldest fighting in the guerrilla war with Peader. Her husband had returned to Scotland to help with the planting, leaving her alone to run her tailor shop in Dungloe.

While they all ate a late supper of chicken pot pie and stout in the dining room, Biddy asked, "Tell me how you met this fine lad, Morgan. He seems a game boyo and mighty attentive."

Collin could see Jack was visibly taken aback by Biddy's forward demeanor, but his smile revealed he was inwardly reveling in her comments. He realized that Biddy was a challenge that he would have to neutralize. He wasn't sure how his sister would react to his Auntie's use of levity to deal with Tadgh's death.

Morgan scooped up a piece of flaky pie crust and savored it in her mouth. "Oh, Auntie. We're just friends. Jack saved me from drowning when the *Lusitania* sank. Got me to the last lifeboat."

"Did he, now? Jumped in that boat with you, then?"

Morgan flushed. "No. He stayed behind to help the others. I believe he jumped off the stern just as the liner was going under and broke his back."

The matron of the house raised her eyebrows, her eyes wide with the gravity of Jack's predicament. "I'd say you'd be a lucky man to be alive, lad."

"Yes, Ma'am, and happy to be here with you all."

"Any residual pain?"

"Nothing I can't handle compared to before."

"Welcome to the family, my boy. Any good friend of my niece is a part of our clan."

Collin didn't like how friendly Morgan and Biddy were getting with Jack. He likely wouldn't go to Canada, and the longer their familiarity kept up, the less likely Morgan would agree to go.

Collin handed his sister a glass of burgundy and commented, "Jack is the manager of a grocery in Dublin now, Auntie. He's good friends with the owner. You remember Deirdre, don't you? The surprise bridesmaid at Morgan's wedding."

"Oh, yes. The pink dress I made. Busty, I remember A looker. Wasn't she the pub owner, though?"

Morgan chimed in. "Long story, Auntie. She owns a grocery now."

Biddy looked at Jack. "You like it there, son?"

"Yes, it suits my business background."

Collin quipped, "It suits you more than that, eh, Jack."

Jack looked sheepish. "I like it here, too."

Aidan announced during supper that he would like to meet up with Peader and join his flying column.

Morgan frowned, stopped eating, and thought about admonishing her brother-in-law. She wanted to save Aidan but realized he needed to support the Cause. *What's the use?* It was all too much for her to bear.

Biddy had not talked about her son, but this forced her to speak. "Ever since Peader decided to take up arms, I've worried night after night, especially when we house the Volunteers. They almost caught him on his first raid of the RIC barracks at Falcarragh on March 21st. Since then, he's been on the run in the hills."

Aidan finished his stout and burped. "Excuse me. Near here?"

"No. He's responsible for the area around Derry fifty miles east, and I've heard that he stays up in Glendowan, about halfway to that city. It was after that raid by his flying column that the Limey bastards brought several thousand troops to our shores in early April. They set up between our town and Crolly and created detention centers in Dungloe and just north of us at Burtonport. They've been hounding us ever since. I can have one of the lads take you to Peader after the memorial service if you're hell-bent on getting yourself killed."

"I have to continue to fight to help free our country and to avenge my brother's death."

There it was. The subject they had been avoiding throughout the meal. The harsh truth of it.

Surprisingly, Morgan made the first comment. "Even though I disagree about the killing, Tadgh would have wanted Aidan to continue to fight for the Cause, Auntie. He's a fine lad, so he is."

Aidan blushed and put his arm around his sister-in-law. "She knows me better than I know myself, Ma'am."

"Yes, I can see that."

Biddy offered her guests an after-dinner drink, but they declined. She got up from the table to clear the dishes and said, "We'll talk more of this tomorrow. Now, you young fry need to get to bed. You must have had a tough few weeks."

As they stood there, she added, "Before you go up, be aware that you might have to head into the hills yourselves if the sweep is on."

Sleeping arrangements were cozy at the O'Donnell residence. Biddy had reared several children, but they had shared two bedrooms and the one bathroom in this modest three-bedroom home. Plenty of room now. Jack bunked in with Collin and Aidan while Morgan was given her own room.

From the village's tailor shop on Monday, Collin contacted the *Tely* and *Irish Times* publishers to update his family situation. Robertson understood, but Healy insisted Collin return to Dublin as soon as possible. Collin explained that he was pursuing the story of the flying column in Donegal. Luckily for him, Healy did not ask for details. He simply relented and allowed his reporter to stay in the area for a fortnight.

The telegraph communication with Kathy in Toronto posed even greater jeopardy for Collin. How could he explain he was seeking treasure and thereby breaking his promise to her? Instead, Collin focused on telling her the plans for Tadgh's memorial service. How could she take umbrage with his attendance at that important milestone, given the similar wake they held for Claire when they thought she had died. Almost five months had passed since he left Canada and bid his family farewell. It seemed like a lifetime with all that had happened. Someday he would share the memories with Kathy, but not now via telegraph.

Collin justified his familial avoidance with the belief that what Kathy didn't know wouldn't hurt her. In truth, he was only protecting himself from her and only temporarily. He'd be going home soon, hopefully with a few of the O'Donnell riches to show for his efforts.

On Tuesday, Aidan was introduced to Kyle, a village baker when the man was home in Dungloe. He was a member of Joe Sweeney's local No. 1 Donegal Brigade.

When asked about Peader's whereabouts, the local rebel said, "There's trouble between O'Donnell and the commanding officer of the 1st Northern Division, Frank Carney."

Aidan remembered Peader and thought that he hadn't seemed the kind to cause trouble in the ranks. Then again, he hadn't seemed the type who would take up arms and lead a flying column either. "Why?"

"Carney has been living the life in Derry, and Peader wants him to engage with our Brigades and lead from the field."

"That's essential, I can tell you from my time in West Cork. Tom Barry is an excellent leader."

"Carney's been making trouble for Peader with his superiors, all the way up to Collins. Until now. Joe Sweeney, our No. 1 Brigade C/O here in Donegal Town, has supported Peader, but they consider him a renegade, so they do."

Aidan was quick to respond. "The guerrilla fight is in the hills, and the local commanders need to be a bit renegade, now, don't they."

"You're preaching to the choir there, Aidan, but I'm not a muckety-muck."

Aidan couldn't wait to meet up with Peader again. "Can you take me to him, Kyle?"

"Aye, when you're ready."

On May 1st, the memorial service proceeded smoothly after Sunday church in the graveyard of the Catholic church in Dungloe. The attendees sat on three rows of folding chairs by the graveside in the sunlight after passing by the raised simple pine casket to pay their respects. Collin had produced a photograph that he had taken of Tadgh with the Finlays and the O'Donnells in Toronto, which was placed on the coffin for the mourners to see. Unfortunately, there weren't many snapshots of Tadgh and Morgan together since Tadgh favored anonymity, so only Morgan's wedding photo lay alongside.

The spring crocuses and daffodils were in bloom, and the majestic oak trees sported new shoots of light green. For a moment, at least, there was a respite from the ugly war, except for their reason to be there.

Several of the older citizens of Donegal Town attended. A couple was related to the McCarthys, but sadly they didn't know the deceased. Half a dozen, however, had been friends of the cobbler Finian, Morgan's father, and his wife, Shaina. One even remembered little Claire and Collin running around the boot shop on the Diamond in town.

After the priest gave the blessing, Aidan spoke on behalf of Tadgh while Collin held Morgan's hand in the front row.

"I envied Tadgh when we were young. After our parents were murdered, I couldn't match his strength and discipline. I fell apart, drinking too much, losing my job at B&C. He didn't give up on me. He and Morgan saved me from myself and taught me to be a man. I have loved him dearly."

Aidan choked back tears. "My brother fought valiantly for what he believed in, one free Ireland, whether it was in the hills of West Cork, the streets of Dublin, or the hunger-strike depths of the Joy. He never wavered, never succumbed to the evil British."

Morgan could hold back no longer and began to weep. She dug in her bag for a handkerchief. Collin wordlessly offered his.

"Tadgh loved one woman who stood beside him, one of the most caring people I know. Morgan was Tadgh's moral compass, and she is mine as well. I love her as deeply as a brother can. Thank you, Sis. Now, in Tadgh's name, I am dedicating myself to achieving one free Ireland. If necessary, I will gladly lay down my life to achieve that goal, just as my brother did."

Then Aidan read a short message from Michael Collins that Tom had given him before leaving Creagh.

> *My school chum Tadgh is the epitome of a free Irishman; patriotic, loyal, and self-sacrificing. Through his efforts and thousands like him, we will rid Ireland of the British menace. God rest you, Tadgh McCarthy.*

Morgan got up and hugged Aidan before he sat down. It was her time to speak, but the words wouldn't come, her eyes streaming, throat choking.

Collin stood up, put his arm around his sister, and addressed the mourners.

"I know Morgan loved Tadgh as much as God loves us all, enough to sacrifice his only Son for us. Yet He lets us take our own path, just as Morgan let Tadgh pursue his mission in life despite her Florence Nightingale nature. I came to appreciate and love this man for his battle skills and conviction to his passion for justice for the Irish people. May he rest in peace forever with our Lord. I have words of respect to read to you from my relatives in Canada who met Tadgh several years ago."

After reading the telegrams of remembrances, he turned to Morgan and whispered, "Your turn, Sis."

While Collin still held her hand, Morgan dried her eyes, swallowed, and spoke softly. "I loved you, Tadgh McCarthy, with all my heart and soul. You rescued me many times. My only regret—I could not save you when you needed me most."

Morgan sniffled a little and continued. "Tadgh, you are my everlasting love. I am extremely proud of you. Rest in peace, dearest." She glanced at the coffin, and her eyes lingered there.

Then Aunt Biddy stood up and handed her one early red rose which had just bloomed in her garden. Morgan kissed its flagrant petals and gently laid the flower on the coffin. Collin guided her back to her seat.

Just as the priest was signaling for the coffin to be lowered into the grave, Auxiliaries in a Crossley tender lorry drove out into the cemetery and disrupted the proceedings.

The officer in charge jumped down and walked over to the graveside. "Who are we burying here, O'Donnell?"

Biddy rose from her seat and stood up to the man. Her face was red as she crossed her arms to bar his way. She spat out the words, "Have you no decency, Tavis?"

"Not when your son and his traitors are raiding and killing my men." Her eyes narrowed.

Morgan stood to join her. Biddy pulled her close and snapped at the man, "We are burying a good friend, if you must know."

"His name, woman. Don't lie to me!"

"Tadgh McCarthy, not from around here."

The officer returned to his vehicle and scanned pages of names. He came back to Biddy, who was standing with her hands on her hips.

"The notorious playwright rebel from Cork, I see. Killed two RIC officers. What's he doing up here in Donegal?"

Morgan shook her fist and shouted, "Burial, after being executed without trial."

"Serves him right. Good riddance. And who are you, madam?"

When Morgan didn't answer immediately, Jack stood up. "She's my wife, sir. Agnes Jordan."

"And you are—?"

"Manager of the Cunard Shipping Line, in Queenstown, and friend of the O'Donnells." Jack produced an old business card from his wallet.

Removed from the details of the Cork penal system, Tavis handed the card back, turning to Biddy, "You give your son a message from me, madam. He won't live to see the new moon."

With that, he turned on his heel. In a cloud of exhaust, his vehicle trundled out of the cemetery leaving tire marks on the graves of the innocent dead.

The mourners stared, shocked.

Morgan stood there like a rock, her head held high. "Damn them all to hell. Aidan, you make sure you execute that devil for me."

Jack realized at that moment that he must be with Morgan for eternity. The way she stood up to that bully policeman under extreme duress, how she held her own. He would need to explain his feelings for Morgan to Deirdre.

Biddy brought Morgan to the coffin, and the rest of the family gathered around while the memory of Tadgh was lowered into the ground.

They dispersed after the interrupted service and went back for drinks and dinner at Meenmore. No one was in the mood for a wake. The war hung over them all.

The opportunity for Jack soon arose. Monday morning after breakfast, Biddy let him use the telephone in the tailor shop where she was offering him warmer clothes.

Deirdre would be busy in the grocery. He decided to wait until after the morning rush to call. *Come on,* he prodded himself. *Stop procrastinating.* He didn't know what he would say or how to say it.

Deirdre answered the telephone at the checkout on the first ring.

"Hello, Deirdre. It's Jack."

"Jack, I'm glad you called, darling. I've been worried sick. Are you all right?"

"Yes, yes, I'm fine. I'm sorry that I didn't call sooner, but we've been busy. How are you and Derek?"

"Eking out a living, Jack. If the war's not driving people away, the threat of the curfew is."

"Your health, I meant."

"We're fine. When are you coming home?"

Jack ignored the question. "I have bad news. It was Tadgh who was captured, and now he's been executed."

"Oh no! Morgan must be devastated."

He saw his opening. "That's why I'm calling."

"Was she hurt?"

Jack explained that she was physically fine but that he, Collin, and Aidan were providing her much-needed moral support.

"I miss you terribly, Jack. When can you come home?"

"I miss you too, Deirdre, but—"

"But nothing. I need you to come back to me, love. The grocery needs you."

Jack twirled the telephone cord in his fingers. He wracked his brain for the right words, but they wouldn't come. He loved Deirdre, too.

"Are you still there, Jack?"

He couldn't tell her that way, not over the telephone. "Yes, I'm here. I'm not sure when I can get away from here, lass."

"Where's *here,* and why not?"

"We're in Meenmore, Donegal, just north of Dungloe. It's a long story, Deirdre. We came to Morgan's Aunt Biddy's home to hold a memorial service for Tadgh, and now it looks like this will be Morgan's new home. The war has erupted here, and it is best that I stay out of harm's way."

There was silence on the other end of the line.

Now it was Jack's turn to wonder, "Are you still there, Deirdre?"

"Yes, I'm here for you, darling."

"The police raided Tadgh's home. They set it on fire. Destroyed it."

"You've had a time of it, then."

"I'll say."

Deirdre paused to think, then said, "Jack. It may not be the best time to bring it up, but since I have you on the telephone . . . ah . . . you *did* promise to inform me about the *Book of Ballymote* and William Temple's papers."

At his silence, she prompted, "Anything new?"

"Only that Collin found a pirate chest at Tadgh's house. It contained an old journal with Arabic writing in it. They think it was the same pirate that attacked the Temples."

"What? Such a coincidence. What does it reveal, Jack?"

"We're looking for an Arab to translate it. Collin thinks a researcher named Lawlor can do that for us in Dublin. He does research at the Royal Irish Academy and teaches divinity at Trinity. Do you know him?"

Deirdre knew that she and Morgan had spoken about the professor but without Jack present.

She took a chance. "Not the kind of man I usually see in my grocery, Jack, is it?"

"I suppose not. Collin should be coming back to Dublin for work tomorrow, I think. I'm sure he'll stop by. Oh, and they found another document with the journal, about an old Knight's visit to Patrick's Purgatory here in Donegal."

"Did they. How odd. When can I see you, Jack?"

"I'll have to let you know, Deirdre."

"Don't stay away too long. I love you."

"I know you do. We'll talk later, Deirdre."

"Be safe."

Jack was mad at himself for his weakness. Not telling her the truth about his feelings for Morgan. He vowed that he would confess them to her when he saw her next. He was so confused about that predicament that he didn't realize that he had betrayed the McCarthy's trust and spilled the beans.

Deirdre handed the checkout duties off to her new salesclerk, Yvonne. The young woman had answered an ad placed by Derek at his boss's behest. There was something about her that struck Derek's fancy as he interviewed candidates. She seemed to be a smart extrovert and would be a good saleswoman for the grocery. He couldn't get her stunning five-foot-five hourglass figure and captivating face out of his mind. He thought he had kept his interest in a woman twenty years his junior out of his decision and that it was her last name, Swift, that had finally made him recommend her to his boss. Deirdre agreed with his assessment, and she was hired. It had been a month now, and she had proved herself more than capable of handling the storefront.

Deirdre headed for the storage room, where Derek was instructing the stock boy on how to do inventory.

Taking her compatriot aside in private, she relayed what Jack had inadvertently divulged. "They've found a journal at Tadgh's house. Amazingly, it may have been written by the pirate who attacked the Temples back in 1627. They're up in Donegal and interested in Patrick's Purgatory."

"Didn't Temple write FP or PP in his book notes, Dee?"

"Yes. PP, Patrick's Purgatory. As a puzzle goes, this one's a lulu. I'm even starting to believe in Divine destiny."

"What do we do now?"

"The war has devastated our business, what with the curfew and random killings. It is hard to get fresh produce. Almost not worth staying open until the war ends. We could shut up shop and head to Donegal. I need to see Jack."

"Deirdre, we both knew there might come a time when our duty to find and protect would take precedence over your business. There is a lot at stake."

Deirdre remembered her father's instructions on his deathbed. "Just the future of the human race is in the balance." She looked at Derek full-faced. "Collin O'Donnell is coming back to Dublin tomorrow. He's bringing the journal to get it translated by, of all people, our fellow Templar, Hugh Lawlor. More Divine Providence. Let's wait and see what develops before deciding about the grocery."

"Whatever you say, boss."

The O'Donnells heard about the new onslaught. Kyle, the baker, brought the news from Sweeney at the Brigade level to Aidan on Monday evening. Thousands of British troops had just landed in Derry from England.

They were eating supper at the dining room table, a kind of delayed-wake special meal of roast beef, tatties, and neeps, a dish Biddy's husband brought back with him from Scotland one time. She invited the Volunteer to join them.

Morgan was in a better frame of mind than she had been during the service. "Isn't Peader responsible for Derry, Auntie?"

"He'll be for it now, that's certain. Aidan, can you go to him? Let him know what he's up against?"

Seated adjacent to Morgan, Aidan finished the last bite of his apple pie and got up from the table. "Kyle, you said you'd take me to Glendowan."

"We can leave this evening."

Morgan knew better than to protest his going. He was Tadgh's brother. But she hated the thought of losing both of them. "Aidan, I know better than to ask you to stay. I am very proud of the man you have become. But with Tadgh gone, I feel responsible to him to help keep you safe. Promise me that you won't take any unnecessary chances and that you will come back to me if you are hurt."

Aidan turned and looked down at Morgan. "Of course, Sis. Understood."

Morgan took his hand and pulled him back down next to her. "Tadgh and I didn't let you down. Now you must make sure that you don't let *us* down."

"It is because of Tadgh and the murder of our parents that I fight on."

Biddy chimed in. "You make sure that Peader is safe, Aidan. We're all counting on you."

Aidan caught the sharpness in their hosts' eyes and held her gaze. "Yes, Ma'am."

Collin observed the interchange and realized *Morgan's not coming to Canada anytime soon unless the war situation changes for the better.*

Collin, too, had his duties. He hoped Morgan could cope. "Now that Tadgh has been laid to rest, I need to go back to Dublin tomorrow by train, at least for the next week. I'll take the chest and try to get a translation of the journal from Professor Lawlor."

"Good idea, Brother," Morgan said, stirring sugar into her tea and spooning a sip to check its temperature. "Last time I saw him, he brought a bright graduate student to help decipher the *Book of Ballymote.*"

"But we need a translator of Arabic, lass."

"The professor told us his student is studying the Knights Hospitaller and their movements in the Mediterranean and Ireland. The Knights fought the Barbary Pirates, so maybe he has studied Arabic countries. He seemed like a responsible lad, Collin."

"To be trusted?"

"I suppose. I'll leave that to your judgment if you get to meet him."

"Will you be all right here, Sis?"

Jack came around behind Morgan, seated at the table, and placed his hands on the back of her chair. "I'll stay with her, Collin. We'll be fine until you return."

Morgan looked up over her shoulder into Jack's hazel eyes. "You're a good friend, Jack Jordan."

"It's sorted, then," Biddy declared as she put the cozy back on the teapot. "I have my new family with me at last."

Aidan reached Peader's No. 2 Brigade hideout in Glendowan on Tuesday, the 3rd. Peader already had the news about the troop concentration in Derry. Aidan filled him in about the family. He tried to be brave with this flying column leader when he came to the part about Tadgh's death, but his emotions got the better of him. "I should have been the one, not Tadgh. It was my fault."

Peader winced when he heard the details but said, "Nonsense, Aidan. You were taking Morgan to Dublin at Tadgh's request. I'm new at this guerrilla warfare, but I've learned that it is God's will who should live and who should die. The vindictive British must be stopped. We soldier on."

Peader clapped him around the shoulder. "Tadgh was a grand comrade. We should be that grand. I'm glad you're here with me. We must see this through."

Aidan locked eyes with the flying column commander. "Aye, that's why I'm here. Tadgh is my hero. I hope I can do him justice by supporting you in this fight."

"You're welcome here, lad. How's Morgan taking it?"

"It hit her hard, with Tadgh's death and the burning of our safe house in West Cork afterward by the infidels. But she's a game lass."

"That she is, Aidan. That she is. I'm truly relieved she is with my Ma at a time like this."

♣ ♣ ♣ ♣

Collin had arrived mid-afternoon on Tuesday at the Shelbourne Hotel in Dublin. His colleague at *The Irish Times*, Maureen O'Sullivan, was waiting for him in the lobby with a report on the skirmishes throughout Ireland. They sat for a drink in the Lord Mayor's Lounge.

"Churchill is angry with his troops. He's threatening all-out war, Collin. They are never going to give up Northern Ireland."

Collin nursed his Redbreast whiskey. "I can tell you that the retribution on both sides is killing any chance for a peaceful resolution. The age-old British tactic of ravaging the land and razing the homes only fuels the fight, not resolves it. All the Black and Tan soldiers tainted by the horrors of war in the trenches are now taking it out on the populace. They're stoking the hatred."

Maureen sipped her sherry. "Healy wants us to concentrate on any initiatives for bringing the parties to the negotiating table. This conflict now has international exposure and condemnation. Pope Benedict XV has just sent a letter to Buckingham Palace and Mansion House here in Dublin imploring, and I quote, 'the English as well as the Irish to calmly consider some means of agreement.' I have a contact at the Castle that we can call on to give us updates on their deliberations."

"That's fine, lass," Collin responded, staring absentmindedly into his whiskey.

Maureen changed her approach. "We've not really talked about our families since you came back to Ireland. How's my cousin Kathy doing now that you have found your sister?"

"Fine, as far as I know, but I've been gone for five months now."

She stared at him. "That's a long time, Collin. When do you expect to go home?"

"I don't know. Depends on this war. I'm hoping to take my sister Morgan back with me."

"Morgan? I thought her name was Claire."

"It is. Well, it *was*. Long story, Maureen, best saved for another time. Suffice it to say her husband was recently killed by the British. I will be encouraging Morgan to come to Canada when I return."

"Make sure you stay in close touch with your wife, Collin. Take it from me. Women need that."

"What happened to your beau, the one in the great war?"

"Jock? He survived, luckily. We're married with one little boy now."

"You won't be after my body this time, will you?"

"Of course not, silly, though it's a fine body, I must say."

"You're looking lovely as always. Motherhood must agree with you."

"Flattery will get you everywhere, lad. Let's meet at *The Irish Times* tomorrow at ten o'clock. Healy would like to coordinate our efforts and talk to you about Robertson."

That evening Collin walked to the Temple Bar pub for supper and stopped by the grocery.

Deirdre rushed out of the office and threw her arms around him. "Oh, Collin. You're finally here. I had been very worried before I received a call from Jack. Are the others with you?"

"Tadgh's dead, Deirdre. Captured and then murdered in Cork jail."

"Jack told me about Tadgh yesterday in his call from Dungloe."

"Did he, now? It happened two months back. The rest are all right, up in Donegal with my aunt and Peader. You remember Peader, don't you?"

"He's the one who came in with Tadgh during the Rising, the both of them dressed as women. The two dolls, I liked to call them." She caught herself. "But I shouldn't laugh about Tadgh and his antics, now, should I."

"I don't know. It might help."

"I miss Jack. How is he?"

Collin seized the opportunity. Jack was a fine fellow and a good match for Morgan, but he seemed motivated to stay in Ireland, maybe even get his old job back. If Collin could motivate Deirdre to win the man over again, Morgan might come with him to Canada. He decided to tell her that Jack was getting chummy with Morgan.

"He's fine, trying to help Morgan get through her ordeal."

Deirdre's pretty eyebrows went up.

"He has the best of intentions, I assure you, my dear."

"I'm sure he has. She's a looker, I'll say that much."

Collin wanted her to go after Jack. "Deirdre, you're the one who's a knockout, lass."

"You don't need to pay a lot of money to stay at the fancy Shelbourne, Collin. You could stay here with me. I've plenty of room, you know."

Collin realized his compliment had been taken the wrong way. "I'm married with three children, Deirdre."

Deirdre laughed, "I was joking, Collin. A girl can dream, can't she?'"

Collin looked around. "Where are your patrons?"

"The war in Dublin is killing my business, what with the daily firefights and all."

"People have to eat, don't they?"

"They don't come this close to the trouble, Collin. Did Morgan satisfy her curiosity about the possible secret in the *Book of Ballymote*?"

The last comment piqued Collin's concerns. The woman had slipped in that remark. "Not yet. Tadgh's death has sapped her interest. That reminds me, Deirdre. Do you still have the papers they found in Temple's chest?"

"Of course. Is there a reason you need to see them?"

"No, just checking. Could I take the documents with me when I return to Donegal?"

Deirdre answered curtly, "As I already agreed with Tadgh, rest his soul, I prefer to keep Temple documents here with me."

"Could I photograph the table of contents from the Swift manuscript?"

Deirdre's eyebrows went up, her eyes focusing on Collin's. "Why that one?"

"It is quite confusing, lass."

Deirdre seemed to like the sound of that. "Of course. I'll fetch it after you eat. Going across the way?"

"Yes, care to join me in your granny outfit?"

"I'd better not, Collin. Haven't been in there since—"

"I understand, lass. It must be awful."

She turned away and took her handkerchief out of her sleeve.

Deirdre had passed Collin's test. But he was still skeptical of her motives even though Morgan didn't share his concern.

Collin returned to the grocery through the back alleyway when he finished his supper. Deirdre fetched the Swift manuscript and asked him to sit in her kitchen. As he took out his No. 2 Autographic Brownie to snap the pictures, Deirdre asked, "Is there a specific part in this document that you need for your evaluation of the *Book of Ballymote*?"

"The documents are not related as far as I know, but I do need to consult an expert."

"Really. Who is that?"

"A scholar you likely don't know. Professor Lawlor at the RIA. Ever heard of him?"

Deirdre wondered if this was a test. "I heard his name from Tadgh and Morgan, Collin. Can I get you a whiskey?"

Collin frowned, then looked away, stowing his camera so he would not alert her. He had seen her eyebrows raise, and he wondered if there was more of a connection than met the eye. "No, I've had my fill of victuals and drink, m'lady. I'll take my leave since it's getting close to curfew." With that, he got up and headed for the stairs.

"Don't be a stranger, Collin."

He waved as he reached the bottom step and disappeared without looking back.

The Volunteers were still an annoyance in the Dungloe/Burtonport area despite large military and police sweeps. London was advised that West Donegal was effectively functioning as a small republic. By May 6, just six days after Tadgh's memorial, the British closed most routes west of the boundary road running from Mulroy Bay through Donegal Town, forcing all flying columns into hill country.

That morning, Tavis brought reinforcements and swooped down on the O'Donnells. Biddy, Morgan, and Jack met him at the door.

Tavis put his foot on the door threshold. "It's getting near a new moon, woman, and we are closing in on your son and his murderous outlaws."

Biddy tried to slam the door in his face, but he held fast. "Get off of my property, you lout."

Morgan tried to help her close the door, but the man used his foot to keep it ajar.

Jack sized up the situation. There were a dozen hoodlum soldiers on the front walk and situated around the side of the home that he could see. Some carried lit torches, and others held cans, presumably filled with petrol. He held up his hand and stopped Morgan from resisting. "What is it that you want from us, sergeant?"

"Remind me who you might be?"

Jack guessed the sergeant's experience. "As I told you, I am the manager of the Cunard line in Queenstown, responsible for bringing Americans and Canadians to fight alongside you all in the trenches of Belgium during the Great War, so I am."

This took Tavis aback, as he had survived the agony of trench warfare when many of his comrades had died a horrific death.

Jack saw he was having an effect. "I am not your enemy. What do you want here?"

"We're going to search this residence. If we find contraband weapons or any Auxiliaries, we will burn this home to the ground." Tavis raised his

Webley at Biddy's head. "Now, step aside."

Jack held the women back and let the sergeant and a few of his men into the home. They spent fifteen minutes ransacking the building, finding no weapons or rebels.

On the way out of the house, Tavis met with Jack, who was sheltering the women. The Britisher spat out his remarks at Biddy. "Your son will be dead in a few days, and I'll be back when his men return here. Then you will pay the price for treason."

Biddy and Morgan looked like they would like to claw Tavis's eyes out, but Jack held them fast. He stared at the sergeant and said, "You are a foul-mouthed bully, sir. Next time, you'd better come with a search warrant."

Tavis's eyes blazed with hatred. "You are an English traitor, supporting rebel dogs. I will ferret you all out and exterminate you." He raised his rifle as if to shoot but must have thought better of it. Instead, he struck Jack hard on his right side with the butt of the weapon.

Jack held his ground, ramrod straight. Through clenched teeth, he said, "Now that you have done your search, I will ask you to leave these premises, sir."

Tavis stared at the three for a minute and then waved his men off before turning on his heel. Once he was outside on the sidewalk, they saw him turn back and shoot the glass out of the front picture window, not fifteen feet from where the women were standing. Morgan pulled Biddy down with her as she dove for the floor, glass shards exploding above them.

"This is a warning!" Tavis yelled at them. "Next time will be the end of you and your home."

Biddy jumped up and waved her fist at him through the gaps in the broken window. "Get off my property."

Jack closed the door, then bent over and collapsed on the floor, holding his side in pain. Morgan knelt beside him, gently touching just above his hip. "Your back again, Jack?"

"Y . . . yes."

"Let me check." Morgan reached around and ran her fingers down Jack's spine. The muscles were in spasm, but there were no significant misalignments. When she reached the lower vertebrae, Jack flinched.

"Do you have any numbness in your legs, Jack?"

"No, Morgan, thank God. But it's hard to breathe."

"Can you move your toes?"

Jack tried to wiggle his toes and winced. "Yes, I can do that, but there's a shooting pain up my right leg."

"That's natural, under the circumstances. Biddy, are you cut by the glass?"

Biddy checked her face and arms. "No."

"Fine, then can you get me a cold compress, please?" Morgan put her arm under Jack's, asking, "Can you get up?"

"I don't think I can, Morgan."

"Can I help you get to the chesterfield in the living room?"

"I don't know."

"Let's try."

Together, they hobbled across the room to the chesterfield under the front window of the parlor. She struggled with his weight. The floor was littered with glass shards.

Morgan called out, "Biddy, I need you."

The matron of the house came running, compress in hand.

"Please clear the glass off the chesterfield but do be careful of the splinters."

Biddy swept the chesterfield clean with the compress, and Morgan laid Jack down softly on his stomach.

"I'll get another cloth." Biddy ran to the kitchen.

An hour later, Morgan confirmed that the problem was likely muscular and not skeletal. She wasn't sure about his right kidney. The cold compress had reduced Jack's pain level, but he could not sit up without assistance.

Morgan helped him to her bedroom on the main floor since he couldn't navigate the stairs. She would move into the boys' room. While propping him up in bed against pillows, it was then that she remembered what he looked like that night when he was stripped naked in the street. She chastised herself for having these inappropriate thoughts about him, especially when he was hurting terribly.

"What do you have for pain?" Morgan asked her aunt once they had him settled. Biddy took down a glass jar of coca leaves from the upper kitchen cupboard.

"I make a strong tea with this plant to help my sciatica."

Morgan had seen this used in the hospitals of Belgium in a more addictive form, cocaine. She knew that the raw leaves would not hurt Jack. Biddy brewed the herb, and Morgan filled him with fluids to see how his kidneys would react.

Half an hour later, Jack announced that his side and lower back pain was subsiding. Morgan checked, and the muscles were starting to relax.

"You were brave today, Jack." Morgan felt his brow for temperature.

Normal. "Especially with that lout, Tavis. He deserves to be dead and gone."

"This house would have been torched if we had reacted physically to that bastard," Jack winced as he shifted his body posture. "I was afraid that you or Aunt Biddy were going to strike him or worse. By the way, that's not Florence-like language, my dear."

"I must say, I don't feel like Florence Nightingale today."

Jack saw his opening. "You are very attentive to my dilemma, lass. Much appreciated." He reached out to hold her hand, and she did not pull away.

"I'm here to help, Jack. Me and Auntie."

Dinner time came at noon. Jack said he could not stomach any solid foods. Morgan and Biddy went to the backyard after Jack nodded off. The grass lawn near the back kitchen door was lush green, although a little unkempt. The plantings Biddy had made in April were just starting to shoot up in the vegetable garden. Beans, carrot tops, potatoes, and peppers. Morgan was heartened by the promise of spring—new beginnings. The air was fresh, the breezes light, and the sun warm. They had donned sweaters, but now they seemed unnecessary. Within the confines of Biddy's hedged property, there was a momentary peace.

A row of peony plants flanked biddy's vegetable garden near the cedar hedge with a border of lilies of the valley. The two fragrances were intoxicating. With the tree swing from the overhanging maple tree on the lawn, Morgan knew this would be her place of solitude.

Biddy knelt, and as she talked, she pulled up tubers from the plants that had survived the winter. "I was relieved to have a strong, articulate non-Volunteer man as our champion today, I can tell you. Jack exuded confidence and impartial respect for the rule of law. The nerve of those belligerent soldiers threatening to burn us out."

Morgan took the potatoes and put them in her wicker basket. "Yes, he was marvelous, Auntie. I would have struck Tavis dead if I could."

Biddy jammed her trowel into the soil. "I would too, Morgan, except that it would have ended with us being homeless or worse. Jack's a fine man. The strong, silent type, to be sure."

"He's been a good friend, Auntie. I don't know what I would have done without him these last few months."

Biddy picked some basil shoots and handed them to her helper, looking her square in the eye. "I know, dear. It's too soon. But he's a fine catch, he is. When the time's right, you know. You want to have children, don't you? They're the joy and agony of life, so they are."

Morgan thought of the pain of losing Tadgh's child, and a chill ran down her spine. She put the basil in the basket and decided not to speak of it. "Of course, Auntie. I want to have at least two."

"Then, that man there would make a sterling father, I'd wager."

"It's not the time or place, Biddy. But then you've always been one to get on with living, haven't you?"

Biddy stood up and wiped the dirt from her knees. "Life's precious and short, as we are all too aware of these days, darling."

Morgan took her auntie's hand in hers, "You're right. He is a courageous lad, and I think he would make a wonderful da, to be sure."

As they turned to go back into the house, Morgan looked beyond the hedge. The trees in the yard were blackened and dying. A neighbor's home lay deserted, burnt to the ground.

After supper, Biddy produced a bedpan since the only bathroom was on the second floor. Morgan offered to stay with Jack overnight to help with his ablutions. While he was sleeping, she had the opportunity to think. Now that she was in her family's home with her ever-positive Auntie, she was coming to grips with Tadgh's loss. The agony of his demise was still raw, but she accepted it. The human mind had to move on. It wasn't that she loved him less. Instead, she realized she had to love herself more. For years she had supported his aggressive behavior, for an albeit good cause, at the expense of her beliefs. She had to pick up the pieces. Now she was free to be her own woman, chart her course.

What about Jack? He was Deirdre's beau, wasn't he? Morgan looked at him, sleeping peacefully. She could see herself with this man. He would make a good father. But he'd want to stay in Ireland, and she was still a wanted woman who the police thought was his sister. It was way too soon to contemplate such things. *What a mess. But Biddy was right. Life was preciously short.*

Just after midnight, Jack awoke in a sweat but had no fever. Morgan assisted him to the washroom, and thankfully there was no blood in his urine.

♣　♣　♣　♣

A large contingent of military and police left Letterkenny east of Derry on Tuesday the 10th. They caught part of Peader's column unguarded at

John Mullen's home. Peader, Aidan, and Con Boyle escaped up Glendowan Mountain with six soldiers scrambling after them. Although majestic and windswept, the boulder-strewn heather foothills were mostly barren of trees affording little cover from the marauders. Peader was hit, once in the arm and again in the hand, but Aidan managed to fireman-carry him up the hill. Boyle was shot in the ankle and fell back down the mountain into captivity.

When Aidan and Peader reached the safety of the dense pine woodland near the top of the mountain, they managed to give their pursuers the slip by hiding in an overgrown cave. Aidan stopped to examine Peader's wounds. His arm was hanging by the flesh of his bicep since the bullet had smashed the humerus bone above the elbow. He was suffering badly from shock. Aidan tied a tourniquet above the wound with his belt and used his shirt, ripped in strips, to stop the blood flow and secure a sapling splint from the brush covering the cave entrance. Then he bound the hand tightly with the last strip of cloth. He had learned these triage skills by watching Morgan in action.

Aidan kept poking his head out to check the whereabouts of their pursuers. Once, he had to duck back in to avoid being spotted by an Auxie passing not fifty yards from their hiding place. They waited almost an hour for the Auxies to give up the search.

Although incoherent at times, Peader then managed to direct Aidan, who propped him up as they struggled, to fellow Volunteer John Bonner's home in Commeen, a mile away from the attack. John drove them back to Meenmore with no running lights. The evil Tavis had been partially correct. Peader was disabled by the time of the new moon but not killed.

Biddy slept with one eye open these nights and heard the engine coming off Pole Road. *Tavis again?* Peeking past her bedroom drapes, she saw two men carrying another man toward the front door. It wasn't unusual for Volunteers to show up unannounced in the dead of night, but this man looked in bad shape. She rushed downstairs and switched on the outside light before opening the door.

"Sweet Brigid, Aidan. It's Peader!" Turning back toward the house, she yelled, "Morgan! You're needed over here!"

Morgan slept in the chair beside Jack's bed, deep in a dream. She lived in the yellow cottage above Queenstown Harbor, where they stayed the night before her wedding to Tadgh. She had two lovely small children, and they all waited for Tadgh to come home from the day's catch. Someone yelled out that Tadgh had been lost at sea. Morgan awoke in a cold sweat. It took her a moment to gain her bearings.

She heard the yell for a second time. "Morgan, hurry! Peader's been shot!" Morgan needed no further urging. She jumped off the chair and hurried into the parlor.

Peader was lying semi-conscious on the chesterfield in the parlor, with Biddy hovering over him. Uncharacteristically, the matron of the house was wringing her hands, at a loss as to what to do. Morgan quickly assessed the damage as a bullet wound with a compound fractured arm. Peader had lost a lot of blood. He was in serious condition but nothing like the horror of the Belgian hospitals where she had worked.

"Aidan, did you do the triage?"

"Yes, Sis. Pretty sloppy."

"Not at all. You stopped the blood loss. Good job. You may have saved Peader's life!"

Biddy was crying but wiped her eyes with her nightdress and asked what she should do.

"Get me some clean cloths and disinfectant," Morgan ordered. "Then get boiling water and sterilize a sharp knife."

Her aunt raced to the kitchen.

Half an hour later, Morgan had removed the bullet still lodged in the arm, reset the humerus bone, cleaned the wound as best she could, then bandaged it and splinted the bone with wooden spoons. She knew that infection had already set in from the redness spreading in the flesh around the wound. Then she turned her attention to the hand where the bullet had passed through, puncturing the dorsal muscle between the thumb and the first finger. Fortunately, no significant tendons appeared damaged.

Chapter Eleven
The Journal

Wednesday, May 11, 1921
Dungloe, Donegal, Ireland

Biddy brought coffee and rolls to the parlor. "I don't know what I would have done without you, Morgan."

"I'm glad I was here to help, Auntie. I wish I had bacteriophages, the kind we used in the hospitals during the Great War. Peader has lost a lot of blood, and his arm wound is infected, but I think he'll live and be able to use his arm again when it heals. We'll need to ensure the infection recedes in the next few days by changing the dressing frequently." Morgan didn't want to tell her that a red line heading up his arm toward his heart, if it occurred from either wound, could prove deadly.

Biddy hugged her niece. "Thank you, dear. You were in the Great War?"

"Yes, Biddy. It's a long story I'll tell you about some time. Peader won't be able to use his arm for at least three weeks, I'm afraid, even if the infection doesn't take hold. Can you get a couple of blankets for him, please? I think it best not to move him for the time being. It might open the wounds again.

When Biddy returned with the blanket, Morgan asked, "Do you have a place to hide him if the British come again, Auntie?"

"I have a root cellar with an entrance I can board up."

"Hopefully, we won't have to use it."

Aidan overheard their last exchange. "What do you mean by 'come again,' Sis?"

"Tavis was here yesterday, looking for you Volunteers."

"That goon. Here?" Aidan interrupted. "In this house?"

"Yes, he hurt Jack. This house is still standing because he and his goons didn't find any of you here."

Morgan was conflicted, not about killing the British blaggard, but about the risk to Aidan in the attempt. Tadgh would never forgive her if they killed Aidan. How far she had come away from her lifesaver beliefs when her own family was mortally affected. Then she remembered the immoral incident at the graveside and the bastard's bullying at this home that injured her dear friend. "I need you to take care of him like you said you would, Brother."

Aidan was livid. "I will kill him. How badly is Jack hurt?"

"I don't know yet. He took a mighty blow to the kidney and lower back."

"That doesn't sound good, Morgan, with his history and all."

"We'll have to see, Aidan. I am hopeful."

"You always are, Sis."

Jack had heard these proceedings from his bedroom with the door open. He was in awe of Morgan's skill as a nurse, including how she comforted her aunt. It was amazing how she could spring into action, subduing or forgetting her woes when confronted with a medical problem. Deirdre had given him love when he needed it, but here before him shone the love of his life in all her glory.

Collin and Maureen made a good team. By Friday, May 13, they had infiltrated the Castle organization and were getting daily reports of the British war strategy and operations. As a result, Collin could keep abreast of happenings in Donegal. Their newspaper articles protected their source.

On Saturday, among other skirmishes in the city, the IRA commandeered an armored car killing two British soldiers. They drove it into Mountjoy prison to liberate Sean MacEoin. Their plot discovered, they had to shoot their way out of the Joy without Sean. It reminded Collin of the botched attempt to spring Tadgh out of the same punitive institution.

Collin's Castle source relayed the news that the IRA flying column leader at Glendowan had been ambushed and shot. Calling the tailor shop from his hotel, Collin was relieved to hear his cousin was safe for the moment in Meenmore and that Morgan had stabilized his condition.

Together at the Shelbourne bar on Sunday evening the 15th, Collin told Maureen, "I've got to get back to Donegal soon, lass. The situation there is deteriorating."

"That depends on which side of the fence you sit, doesn't it, my boy?"

"Like the situation in the rest of the country, I think both sides are struggling. This war may be coming to a head."

"What do you mean?"

"I don't know. Call it reporter intuition. I predict a major clash is imminent in response to the Pope's plea."

♣ ♣ ♣ ♣

On the 15th, with his mother's good food in him, and Morgan's care, Peader was starting to recover. The two invalids were sharing the same downstairs bedroom. Morgan checked under the bandages and saw that the infections had receded. "Your arm looks better this morning, cousin. I think you'll live to fight another day, as they say. Although I wish you wouldn't."

Peader pumped the fingers of his injured arm to get the circulation going. "I'm feeling human again, thanks to you and Ma. Where's Aidan? I've got to get back to Glendowan."

"You'll do nothing of the kind. You're not fit enough to travel yet."

"Nonsense, Morgan. I may not be fit to fight, but I can still lead my men. Besides, you all are not safe when I am around."

He was right. Morgan remembered all the Auxies with petrol cans the last time Tavis paid a visit. Even Peader, incapacitated as he was, would be better off at his hidden safe house with his men to look out for him. All right, I'll let you go if Aidan agrees to tend to your wounds and if you stay in hiding for the next two and a half weeks. If you reinjure your broken arm, you may never be able to use it with strength again. Do you promise?"

"If I don't get out of here before Tavis shows up again and torches our home, none of us will be needing arms or legs, for that matter, if we're dead."

"Do you promise?"

"I'll do my best."

Before they left later that afternoon, Morgan checked his bandages again and then made sure she strapped the arm sling firmly to his chest. She handed Aidan a bag with gauze, bandages, ointment, and a second homemade sling.

Biddy provided a bag of food for the men. John Bonner arrived to take them just before dusk. Biddy, Morgan, and Jack, standing up with the aid of a crutch, bid them Godspeed from the doorway as they drove off up into the darkening mists of the eastern hills.

♣ ♣ ♣ ♣

Peader was glad to be back. At least at his safe house, he could direct operations. His men had prepared a cot in the parlor for him. He was in no condition to accompany his men on missions. Aidan became his nurse for the time being.

That night, on his return Peader received informal word through a courier from Derry that Carney was suspending him as OC Brigade No. 2. He ignored the information.

Carney finally engaged with the Volunteers by coming to Joe Sweeney's home in Burtonport that night. At two the following day, the house was surrounded by the military. Carney and two other senior officers were arrested, but Sweeney hid and escaped capture. So much for Carney's active military leadership.

The following morning, the British landed the destroyer *Byfort* at Burtonport Harbour, five miles north of Meenmore, and Head Constable Duffy initiated an extensive sweep of the western Donegal area. It was a good thing that Peader and Aidan had left.

During the painful ten-day round-up, Peader, farther east toward Derry, ordered raids in Letterkenny to divert attention away from Sweeney's western Brigade No. 1 area. Though successful in redirecting the enemy's attention, the people of nearby Letterkenny paid the price with lootings, burnings, and murders.

On Friday, May 20, the British moved their round-up operations from the west of Donegal to the southwest. Most of Peader's flying column returned to Meenmore without their leader and Aidan, much to the consternation of Biddy. She fed them and sent them on their way just before Head Constable Duffy arrived with his Black and Tans. Tavis was not with them. By then, Jack was walking with a cane, but Morgan insisted he stay in his room during the raid. Once again, the house survived by luck and chance.

With the incarceration of Carney, Joe Sweeney was appointed General, OC of the 1st northern division of the IRA.

In May 1921, ten thousand British troops and sixteen hundred police, including four hundred men of the RIC Auxiliary Division, patrolled the streets of Dublin. Michael Collin's squad focused on assassinations of selected police, military, or administration figures. The four Active Service Units of the IRA's Dublin Brigade ambushed British forces with hit-and-run tactics using grenades and handguns. Altogether, the rebels numbered less than two hundred men. Collins gave strict orders to avoid prolonged engagements with the better-armed British forces.

Under the new, controversial British partition law, Southern and Northern Ireland had held parliamentary elections on May 15, called Black Whitsun. The President of the Republic and of the Sinn Féin political party, Éamon de Valera, was emboldened when his party won 124 of the 128 seats in the south.

On May 21, his clandestine government, the Dáil Éireann, met to discuss military operations in Dublin. De Valera wanted a powerful show of force by the Volunteers of the Dublin Brigade against the British to demonstrate that it was an army representing the Irish government. Two possible targets were debated; either the Custom House, headquarters of the Local Government Board for Ireland, an agency of the British administration in Ireland and custodian for many government records, or British Auxiliaries Beggars Bush Barracks. Remembering the disastrous military consequences of the pitched battles during the Easter Rising, Michael Collins strongly voiced his opposition to such an attack.

He was overruled.

In broad daylight, just before one o'clock on Wednesday, May 25, approximately one hundred and twenty plainclothes IRA Volunteers assembled in small groups around the Custom House on the north shore of the Liffey River. They were located less than half a mile along Custom House Quay east of Liberty Hall, where many of their rebel heroes had launched their Easter Rising five years earlier. Tom Ennis led the 2nd Battalion, Dublin Brigade, a group of guerrilla fighters short on experience, armament, and ammunition.

Collin, out for his constitutional walk along the south shore east of Butt Bridge between the two landmarks, stopped to examine the imposing domed architecture of the Custom House with its central Corinthian columned entrance. He wondered if the central repository of historical records in the library of this imposing edifice contained information on the British shutdown of the pit at Patrick's Purgatory in 1632. As he crossed the bridge, he wondered why so many men were loitering in front of the building, certainly in contravention of the martial law restrictions. He passed through their ranks, went inside through the main hall to the library, and asked to see their records.

Suddenly, shots rang out.

Collin heard the commotion and gunfire inside the main hall. He ran to the corridor, then saw the caretaker, lying in a pool of blood beside the front desk, the receiver of the telephone still clutched in his hand. He quickly snapped a picture with his No. 2 and retreated into the library. About sixty of the hundred bystanders on Custom House Quay had rushed into the building. The armed Volunteers brandished revolvers, shooting indiscriminately. They rounded up the staff and marched them to the main hall. One rebel burst into the library and ordered the two librarians out at gunpoint. He failed to notice the reporter peering out from behind the stacks.

Still hidden behind the books, Collin went to the window facing the Liffey. Two men emerged from a lorry carrying petrol cans. Out of the other side of the vehicle came two men with bales of what looked like cotton. *Jaysus! They're going to set this national treasure on fire!*

Another sixty men were taking up strategic positions outside the building with pistols drawn, having now shown their colors.

It took less than five minutes before squads of Auxiliaries drove up in three lorries and an armored car. They jumped out and took cover. A firefight started outside the building. With his camera clicking through the window, Collin watched the scene unfold. A few stray bullets pierced the library's windows as the police peppered the building with three Lewis machine guns, returning fire to the pistol shots coming from within.

Within minutes the Volunteers ran out of ammunition. Collin realized the situation was becoming dire for the rebels. He saw them spreading the petrol and cotton throughout the main hall. Collin thought about trying to lock the library doors to save the precious written history of southern Ireland but quickly realized that the wooden doors would burn and there would be no other way out of that section of the building. The windows had too much lattice iron to allow his escape. Collin stepped back into the stacks as three Volunteers rushed in and started pushing the stacks over, scattering the books and papers. Then they doused the piles with petrol and set them ablaze before running back into the main hall.

All the while, Collin took photographs from his hiding spot in the furthest recessed alcove.

The fire engulfed all the flammable materials in the library. It took scarcely a minute. The records of centuries, and potentially any information on the shutdown of Lough Derg by the British in 1632, were rapidly turning to ashes. Collin realized he was trapped, with a wall of flame between himself and the single burning exit door. He thought of Kathy and the children, safe at home, and her warning for him to steer clear of the fighting.

Panic set in, and he froze, his neck stiff, muscles atrophied. Returning images of the burning warehouse on the Toronto waterfront in his youth and Sam's face as he peered down at him. What did Sam do to save him then in the warehouse? He couldn't remember because he had been unconscious at the time. Then the other devastating fire, the attempted immolation of the Clans in the Cashel Cathedral ruins with gas-fueled flames—all the images returned to him in the searing heat.

There was no water source to wet himself down and nothing to douse the fire with. He coughed as the intense smoke and ash particles filled his lungs. Blood pounded in his temples as the heat rippled his face. He had only seconds left to act.

Collin did the only thing he could do to save himself. He located the door, pulled his coat up over his head with his hands in the sleeves, and darted through the flames. He could feel his garment on fire, and his feet burned as he pushed past the flaming door and out into the main hall.

One of the staff immediately pushed him down on the terrazzo floor and beat the flames out with his own coat. Collin's shoes were still smoldering; the staff member pried them off.

Collin had survived the ordeal with singed eyebrows and blistered feet. He thanked the man profusely and looked around the hall. Volunteers were fleeing through the fire. The staff rushed out, arms in the air. The gunfire seemed farther away now. Perhaps the British were chasing the escaping Volunteers? Both wings of the stately historic building were ablaze. Flames ravaged the main hall and were rapidly consuming the cupola roof high above. Embers and flaming debris rained down on the terrazzo floor all around them.

"C'mon. Let's get out of here," Collin's rescuer yelled, taking his hand and pulling him up. Collin needed no further encouragement. They rushed out among the crowd, their arms in the air.

Once outside, British military forces of the Wiltshire Regiment from the castle coerced the staff away from the building at gunpoint, moving them to the guardrail at the Liffey River. Collin lowered his arms long enough to take a photograph of the burning Custom House conflagration. A British soldier ordered him to get his hands back up. A couple of Volunteers in civilian dress had posed as members of the staff and tried to make a run for it. The police gunned one down as he tried to dive into the Liffey.

Tom Ennis was shot twice in the leg but managed to limp away.

The fire brigade had been busy with other IRA actions and arrived on Custom House Quay just in time to see the massive building being consumed by fire.

"Papers!" Collin ascertained that the burly policeman was talking to him. He decided to comply since there was a rifle pointed at his head.

Collin produced his Canadian *Tely* identification.

"What's this, a joke? You're coming with me, lad. Hands up."

Collin spent the better part of twenty-four hours in the lock-up. He was allowed a telephone call that he made to Maureen, who summoned Healy to convince them of her colleague's newspaper credentials. Even with that support, Collin was asked rather rudely to return home to Canada. He had no intention of doing so. Not now, certainly. His camera was confiscated for the battle pictures it contained, but he got it back without the film two days later.

He heard that over seventy IRA Volunteers had been arrested, one hundred and eleven people overall. Five IRA men were killed, along with three civilians. Only a few police had been wounded, but the Custom House had burned for five days and was completely gutted.

The *Irish Bulletin*, the official gazette of the government of the Irish Republic, published the following statement,

> *A detachment of the Dublin Brigade of the Irish Army was ordered to carry out the destruction of the Custom House in accordance with a decision arrived at after due deliberation of the ministry of Dáil Éireann. We, in common with the rest of the nation, regret the destruction of historical buildings. But the lives of four million people are a more cherished charge than any architectural masterpiece. The Custom House was the seat of an alien tyranny.*

Collin realized that de Valera had achieved his spectacular propaganda victory but at a terrible cost in human resources. As with the Easter Rising in which he participated, this had been a military debacle, one that the savvy Michael Collins had predicted. And the worst outcome for future generations was centuries of local government records were destroyed in the blaze.

As they exited the RIC barracks and jail on Thursday the 26th, Maureen commented to Collin, "You certainly have a nose for trouble, Collin. You could have fried in there."

Collin saw that she looked concerned.

"I've been in scrapes before, lass." He told her about Tadgh's silencing of the sniper hampering the fire brigade during the burning of Cork and how they were almost shot until his brother-in-law dispatched the police crazies. Collin hadn't included that spicy detail in his newspaper report. As Collin talked, he thought, *There was no point in worrying the family on the home front.*

Maureen squeezed his hand. "You need to be more careful."

"You're right, Maureen. These are dangerous times, to be sure."

When they arrived at the Shelbourne, Maureen said, "You've never shown me your fancy room. May I come up?"

"I don't think that's wise, lass. And I'm exhausted, that's certain."

"Another time, then?"

Collin changed the subject and pointed at the restaurant. "I've time for tea. Shall we?"

"Umm."

While they were sipping, Maureen said, "Maybe this Custom House burning is the big event that you predicted. Do you think it will make a difference?"

"It has depleted the IRA ranks of men here in Dublin at least. An unfortunate turn of events for Mr. de Valera, I should think."

"I hear the opposite, Collin. He's strutting around like a peacock."

"Such is the folly of non-military politicians. My money's on Michael Collins, and not just because his name's like mine. Mr. Healy has directed me to leave Dublin after this, Maureen, so I'll be going back to Dungloe on Saturday."

Maureen's eyes lowered, and Collin noticed. He gave her the telephone number at the tailor's shop. When they got up to leave, Collin held her chair and said, "Keep me informed of developments here in the city, please."

Maureen turned around, leaning in, and tried to kiss him. As he spun his head away, her lips grazed his cheek. "I think you're grand," she said.

Reeling from her fragrance and fighting to regain his balance, Collin stuttered, "And you're—beautiful." It was all he could say in the jumbled thoughts and confusion.

The women in his life made things complicated. Alone in his room at the Shelbourne, Collin reflected on his close scrape with death and with love. And then the vision of his wife's face rose up, her expression punitive, accusing. Another woman, his sister, came to mind. It was time to go to Morgan and take her back with him to Canada.

Collin had inquired at the Trinity College Provost's office about a translator of Arabic and had been directed to contact their affiliate Université Mohammed V in Rabat, Morocco. That was not feasible or advisable, so he took the only route available to him and arranged a meeting with Lawlor. Before leaving for Donegal, Collin met the professor at the RIA on Friday morning. This time he was bringing the journal in Arabic for translation. The bespectacled paleographer met him at the front door with one of his students.

"Collin O'Donnell, may I introduce you to Fazaar Gascony? He is pursuing his doctoral degree in the religious confrontation between the Muslim pirates of the Mediterranean and the Catholic doctrine of the Papal dynasty."

Collin noticed the lad's muscular features. Well-dressed in slacks and a blue blazer, he looked studious. "My sister mentioned meeting you. I understood you are studying the Knights Hospitaller."

"That too, sir. It all runs together now, doesn't it?"

"I presume that the professor brought you here because you are conversant with the Arabic language, am I right?"

Fazaar answered smartly and politely. "Yes, sir, I can translate that language, sir. Had to learn it for my studies, don't you see." He was happy that he had doctored his academic record to change his last name from al-Khattabi to Gascony, with no man the wiser.

Collin shook his hand, noticed a firm grip, and eyed the lad closely. He wished there was another way to get the journal translated since he had no idea what secrets it would hold, but he had no other choice. Morgan had told him that the professor and the student were trustworthy, and Lawlor had seemed knowledgeable and straightforward when Collin had met with him years ago.

Lawlor saw the interchange and said, "I can vouch for Fazaar, Mr. O'Donnell. He's been with us throughout his college studies. I trust him explicitly."

Collin still wondered about that. "Yes, I see." But there was something mysterious about him that he couldn't put a finger on. "How's your brother's shoulder, Fazaar?"

Collin eyed the student closely as he asked the question. No flicker of reaction. Nothing.

"I beg your pardon. I don't have a brother. I'm an only child," Fazaar lied.

The professor nodded. "That's what our records show, Mr. O'Donnell."

Collin wondered if there was any way to confirm what the student was telling him. Not likely, and he was running out of time. He needed to know what was written in the journal.

The professor led them to a ground-floor conference room. "Are you all right, lad?" he asked as Collin walked down the corridor.

"I had a bit of a run-in with a fire, sir," Collin replied, pointing to his feet.

"Here in Dublin?"

"Yes. You'd have cried had you been there to see the destruction, to be sure."

"I don't understand. Oh, no. Not the Custom House."

"Aye, I was in the library checking out some facts when it was torched."

"It's a travesty. Those rebel bastards have no idea about the loss to humanity."

"I agree with you, sir," Collin said as they entered the professor's office.

"Before we begin," Lawlor asked, "did you ever find what you needed in the *Book of Ballymote*, my son?"

"No, sir. We're still mystified about its significance, if any."

Collin had brought a contract for the professor and his translator to sign. "Whatever information we discover here is private to my sister and me. Is that understood? I need both of your signatures."

Lawlor looked at Fazaar before they responded in the affirmative. They both signed the document without reading it, and Collin folded and pocketed it, thanking them.

Fazaar said, "Professor Lawlor, there's no need for you to stay. I know you are busy. I'm sure this is a simple translation task."

Collin realized that was a good idea. *The fewer people who know about the contents of this journal, the better.* "I agree with Fazaar here. No need to bother you, Sir."

Lawlor laughed. "Are you kidding, boys? You told me over the telephone that you have an ancient manuscript in Arabic!" The professor reached for the envelope in Collin's hand, which contained the journal. "What do you have here?"

"Not so fast, sir. You had us don gloves to examine your document when we were here last." Collin explained that he thought the document needing translation was an old journal from the 1600s found there in Ireland.

"Then we'll go to the clean reading room," Lawlor said, leading them back to the room they had been in before. They donned gloves, and Collin carefully removed the journal from its envelope.

"Let me see it, please," Fazaar said, noticing the initials carved into the leather cover. He tried not to show his enthusiasm. *So, Abbad was right. He almost lost an arm trying to steal the very document that this imbecile brought right to me.*

Collin thought it odd that the professor did not ask where the journal was found.

Fazaar read to himself for a minute as he gently leafed through the first three pages.

Collin put his gloved hand on the page, interrupting him. "Read it aloud, please, Fazaar."

The lad stopped as if transfixed in thought.

Praise Allah. This is the diary of my ancestor, the one our father and we have been searching for these many years. What would my relative have me say?

Then he remembered Abbad's instructions.

Give any of them the truth as you know it. We will use them to find what we seek. But try to keep it from Lawlor. If not, we will take care of him and the grocery woman later.' Should he just snatch the family journal now and steal it? He would not be able to mine information from Templar Lawlor in the future. Abbad would be incensed. Better to share the contents and let the O'Donnells do the searching for the al-Khattabis.

Collin balled his fists. "Well, Fazaar? What does it say?"

Lawlor seemed to be all ears, too, as he leaned forward.

Fazaar decided. It couldn't be helped. They would also use Lawlor and the grocer woman when the time came.

Slowly he said, "Amazing."

Collin bent over him to see. "I couldn't understand any of the characters."

"Let me summarize the first three pages of this journal. The author Flooren Janszoon van Haarlem was the second brother of Jan Janszoon von Haarlem, the infamous Barbary Corsair, Murat Reis of the Salé Rovers."

Collin had done his research but didn't let on. "An important pirate, then?"

Fazaar answered, "This is my specialty. He founded Salé and became one of the most feared Barbary Pirate leaders in the 1600s. Flooren describes the attack and pirate settlement on the island of Lundy off the coast of England in 1626. It says he and his brother established a northern base of operations to search for a special treasure."

Collin noticed Lawlor cup his ear as he pored over the journal. "What special treasure?"

"I don't know. Flooren writes that this search was based on some handwritten note Jan acquired when he attacked and looted a galleon of the Knights Hospitaller out of Malta in 1624." He flipped over to the fourth page. "The courier was the Hospitaller commander's brother, Denis Polastron de la Hilliere, who was on his way to meet with the militant Pope Urban VIII."

"He wrote all that here?" Collin gestured at the page with a gloved finger.

"Yes, Mr. O'Donnell." Fazaar read on. "It says here that he was part of the boarding party who tortured the courier. Apparently, the Grand Master of the Knights Hospitaller, Antoine de Paule, was out of favor with the Pope, who considered him a man of loose life and conversation. He was purported to be guilty of simony, having bought his dignity with money."

Lawlor rubbed his chin. "I have read somewhere that de Paule was not liked by the ruthless Pope of the day."

Fazaar consulted the journal again. Pointing at the text, he quoted it verbatim, "The courier, a man of integrity, was sent to speak of The Grand Master's probity and virtue and to justify him in the most honorable manner."

Collin tried not to look amazed. "What was this all-important note?"

The Arab translator consulted the journal again. "Flooren writes that the courier tried to throw it overboard when the pirates started searching him, but Jan plucked it out of his hand before he could get to the rail. Under torture, he finally divulged what he knew of the document to have his life spared."

"And?"

Lawlor seemed to be straining forward to hear.

"The courier finally said this note had come into the possession of the Grand Master Adolf de Wignacourt in Malta at the end of 1601. It says here that a fisherman delivered it from Ireland's west coast who stowed away on three ships to get it to him."

Fazaar pointed at the page and locked eyes with Collin, paused, then turned back to the text, continuing. "According to Flooren, the writer of the note pleaded with the Grand Master to seek an epistle in Ireland to protect the faith."

Now Collin knew that the yellowed handwritten note they had found in the journal pocket was what Fazaar was reading about. *Should I stop the translation now? If I do, I won't find out anything more.*

While Collin was deliberating, Fazaar continued to read and talk. "The Grand Master was heavily involved with battles with the pirates, Flooren brags, and nothing was done to respond to the note during his reign. De Paule came to power in 1623. He had no idea how to deal with this note either until he tried to use it as a peace offering to the Pope as part of his penance."

Collin was mesmerized. He had to find out if Fazaar was truthfully relaying the journal's contents. "What did the note say, exactly?"

Fazaar read on and hurriedly opened the back cover to view the pouch. He raised his arms and shrugged. "Flooren writes that the note is tucked in the back of the journal, but this pouch is empty."

From Fazaar's lack of facial response, Collin believed him.

Lawlor engaged in the conversation. "There must have been more to the note that was damned important enough for the Janszoons to capture an island in the English Channel four years later in order to seek whatever was written on it."

Fazaar read on, silently turning through more yellowed pages. "There are many entries about raids in that period, 1627 to 1631, none of them around the British Isles. But these two curious entries shed some light." He read aloud one entry—

> *November 12, 1626. Jan sent me to Ireland to interrogate the Irish Knight Hospitaller, Thomas Fitzmaurice in Kerry. He professed to know nothing of the all-important epistle of the Christian faith and drove me off his land.*

He flipped forward in the journal. "The second entry was on January 27, 1627." I will read it for you.

Jan sent me to Dublin to meet with Trinity Provost William Temple. He was cited by De Paule in his letter to the Pope, which was attached to the note. Temple claimed to be a Knights Templar. Under duress, he provided a letter from Niall O'Donnell to the British commander in the north in late 1601 that talked about an epistle and an all-important gospel given to St. Patrick by God when he showed him purgatory.

"It all sounds like a fanciful, imaginary tale to me," Collin said. "Kind of like the strange tale about Knight Owain you shared with my sister, professor."

"Nothing fanciful about it, Lawlor retorted. It truly happened."

As he continued to read forward, Fazaar wondered, *Could this be what we have been fighting to find in our crusades? From Jerusalem?*

"Wait, here's another interesting statement," Fazaar commented. "Flooren wrote *Niall O'Donnell's letter says that this epistle is buried somewhere with the O'Donnell treasure.* I wonder if he meant that the epistle was the O'Donnell treasure? It is not clear."

"This is a more important find than any of the books we've been talking about. Imagine it. An O'Donnell treasure," Lawlor said, beaming.

"I think that Fazaar is right, that the epistle is the treasure," Collin interjected, carefully turning the pages ahead in the notebook and having no idea what was written. "Scribblings of a lunatic."

Fazaar asked, "Should I continue?"

Lawlor immediately responded. "Yes."

"Flooren writes he was slashed by his own cutlass, which he left at the scene when driven out by the burly son of the provost."

Collin noted he hadn't mentioned that the wife had stabbed him. "Wasn't there an attack on Baltimore by the pirates?"

"Oh, you know of that." Fazaar turned pages until he found what he was looking for. "Here is an entry dated June 20, 1631. Along with his brother, Flooren captained one of the ships attacking Ireland and took away slaves. This is famous in Moroccan history."

Collin clenched a fist at his side. "Do you mean the rape of Baltimore in 1631?"

"Yes, sir, that's right, if you want to put it that way."

"What other way could you put it?"

Fazaar ignored the question. He was busy remembering what his father had taught him. "The history books say that Flooren never returned to

Morocco from that raid. It was always assumed that he had died during the attack. But now we know differently. This is exciting. It changes history. Where did you find this book?"

Collin could see the young man squirming in his seat and wondered if the student was just excited at this information or whether there was something else, something more personal. He answered. "It fell out of the sky, so it did. The light of God shone down from heaven and illuminated it for the first time in centuries." Then he waited for a reaction.

The other two men waited for Collin to explain, but he didn't.

Lawlor spoke up. "You can't leave it at that, son."

Collin shrugged his shoulders. "That's all I can say about it. But I have spoken the truth."

Fazaar frowned but continued reading, where he found another interesting entry. "Flooren writes he was ordered to stay in Ireland to find the grand prize that would make the Barbary Corsairs omnipotent."

Collin could see that Lawlor could hardly contain himself.

Fazaar's eyes were dancing across the vellum. "Murat Reis had instructed him not to come home without it for fear of death. See here. That statement is written in all capitals." He jabbed a gloved finger at one point in the journal. Collin couldn't tell all capitals among the squirrely markings.

Collin nodded as if he understood. "Was that normal for pirate brothers to threaten each other?"

Fazaar spoke the obvious. "Power begat power and outranked family blood in those days. You didn't get to be Murat Reis of Salé without stepping on many toes. Jan was ruthless. He had to be."

Collin looked up at the student from the journal and commented, "I see no difference in today's world, lad."

Lawlor got up from the table and stared out the window momentarily. Then he turned to his student. "How did they get from a note about an epistle in Ireland to a grand prize that would make the Barbary Corsairs omnipotent?"

Fazaar skimmed the pages and said, "I have no idea, sir."

Collin was getting concerned that these men had already gleaned information that materially affected his private search. But what could he do? He needed the translation, and the subject of the information didn't seem to be pointing toward the O'Donnell treasure. Yet it fascinated him.

"Does he write about what happened after Baltimore?"

Fazaar scanned ahead again. "Yes. The people moved inland away from the sea. Flooren changed his habit and blended in with the natives. Having been educated in Europe along with his brother, he looked more European and knew the English language. He brought gold given to him by Jan in a pouch, sufficient to build a house on the Ilen River. That's as far as I got at this point."

Collin was suspicious. Although he could look it up, he decided to test Fazaar. "What part of Europe, do you know?"

"Not exactly sure, sir, but I think maybe the Netherlands."

Collin was watching the lad's gestures and facial features when he asked. "That's where you're from, isn't it, Fazaar."

The student was non-plussed as he answered, "That's right. That is why I take such a keen interest in the history of Janszoon's Salé Rovers." He hoped the other men couldn't see through this lie.

"What are you getting at, Mr. O'Donnell?" the professor asked, adjusting the pince-nez on the bridge of his nose. "I can vouch for this lad. He is above reproach."

"I'm sure he is," Collin said, smiling but carefully watching Fazaar. "As a good newspaperman, I was just drawing a conclusion as to why you would know such a lot about this pirate. Thank you for clearing that up, lad." In truth, Collin had mixed feelings. Maybe he was just remembering the evil Boyle and thinking the worst. He pointed at the next page. "Read on, please, aloud."

Fazaar voice had an edge to it as she read—

July 18, 1632. I have researched the location where St. Patrick was shown purgatory. Niall O'Donnell's note said that is where God gave the saint a gospel. The story of Sir Owain in that same box as Niall's note must be significant. This must be the location of the epistle and possibly the gospel. Back to where it came from in the first place. I am leaving on a pilgrimage to Lough Derg, which I learned about from the local parish priest. I will gain access to the pit and dig to find what we seek.

Collin realized the pirate had been getting close to the possible location of the O'Donnell treasure. Should he let Fazaar continue to read? He decided he could handle the situation and needed to know what the journal said. "Go on."

Collin tried to remain calm as Fazaar scanned again for a minute before speaking. He concluded *this student would have lied if he were thinking of going after the treasure himself.*

"There are several entries about his travel to Donegal, his acceptance by the friars, his fifteen-day preparations, and his plan to spend a night in the pit. My, my. Look at this. He says he overheard British mercenaries on Saints Island discussing a dispute between these friars and those at Donegal Abbey. On October 24, the friars rowed him from Saints to Station Island just before sundown and left him alone to enter the pit overnight. Fortunately, Flooren was the only pilgrim on that island that evening. He dug into the backside of the pit all night."

"What did he find?" the professor wanted to know. Collin saw the fire in Lawlor's eyes.

"He writes here that he didn't find any box with an epistle or gospel; nor was he hounded by hellish ghouls."

Fazaar read on and then described his ancestor's words. "In the morning before dawn, he came out of the pit expecting to still be alone. The friars landed and caught him desecrating the area. Then the hounds of hell broke loose. Not from within the pit, but without. He described the violence of those men of the cloth after their sacred site was violated. While he was being beaten by staves, Flooren saw a landing party approach the pit, led by a religious leader dressed in flowing white robes. One of the friars shouted out, "What's Bishop Spottiswoode doing here?" The bishop yelled out for Flooren to be held and announced that all the buildings on the island were to be leveled and the pit filled in. The normally sedate and spiritual friars stood their ground. In their frenzied state over Flooren's actions, some started to attack the bishop's men as they took shovels to the pit."

Collin was startled at this revelation and confused. "The pirate made his escape, or the journal would not have been recovered, right?"

"Flooren writes that he was badly beaten with staves but managed to slip away in the confusion by stealing the bishop's boat. From there, he walked to Pettigo, where he stole a sheepherder's horse and managed to limp home."

The student flipped through the last three pages of scribblings. "Flooren's handwriting gets pretty sloppy from here on. Back at home on the Ilen River, his health deteriorated. He says the beating he suffered had damaged his internal organs. He thought of trying to contact his brother on Lundy to come and get him, but it appears that his pride stopped him. It all seemed like a dead end. He says here that Patrick's Purgatory was obviously not the hiding place. The Temples must have been wrong. In a very shaky hand, his last entry is on November 1, 1632."

The professor interrupted reverently. "All Hallows. The beginning of the Druid new year. Feast of Samhain, lord of the dead. How appropriate. What did he write?"

The student read aloud.

> *Wiliwiliwiliwiliwili. British forces have arrived at my door. They must have followed me from Lough Derg. They don't know I'm in here yet. I think they are looking for the epistle. Getting weaker. I have retreated to my hideout to secure this journal in a safe place before my strength gives out. I will protect it at all costs. Have sent a message to Jan to get it. Sorry, Brother, that I failed my mission. I trust they won't burn me out.*

All three men just stared at the relic, speechless.

Finally, Collin spoke. "What does *wiliwiliwiliwiliwili* mean?

Fazaar spoke. "It means, 'Oh, my God!' I learned in school that the great Jan Janszoon was captured in a raid by the Knights Hospitaller of Malta in 1635, near the Tunisian coast. He was imprisoned and tortured in the island's notorious dark dungeons of Fort St. Angelo until 1640, when a Corsair attack freed him. By then, he was an old and broken man and died a year later."

"He likely never got his brother's dying request," Collin said.

Lawlor added, "Or since you have it, he never found his journal if he made an attempt."

Fazaar scratched his beard. "That's right. What an exciting tale, but with a profoundly sad ending."

That's not the half of it, Collin thought. *If you'd seen Flooren's pitiful decapitated skeleton, you'd know.*

Fazaar closed the diary and handed it back to Collin, saying, "Professor, this would make an excellent thesis."

Collin thought for several moments. Now we have confirmed the history of Tadgh's home, the connection to St. Patrick's Purgatory, and how the pirates got MacSweeney's note. This also confirms that the notes from Niall O'Donnell and the scrap of paper from Brian MacSweeney, both from 1601, are likely authentic, and Flooren did not find the treasure. It also explains why Flooren died hiding in that attic, protecting his notes and documents, presumably from wounds he received from the friars on Lough Derg. He must have been deathly afraid of trying to go home empty-handed.

"I want to thank both of you for helping me understand what was written in this journal," he said as he leaned over the table and shook their hands. "It certainly is a bizarre story, I must say. What we've learned from this pirate Flooren is that the epistle he was seeking was not at the place he called Patrick's Purgatory. He dug up the pit and died for his efforts, at the hands of the meek friars no less."

"If indeed it is a true story at all," Fazaar offered. "It sounds like a weird fiction writer's nightmare."

Collin agreed with the lad as he packaged the journal safely into its envelope. The professor was lost in thought, fiddling absently with his pince-nez.

"I'll remind you that what you learned today is private O'Donnell information. I believe that this story is too unbelievable to be true. As a reputable newspaper reporter, I don't want to bear the brunt of jokes among my peers for promoting false fiction."

Both men answered. "Understood." Then as Lawlor showed Collin the door, the professor said, "I hope you find what you're seeking, my son."

"I think we can put this down as a made-up tale of a madman," Collin said over his shoulder as he walked out into the rain.

Collin knew he had taken a significant risk to involve the professor and his student in the translation of the journal. But he had no other place to turn, and Lawlor had been very helpful in the past. And now, with these revelations, he had to assume this historian might act on the information he heard. That man loved a religious mystery, yet he had acted too nervously, as if he was trying to be deceptively disinterested. Even if he didn't turn out to be a risk, the little squirrel, Abbad, would certainly still be lurking out there with his injured arm. Morgan would never agree to move to Canada unless they would find the O'Donnell treasure or exhaust the clues. Then there was the commitment he made to Kathy to avoid searching for treasure. Collin knew he couldn't stay in Ireland much longer.

Although he hoped Flooren's failure at the pit would throw them off the scent, he concluded the Adventurers had better move fast if they were going to be first to the treasure.

After O'Donnell left, Professor Lawlor picked up the telephone and called Gilroy's Grocery. Deirdre decided that the time had come to act.

Fazaar al-Khattabi ducked out and telegraphed his brother Abbad in Donegal Town.

Chapter Twelve
Lough Derg

Friday, May 27, 1921
Donegal Town, Ireland

*T*he wound in Abbad's shoulder healed nicely with Molly's expert care. She loved him despite his authoritarian ways. It made her weak in the knees to think of their lovemaking.

In their hotel room at the Abbey Hotel on the Triangle, Abbad discussed their course of action with his concubine. "That bastard Collin should be coming to the train station tomorrow, Molly. Fazaar has been following him in Dublin."

"What does that mean?"

"He went to see the professor at the RIA about Flooren's journal. He gave him the true contents, as we agreed, to help them in their search. I told the head of the Association that we were stalled in our search. After O'Donnell leads us to the location, we'll dispose of him and his whole team for slashing me."

"What about the grocery owner?"

"Since Fazaar had to translate my ancestor's diary in front of Lawlor, then he'll have told the grocer. She'll be nosing around. You can count on it. We'll have to take care of her and the professor once the prize is ours."

Molly had no idea how they could do all that, or what the prize was, but she had the utmost confidence in her man.

Michael Collins had gotten Peader's message to GHQ that Carney was not leading in the field. He finally sent Liam Archer, OC 5 Battalion, Dublin Brigade, to Glendowan to investigate this problem flying column leader. By the beginning of June, Sweeney and GHQ decided that the rift between O'Donnell and the Derry commander who had supported Carney was too great. Headquarters established a new Derry command but left Peader as OC No. 2 Brigade east of Glendowan.

On June 5, Peader was well enough to lead his missions. He and Aidan convened a meeting of his column in Letterkenny in preparation for renewed action to disrupt the British infrastructure in the No. 2 Brigade area.

Meanwhile the British moved eight hundred men farther south into No. 4 Brigade's area, which included Lough Derg.

Collin returned from Dublin to report on the progress of the expanding war in Donegal. At Meenmore, he immediately briefed the others about the journal's contents to devise a plan to find the treasure.

Morgan looked at the closed leather-bound journal before her on the glass-topped table as they sat together in the garden. June was a glorious time for the flowers, and she could smell the honeysuckle in the hedge bordering the property. At least here, when the British didn't threaten them, they could still find solace in the sunshine.

When Collin finished, Morgan said, "Clearly, the pirate Flooren made a penitent journey to Lough Derg in 1632 and tried to find the epistle in the pit, or whatever remained of that entrance to purgatory in those days. It appears he created a conflict causing the British to shut down the facility temporarily that year, and he escaped empty-handed."

"I guess he wasn't very penitent then, was he?" Jack chuckled, sitting on the garden bench beside Morgan, cane in hand.

Morgan laughed and turned to his sparkling eyes, realizing once again how important he was becoming in her new life. She reached over and took his hand, noticing the strength and warmth in his returned grip.

Collin saw the interchange and frowned but answered, "As a Muslim warrior, I don't think so."

Morgan turned back to her brother. "He made no mention of the O'Donnell treasure in his journal, did he, Collin?"

"Yes, he did, based on what he read in Niall's letter to Docwra."

"Do you think—?" Morgan's eyes darkened.

"I don't know, Sis. I suggested that the epistle was the O'Donnell treasure. Then I tried to deflect all this and attribute it to a madman's scribblings."

"Just the same, Brother, we'd better hurry if we want to find our birthright."

"I'm sure that Flooren was searching for the Epistle of St. Columba created more than a thousand years before Red Hugh buried it with his treasure."

Jack interjected. "What about the note sent to the Grand Master?

Because it caused Janszoon to start his mission in Ireland, it must be important."

Collin worked his fists. "That's an area to pursue for another time, Jack, surely. Right now, it is urgent that we find the O'Donnell treasure at Patrick's Purgatory, if indeed, it is buried there. Poor Flooren was convinced the epistle wasn't there after his digging failure."

Jack wasn't giving up. "But what if that clue is crucial for the location at Lough Derg?"

"I don't think it is. The inscriptions in the lockets are maps that pinpoint the treasure, and we're the only ones who have them. The rest is for the epistle and gospel, whatever they are. It would seem Red Hugh had two entirely different motives for the Clans Pact. I doubt he shared his religious objective with the McCarthy Clan Chieftain."

"Hopefully, it doesn't pertain to our search for the treasure, then. But I'm still confused."

"About what, Sis?"

"The inscription in Tadgh's locket. It said something about *an Cathach*, didn't it?"

"But his locket was presumably lost when he was arrested," Jack said.

"I've got it written down," Collin said, taking out his reporter's notebook. He scanned back to the information regarding the curious notations behind the mothers' pictures. "Tadgh's inscription is *PPPCCathaoir, BSt, L2284-5, H20, WN99D.*"

Morgan peered over Collin's page. 'That's it. There should be a clue in *an Cathach*, surely to confirm the location on Lough Derg if that's the correct location. Otherwise, it could just be a coincidence that Niall's note talked about an epistle and gospel associated with where God showed St. Patrick Purgatory. We're jumping to conclusions just like Flooren did. The letters PP could mean anything. Peter Piper picked a peck of pickled peppers, for example. The pirate could have been misled. He didn't find anything."

Collin paced the garden perimeter for a minute, lost in thought, before returning to the table. The only sounds in the area were the goldfinches singing in the willow tree. Finally, Collin asked Morgan, "You told me that the small chest Flooren got from the Temples contained their copy of the tale of Sir Owain. We now have it, but why did Temple have it?"

Morgan answered, "Maybe it was Temple who came to the wrong conclusion in his failed search, and Flooren followed him down the same false path."

Jack loved how her mind worked. So perceptive yet logical. He squeezed Morgan's hand and tried to make eye contact. "Aren't you the one who is always going on about Divine intervention? What is Sir Owain telling you this evening?"

Morgan withdrew her hand, laid it on the Tractatus de Purgatorio Sancti Patricii document on the table, and cupped her ear with her other hand. "He's whispering, '*Go to an Cathach.*' We never understood whether there was a clue in the first verse of that relic as there was in the last verse for the McCarthy treasure." She looked over at her brother. "Remind me."

He found the reference in his notes. "Professor Lawlor told you the first undamaged folio had Psalm thirty, verse ten on it, which reads, *Hear, O Lord, and have mercy on me; Lord, be my helper!*"

Morgan tucked her hair behind her ear. "Clear as mud, but what if there is another verse on the same folio, Brother? I wonder what verses nine and eleven say?"

Collin jumped up. "That's easy." He disappeared into the house and returned a few minutes later. "Found it in Biddy's Bible, the one she keeps on her nightstand. You're smart, Sis."

"What does it say?"

Collin opened his notebook to where he had copied the verse down word for word. Verse nine said this—

> *What profit is there in my blood,*
> *When I go down to the pit?*
> *Will the dust praise You?*
> *Will it declare Your truth?*

Jack leaped up. "That's it, then. We'll find the treasure in the pit on Station Island."

Morgan's arm shot out to lend support. "Are you all right, Jack?"

"I guess I got a bit too excited by the news."

Morgan touched his right kidney area. "Does this hurt?"

Jack loved her hand there and would have loved it on other parts of his body. It hurt where she touched, but he answered, "Not at all."

"Even though the pirate didn't find it there?" Morgan massaged his side for a short time, then stopped.

"Maybe he couldn't search thoroughly at night?"

Collin shook his head. "I don't think it's there, Jack. It would be too difficult for Red Hugh and Rory to hide their treasure around that pit back in 1601. At Ardfert, Fuller spoke of the pilgrimage being quite popular in the early seventeenth century. The pit was expanded with a long structure over it to allow three or four pilgrims to occupy it some nights. See? Look here."

Collin dug in his satchel and produced the photo he took at Ardfert that he had processed with the help of *The Irish Times* photo department. He gave it to Jack.

Morgan shook her head. "Flooren's journal says he was alone, and that was just thirty-one years after Red Hugh hid the O'Donnell treasure. He likely waited until night with no other activity on Station Island." She thought a moment. "Lough Derg is in Donegal, right?"

"Barely, Sis. Pettigo is the nearest town, just four miles south of the lough, on the border between Donegal and the newly partitioned Northern Ireland county of Fermanagh."

"But in 1601, couldn't Red Hugh have ordered the pilgrims and friars off the island while he hid his treasure?" Morgan's eyes were luminous. She thought she had the answer.

"No, I'm afraid not. They would still have seen his actions from neighboring Saints Island. Our ancestor would have crossed to the island by boat, remember? And by then, the British were in control of Derry and moving west toward Donegal Town."

Jack had been listening to the sibling exchange. "In that case, where is your treasure and the epistle buried, Collin?"

"That's the mystery the pirate couldn't unravel."

Morgan urged, "We've got to go there, Brother."

"All right, Morgan, but I need you to stay here with Biddy while Jack and I visit and reconnoiter. I read that there are British troops stationed in Pettigo now, and you could be spotted."

"I'm going, Collin. Kathy would never forgive me if anything happened to you and my not being there to help. Besides, Jack is still hurting even if he doesn't admit it, and as I used to tell Tadgh, where you go, I go."

Collin smiled at that statement while Jack glared at him.

They finally agreed that Collin would become a pilgrim for the three-day penitence program on Station Island. Biddy's priest organized the visit for him. Morgan and Jack would take up temporary residence disguised as a local farming couple at the hotel in Pettigo as a headquarters for their investigation.

They left for the lough early on Tuesday, June 7, against the wishes of Aunt Biddy, who wanted her niece to stay put. Morgan's main concern was whether Jack's back would be reinjured in the rough ride of their two-horse Jaunting cart. Jack drove the cart from the front seat while Collin and Morgan occupied the two side-facing rear seats that were back-to-back, with footrests down over the high wheels. Their minimal luggage and tools were stored in the space between those seats. If they found treasure chests, depending on their size, they would have to leave their tools behind to fit them in.

The horsehair seats were particularly prickly on the long journey, but at least there were leaf springs above each wheel on the axle to soften the bumpy ride. Even though this rural cart was intended to reduce the risk of detection by any British troops in the area, it still could pose problems. The speed of the vehicle was a mere five miles per hour, which wouldn't fare well if they were chased by the British.

The route took them fifty miles, first southeast to Donegal Town, and then east to Pettigo on the border. When they passed through the Diamond in their hometown around noon, Collin noticed the nationalist *Donegal Democrat* newspaper for June 6 carried a bold front-page headline:

HOUSE BURNING REPRISALS TO STOP. Below it in smaller type, he read,

British Prime Minister George Orders.

"That's good news, Sis, if it is true. But I think the Limeys are up to no good. We can hope that they've had enough war for the time being."

Morgan shifted uncomfortably on the rough cart seat. "I doubt the order will stick. A lot of angry Auxiliaries and Black and Tans may have something to say about it."

They checked in to Donegal's Pettigo City Hotel on Main Street just before curfew. British soldiers milled about outside and inside its bar. Jack insisted on walking the horses to the livery stable behind the RIC barracks, a quarter of a mile away. He said it would help get the kinks out.

That night, Morgan took one room while the men occupied the adjoining one. Upon Jack's return, they had their late supper of rabbit stew in the hotel restaurant, with soldiers carousing at nearby tables. Feeling the tension during dinner, the pair kept their conversation to a minimum.

Returning upstairs to Jack and Collin's room, they finalized their plans for the next day.

Jack, who turned out to be a respectable horseman from his youth in Surrey, took charge of the logistics. He had asked the hotel clerk for information about the Lough Derg Retreat and had been handed an illustrated brochure. Consulting the document and pointing, he said, "See here. It looks like a grand place to spend a few days. We'll drive you up to the dock on the south shore, where their boat will take you to the island. Then we will come back and stay out of sight in the hotel until your penance is over. There's no point in risking exposure for Morgan now, is there, Collin?"

"Agreed."

Morgan knew that Jack would not complain about his condition. He had been through so much to overcome his paralysis after the *Lusitania* sinking. Before retiring for the night, when Collin went down to the bar for a whiskey, she insisted on examining her patient. Jack delicately said that his kidneys seemed to be working as they should, but she could still invoke a twitch reaction when she prodded his lower spine. She checked his knee and leg reflex. Normal.

"I want you to keep your cane handy on this trip, Jack, in case your back acts up."

"Morgan, you are an angel. I don't know what I would do without you."

Morgan sensed what he was about to say and turned away. "Deirdre must be extremely worried about you. I imagine you miss her company."

He turned her back around and stared into her downcast eyes. "I don't miss manhandling all those vegetables, lass, but I do miss her, yes." Then he lifted her chin and smiled broadly, his dimples showing. "I miss you more when you are out of my sight, Morgan. We need to talk."

She pulled his hand away and stepped back. "Not tonight, Jack. Collin will be right back, we're all tired, and we've got a big day tomorrow."

"Fair enough, lass. But while Collin is away on Lough Derg, then, please."

"We'll see. Now I'm going to bed in the next room. Good night."

So as not to altogether reject him, Morgan gave him a peck on the cheek before departing. Jack was in heaven.

Morgan lay in a strange bed, and sleep wouldn't come. By midnight all the talking by her men next door had subsided, and she thought she could hear snoring. She wondered if they had been talking about her.

That's when the melancholy of uncertainty took hold once again. She ached for Tadgh as the memory of him waned. She knew this was the mind's way of coping with the disastrous loss of a loved one. She struggled to revive him, conjure him again, as he was. Not the emaciated prisoner memory, but the one of him with his tousled hair and tender, amber eyes that only softened with her. His hawkish countenance and jutting chin, and the rebellious set of his jaw, flashed before her. He had a proud, fierce anger that flared when defending the rights of his people. Much like Aidan was now. For a few minutes, she was back in his bed after he saved her from the sea, with his awkward yet gentle healing ministrations, falling in love again with a ghost.

She hated thinking this way because she was in agony when she returned to the reality of his death. This vicious cycle.

Then she remembered Bryon, her first love. The gentle nurse had saved her from imprisonment at Fredricson's orphanage and Lippitt's Woolen Mill. He was like Jack, caring and supportive of her plans for her future as a nurse. They were headed to Europe to save lives, not to take them, when the tragedy of the *Lusitania* caused his premature death and changed her life forever. They had been trying to save those twenty-nine babies in their care, all of whom died because of the war. It was Byron she had seen in the dark waters off Skellig beckoning her, not Tadgh.

Was this her subconscious drawing her back to a life devoid of a death wish for a cause, to a normal life with children and a dedicated service to mankind? What would have happened if the ship had not been torpedoed? With the Great War over, would she have made a peaceful family with Byron in New York? That idyllic thought seemed wonderful, albeit unattainable.

She loved Tadgh fiercely as a man, but he had dragged her into his murdering world, where she had almost died. Where she had been swept up by him, and her wishes for her future had been buried by his own dangerous needs.

She suddenly realized that she resented having her life turned upside down for the last six years. My God, she would have to meet her maker now, having killed a man, albeit having been compelled to do it to save Tadgh. She had killed the man in cold blood when he was just doing his job. As a result, she was now a wanted criminal and could be hanged if caught.

Now Aidan and Peader, for god's sake, were drawn into this blood-thirsty, tit-for-tat struggle. She had become *one of them*. Look at how she now wished for her adversary's death, first Shields and now Tavis. Her moral compass was deflected. She would never have been this way before she met

Tadgh, and she couldn't think of her own needs until after he was gone. The fight for freedom was just, but she agreed with Sean O'Casey. The pen should be mightier than the sword.

Let Michael and Tom, and all the others, run headlong into danger and death, but spare Aidan. She shuddered at the thought that her beloved brother-in-law could, and likely would, suffer the same fate as her Tadgh. Because of Aidan and her cousin Peader, she was still being sucked into the deadly fray as a result of her life-saving morals to heal the injured. Damn those men and their infernal war.

Morgan got up and took a sip of water from a glass she'd placed on the bureau. She was angry, and her throat was parched in the stuffy room. Her brain continued to churn. She sat up in the chair to see if sleep would come in that position.

She thought of Jack, a wonderful, strong, level-headed, peace-loving man. He obviously had feelings for her—intense feelings, it would seem. Morgan knew she could fall in love with him if she let herself feel again. There had been a spark that night of the Cork burning. To date, she had not entertained this possibility because of her loyalty to Tadgh and her other responsibilities. Jack's only involvement with this bitter war was to get caught in its crossfire. His motivation was to win her love and help find the treasures, simple and true. He wouldn't cause her to continue down the rathole of death and destruction. He would save her from it, given a chance.

And what of Deirdre, who obviously had genuine feelings for him? Would it be right to deprive her good friend of a happy future by luring away the love of *her* life? Yet in her heart, Morgan knew Aunt Biddy was right. Jack was a good man for her, and life was short, these days, perilously fleeting. Why shouldn't she think of herself for a change? What would make her happy and safe? Biddy had told her, "The best antidote for sorrow is a new lease on life." The woman was right.

Leaving with her brother would be the easy choice, but not necessarily the right one. Despite the argument she had used with him about her Ma's death, she knew Canada would be significantly more peaceful than Ireland. She remembered Charlotte Perceval's admonition that Ireland would be in strife for many years to come. The thought of the opportunity to become a doctor in Toronto was tantalizing. If she chose to love Jack, would he leave his homeland, Ireland, and a thriving career if she went to Canada to become a doctor, as Collin urged?

All this clouded her thinking about her future. The choice between Tadgh and Canada had been difficult but clear-cut five years earlier. Now, with her husband gone and Jack, Collin, and Aidan remaining in her life, there was no distinct choice. Collin would be heading home to Canada soon, and she would have to decide—to stay or go. She hated being indecisive. That, too, was against her nature.

She went back to bed and pulled the covers up to her neck, mentally exhausted. The image of resilient Jack standing at Dillon's Cross in his stark nakedness would not leave her mind. She drifted into a fitful sleep.

Keeping in the shadows, Abbad and Molly had tracked Collin after he arrived at the Donegal Town train station. The spy with sallow cheekbones and squinty black eyes was listening just outside Biddy's garden hedge when the three Adventurers planned their trip to Lough Derg. He heard it all and made his plans—he and Molly would go ahead by motor sedan to Pettigo. They took a room on High Street across the border in Northern Ireland. They were joined there by Abbad's brother, Fazaar, who wanted to be present when the epistle was found.

After spying on the Adventurers entering the hotel, Abbad was furious. Back in his room, his temper got the better of him with Molly. "I'm going to kill that bastard O'Donnell who slashed me. That journal is mine, right enough. The last will and testament of my poor ancestor. I've lowered myself to that crazy British Israeli Association cult and dedicated my life to pursuing the prize so we can rid North Africa of the invading European infidels. I shall not fail my uncle Abd el-Krim al-Khattabi and his ancestor Murat Reis like Janszoon's brother Flooren did."

Abbad remembered how his father had told him the story about his sacred ancestor, who had been captured when he boldly infiltrated the enemy's stronghold Fort St. Angelo in Malta back in 1635. He had planned to pressure the cowardly Grand Master Antoine de Paule to divulge the whereabouts of the sacred epistle. But his plan was exposed by a traitor in his employ. The great rover was incarcerated and tortured in the fort's dungeons for six years before escaping during a pirate raid on the prison. By then, sadly, his mind had gone.

And now Abbad, through his al-Khattabi heritage, was the last true descendant of Murat. He had been charged by his dying father to carry on the search that the great one had started by tracking the last known Irish Templars led by the bar-owner daughter. He was pleased that he had robbed her of her Temple Bar but angry that she had escaped death from the fire he'd set. It was comforting to know that the one who saved her was dead.

Fortunately, when Abbad found his well-educated Moroccan brother to aid him, Fazaar had been easily drawn into the search. Abbad had infiltrated Deirdre's pub, overheard her discussions with the McCarthys, and intercepted her communications with the Templar professor. Fazaar had been assigned to ingratiate himself with Lawlor.

She had been Fazaar's girlfriend, a good-looking, buxom concubine whom Abbad instantly charmed and seduced. He remembered this with the pride of conquest. Now she was putty in his hands. She had been tasked with getting close to the McCarthy woman, the one they called Florence Nightingale of the Cumann na mBan.

When the time came, Molly would be expendable.

The following day, June 8, at seven sharp in drizzling rain, Collin stepped onto the rowboat with seven other pilgrims for the half-mile trip to Station Island from the south shore departure dock. He was dressed in gray worker's garb with a wide-brimmed hat. He carried the Bible Biddy lent him.

"Poor Collin," Morgan said as they sat in the cart, watching the boat recede into the distance. "He doesn't look happy."

Jack tugged at the reins, steering the horses south in the morning mist. "He'll be fine, my dear. He's trained to be observant. He'll crack the puzzle if any of us can."

At the outset of the three-day waiting period, Jack had a golden opportunity to be alone with Morgan. As they drove the four miles back to Pettigo, mostly in silence, their bodies touched in the strict confines of the wagon's seat. He wanted to stop the cart, hold her tight, and profess his love. But he was conflicted. If he made his move too soon when Morgan was still in mourning, that could ruin everything. If he waited, they might never get another chance. Anything could happen in this murderous war. It already had. Collin would pressure her to go to Canada with him if they survived. That day was not far off. And he did not want to leave Ireland. Hell, it was now or never.

Morgan was nervous about finding out why Jack wanted to talk to her. If it was what she expected, a squeaky, bouncing cart was neither the time nor the place for such a conversation. And besides, it was Jack's move, and she had no idea how she would respond.

The first night Jack brought supper up to his room. He lit a candle and poured the local red wine. They sat at a small side table by the western window, with the purple glow of twilight fading over the moor.

"Morgan, dear, I'd like to talk to you about something important to me."

She looked up from her steak and kidney pie. "About the treasure?"

"About the most important treasure. You."

Morgan laid down her utensils and folded her hands over the plate. "What do you mean, Jack?"

Jack saw the confusing signs, her eyes squinting, lips parted. *What is she thinking? I'm bursting to tell her that I love her and have loved her ever since I saw her trying to save that woman on the boat deck of the Lusitania. She needs to know that. But when?*

"I have felt guilty about my obsession with you while Tadgh was alive and tried not to let it show. Deirdre has helped me fill the loneliness that I've felt."

"I knew you cared for me, as I was an inspiration for you to get better after your back was injured. But you know I've always loved Tadgh. He was my whole existence, Jack. We have been through a lot together. I can't just let that go."

"But he's gone, and I'm heartbroken for you because of it. How can I better help you through this terrible time? You will get through it, you know. You are a wonderful, vibrant woman."

Morgan inhaled slowly, and her hand swept a lock of hair behind her ears. She took time to collect her thoughts before she said, "I'm not myself these days, I'm afraid. You've been a great comfort to me these last six terrible months, ever since Dillon's Crossing. I like you, Jack, really, I do."

Morgan got up from the table and walked toward her bedroom. "But it's too soon. Tadgh—" She couldn't finish speaking, her hand on the doorknob.

Jack went to her and spun her around, wanting to capture her gaze, his hands on her shoulders. "Come back to the table. Let's enjoy the easy companionship we have." He could sense a release in her as he turned her around and gently guided her back to the table where the wine carafe beckoned.

When they were seated, Jack handed Morgan a glass of wine, saying, "I know it's been just four months, an eternity in these dangerous times.

Life is short, my dear, and the war brings that fact into focus for me. Who knows if any of us will see the years ahead."

Morgan sipped slowly, reflecting on possibilities—Canada, working in a hospital donning a white coat with the title of Doctor in front of her name, or staying in Ireland—many years of patching up Aidan and friends and worrying about her ending up in prison when the police finally locate her. She quaffed the last dregs of the drink and set the glass down. "Don't push me, Jack." She changed the topic of conversation to clear the air. "I believe in God, Jack. He put us on this earth to serve a purpose, and I don't think we have fulfilled His wishes."

"You mean finding the O'Donnell treasure and using it to help the revolution?"

"At least that, Jack. That must be our focus, don't you see? For the time being, anyway, during this dangerous war. Aidan, Peader, we're all at risk."

"Aye. I hear you and agree. Let's get through that and then talk."

"Thank you, Jack. Do you think you can get your job back at Cunard after this ghastly war is over, if it ever is?"

"Possibly, lass." He knew that couldn't happen if he were with Morgan. She was supposed to be his sister and a killer. If he could eventually win her over, they could likely live near Biddy in Donegal, far away from the glare of their past. "I want to stay in Ireland, at least. It's my home despite what's going on right now."

"If we live through the war, Jack."

Jack had been questioning their likely longevity earlier. Now it was time to show strength. "We will. I'll make sure of that."

She winced. "That's what Tadgh used to tell me."

"But I am not Tadgh."

"No, no, you are certainly not like my Tadgh."

"Should I take offense, lass?"

"Not at all, Jack. I meant it as a compliment." Morgan resumed eating. "Now, as your nurse, I order you to eat your supper before it gets cold, or you'll be too weak for the life you seek."

Jack took her hand and cradled it gently. She didn't pull back. "Ah, the agony of unrequited love," he sighed, his eyes raised to the ceiling.

"Eat your supper, silly."

Later, alone in his room, Jack realized he had held back and said the right supportive words. She wasn't ready. But he desperately wanted to tell her, to hold her, to hear her say the words, "I love you." But when would that be? Collin would not wait much longer to convince her to go back to Canada with him, not if they found the family treasure.

They spent the next two days in seclusion, waiting for Collin to complete his pilgrimage. The British were bristling in Pettigo. Jack was careful not to jeopardize his possibility for future happiness by stepping on the grave of the deceased.

Collin was experiencing a whole new world. Sure, as an Anglican parishioner, he regularly attended St. Aidan's by the Lake with his family and the Finlays at home, but he was ill-prepared for the rigors and Catholic ceremony of the three-day penitence program.

There was no fifteen-day fasting preamble, no dark pit representing the gate to hell to be locked in overnight like Sir Owain was reported to have endured. But the fasting, the walking around the circles called stations for hours on end—in bare feet, the repetitive kneeling prayers at the crosses at the center of the stations, and above all, the lack of sleep and food, tested Collin's fortitude to the limit. He was only given a glass of water and one piece of bread on the first day. Yet it gave him the opportunity to scout out Station Island to try to determine where Red Hugh had hidden his treasure.

When told to rest, he couldn't. The chants he had been reciting kept resounding in his head. By two in the morning, even the obsessed pilgrims had stopped their incessant rotations and chanting.

On the second night after penitential activities ceased, Collin slipped out of the dormitory trying to find the spot where the pit had been located. He had donned his shoes, a taboo on the island. The soles of his feet were aching from all the barefoot walking he had done on the uneven, rocky ground. The silence in the night air helped him sweep away the numbing effects of the religious rituals of the day.

Pulling the photograph of Carve's 1651 map from his jacket, he confirmed that the long house over the expanded pit had been located between Saint Mary's church and the penitential circles. The ones that had once housed the beehives for the accolades after the time of St. Dabheog. There was no evidence left of the pit and its superstructure. Eyeballing the map, he determined it must have been under the hill surmounted by the bell tower. That's probably why they built that tower there, its chimes calling the pilgrims to the entrance to purgatory. Collin wondered whether the O'Donnell treasure might have been buried in the pit after all and had been found when the facilities on the island had been expanded. He had been taught by the historian Fuller at Ardfert that the island was now fifty percent larger in area because of reclamation. Saint Mary's Church had not been there at the time of Red Hugh, nor were the dormitories and offices occupying the south-west end of the island, away from the circles.

It seemed a hopeless task to find any vestige of the old configuration that could give him a clue to the whereabouts of the treasure. Then he focused on an ancient, fluted stone pillar surmounted with a small iron cross beyond the circles, away from the bell tower, on the way to St. Patrick's Chapel that they called Prison Chapel. He vowed to ask the prior, the facility's spiritual leader, Dean Patrick Keown, about it the next day before he left.

On the third morning, the stations took place in St. Patrick's Chapel in the rows between the pews in preparation for the final church service led by the prior. Once again barefoot, Collin scraped his ankles on the retracted footrests as he trudged by them hour after hour. He couldn't tell whether it was lack of food or sleep or the endless repetition of the religious incantations that was causing most of the pilgrims to be in a trance-like state.

Despite his ordeal, Collin found the whole phenomenon fascinating. He decided that he could write a compelling narrative about this place for the *Tely* at some point. But he was failing in his mission.

After both the final service and picking up their meager belongings at the dormitory, the penitents were shown to the boat dock. The prior came down for the benediction and to see them off.

After most of the pilgrims had already boarded the boat, Collin held back on the dock and asked him, "What's the story about the fluted pillar and its old cross, Father?"

Dean Keown put his hand on the novice's shoulder. "You noticed that did you? The last post in our circles walk. I've heard it was St. Patrick's Cross, don't ya know. We've been taught this oldest relic was erected on Saints Island in the early days when the monastery was there. This religious monument was torn down and thrown into the lake in antiquity, perhaps during a Viking raid. The friars finally rescued and erected this most sacred cross on Station Island near where the pit was located."

Collin was facing the circles. *Cross—of course!* Collin turned toward the prior, fingering his locket. The inscription in Tadgh's locket popped into Collin's head. *PPPC . . . My God. PC, Patrick's Cross. Could it be Patrick's Cross for both treasures?* "Do you know when the cross was installed on this island, sir?"

"I've been taught it was just after the 1487 temporary shutdown." The prior looked at his watch. Collin pressed him. "Could the date instead have been after the British shut your facility down in 1632?"

The prior responded, eyes narrowing, "The recovered base with a new cross was re-installed in the early 1500s, I believe. You heard about that conflict, did you?"

Collin returned the stare, looking for a reaction. "With a Barbary pirate?"

The prior's lips pursed, and he shook his head, "I never heard that. There was a pilgrim, however, who caused quite a stir. But the island was leveled by the Bishop of Clogher, I believe. You seem to know a lot about our little island, sir."

"I've studied the history of Lough Derg."

"I noticed on our registration sheets that your name is O'Donnell. Perhaps you can tell me why the great Chieftain Red Hugh O'Donnell back in 1601 came to do penance before he led his troops to Kinsale?"

It was Collin's turn to be surprised. "Did he spend time on Station Island, do you know?"

"I suppose he did, my son. More time on Saints Island in those days but a day and night here at the pit."

"Didn't the religious leaders pray for victory before major battles? Don't we all pray for our major challenges in life?"

"I see what you mean." Looking back at the dock, he added, "It's time to go, then, isn't it? They're waiting for you on the boat."

Collin wasn't entirely sure how to thank the cleric. Should he bow, shake his hand? He reached out, and the prior clasped his hand. "Thank you, Dean Keown, for all your guidance. I feel physically, if not spiritually, cleansed."

Lough Derg

Station Island, Lough Derg
Courtesy of Lough Derg Priory

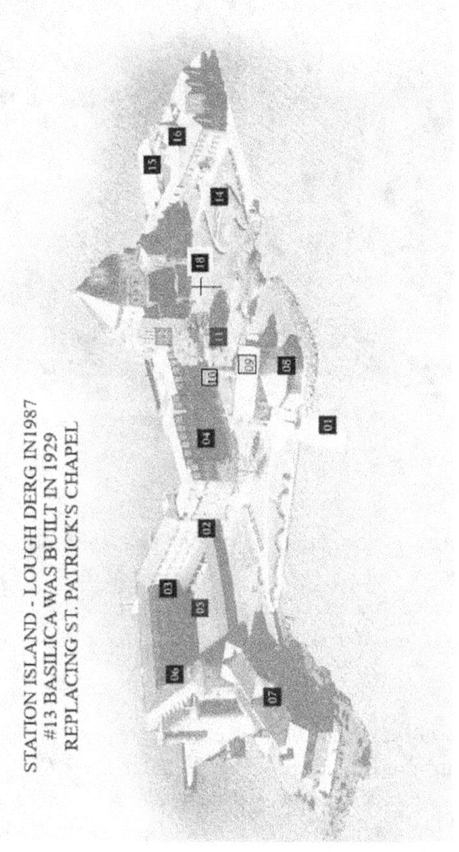

Saint Patrick's Ancient Cross
Station Island, Lough Derg

"Off with you now, lad, before they leave without you. Come back again when you see fit."

Collin turned and waved before stepping over the gunnels among the impatient pilgrims. Now that their penance was over, they wanted to get off the island.

Collin watched the island receding in the morning mist as the boat eased away from the dock. What a religious treasure, kept vibrant through centuries of turmoil and danger. *Is this the place where Red Hugh had hidden his wealth?* He was inclined to agree with Flooren's assessment and wished he had found out about the cross a day earlier.

♣ ♣ ♣ ♣

While they waited for Collin's return that morning, Morgan and Jack had acquired a local lough map from the attendant at the dock-area welcoming shack. Then they hiked the pilgrim's path from the dock clockwise around the south shore. Jack was nimble enough with his cane to make it a mile as far as St. Brigid's Well and her rock chair at the shoreline. From there, they climbed to a large rock marked with a sign as St. Dabheog's Chair up the mountain to the south. The notes on the map indicated that the founding prior went there seeking solace with nature.

Morgan's leg ached from her old bullet wound suffered during the Rising, but she paid it no mind. Instead, she watched Jack as he winced, periodically bending over to stretch his back. "You are quite spry, Jack, given what you've been through."

"When it hurts, I try to remember that I was incapacitated just five years ago."

Morgan came over to where he was sitting on a rock and asked if she could put some direct pressure where his back hurt. Jack was elated. It felt wonderful pressing her hands down on his lower back. She stood behind him, bending forward with the task, and her long black ringlets fell around his head and ears. Sweet-smelling despite the rigors of their trek. When her shirtwaist covering her breasts innocently brushed past his shoulders, it sent shivers down his spine.

"Am I hurting you, Jack?" Morgan asked after one of his tremors.

"Quite the opposite. Your touch is sublime."

Jack had his head down when Morgan looked out at the lake below them and announced, "The little boat is leaving the dock on Station Island."

Jack took her hand, and together, they hurried down the path about a mile and a half from the dock. What a difference between now and the days when he was a slave to a wheelchair, Jack thought. He was walking, albeit with a cane, and holding hands with the woman he dreamed about every night. Life was good.

They got back to the road out of breath but laughing before the boat landed. In the flush of the moment, Jack took Morgan in his arms and kissed her. She pulled away at first, then settled into his arms and kissed him. He could feel her body softening into his embrace.

From the boat, Collin could see the clinch. He didn't like it. Maybe it was time to talk to Morgan about coming to Canada before she became too attached to Jack.

High up on the hill overlooking the boat dock, another interested party was seething at the sight.

Back in her room two hours later, Morgan was restless. Her mind and heart were racing. That kiss at the lough had taken her unawares, but it had been delicious. Jack's arms had been so strong. But what had surprised her most was her wicked reaction. He had made her knees go weak.

Her confounding thoughts from the other night flooded back, but now with more focus.

Most importantly, it finally crystallized in her mind that her whole life had been one of service to others, voluntary and imposed. She had learned obedience early with the abduction and imprisonment at the orphanage and mill. She loved Tadgh unselfishly for years and had supported him in his dangerous, murderous ways if only to keep him safe. Her rebellious and violent actions and the lifestyle she had become embroiled in were not what she would have chosen.

What *did* she want? A future that she directed herself! Morgan had not thought about her life in this way. She was ashamed to have these thoughts with her husband recently dead and gone. She shuddered.

Yet Tadgh had chosen his obsessive kill-or-be-killed path of existence, and it had caught up with him horribly. For a noble cause, she understood. She now comprehended the emotions of hatred and revenge that possessed these men on both sides of this ugly war because she felt them herself. What was the world coming to? Just like the Great War with seventeen million dead. For what? The countries still existed as they had been before a generation of men had been slaughtered.

She had a right and now the opportunity to choose her path, but what was it? The life she'd led up to this point made it hard to think clearly.

Then she remembered her recurring dream. Not the one where the giant squid was strangling and pulling her down to the depths and death. That was her past life of servitude. No. It was the dream where she and Tadgh were living peacefully in a painted cottage by the sea in Queenstown with their children around them. Those dreams always ended with anxiety.

Why? Because if she were being honest with herself, she could not see Tadgh settling down without a war to wage.

There it was—the truth. She wanted a peaceful marriage and family by the seaside, in safe surroundings. Not a life on the run. Yet this is what Tadgh had turned her into—a fugitive. The resentment bubbled up from beneath again.

Muddled thoughts from her previous night's anxieties swirled again. Morgan pondered the variables. She had worked hard to be a good nurse, from the early days at the orphanage through all the deadly turmoil—until today. She wanted to continue her medical career, to help others, but not just to salvage broken bodies from the ravages of war. The thought of becoming a doctor in a peaceful new land was appealing. But if she followed her brother to Canada, he would take her away from those she cared about in her homeland, including Aidan and Jack.

That's when Aunt Biddy's recent guidance re-entered her mind. Life was short, and Jack was a good man. And his kiss was alluring. But what about her friend, Deirdre? And Jack's attraction to her? She wondered what their lovemaking had been like and whether that relationship was still smoldering, ready to flare up once more.

She would have to mull things over before she could make her life-altering decision. If she lived that long. At least now, Morgan could see choices for her future that didn't include war.

Some of the cobwebs in her mind had been swept away with a powerful kiss.

Chapter Thirteen
Treasure

Friday, June 10, 1921
Pettigo Hotel, Donegal, Ireland

*T*hat night, **Collin** wolfed down a steak with potatoes supper in the men's bedroom. Afterwards, he briefed his companions on his ordeal.

Morgan sat cross-legged on the bed with her plate before her while the men ate at the table. She fiddled with a morsel of meat and poked at it with her fork. "People pray for three days straight of their own volition?" she asked. "Why? Tradition, maybe?"

"I talked to one pilgrim lady who had been there nine times. She goes every summer."

Morgan chuckled. "She must lead a wicked life, then, to need that much penance."

"Or at least she thinks she does, Sis. What I endured is minor compared to the pilgrims in the Middle Ages who fasted for fifteen days before, and then again after dwelling in the pit, not to mention the night they are kept in the gateway to hell."

Morgan speared another chunk of meat, chewed, and swallowed. "Is it possible that the treasure is buried at the base of St. Patrick's Cross, much like the McCarthy treasure located on the Rock of Cashel?"

Collin gulped his stout. "There is an elegant symmetry to that possibility. And the timing is right since the cross was moved to Station Island over a hundred years before Red Hugh came there to bury his treasure. But I am still convinced he couldn't have secreted it onto the island without the friars knowing."

After he finished his meal, Jack urged, "Let's have another look at the inscription, Collin."

Collin moved his plate out of the way and then opened his notebook, thumbed through the pages, stopped in the middle, and read the characters aloud. *"PPPCCathaoir, BSt: L2284-5, H20, WN99D."*

Morgan added, "The Blarney Stone was the key that opened the door to both these treasure maps. Its length, if you will recall, is 27 inches." She set her plate aside and found an envelope to calculate on.

"That's right, Sis. Here the distance would be considerable, 27 times 2284."

Morgan calculated on paper. "5,139 feet, to be exact."

"What about the fact that they measured in nautical troighids in those days?" Collin asked.

Morgan fidgeted with the paper and pencil. "Remember, the conversion doesn't matter for distance; it cancels out. It does matter for the angle."

Jack looked at Collin's photograph of the map of Station Island in 1651. "That's ridiculous. If it were that far from St Patrick's Cross, it would be at the bottom of the lake or further out, not on the island at all."

Morgan turned the photograph around so she could see it right side up. "This doesn't make sense. The chieftains would have used consistent dimensional units, surely. Maybe the word *Cathaoir* doesn't refer to *an Cathach* after all."

Sudden inspiration struck Jack. He jumped up and hurried out the door, then quickly returned, nearly out of breath. "I asked the bartender. The word means 'chairs' in Gaelic."

Collin scratched his head. "Chairs? You mean the pews in the church? Saint Mary's Church wasn't even there in 1601."

Morgan bolted upright. "The rock chairs, Jack. We saw them today. Could that be it?"

Collin shook his head. "What chairs?"

"Jack and I walked the pilgrim's path from the dock to the sign for St. Brigid's Well and Chair and back today while we waited for you to return from Station Island. There are two large rocks that look like chairs, with sign markers set by the path. One is attributed to Saint Brigid at the shoreline, and the other up the mountain to the south is where St. Dabheog was said to have communed with nature back in the 400s. We went to see them, Collin."

Collin's face lit up. "Could it be that simple? It would have been off the island somewhere up in the woods."

Morgan answered. "Stands to reason, Brother. Red Hugh could have buried his treasure in private up there with no one watching. You say that Red Hugh went there in 1601?"

"Yes, Dean Keown told me. Likely to Station Island to pray before heading to Kinsale."

Morgan pushed her index finger down on the map of the island.

"And remember the Clans Pact? This would certainly be a sacred religious location for Red Hugh."

"That's right, Sis. How can we figure this out?"

Morgan thought for a moment. "The guide at the shack by the boat dock gave us a map of the south end of the lake with the pilgrim's path marked on it. Do you have it, Jack?"

Jack checked his back pocket. He was sitting on the paper. They spread the wrinkled document out and stared at it. Their mouths fell open. Collin took the pencil, and Jack offered the straight-edged tray from their supper. Together Morgan and Jack held both ends of the tray while Collin drew the line on the map. The solution revealed itself. Dabheog's chair, Brigid's chair, and the location of St. Patrick's Cross on Station Island were collinear, in a perfect straight line.

Collin said it first. "That's got to be it! Now, how can we calculate the distances involved?"

Jack pulled out their map of the area, including Pettigo, the road to the lough, and the lough itself.

Morgan quickly went to her room, retrieved Aunt Biddy's cloth measuring tape, and handed it to Collin.

They crowded around the maps on the bed as Collin unwound the tape and measured the distance. Checking the scale on the map of the area, he announced, "The distance from Pettigo to the dock in a straight line is four point zero miles. Let's look at the distance from the cross to Brigid's chair. He measured the distance off the maps, careful to get the ratios right. Then he scribbled numbers in his notebook. "By my calculation, that distance is 3680 feet."

Morgan said, "The inscription distance was 5,139 feet, so that can't be the location. What is the distance from the cross to St. Dabheog's chair?"

Collin went to work calculating the distance. "5,150 feet!"

Morgan slapped her brother on the shoulder. "That must be our answer."

"Jack scratched his head. "It all seems to come together, but how would your ancestor have been able to measure the distance, Morgan?"

"Like we did," Morgan surmised. "That map that Carve drew of Station Island back in that century looked very detailed and was likely accurate. Being on Red Hugh's land, he probably had a similar map that included the pilgrimage points of St. Brigid's and St. Dabheog's chairs accurately located."

Collin consulted his notes. "Let's check something else. What was the width of the Blarney Stone, Morgan?"

"Sixteen inches. Why?"

"Give me a second, Sis." Collin scratched out the numbers. "If I use Tadgh's nautical measurement of ten and a half inches per troighid, then the Blarney stone is one-and-a-half troighids wide. Aha! The end of the inscription is *WN99D,* which translates to North 151 degrees."

Jack noticed that Morgan did not seem to be bothered by the mention of Tadgh's name. *Good.*

Morgan refocused on the map of Lough Derg with the pilgrims' path, and they drew a straight line, north-south through the cross. Using her logical mathematical skills, she had exhibited during the McCarthy Gold search, she offered, "I'll bet my bottom dollar that the angle between the two lines will be about thirty degrees. It sure looks like it, that's certain.

Map of Lough Derg Pilgrim's Path
(www.eastwestmapping.ie)

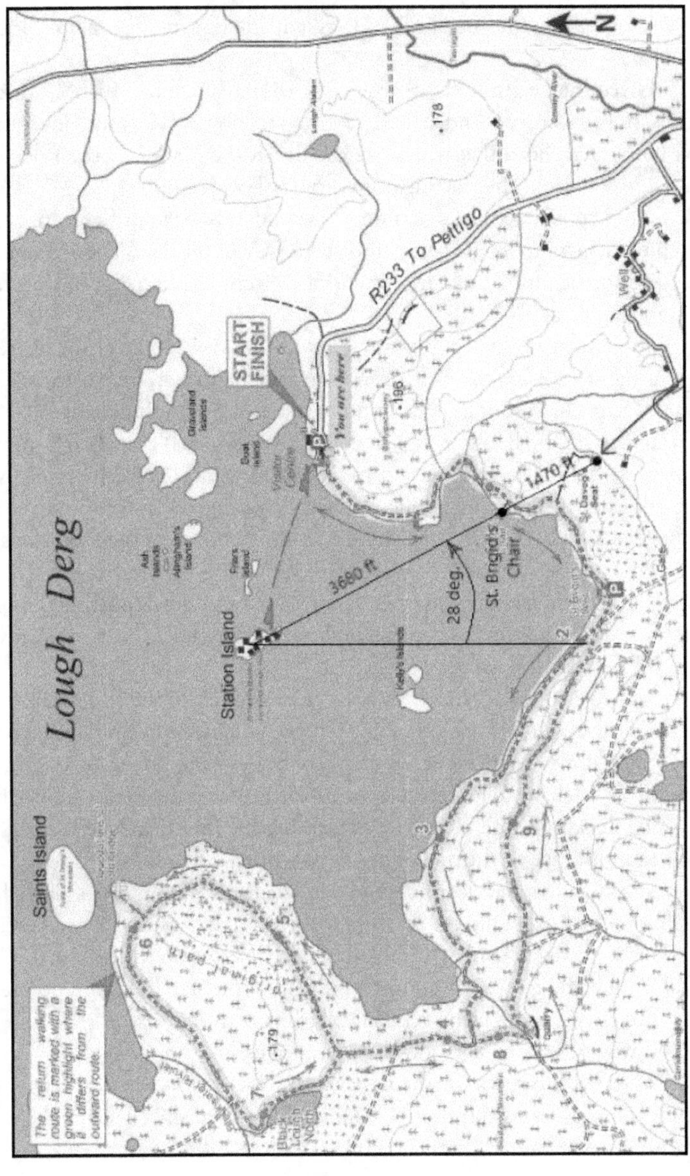

"I think we have found the location of where Red Hugh buried his treasure. It's not on the island at all but rather at the very sacred St. Dabheog's Chair."

"What about the height?" Jack asked, holding up the map. "H20 would be—"

"Given the height of the Blarney Stone is ten and a half inches, which means it is seventeen and a half feet down, boys," Morgan piped up. "Wouldn't that mean that the treasure is under the island? At the Rock of Cashel, it was from the starting point on the Tympanum."

Collin considered the situation. "It would have been difficult for Red Hugh to determine the height from Patrick's Cross on the island, Morgan. I'd guess the beginning of this dimension is from the location of the seat of Dabheog's chair."

Morgan concluded, "The first clue was from verse nine at the altered beginning of *an Cathach*. With *PPPC* in Tadgh's locket, which led us to Lough Derg, the rest of the inscription gave us the map. Ingenious!"

Collin said, "If we're right, then Florence and Red Hugh must have been master puzzle makers to invent and intertwine the clues so mysteriously with their own relics. Especially during a war for the survival of the Clans. There is true, symmetrical beauty in the combined solutions."

"Divine intervention," Morgan offered, folding up the maps.

"Then we must be master puzzle solvers," Jack added, puffing out his chest. He took the pencil and paper and started to make a list. "Tomorrow, we'll get the supplies we need to excavate."

Collin asked, "Can we get the cart close enough to the rock chair?"

Morgan thought for a moment. "The woods are dense on that hillside above and down to the chair but open below that down to pilgrim's footpath. We'll have to leave the Jaunting cart back up the road out of sight from the dock opposite the chair. Consulting the trail map, she added, "I guess that distance to the rock is about two-thirds of a mile."

Collin looked over Jack's shoulder at the list. "Sounds like a daylight digging activity but a night operation for removal if we find the treasure."

Jack looked at the map. "If the friars don't see us on the hill, that is."

"We'll be digging away almost a mile from the island," Collin pointed out, "and they'll be focusing on their pilgrims at the circles."

"If we use torches at night, they may see us."

"True. We'll have to use them sparingly. Now, if you two heathens will excuse your righteous compatriot, I need a little sleep since I've hardly had any in four days."

Collin headed for the bathroom down the hall, and Morgan got up to go through the adjoining doorway to her room. She stopped at the threshold. "If you fancy a drop of whiskey, Jack, I have some in here. We need to talk." She disappeared through the door, leaving it open.

Jack wondered if she was batting her smoky green eyes at him. Probably just his imagination.

A minute later, Collin returned. "Shall we turn in, Jack? We've a full day ahead of us."

Jack moved over to the adjoining room door. "You go ahead, Collin. You deserve it. I'm just going to pop in to talk to Morgan about our plans for tomorrow."

"Are you sure that's why you're going in there?"

"She's a big girl, Collin, and I'm a respectful lad. I know that being a widow, she needs time to mourn."

"Remember that, Jack. Don't get her muddled by your attentions. Not now."

Jack turned to go. "Good night, my friend."

Collin heard the warm welcome that Morgan gave Jack as he stepped through the doorway. The door closed, and Collin was left alone with his thoughts. He worried that his sister was in danger, this time with a man he now knew very well and liked. Should he interrupt them? Or was his concern more selfish since their budding friendship threatened his plan for Morgan to move to Canada as soon as the O'Donnell treasure was unearthed? He was too tired to worry about it tonight. He could hear those incessant incantations drumming in his head again.

Once Jack had been served his promised Jameson, Morgan took charge of the conversation.

"How's the back?"

"Better with this whiskey trickling down my throat."

"I worry about you, my lad."

Jack liked the sound of that. "Do you now, Morgan. I can assure you that I am fit as a fiddle."

"Maybe one that is slightly out of tune."

"Then you need to tune me up." From the corner chair, Jack extended his arms wide, but Morgan sat still on the edge of the bed.

"We need to talk about that kiss today, Jack."

"Too impulsive, that was, and I apologize."

"No, Jack. That kiss meant something; I must admit."

Jack rose and sat beside her on the bed, hips touching. "Then that's grand, isn't it? Because I feel the same way."

Morgan slid away from him. "That's my dilemma, Jack. In a manner of speaking, I'm still bound to Tadgh, as we've already discussed. You can understand that, can't you? And you are close to Deirdre, am I right? The two of you, a couple?"

"Ah, yes, in a manner of speaking. But that was before—" He stopped, not wanting to bring up Tadgh's death at this critical juncture.

He stared at her green eyes, lovelier than ever in the soft light, and listened to her lilting voice.

"Are you sure the attraction isn't because I am unavailable, the lure of forbidden fruit?"

Jack searched her eyes, intoxicating with the bedside candlelight dancing in them. "You have always been in my thoughts since I first saw you."

Morgan found a flaw in the embroidered bedspread, a loose thread in the edging, and toyed with it to restore the pattern. "You know that Collin wants me to go to Canada when this war is over. I have to decide soon." She didn't look at Jack but fussed with the thread.

"He's mentioned it. But I need you here." Then he added, "In your homeland with your family."

"Collin is family. Besides, I can become a doctor if I go back with him."

Jack tried another approach. "What would Tadgh have had you do, Morgan?"

She stopped fussing with the thread and looked up at him. "That's easy. Stay in Ireland, fight for the Cause, come what may, and protect Aidan. But the man's gone."

She smoothed out a wrinkle in the coverlet. "That's a reality I struggle with."

"Then why not stay here, with your Irish family and me? This war will be over soon, and we can settle down. We can live up here in Donegal, near your Auntie." He tried to tone down his eagerness and instill calm.

Morgan got up to sit in the chair, leaving Jack on the edge of the bed. "I haven't sorted anything out yet. For the sake of discussion, what about Cunard?"

He had to work this carefully. "Might be a problem, what with your, ah . . . notoriety."

"Donegal, Jack? Is that what you want?"

Jack came over to the chair, facing her. "Since you asked, I want both you and a career, right here in our Ireland."

Morgan took the hand he offered and asked, "If that were to happen, what about children?" The agony of losing Tadgh's child flashed through her mind. She desperately wanted babies but was concerned about her ability to complete a pregnancy.

Jack asked, "Are you all right, my dear? You look as if you're in pain."

Recovering her composure, Morgan said, "I'm fine." She waited for an answer.

"Three would be nice."

Morgan withdrew her hand. "Only nice?"

"I don't know. I haven't given that much thought to children—until now."

After he blurted that out without thinking, Jack could see Morgan's eyes narrowing, the pupils turning black. Was her melancholy setting in again, that sadness he couldn't penetrate? Should he attempt another kiss? He remembered Collin's admonition, so he said, "When you are ready, we will talk again."

Without warning, Morgan erupted. "You're pushing me too fast, Jack. You need to give me more time."

Jack was shocked by Morgan's outburst. He thought they had been making progress. *I guess children are a problem with her.* He stepped back and realized he was handling this poorly, and he was so clumsy at love. Time to reconsider his approach. "Of course, my love." He opened the adjoining room door and closed it softly behind him, leaving her alone.

The conversation had left Morgan demoralized. No easy answers to her dilemma. Flopping down on the bed, she cried herself to sleep without even changing into her nightdress.

While Jack was purchasing the needed shovels, ropes, buckets, and torches at the general store the following morning, he overheard soldiers in the next aisle talking about their expectation that a newly appointed Donegal rebel leader was expected to be visiting each of his lieutenants within the southwest area. One said they were on guard, and more British reinforcements were expected to arrive in Pettigo shortly. It was crucial this man named Joe Sweeney be intercepted and arrested, not to be killed unless absolutely necessary. Lough Derg was considered the kind of secluded location where the rebel leader might try to hold a meeting.

On his way back to the horse cart, Jack passed the livery and saw a four-wheel hand wagon the size of a children's baby buggy for sale. He bought it and threw it in the horse cart.

Arriving back, Jack explained what he had heard. Then he said, "I think we should hold off for a few days. The police will be swarming all over Lough Derg looking for Sweeney."

Collin disagreed. "I say we proceed. I need to check in with both newspaper owners soon, and I'm sure they are going to order me back to Canada as soon as I contact them."

Morgan wasn't confident about moving forward quickly. "We spent a good deal of time on that mountain yesterday, Brother. There were military personnel in the neighborhood, that's for certain. Look at all the British soldiers here in Pettigo. I agree with Jack. Give it a few days."

Collin didn't like being the odd man out, especially with Jack. "We'll wait one day, and then I will go out to see if we can explore the place safely."

Jack stood up, met the challenge, and approached Collin, nearly jutting up against his face. "Excuse me. Who made you the leader?"

Collin raised his arms as if to ward off a foe. "I'm not. I just want us to use the time we have productively." He turned away red-faced, not wanting an altercation. He needed Jack, so he turned back around. "The other reason that I'm anxious to get going is the possibility that we may have company, that bandit at Barrow House, for instance."

"I'm no leader," Morgan butted in, "but I've got good ideas. Why not wait two days and see how active the British are up north? If the treasure is there, another day or two won't make any difference, will it? It's been hidden for three hundred and twenty years."

Collin answered, "You're right, Sis. We're the only ones with the clues from Tadgh's locket."

That caused Morgan to tear up again as she thought of what had happened to her man. "Except that the bloody Brits got Tadgh's locket."

Jack put his arm around her shoulder. "I know what you are thinking, that the British are still looking for the epistle. But that's very unlikely, I should think. The inscription was just one part of the clues, lass."

"The cornerstone, Jack. What if one of them found Boyle's copy of the Clans Pact after he died? We don't know what happened to it, do we."

Collin interjected. "That seems remote, Morgan. I think we are much more likely to have Abbad as an adversary. Let's focus on getting to the treasure before anyone else has an opportunity.

Morgan poured each of them a shot of whiskey, handed out the glasses, and they raised them in unison.

♣ ♣ ♣ ♣

The next day on Sunday, the twelfth of June, Peader's commander, Joe Sweeney, rode his bicycle to his No. 4 Brigade OC O'Flaherty's home in Castlefinn. This isolated market town was located ten miles northeast of Lough Derg and twenty miles southeast of Letterkenny, just inside the newly divided Northern Ireland boundary. It was the ancestral home of Niall Garve O'Donnell. Could it be that the treasure he sought and never found was only a few miles from his castle? If so, that would be the ultimate irony.

Sam O'Flaherty had just been ordered back to Donegal from his Dublin post by Michael Collins. He and Joe discussed the lack of armament for the Southwest Battalion and the annual problem of men leaving for their six-month Scotland work commitment.

At two a.m., the military raided the home. Joe scrambled out a window and plunged through a creek before he could put on his britches. Sam hid in the rafters. When the British finally left, not finding either man, Sweeney scampered back and rode off on his bicycle. A few miles out, the front wheel came loose, and he fell, scraping his face badly on the gravel road. He needed to withdraw to heal, so he chose Lough Derg, normally an isolated spot. An informer got word of the destination and sent a runner to Pettigo to alert the troops.

♣ ♣ ♣ ♣

The three Adventurers decided that Monday morning to go treasure hunting. Collin observed that the military was not headed north toward Lough Derg at their regular mustering hour of seven o'clock. The O'Donnells started for the lough at eight, with Jack driving the rig. It would be eight hours before the runner would bring news of Sweeney's plans to the Pettigo Auxie detachment.

Jack brought the cart to a halt an hour later on an abandoned dirt track off the Lough Derg Road, about a third of a mile from the dock. A stream alongside a hiding thicket of mulberry trees afforded relief for the two horses. He slackened their reins to allow them some freedom as he tied them to a tree by the water. Then he patted them down but kept them loosely harnessed to the cart in case the group needed to leave in a hurry. "I scouted out this hiding site when we came to pick you up, Collin," said Jack. "This should be about even with the St. Dabheog's chair, I think.

We'd better not be seen at the boat dock." Pointing up the slope parallel to the shoreline, he announced, "We hoof it from here."

Together they hefted the shovels, rope, buckets, and torches up the hill to the west, through the trees, leaving the hand wagon behind in the horse cart.

Abbad and Fazaar snuck up on the horses after parking their vehicle down near the dock out of sight. Abbad smiled when he saw the toy hand wagon in the back. "Looks like they're expecting to find their treasure," he chortled. Molly followed soon after with the binoculars hanging from a strap around her neck. Together they settled into stalking their prey.

Once they had crested the hill, taking a breather, Collin asked, "Are you sure you know where this chair is located?"

"I'm trying to get oriented," Jack huffed. "We came to it from the shoreline." Looking down through the trees from the top of the hill, he swept his arm across the scene below him. "All those rocks down there below the edge of the tree line look the same from this distance."

Resting her arms on her planted shovel, Morgan suggested, "One of us needs to go down to the path by the lake and find St Brigid's Chair. Then we can follow the line from Station Island up to St. Dabheog's Chair."

The men couldn't fault her logic. After descending from the trees, they looked out across the lough at Station Island. They were about two thousand feet from the shoreline, maybe up two hundred feet from its surface, and the hillside below the tree line was open ground, boulder-strewn, with occasional weathered pine trees leaning bravely against a prevailing west wind.

Morgan breathed in the view. "It's a beautiful, tranquil view, lads. I can see why St. Dabheog would hike up here from Saints Island to pray in solitude. Can you imagine it, sitting up here fifteen hundred years ago, contemplating the will and grace of God, barely four hundred years after the resurrection and before the Romans were defeated in the ancient world? St. Dabheog and his monks created an important Christian pilgrimage site that would survive long after the Romans, the Vikings, and medieval societies that were eventually destroyed through their greed and avarice."

"Still providing sanctuary and penitence for all Christians even during terrible revengeful wars erupting all around it," Jack remarked.

"Yes, and we'd best get at our business before any of those forces of evil descend on us," Collin said. "Where is that stone chair?"

Morgan pointed downward. "I see the footpath down there. I'll go since I saw it before."

"I'll go with you," Jack said.

Morgan put up her hand and then pointed at the island. "You see those people over there?"

In the distance, they saw pilgrims walking the circles with a few friars watching them intently.

"Jack, with your bad back, you should stay here in the trees with Collin. One person in the open is more than enough. I don't want to attract attention. The British might be about. Here. Hold my shovel."

Collin said, "If you stay at St. Brigid's chair where we can see you, Jack and I can bring the tools and stay in line with you and the island while you come up. We should meet at the saint's chair."

The men watched Morgan as she picked her way down among the boulders and trees to the lakeside path. She darted to her left until she found what she was looking for and waved. "Let's go," Collin said, heading left, into the trees. We can start to descend when Morgan is in line with the island."

A few minutes later, they met at a set of rocks that, with some imagination, looked like a stone chair. A small wooden sign signified that this was indeed the chair of the founding saint. Was it a coincidence that they were just below the tree line, or had the monks over the centuries cleared the hillside to give a clear view from St. Dabhoeg's chair? An isolated, gnarled tree just below the rocks partially hid the site from Station Island and the path below.

Morgan sat down in the saddle of the rocks where the saint might have rested his weary bones and looked down and out at the island. She felt the rocks surround her body. "Can we assume these ancient rocks have been in this exact place for at least three hundred years?"

Collin answered, "They were probably deposited here when the last ice age receded many thousands of years ago, so yes, Sis."

She surveyed all around. "Where should we dig, fellows?"

Collin said, "We need another clue." He pulled his notebook from his jacket pocket and stared at the inscription from Tadgh's locket.

It was Jack who saw it: *L2284-5*. "What if the -5 after the number

2284 refers to the distance from the rock to the treasure?"

Morgan leaned down from her perch to see the notebook and said, "That would be about eleven feet, given the Blarney Stone length." She pointed forward. "Look at that hollow down there towards the lake, between the chair and that old pine. It's about ten feet north of the front edge of the chair rock, and it appears to be sunken down."

Collin walked down into the depression. "This is as good a place as any to start, my dear, right in the middle of the depression, directly in line with the cross. Everywhere else looks rocky."

Jack stood to the side and eyed the terrain. "All right, Morgan. Your seat is about ten feet above the bottom of the depression. If our calculation is right, then the treasure should be about seven or eight feet down if it hasn't sunk even lower over the years."

Collin gripped a shovel. "Fine, Jack. Why don't you and I start digging here while Morgan keeps watching from on high in the chair."

Morgan liked that idea. "I'm happy to have you two blokes do all the heavy work. If your back starts to act up, Jack, you need to stop. I will take over. Otherwise, I'll just supervise from up here."

Abbad, Fazaar, and Molly crouched in the dense pine forest two hundred feet above the toiling group. Molly whispered to her mate. "I'm happy to let them do the heavy work, too."

"That's been the idea all along." Abbad opened his pack and took out a bottle of stout as the sun broke through the trees by ten o'clock.

Around two in the afternoon, Collin was beginning to doubt they had the correct location. They had excavated a six-foot-square hole to a depth of about four feet. Along the way, Collin had to remove rocks and chop away roots from the tree that hovered over their dig.

Morgan returned from the cart with the picnic hamper she had prepared.

While they ate their ham and cheese sandwiches sitting on St. Dabheog's rock, Collin said, "I'm not sure about this location—all these rocks and roots." He scanned the area but couldn't come up with any other location close to the chair that could support any soil depth.

"That tree would not likely have been there in 1601."

"True, Morgan, but what about the rocks I dragged out of this hole?"

Morgan stuffed a pickle sliver into her mouth before answering. "Pirates used to booby-trap their hiding spots. Maybe Red Hugh placed these boulders to discourage treasure seekers that may have stumbled on the clues. You sound like you're discouraged already, Brother."

"Not at all, lass. The message in the locket was pretty specific once we deciphered it."

Jack swigged some water from the canteen Morgan had brought. He turned to Collin and said, "I think we should keep digging, but we're going to need a ladder if we are to go much deeper."

Collin pointed toward the dock in the distance. "I noticed equipment behind the shack near the dock when I checked in as a pilgrim. There may be a ladder we could borrow."

"Without their knowledge, Collin?"

"Of course, my dear sister. Jack is an excellent scrounger, aren't you, Jack."

"Then we agree to continue with this hole?"

"At least until dark." Collin sat down on a nearby stone.

"How's your back feeling, Jack? You've been digging—"

"I feel fine, Morgan. I can do this. I'm on my way to get us that equipment."

While Jack was gone, Collin chose to talk to his sister alone. "Do you remember our discussion when I first found you, the one where I spoke of the opportunities to become a doctor in Canada where I live?"

"Of course. Your glowing description of the wondrous new frontier in Canada." Morgan had been expecting Collin to pressure her again. But why now?

"That's right. It is magnificent there. I've been waiting to ask you to come back with me until you've had enough time to grieve. It's been four months, and Tadgh is not a reason for you to stay in Ireland now. Who knows how long it will take for this war to end? I'm asking you now. Come back with me, please, Morgan. You'll not regret it, Sis, I can assure you."

"What about Jack, Aidan, Aunt Biddy, and Peader, Collin? I have family here, too, and they need me."

"Jack could come with us."

Morgan started putting the picnic things away to distract the conversation.

When she didn't answer, Collin repeated his question.

She turned and said, "I think Jack wants a life here in Ireland, Collin. And I can't just walk away completely from the Cause that is sure to liberate Ireland, Brother."

"But is it *your cause*, Morgan?"

"Aidan and Peader are committed to it. There is grave injustice here."

"You didn't answer my question, Sis. Is it *your fight?*"

"Until recently. I didn't agree with the revengeful killing, and I still try to preserve life wherever possible. Ireland should be rid of the English overlords, true."

"But is this what you want or deserve?"

There it was. The question she had finally answered for herself. The answer was an emphatic no. But she was not ready to vocalize it yet. Instead, she said, "This is hardly the time and place for this discussion, Collin."

"All right, but I won't give up on persuading you, Sis."

"What persuasion?" Jack asked as he lumbered toward them, back from his trek over the hill and edge of the woods, carrying a ten-foot ladder over his shoulder. "You were right about the tools." He lowered the ladder into the hole.

"Collin wants me to go and live in Canada with him when he returns, don't you, Brother."

"Yes, and I mentioned that Jack could make the trek with you."

"But I have my position at Gilroy's Grocery to close out and would like to make a new life in Donegal," Jack reminded her. "I can't just leave my country behind."

Morgan munched on a carrot. "You weren't invited yet, Jack."

He grabbed his shovel. "Can we talk about this later, Collin? We have more pressing matters at hand."

Collin pulled his locket from under his tunic and stared at it. "I just thought of something. Since the inscriptions were cross-referenced between the O'Donnell's and the McCarthy's, then the lockets had to be produced by one or the other of the chieftains in 1601. That would have been before Florence was incarcerated but after they had determined precisely where their treasures would be buried."

Jack offered his thoughts. "That's right. I would imagine that Florence had them secretly made. And since we suspect that the McCarthy treasure was not buried until the siege of Blarney Castle, then the inscription must have been passed on secretly from the MacCarthaigh Reagh to the McCarthy Mor after Kilbrittain Castle was taken by Boyle in 1642."

Collin added, "And Red Hugh must have communicated the

inscription for the McCarthy locket after he buried his treasure, sometime between forming their pact in October 1600 and when Florence was arrested in mid-1601. It seems strange that we are uncovering the past of our own ancestors when they were locked in mortal combat for the country that they loved, a battle that we know they lost."

Morgan thought of poor Auntie Biddy and said, "We're locked in the same deathly battle now, with the same foe treating us in a brutal way. Burning us O'Donnells out, just like Inchiquin burned all those people to death in the cathedral on the Rock of Cashel back in 1648. We can't let them win again." Morgan heard her voice spout off Tadgh's words. It was as if he was still within her, speaking through her. Her spine tingled for a moment, and she thought *how easy it was to get sucked back into revenge. Lord, help me break free from this hateful evil.*

Collin guessed that Morgan's comment was meant for him, and he needed to change the subject.

"Let's get to work." He took his shovel and climbed down into the hole.

Jack joined him, and they resumed digging.

An hour later, they needed to use their buckets to get the dirt out of the deepening hole. Morgan was tasked with hauling the dirt-filled buckets up by a rope, then dumping them down the hill.

By eight-thirty, the sun was dipping to the western hills. Morgan peered down into the eight-foot-deep hole. Collin was struggling with yet another large rock in the bottom of the pit as the light waned.

Collin looked up. "We could dig to China and never find what we're looking for down here. What if the treasure's here but just twenty feet on one side or the other? We could dig up the whole hill and never find it. We'd better stop for tonight before it gets too dark up here on the hillside."

Morgan shone her torch down on the men. "There you go again. Kathy told me how you look at the glass half empty, Brother. Keep digging. I feel that we are close to our birthright."

Collin cursed himself for falling into his former bad habits. But he was tired. Dog tired.

Morgan came around to hold the top of the ladder. As she grasped its uprights and pulled them back toward her, the top edge of the hole caved in behind it. Earth rained down on the men, filling the pit back up to their knees.

Collin pulled one foot and then the other out of the dirt to free himself as he headed to the base of the ladder. "Watch out, Morgan. Now we need to get out of here and start again tomorrow." He clambered up out of the hole on the downhill side. The sun was slipping from view behind the western hill, and the crickets started their evening song.

Morgan heard Jack's startled voice from below. "What's this?"

She switched on her torch and shone it down on her suitor. Jack already had his torch on and was examining something he found in the pile of dirt that the ladder had dislodged.

"What is it, Jack?"

"An old coin I found here in the dirt," he whispered in awe.

"Bring it up, Jack."

He started up the ladder with his torch, then stopped, transfixed. "You've got to come down to see this."

Morgan backed down the ladder. Jack was standing at its base, scooping the dirt away from it. She turned her torch on the collapsed wall behind it. There, glistening in the light, was a cache of coins just at the level of the caved-in dirt. The end of a rotten chest was torn open, exposing the treasure.

"We found it, Collin!" Morgan cried. "It was just a little farther down the hill than we guessed." Her brother peered over the top of the hole, holding his finger vertically to his lips. Speaking softly, he said, "Quiet, down there."

At that moment, four Crossley tenders full of Auxiliaries came rumbling down the Lough Derg Road toward the dock, passing by over the hill to their east. In the still night air, they heard men barking orders to get out of vehicles and search the area.

Collin crept east along the edge of the tree line to where he could see torches flickering below. An officer marshaled his fifty men to spread out in their search. He yelled the name Joe Sweeney and the men started to move faster. A group of them had boarded the boat, and they were headed to Station Island, while others started down the pilgrim's path toward Saints Island.

He scrambled back to the hole where Jack and Morgan were still probing at the old casket end. He whispered down to them. "Get out of there! Now! Turn your torches off! Quick! We need to bury the end of the casket."

They scrambled out, pulling the ladder after them. Fortunately, there was no moonlight to illuminate them. They all started shoveling dirt from the piles beside the hole back into it as quietly as they could. Fortunately, the gnarled tree partially hid them from the path below. Half an hour later, with all three shoveling, the depth was reduced to two feet, just a deeper depression, and the treasure was once more buried. They couldn't get rid of the pile of rocks they had hefted out of the hole. Up until now, the Auxiliaries had not ventured up towards St Dabheog's chair from the pilgrim's path. Ten of the enemy not a thousand feet below their position had turned up the hill wielding their rifles.

Collin whispered, "We need to get out of here. The treasure will be safe overnight. Let's take the ladder and all of our equipment."

They headed southeast, off into the woods, walking as silently as possible, feeling their way in the dark toward the hiding place of the horse cart. The three passed within a hundred feet of Abbad, Fazaar, and Molly, who were lying prone in the underbrush, silently waiting for their chance.

The horses snorted softly at their approach. They could hear the Auxiliaries out on the lough reaching the island. They were met by the furor of friars and pilgrims all shouting. Collin snuck down the road and around the bend toward the dock to find out the troop movement while Morgan and Jack loaded the cart. They left the ladder in the woods near where the horses were tied.

Jack was getting up into the cart and taking the reins, and Collin appeared, muttering, "We'd better go. There are still a few of those bastards hovering around their lorries, and it'll soon be after curfew. Who knows when they will come back this way."

Jack walked the horses until about a mile south on the Pettigo Road. That way, he could muzzle the horses if they made too much noise. At least it was pitch-black. He hoped there wouldn't be any more police lorries arriving at the lough.

Finally, judging that they were at a safe distance, Jack got their horses ambling down the road, leaving the treasure behind them. If the Auxies came across the pit, they might wonder about it but probably wouldn't dig deeper. A rebel leader was the treasure they sought.

Jack gave Morgan the one coin he picked up. She turned it over and over in her fingers as they headed back to Pettigo, worried that the digging was fresh and the risks of exposure were real. She cautioned, "We'll have to come back tomorrow morning, boys, as soon as the Auxies are gone."

The two men nodded in agreement.

♣ ♣ ♣ ♣

Abbad followed the Adventurers to their cart in the darkness and watched them leave. Then he returned, picking up Fazaar and Molly. They climbed down to the pit and peered at the newly disturbed depression. The darkness held what they wanted.

"The epistle is down there. I can feel it," Abbad whispered. "Under all that dirt. I heard them say they found something."

Fazaar saw the ten Auxiliaries shining torches and spreading out three hundred feet below. One was starting toward their location. He tapped his cousin's shoulder and forced him to look down the hill.

Molly whispered, "Abbad, we need to move higher to the shelter of the trees."

The three scampered back upslope and saw lights in the trees to their left coming from the road.

Abbad scanned all around them. He hated to leave the coveted prize, but his revolver would be no match for even ten of them. Besides, his shoulder was still too sore for fighting. He couldn't risk drawing the Brits to this disturbed location. "We've got to get away from here tonight. But after centuries of searching, we're going to get the epistle and treasure tomorrow before those O'Donnells and McCarthys come back. We'll retreat overnight farther up in the woods or until the damned mercenaries leave since our vehicle is at the boat dock where they parked their Crossleys."

Chapter Fourteen
Escape

Monday, June 13, 1921
Pettigo, Donegal, Ireland

The Adventurers slipped back into Pettigo after curfew, leaving the horses and cart at the livery. They overheard the police drinking in the Pettigo Pub as they crept by in the dark.

At six the next morning, Morgan, already dressed, knocked on the adjoining bedroom door. "Rise and shine, lads. We need an early start."

She heard a muffled response through the woodwork. "Give us a few minutes, Morgan."

"I'll meet you, sleepyheads, for breakfast downstairs in the restaurant. Get a move on."

Twenty minutes later, alone in the just-opened restaurant, a brazen waitress was taking Morgan's order for coffee and rolls when the first two Auxiliaries came in and sat down in a booth nearby. Morgan wondered if she should leave but decided to stay. She and her men had avoided the attention of the enemy until now.

The Auxiliaries became annoyed the waitress wasn't immediately attending to them. One got up and came to Morgan's table. "We're waiting, woman."

The waitress looked up from her notepad. "I'll be there when I finish up here."

The soldier took hold of the waitress's arm and tried to pull her away.

She tried to break away. "You're hurting me."

The Auxie tightened his grip. "Leave off, woman."

Instinctively, Morgan stood up, coming to the woman's defense. "Let her go. You're bruising her arm."

Still holding the waitress like a vise, the soldier spun around, spying Morgan with a lecherous eye. "You're a comely lass with a big mouth. Sit down."

Morgan's green eyes flashed as she stood her ground.

The Auxie let the waitress go and turned on Morgan. "I like a girl with spunk, and you're a grand colleen. It's been too long. I have an hour before reporting for duty. We could have a good time together." He stepped forward and tugged at her shirt collar.

The top two buttons popped, exposing her breast. He grasped her blouse and held on as she struggled to get away.

"I've got a real live one here, George," the Auxie yelled at his mate just as Collin and Jack entered the restaurant. Jack was on him in an instant. He punched the Auxie square in the stomach.

The man's cohort got up from his seat and pinned Jack's hands behind his back. Two more Auxiliaries walked in and went toward Morgan.

Collin assessed the situation. His two compatriots were going to be arrested, no question. He could probably knock one of the bastards out before the others drew their Webleys, but then they'd all be incarcerated. He hated to see the lout lay his hands on his sister, but he had to be smart.

He pulled out his No. 2 Brownie camera. "What's going on here, officer? I am a newspaper reporter with *The Irish Times*." He snapped a picture of the Auxie manhandling Morgan. "It looks to me that you are accosting an innocent woman."

Another Auxie demanded, "Show me your papers."

Collin flashed his credentials.

The lout holding onto Morgan sneered, "This woman resisted an officer. I'm teaching her a lesson."

Collin shook his head at Morgan to get her to stop squirming. "A lesson in what, might I ask? You are manhandling her."

"To exact obedience from her."

Collin moved forward and took a close-up of the policeman's hands entangled in her blouse, ripping it open. "My newspaper will be very interested in your lessons, I should think. Especially since I witnessed your technique myself."

The Auxie let go of Morgan's shirt, then grasped her left hand, pulling her away. She used her other arm to cover herself and dragged her feet.

Jack tore free and went to Morgan's aid, but the attacker would have none of that. The bruiser punched Jack in the face and regained control of his prisoner.

"Let's take these two to the barracks, George."

Collin stepped in front of them. "On what charge, officer?"

"Attacking an officer and resisting arrest." He drew his Webley and pointed it at Collin's heart. "Take the film out of your camera."

Collin couldn't do anything about the situation. The other soldiers were amused by the proceedings, their eyes on Morgan trying to cover herself. He opened the camera, stripped out the roll of film, and handed it to the officer. At least this way, he could keep the camera.

The officer holding Morgan snatched the film and pushed Collin out of the way. Collin feigned weakness and let the man do it. He resisted the urge to threaten the man by mentioning the clout that the newspaper had in the community.

When the Auxiliaries departed with Morgan and Jack, Collin followed at a distance to the barracks where the jail would undoubtedly be located. Then he went back to the restaurant.

He learned from the Auxiliaries streaming in for breakfast that they had not found Sweeney the night before. If he'd been on Station Island, then the prior must have hidden him well. They were going back out to the lough in force to search until they found a rebel and apprehended him.

What a mess thought Collin. It would not be a good day to return to Dabheog's Chair for the treasure. The most important action was to free Morgan and Jack. Hopefully, the police wouldn't connect Morgan to Tadgh McCarthy as his accomplice or to her alias, Bernice Jordan, the guard killer. Her peasant disguise was rudimentary but effective. He had two avenues to pursue. First contact Healy and have the paper apply pressure, although he doubted that would work. Second, ask Aiden to send Volunteers to attack the RIC Pettigo Barracks and free Morgan and Jack.

Collin found the hotel telephone. With the help of the waitress, who confirmed the boorish behavior of the policeman, he convinced the owner to let him use the phone. He hoped it wasn't being monitored by the police.

His first call was to *The Irish Times*. The publisher took the call. "Where are you, O'Donnell? Things are developing fast here in Dublin, and you should be reporting on them. Robertson called me and asked why your articles dried up."

Collin knew this phone call was a mistake. "I'm sorry, sir. I am in Donegal. My sister was accosted and arrested by Auxiliaries. I am trying to get her out of jail."

"The same one you were searching for five years ago?"

"The same, Sir."

"There's not much I can do to get her released, lad. My hands are tied. Do an article on police brutality, and I will run it. It might stop them mistreating her in jail and fit well with the talks starting at high levels."

"I will. Thank you, sir. What talks?"

"It's early yet, but I've heard the Pope's admonition and call for peaceful resolution is influencing the powers that be. The escalation with the burning Custom House was a pivotal event. We'll have to see how it plays out. I need you here, Collin."

"That is good news, Sir. I'm encouraged for the first time. But the war up here in Donegal is entrenched. I'll get there as soon as I can. Perhaps you could let Mr. Robertson know my predicament."

"I can do that, lad. Send reports of the conflict in Donegal and get back as soon as you can. I'll cover for you with your boss."

"Thank you, Mr. Healy."

The publisher had rung off. Collin took the risk. He called the tailor shop and talked to Biddy O'Donnell without revealing the plight of her niece.

"Can you tell me where Aidan is right now, Auntie?"

"Do you remember the address and name I gave you before you left?"

Collin knew the Letterkenny address for Cogan. "Yes, Auntie. Thank you." *Isn't Biddy the crafty one?*

"When will you and Morgan come back to Meenmore, Collin?"

"I don't know yet, Auntie. Have there been more raids?"

"Yes, but no more burnings. It was reported in the newspaper that the British have called off burning reprisals as of the sixth."

Collin knew that this was consistent with what the local newspaper and Healy had been saying. "I'll get back to you, Auntie. Stay safe."

"You as well, dear. Be safe!"

Collin went to the RIC barracks and asked to see the prisoners, showing his newspaper credentials. The policeman at the counter confirmed two prisoners brought in that morning were both charged and present, but he shrugged his shoulders. Collin was not allowed to see them.

The officer added, with a foul breath, "With all the commotion, I expect they will be here for quite a while before being transported to the jail in Derry."

Collin doggedly pressed on. "I see. I was present in the hotel restaurant this morning when the incident occurred. The woman was physically accosted by your officer, and I was a witness, Sir. My newspaper publisher approved my writing an article about police brutality in this incident." He handed the officer his card. "As you can see, I represent a unionist newspaper. May I know the names of the Auxiliary officers involved?"

The officer had already turned away, sorting papers on his desk. He spun back around, scowling, "Eh? Are you still here? No, you may not."

"I will note that you refused to give me the names in my article. I trust there will be no more mistreatment of the prisoners, then. This will not look good for your barracks."

The officer at the desk ignored the comment with a sneer curving his mouth.

Collin had to think fast. He hated to leave his companions there, but he was powerless to extricate them from this predicament by himself. He counted at least ten officers in the barracks, and many more spread throughout the town, so he returned to the hotel to plan.

They were both counting on him. While he ate eggs and bacon in the restaurant, he wondered whether Morgan and Jack would be fed. His mind raced. Any thoughts of removing the treasure from the pit were secondary to getting his sister and friend out of jail before something more drastic happened. That meant that he had to go to Peader's flying column hideout for help. He and Aidan would have the men to get the job done. Collin's mind flooded with the memory of what happened to Tadgh when he was incarcerated. If these goons identified Morgan, her neck would be on the block.

There was no time to waste. *What if the Volunteers were out on a prolonged mission?* Consulting his map, Collin traced his route of forty-five miles to Peader's hideout west of Letterkenny.

He wondered whether he could borrow, or in this case, pilfer an automobile for the trip. He walked the town in search of a good candidate. The only motor vehicles that he found were the Auxiliaries' lorries, which were not a viable option. He was stuck with the horses and Jaunting cart at the livery and calculated that it would take ten hours to get there.

It was nearly three o'clock before he could leave Pettigo, having collected the horses, cart, and enough hay to keep the beasts fed, which he tied to the back seats. He placed a shovel in the storage area between them. This was all new to him. He'd never even ridden a horse before, much less driven a rig like this. Fortunately, the blacksmith had been able to hook up the bridle and harness, and he'd watched Jack with the horses.

First, he had an important job to do.

Collin steered the horse cart north on the Lough Derg Road, arriving at the hiding place an hour later without seeing any Auxiliaries. As he started to climb the hill toward St. Dabheog's chair, he found the ladder at the edge of the woods. *Was this where we left it?* He wasn't sure. *Good.* The pit looked the same as he had left it. He couldn't be sure that the Auxies wouldn't come back, and it would have taken him too many hours to excavate he treasure. Alone. Morgan's peril was his first priority.

Instead, using the shovel, he spent the next hour filling the pit with the pile of rocks taken from the hole and stacked above and then shoveling in the remaining dirt. Afterward, he collected pine needles from the nearby tree and scattered them over the depression.

Satisfied he had safely hidden the treasure's location from prying eyes, he headed back to the cart. On the way, he picked up the ladder and took it to the back of the welcome shack. The Lough Derg guard was busy checking out pilgrims returning from the island, so Collin slipped behind the building through the adjacent copse of trees to avoid detection.

He emerged just in time to see a Crossley tender with five Auxiliaries pull up to the dock. They jumped out and started an animated conversation with the guard, demanding to commandeer the boat to Station Island.

Collin used this commotion to slip back into the trees undetected. Once at his cart, he found a pilgrim in a black cloak petting his horses. The man explained he had wandered up from the dock, having heard the horses whinnying.

"Fine animals you have here."

"Thank you. Tell me, are you coming from or going to the island, sir?"

"Coming from. Just waiting for my ride."

"Were you there last night?"

"Quite the disturbance. Policemen came late at night and roused the prior. They searched the island, dormitories, and all. Broke the spell, I can tell you."

"Did they leave with anybody?"

"No. But they seemed upset when they left."

"Do you know if they left a policeman on the island?"

"I don't think so unless he kept out of sight until I left this afternoon."

"Thank you, sir." Collin untied the reins and jumped up into the cart. "Now, I must be off. Good day to you."

Collin steered the horses back south, backtracking past Pettigo before heading northwest toward Donegal Town. Along the way, another police lorry passed him but fortunately paid him no mind.

♣ ♣ ♣ ♣

Morgan lay on the hard, wooden bench they called a bunk in the dank cell of the basement jail at Pettigo RIC Barracks. After the better part of a day, she now understood the routine. At least a matron was decent enough to have brought her a coat to cover her ripped shirtwaist and to ward off the cold. The cell was rough concrete blocks about nine by six feet with one cracked sink and a covered hole in the floor for a toilet. The one blanket was threadbare and of questionable cleanliness. The food was barely edible, consisting of stale bread and a few mushy vegetables twice the first day. She had not been allowed out to exercise.

Morgan kept reminding herself conditions here were far better than what Tadgh endured back at the Joy. She had to fight the urge to dwell on his demise, so she focused on how she could escape after what had been an unwise altercation with the police. But they were infuriating, inhumane. This experience reminded her why her fellow Irishmen were willing to die to get rid of these blaggards. Here she was, sucked right back into the fray.

And Jack, what a gallant friend. How he had come to her aid. At least he was right beside her in the next cell. She couldn't see him, but they could talk. That gave her great comfort. Although they didn't speak of it, she thought that Collin must be doing his utmost to gain their freedom. At least these bastards didn't seem to know who she really was, and she hadn't given them her real name.

At what seemed like it must be near sunset, Morgan finally said, "You were wonderful, Jack, back at the restaurant. Thank you."

She heard him get up off his creaking bench before he spoke. His back must be killing him in the damp cold.

"When we get out of here, and the war is over, we can start a new life together, Morgan. We can buy a house like those colorful cottages that you love near your auntie. Then we can have a brood of children if that's what you want. I'll make you happy, I swear it."

Hearing this, Morgan was still conflicted. It was sweet of Jack to talk of a brighter future to cheer her up. And she had dreamed of those cottages and a family, a big family.

Morgan wasn't up to revisiting her options. "Let's get out of here first, Jack. Then we can talk about the future."

"I'll count the hours."

Collin's backside ached something awful as the horses finally clopped into the outskirts of Letterkenny at five in the morning. The sun was rising past the southern arm of Lough Swilly, painting the rolling countryside in a golden glow. It was as if the world was at peace around him. But Collin knew this was just a temporary respite, very temporary. He'd stopped to allow the horses to feed and drink several times. Not really being a horseman like Jack, Collin wasn't sure how to care for them. They were in better shape than he was, though. In his haste, he had forgotten to bring food and drink for himself. Cogan's farm had to be about five miles west of the town roundabout, according to Biddy.

Collin eased the horses out onto Circular Road, heading away from the town. An hour later, he finally saw a white farmhouse and barn with an attached silo, just like Biddy described. The name on the mailbox was Cogan.

Collin pulled the cart up to the hitching rail in the front yard and descended, tying the reins.

He saw the front window curtain part, and the barrel of a rifle appeared behind the glass. Then the front door flew open.

Aidan rushed out to greet him. "What's wrong, Collin?"

The lad was becoming quite perceptive. "Morgan and Jack were arrested and jailed in Pettigo, and I need your help."

Aidan waved him toward the building, "Come in, come in. We don't tend to stay out of doors unless we're on a mission, don't ya know."

Once inside, Collin's eyes adjusted to the curtained darkness. The parlor was rustic at best, with a stone fireplace built against the outside wall. About ten men were sprawled on various worn-out furniture pieces and the threadbare rug in front of the roaring fire. It wasn't that much different from Creagh, other than this building was smaller and at least temporarily was still standing.

"Cousin, is that you?" Peader got up slowly from his chair by the fire.

Collin grasped his cousin's arm in greeting and noticed that Peader winced at the touch. "Arm still hurting?"

"A little, Collin. But I am getting stronger day by day. We're back at full strength and giving the bloody British fits." He pointed to a large table in the corner. "Sit down and join us."

"I need your help, Peader. It's urgent."

Peader called several of his men to the table and explained, "We're about to have a planning meeting for a mission to blow up a bridge in a few hours. We can talk after I deploy the men."

Collin observed his strong leadership skills, his solicitation of ideas, his confident voice, the attention of his men. He had changed since Collin visited him about five years earlier at his home in Meenmore. His belief in civil unrest was replaced with a vehement hatred of British occupation. Collin decided to ask him how that transformation had come about when they both had a spare moment.

After the meeting was over, Peader came into the sparse kitchen and offered Collin a refreshment. Their icebox was leaking, and the sink unattended. "What brings you here to us, Collin?"

Aidan overheard the question from the parlor and broke free of the column members to join his commander. "Collin says that Morgan has been accosted and imprisoned in the Pettigo jail by Auxiliaries."

"Do they know who she is?"

Collin clenched his fists before he answered. "I hope not, Peader. She's smart enough to give them a false name since she has no identification. I want to break her and her friend Jack out of jail. Doesn't your flying column attack RIC barracks?"

"It is a legitimate target, but Pettigo is out of my brigade's territory down in No. 4 Battalion. Sam O'Flaherty is OC there. I have already gotten the ire of my Derry counterpart and questions from GHQ. As you can see, we are constantly on the run. Our new OC Northern Division, headed by Sweeney, would have to authorize an attack on that barracks."

Collin saw an opening. "They have been looking for Joe Sweeney down at Lough Derg for the last two days, without success, I expect. We could find him."

"I was told he took a tumble on his bicycle and was in need of rest."

Aidan stepped forward and pleaded with his OC to help.

Peader stroked his beard. "I'll tell you what I will do. I'll send Aidan with two of my men to guide you to Sam O'Flaherty's hideout in Castlefinn. If he agrees to support such a mission, then we will make it a combined attack with the men I have provided."

"Thank you, sir."

Collin capped Peader on the back. "Thank you, cousin."

"You can thank me when Morgan's freed. You look like you could do with a rest. Have you slept?"

"Not in the last twenty-four hours."

"Then have some breakfast with us before we head out on our mission. Take your rest until midday before leaving."

Collin shook his head. "I'll gladly take your food, but we don't have any time to spare."

Peader took command. "You'll be no use to your sister if you're dead and not just dead-tired."

Aidan announced that he would be ready to go at one o'clock.

That afternoon, Collin and Aidan headed southeast down Letterkenny Road in the Jaunting cart toward Castlefinn, fifteen miles away, accompanied by two hand-picked Volunteers on bicycles. The flying column boys wore civilian clothing borrowed from a local sheepherder. When they arrived at Sam O'Flaherty's home, they were told that the OC No. 4 Brigade was out on maneuvers with no set time for return.

Agonizingly, the four men had to wait four days for Sam's return. Collin had thought of just proceeding with their contingent, but Aidan reminded him of the need to get O'Flaherty's approval.

Finally, on the night of Sunday, June 19, Sam arrived home, tired, and with two of his men injured.

"Damn those British devils. They laid a trap for us at Kelly's Bridge. We had to scatter, and we've been on the run ever since. Two of my men have been killed."

Aidan started to introduce Collin and his team.

Sam interjected. "They don't think much of your OC of No. 2 Brigade, lad. O'Donnell's a loose cannon."

Aidan came to his defense. "He's getting the job done, sir, and I think he was dead right about Carney, too."

"Is that so, lad?"

Collin was tired of waiting, and this chit-chat was driving him mad. There was no telling what had become of Morgan and Jack. He cut in. "How would you like to strike hard against your enemy?"

"That's what I am trying to do every day."

"You might even save your OC Sweeney in the bargain."

Sam felt guilty that his boss, Sweeney, had been forced to flee from his home and saw the merit of trying to rescue him. Collin explained what he knew of the Auxiliary's search for him on Lough Derg.

"I heard he was going there."

"I want to attack the RIC barracks at Pettigo as well, Sam."

"A valuable target, to be sure, and it would disrupt their operations here in southwest Donegal. Why do you want to do this? You're a reporter, not a freedom fighter."

Collin explained what had happened to Morgan and Jack.

Sam huffed. "Those Limey bastards think they can abuse our womenfolk at will. I'd kill them all if I could get them alone, one by one."

"Well then?" Collin raised his eyebrows.

"I'll join you, myself, with seven of my men. We will search for my superior, Sweeney, and then head for Pettigo with his approval."

"What if we don't find your boss?"

"Then we will attack the Pettigo RIC Barracks anyway."

"Good. Thank you, sir. When can we leave?"

"We'll leave tomorrow morning at first light. Meanwhile, you are welcome to eat and rest here at my home. Just need to keep an eye and ear open for the devils with the berets."

The combined flying column skirted around Pettigo in two nondescript rural lorries before heading north on the Lough Derg Road the next morning, June 20, having traveled a total of twenty-seven miles. There were no Auxiliaries at the dock to Station Island at noon. All the arriving pilgrims had already been transported to the island. The welcoming guard recognized Collin and let him, Aidan, and Sam cross by boat.

As always, the prior was waiting for the boat when it landed.

"O'Donnell, is it? The knowledgeable pilgrim, as I recall."

"Yes, sir. We're looking for Joe Sweeney, a colleague of ours. We were told he might be coming to you."

"You're not policemen, then?"

Sam stepped forward and shook the religious leader's hand. "No, sir. We are Volunteers trying to give our people the right to worship as they see fit without deadly recrimination."

"That's more or less what Mr. Sweeney said when he came to visit almost a week ago now."

"May we see him, Prior?"

"I'm afraid not. He stayed for four days, then left last Saturday once his face healed."

Sam slapped his thigh. "Damn. Do you know where he was going, Prior?"

"I'm afraid not, son. We learn not to ask a lot of questions these days. Better to focus on saving souls here."

Collin asked, "Speaking of that, I met a pilgrim who had been here when the Auxiliaries raided your island, Prior. Where did you hide our commander, if you don't mind my asking?"

"In plain sight, my son. We dressed him as a priest, put on a false beard, and had him sleeping with the other friars in their cells." The prior stared into Collin's eyes. "Did you find what you were looking for, lad?"

"What do you mean, Sir?"

"It was clear to me you are not a Catholic man, although you may be a Christian. And all those questions."

"We're still searching, sir."

Sam, Collin, and Aidan got back in the boat. The prior made the sign of the cross as they pushed off from the dock. "May God be with you, with all of you. We all need to listen to God's word, especially these days."

With that, the three men headed back to the dock where the rest of the column was waiting.

Sam spoke first. "We're not waiting for approval at the division level. This is my brigade now. We are going to attack the RIC barracks tonight and free O'Donnell's relatives."

At eight o'clock, while the integrated flying column waited in the woods opposite the RIC Barracks on Main Street, Collin returned to that police station. The officer at the desk remembered him.

"Did you file your article?"

"Not yet," answered Collin. I'm waiting to see if there is any repeat police brutality. Are the woman and man still here?"

"Until tomorrow. Now that the search is over, some of our men are returning to Derry. The prisoners will be going with them under guard."

Collin thought before he spoke. *Damned lucky we got here tonight, then.* Would it be better to wait and attack when they were on their way and mobile? Too much chance of them being caught in the crossfire, and Sam wanted the prize of destroying these barracks.

"I want to see them and determine if they have been harmed."

"That is out of the question. Now beat it."

"Then I will submit my scathing article to *The Irish Times* tomorrow."

"If I let you see them briefly and they have not been harmed, will you tear up your article and not submit it?"

"There is the matter of the original attempted rape by your officer and confiscation of my film, the visual evidence. I have additional witnesses."

Collin could see that the officer was rattled. He tapped his pencil furiously on his desk. "If I let you see them, you must drop your article on the whole matter."

"And they still go to jail?"

"That will be up to a judge."

"All right. I won't report on this matter."

"You'll be sorry if I see your article in print. They'll pay." The desk officer called to one of the three other policemen standing nearby listening and ordered him to take him to see the two prisoners being held in Cells 4 and 5.

Collin counted twelve stone steps from the main office to the jail below and ten cells behind solid wooden doors, each with a slat to pass food trays through. God, how awful for Morgan. He knew Jack could take it. The smells of urine and mold were pungent, and a rat scurried against the stone walls.

The single bulb in the ceiling flickered intermittently as the officer went to the wall opposite the cells and chose a key off the rack. Collin noted it was on the number four hook.

"Stand against that wall where I can see you," the officer ordered, drawing his Webley. He pointed it at Collin, who complied, with his hands placed where the guard could see them. The guard turned the key and pulled with all his might to move the creaking door on its rusted hinges.

When the door was open enough to squeeze through, he gestured to Collin by flicking the muzzle of his revolver toward the door.

Collin had to decide. Were they luring him into the cell to lock him in?

"Bring her out to me, or my deal with your superior is off."

The guard hesitated and then went into the cell. Collin thought that it would be safe enough to go in as long as the guard was in there with him. He was sure he could handle him if necessary. He stepped over the threshold and into the near darkness. The guard nudged a body lying on the wooden bed.

"Sis, is that you?" He spoke to the figure, who stirred and sat up in a halting motion. "Oh, Collin!"

Collin went to her but kept himself between the guard and the door. The man showed no inclination to bolt. She embraced him and started to cry.

He examined her as best he could in the light. "Have they hurt you?"

"No, other than staying in this awful place with the rats."

"They're going to take you and Jack to Derry tomorrow. I am working with Mr. Healy at the paper to mount a defense in court. We will get you and Jack free."

"Thank God, Collin! I've done no wrong."

"Of course not, lass. They'll be punished. I hate to leave you, but you will be out in the light tomorrow. I will see you in Derry." Collin reached over to kiss her forehead and pushed a piece of paper into her hand in the dark cell.

She closed her hand over it as she gripped his shoulder.

Collin hated to do it, but he turned away. "I have to go now. Whatever happens, don't lose heart."

The guard pushed the door closed, locking her into that black dungeon with the only light blinking through the food slot. He put the key back on the hook.

The process was repeated in Jack's cell, where Collin saw the key on hook number five. Jack seemed in good spirits given the situation but complained that his back pain had flared up due to the dampness and challenging sleeping conditions. He, too, received the same verbal input and written message on a piece of paper, delivered in a similar secretive way, but without the kiss on the forehead.

Collin hoped they could somehow read what he had written in the darkness.

In both cases, they had put the paper at an angle to the doorway light and had barely read the message just before the door slammed shut. Morgan began to cry as she read the words,

> *Aidan and Peader's men are outside. We are going to attack this barracks in two hours to free you. Be ready.*
> *Love, Collin.*

Collin thanked the desk officer and lied through his teeth that the prisoners had been treated fairly. The officer reminded him of his commitment to shelve the article, and Collin exited the barracks. He hoped to hell the guard had not seen the note transfer to the prisoners, that their element of surprise would not be lost.

When he rejoined the flying column in the trees outside town, Collin reported the building layout, including the jail, and the fact that only four policemen were visible in the main room.

"What about the upstairs barracks?"

"I don't know. I couldn't hear any more voices. There were many more Auxies here when I left five days ago." Sam checked their readiness. The flying column had ten men, nine rifles, each man having forty rounds, and a total of three Mills bombs.

As one more check on the situation, Collin walked back down the main street. He poked his head into the restaurant of the Pettigo Inn and then the pub down the road, counting a total of a dozen Auxies enjoying libations. Then he checked on three Crossley tenders out behind the barracks. Noticing keys on the wall behind the officer's desk, Collin speculated they were for the trucks.

At nine-thirty, as dusk settled into the night in the moonlit sky, the flying column snuck to the back of the barracks just before the curfew went into effect. Aidan disconnected and removed the electrical spark plug wires in two of the lorries, throwing them into the woods behind the parking area. They would use the third armored vehicle, conveniently fueled for their escape. It afforded more protection than their vehicles, and it could carry all the men. They'd come back for their vehicles later.

The column had to move swiftly now. The Auxies would be tumbling out of the pub to roam the streets, looking for anyone violating the curfew in a few minutes.

O'Flaherty took the lead. Leaving one sentry to guard the escape vehicles and another to guard the front entrance to the barracks, he took the rest of his men and rushed into the central office, firing their handguns. Two of the three Auxies died where they stood. The desk officer ducked under his desk and unholstered his Webley. Sam calmly stepped behind the desk and shot him in the head before he could discharge his weapon. Then he plucked the keys off the hooks on the wall behind the desk.

Collin realized he had just crossed the line, abetting rebels in their killing spree to save his sister once again. That would only matter if any British enemy forces who had seen him remained alive after this attack. He had no weapon, but he was prepared to support murder if it meant his sister would be released. He had fleeting thoughts of Kathy's warning to avoid risks before he left home but quickly snapped back to the brutal reality of the moment, a time for immediate action.

The fourth policeman darted through an internal door. They could hear him calling up the stairs.

Sam motioned five of his men to follow the Limey. Collin and Aidan descended to retrieve the prisoners from the jail.

A minute later, the first Mills bomb thrown up the stairs caught the fourth Auxie and then five more rushing down the stairs. The back offices and stairs were instantly ablaze.

Down in the dungeon, Collin grasped the number four key and threw the number five to Aidan, pointing, "Next one down."

Collin pulled open the number four cell door, and Morgan rushed out. She'd read the note.

She threw her arms around his neck. "Oh, Collin."

Collin disengaged her and held her hand. "No time for that now, lass."

Aidan opened cell number 5 and rushed in for Jack. He was up but limping badly. Aidan put his arm around his waist. Together they headed for the stairs.

Suddenly, they heard the shouts of other prisoners down the line. Collin hesitated and then said, "Morgan, go with Aidan. I will be right behind you."

Aidan took Morgan's hand in his free hand and helped them up toward the mayhem above.

Collin removed the keys from the hooks. One by one, he opened the remaining doors, then bolted up the stairs, yelling, "Hurry! Follow me. The building's on fire!"

Collin rushed up the stairs and burst into the main office. It was ablaze. Morgan, Jack, and Aidan were nowhere to be seen. Near the other offices and stairs, Sam was shepherding his men out the back door. Some of the men carried stolen Auxiliaries weapons. Collin rushed after them.

The activity in the back parking area was one of military precision. Aidan had Morgan and Jack in the operable Crossley. Jack sat in the middle of the front seat with Morgan beside him, hugging her tightly.

Sam was behind the wheel, trying all the keys. The rest of the column, including Aidan and Collin, squeezed into the back bed of the lorry. One was wounded in the hand.

The Volunteer guarding the front of the building rushed around, yelling that the Auxies were coming out of the pub and restaurant. He scrambled up into the Crossley.

Sam found the right key, and the engine coughed to life. The only way out of the parking area was down one side of the barracks and into the main street.

"Keep your heads down, everyone!" Sam yelled. The main barracks building and its neighbor had both caught fire. Sam wheeled the lorry through the flames between them and pulled onto Main Street. The remaining Auxies from the burning barracks started firing. The Crossley was caught between the group at the pub and the one from the restaurant.

Sam chose to veer left toward the restaurant—fewer of the enemy in that direction.

They flashed by four Auxies firing at them from the restaurant doorway. The front windscreen took a direct hit on the passenger side, with glass flying. Jack instinctively twisted around and threw his body in front of Morgan to protect her.

A few seconds later, another Crossley barreled down a side alley to ram them. Auxies were hanging out the side. Bullets thudded into the side of the vehicle. Aidan snatched up the second Mills bomb, pulled the pin, and let it fly. He timed his throw perfectly. It exploded behind the cab, detonating the petrol tank. The lorry flew up, bursting in flames, and crashed short of Main Street. As they rushed by, an Auxie, his clothes on fire, stumbled towards them, his bomb in hand. As he reached up to throw, it exploded, killing him instantly. Shrapnel rained down on the column.

The remaining Auxies from the restaurant raced to the back of the barracks for the lorries. Without keys, they tried the hand cranks. Without spark plug wires, the engines wouldn't start.

Sam raced north out of town on the road towards Lough Derg, then turned northeast on Inisclin Road, hugging the boundary between Donegal and the county of Tyrone, now officially Northern Ireland.

Morgan noticed Jack sag as he still gripped her front to front. Then a warm liquid oozed onto her right hand. She looked at his face.

"Are you all right, Jack?"

"Been better," he rasped.

"Jack, you're bleeding!"

Morgan put her arm around him, carefully felt around Jack's back, and touched the edge of a sharp piece of glass.

"Can you stop the lorry, sir?"

"What's the matter?"

"Jack has been injured."

"We need to be certain first that we're not being followed."

Sam continued driving for several minutes before pulling into a suitable blind sidetrack. He shut off the motor, hopped down, and came around, opening the passenger side door.

"Your friend has been hit by several pieces of the windscreen glass now embedded in his back. I'm going to lift him out onto the grass."

Morgan was soon administering to Jack, with Aidan by her side.

"Have you got any first aid supplies?"

"The Crossley tenders usually carry a kit under the dashboard. I'll get it, Ma'am."

Morgan realized the meager kit would have to do.

Having checked on his men, Sam returned to where Jack lay on his stomach. "We can't stay here very long."

Morgan had a dim recollection of trying to remove the wood spears from poor Tadgh's leg onboard Fritz's German U-Boat submarine. It seemed eons ago, in another mad world. She shook the vision away. Her thoughts shifted to Jack, who had just thrown his body in harm's way to save her. "Give me a few minutes. I have to remove the glass."

"When you're done, can you make your way over here quickly? One of my men was shot in his hand."

Collin sat with Aidan and the other Volunteers in the truck bed. As he watched Morgan work on Jack, he remembered the pain when the Black Tom shrapnel pierced his lung after shielding Kathy. That seemed a lifetime ago, though it had only been five years. So much had happened. Tadgh was dead. He knew he was losing the battle to convince his sister to go to Canada. Jack was winning her over, and his selfless action was going to help his cause.

Collin chastised himself for that thought, selfish. Looking in the direction of Lough Derg and fingering the coin in his pocket, he wondered when they would be able to return to claim their birthright.

Chapter Fifteen
Bloody Sunday Belfast

Monday, June 20, 1921
On the Road to Castlefinn, Co. Fermanagh, Ireland

ack's wounds were more severe than Morgan first thought. They laid him out on his stomach in the bed of the lorry, with Morgan attending to him for the journey.

She worried that one of the glass spears might have punctured a lung, but he didn't seem short of breath, and his pulse rate was normal. Collin and Aidan stayed with them, and two Volunteers sat up front with Sam. After Morgan had done all she could for Jack, she turned to the wounded volunteer. Fortunately, the bullet passed through the web between his thumb and forefinger without severing any tendons or ligaments.

An hour later, they had passed through Tyrone and stopped outside Killygordon back in Donegal. Here No. 4 Brigade kept lorries in an unused barn. Sam backed the Crossley up to the doors, and they transferred the Volunteers to two of the lorries before locking the Auxies vehicle in the barn. This new truck was too valuable to discard, yet they didn't want to be caught in it when the inevitable manhunt reprisal began.

Once they had reached Sam's home in Castlefinn, Sam cautioned Aidan. "You must leave with your friends as soon as Jack is able."

Aidan knew all too well that invading the beehive would bring on the swarm, at least in southwest Donegal. He hoped they would not seek retribution from the friars on Station Island.

Two days later, on the 22nd, the newspaper's front-page story boldly told that King George V officially opened the first Northern Ireland parliament, where he delivered an impassioned appeal for peace.

. . . I speak from a full heart when I pray that my coming to Ireland today may prove to be the first step towards the end of strife among her people, whatever their race or creed. In that hope I appeal to all Irishmen to pause, to stretch out the hand of forbearance and conciliation, to forgive and forget, and to join in making for the land they love a new era of peace, contentment, and goodwill . . .

Collin realized that this was what Healy had been alluding to—the Government of Ireland Act, creating a partition between the southern twenty-six counties and the six unionist counties of Northern Ireland, was now cast in stone, like it or not. Initially, the King's appeal was scoffed at in the O'Flaherty camp as they planned another road demolition.

Sam received news that their attack on the RIC barracks at Pettigo brought hundreds of incensed Auxiliaries back to the area. Some raced through Castlefinn on their way south. They weren't going to leave anytime soon.

Morgan took Collin aside at Jack's bedside before they left the safe house on Friday the 24th. "I am apprehensive about Jack's condition. At least he isn't coughing up blood, which is a good sign for his lungs. But he has an infection in two of the six wounds, and I don't have proper medicine to treat him."

Morgan had gotten all the glass out as far as she could determine. She looked around to confirm they were alone before speaking. "We need to go back to Meenmore before coming back for the treasure."

Collin realized that just as he had been more worried about Morgan, she was now more worried about Jack. He checked Jack's forehead for himself. He was burning up. "I agree, Morgan. I went back to the pit before I went for Aidan's support. It looked the same as when we left it. I finished filling it in."

"What about the rocks we pulled out?"

Collin explained what he had done to cover the excavation. He parroted Morgan's earlier words, "If it lay there for more than three hundred years, a few more days won't hurt."

Jack writhed as a pain spasm wracked his body, and he coughed out, "I'll be all right if you want to get the treasure first."

Morgan put a cold compress on his brow. "Nonsense, Jack. You need medical assistance, and it is too dangerous to go back to Lough Derg right now."

Sam gave them one of the lorries since he now had the Crossley tender, a vehicle that could be used to infiltrate the enemy once the reprisal rage died down. Sam explained that the column would return to Pettigo to collect their other vehicles.

Morgan and Collin laid Jack on his stomach in the back seat of the lorry with a blanket over him. Morgan hopped in and cradled Jack's head in her lap while Collin and Aidan jumped into the front seat. Then they headed northwest toward Meenmore, leaving the jaunting cart and horses at O'Flaherty's disposal.

Biddy welcomed them back, thankful they were all alive. Aidan left with the lorry to return to Peader and No. 2 Brigade in Letterkenny. Collin decided to return to Dublin and wondered if he would be a hunted man since he had shown his credentials to the officer in Pettigo. What a state of affairs; he had to hope all the Auxies who could identify him had been killed during their attack on the barracks.

Before leaving for the train station, Collin took Morgan aside. "I'd venture that the King's appeal for peace will be the beginning-of-the-end to this war. We should be able to recover the treasure when I come back to Meenmore in a fortnight. I want you to give some thought to the benefit of coming to Canada with me."

"Not now, Collin. Poor Jack."

"As I already said, he can come with us, Sis. I insist."

"He wants to stay in Ireland and make a life here in Donegal, Collin. And I can't just leave Aidan, now, can I?"

"I'm not taking no for an answer this time, Morgan."

"It's not up to you, Collin. Do whatever you have to do and come back here safe and sound. If Jack recovers, maybe I can figure out a way to retrieve the treasure myself."

"Not on your life, Morgan. I can't have you captured again. And how could you dig it up by yourself anyway? No. The treasure is safely buried."

She hugged him and sent him on his way, thinking that big brothers could be a bother.

A week later, on Sunday, July 3rd, Head Constable Duffy led yet another raiding party into Dungloe in reprisal for earlier No. 1 Brigade attacks. He was ignoring orders to stop harassing innocent citizens. Word got back to Peader in Letterkenny, and he sent Aidan to make sure his ma would be protected. By the time he arrived in Meenmore, Duffy had already forced entry into many homes and arrested several townsmen. Fortunately, due to the British order, he stopped short of burning them out.

Aidan questioned No. 1 Brigade OC James Cole as to who was responsible for the targeted raids that threatened his family.

"We suspect a roving fishmonger, name of John Collins, living in Ramelton and traveling around with a horse and van. We notified Michael at GHQ, who is not related, and he checked with his informer at Dublin Castle. The fishmonger is a British agent passing Duffy messages hidden inside the fish."

Aidan was incensed. "What are we going to do about it?"

"I've ordered Collins arrested when he returns to his wife in Ramelton. Meanwhile, protect your family, lad."

On the way through Dungloe, Aidan witnessed another raid happening on Chapel Street in front of the home of Biddy's friend, Tom Slater. Poor Tom had no affiliation with the Volunteers as far as he knew. Yet a single Auxiliary with his back turned to Aidan threw a haymaker at Tom's bruised and bloody face. Tom fell to his knees and covered his face with his hands. Then the Auxie seized the front of Tom's shirt, yanked him to his feet, and landed another blow. All in front of Tom's wife and young daughter.

Aidan rushed forward, yelling, "There's enough of that!"

Suddenly, the policeman turned towards Aidan. The evil lout who callously interfered with Tadgh's memorial service was right in front of him. Aidan remembered Morgan's out-of-character impassioned request and knew he needed retribution.

"Let go of that man, Tavis!"

The brute snarled, and turned to attack, flashing a knife.

"Drop that and fight me like a man," challenged Aiden, with fists raised.

Tavis sneered and lunged. Aidan sidestepped the thrust, seizing the officer's wrist and twisting it upwards. He heard a cracking sound, bones breaking, he hoped. The Auxie flipped the knife to the other hand, howling in pain, and stabbed again.

He scraped Aidan's arm, but O'Donnell managed to get him in a chokehold. The brute kept trying to jab at him until, with a simple twist of the neck, the devil lay dead at Aidan's feet.

"You'll not be bothered by this fellow anymore," Aidan said, staring down at the lifeless hulk. "The poor man must have fallen and hit his head."

Aidan dragged Tavis's body halfway down Chapel Street and flung it into a ditch.

When he returned, Tom was still holding his face and moaning from the beating he'd taken. His wife and daughter helped him to his feet. "You'd better get your family inside, Tom," Aidan advised. "I expect there'll be reprisals."

Returning to Meenmore, Aidan announced that Tavis, the rude disruptor of Tadgh's Memorial, was dead. Aidan had meted out justice for the family.

Morgan threw her arms around her brother-in-law and kissed him on the cheek as she was wont to do. Sitting in the chair by the window, Jack noted that even the most fervent saver of lives can succumb to eye-for-an-eye revenge if the original offense strikes too close to home.

The next morning, Brigade OC Cole stopped by to tell Aidan that the spy, John Collins had been arrested by the Volunteers and was hidden in the Brigade jail. He had sung like a bird about his activities but was court marshaled and sentenced to death. Hopefully, the reprisals would stop now.

Three days later, Jack read in the *Donegal Democrat* that Collins' wife tearfully reported his abduction. Cole was wrong. That brought a new round of reprisals from Duffy and his mob.

Far from the trouble in Ireland that her husband was embroiled in, Kathy was drying the last of the dishes from dinner with Lil. She and her three children had celebrated Canada Day on July 1st with the Finlays at Number Ten Balsam Avenue and had stayed on until the 4th. Lil had not heeded Sam's request to urge Kathy and her brood to stay at her own home more often, but lately, the visiting had outgrown its welcome.

Kathy put a porcelain cup and saucer on the special shelf in her friend's kitchen. "Collin is reporting in the *Tely* that the Irish War of Independence may be reaching a ceasefire soon. I'm hoping he'll be reassigned home. The kids and I are anxious for him to be home, finally." She sighed and shut the cupboard door. "I've been more patient than last time, but six months is too long to be away from the family if you are a reporter. I understood that soldiers in the Great War would need to be away for years, but that war is over, and the men have been home for a long time."

Lil loved her best friend but was tired of hearing Kathy's laments. "Look on the bright side, Kathy, with the glass half full, as you used to say to Collin," she said, handing her best friend the gravy boat to dry. "He's alive and will be home soon."

"He's missing the children's upbringing. Liam is in kindergarten already, for heaven's sake. I miss Collin so."

Pulling out an envelope from an apron pocket and waving it in the air, Kathy said, "Here's a letter I just got from Maureen, my cousin, the reporter. I've taken to writing her to find out what is happening over there. For all his newspaper reports, Collin is not good at communicating with his family."

"I'll give you that," Lil responded. "What does it say?"

"Let's go into the parlor, Lil. I want Sam to hear this."

The two women stepped into the parlor where the children were playing around Sam's feet as he smoked his pipe filled with Prince Albert tobacco in his favorite chair.

Sam looked over the top of his paper. "What are you railing about, lass?"

"A strange letter from Maureen. You remember her, from when you last visited your father's home."

"Of course, your long-lost cousin. What's odd about it?"

"Mostly she talks about assignments that she and Collin get for reporting, routine stuff. But not this time. She must really be worried about Collin, and that frightens me. He's never mentioned any personal danger."

Sam extended his arm toward her. "Let me read it, Kathy." He knew that she usually exaggerated the situation. He read the contents as he puffed at his pipe, a ring of smoke curling around his head.

"Hmmm. I see your point. Maureen does say here that Collin could have died during the Cork burning at the hands of the police if it weren't for Tadgh's intervention. But that was over six months ago. I am sure that he's fine."

"That's not the point, Sam. Married people should share their experiences together."

"He knew that this would upset you if he told you, lass. He is in a war zone, making his mark as a foreign correspondent. He's likely looking into mostly political and not military affairs, building his reputation and career. He can take care of himself. We've both seen him do it. These long absences are to be expected, I'm afraid."

"I know, but I'm frightened when I don't hear from him." Kathy was holding back tears for the sake of the children. "It has been months. What should we do?"

"What's the matter, Mommy?" Liam asked, walking over, holding on to Kathy's skirt, and looking at her with his soulful eyes.

She playfully brushed a stray lock of the boy's brown hair from his forehead, then picked him up. "Nothing is wrong, son. I just want Daddy to come home soon."

Lil was drying the gravy ladle behind her. She brandished it at her husband. "You're going to send Mr. Robertson a strongly worded letter urging him to order Collin home. That's what you're going to do."

Sam shook his head at the women. "He is probably on assignment again, away from the Shelbourne, and isn't getting his telegrams until he returns.

Four-year-old Claire piped up. "Yes, Mommy, I miss Daddy. He'll be home soon."

"Will he, Claire? How do *you* know?"

"How do we know, Papa?" The children now called Sam *Papa*.

"Because it says here in the paper that the King asked for the fighting to end."

They had arranged a sleepover, and the children were all put to bed by nine o'clock. After bedtime stories, the grownups sat in the kitchen for tea.

Kathy wrapped her fingers around her teacup but did not lift it from its saucer. "Ever since the telegram in March saying Tadgh had been killed, I've been worried about Collin's safety."

"He's a reporter, Kathy, not a fighter," Sam reasoned. I'm sure he's fine, just missing home, I suspect."

Lil took a sip of tea and a bite of biscuit. "I liked Tadgh when he visited. A fine Irishman of principle. What is this Jack like?"

Kathy drained her teacup and took it to the sink. "He's not as tall, yet handsome, nonetheless. He suffered a broken back when he jumped off the sinking *Lusitania* and was in a wheelchair for at least a year."

"Is he crippled?"

"No, apparently, he worked hard at recovering. The thought of finding Claire motivated him; we learned that while we were there. He's a decent, peace-loving man. It was apparent to all of us, except maybe Morgan, that he loves her. Despite this, he organized the reception for her and Tadgh at their wedding with no hard feelings. I like him a lot and hope they both move here."

Sam had gobbled down his biscuit. "Kathy, I think it wouldn't hurt for you to take Lil's advice."

Lil laughed, "Really, did I hear you right? Did you actually tell Kathy to take my advice?"

"I think it wouldn't hurt for Kathy to send a letter to Mr. Robertson requesting Collin be recalled home from Ireland on family business. It would be better coming from her, I think."

"All right, I will if you'll help me with it, Sam."

"Let's go to my studio, and we'll write it together." Sam had no expectation that such a letter would sway Robertson one way or the other.

On June 27, before curfew, the first night back in Dublin, Collin had gone to the grocery to find Deirdre. A closed sign hung on the front door, but he noticed someone moving behind its window curtain, so he knocked.

A vivacious young woman looked out the window and pointed at the sign. Collin waved his arm as a gesture to open up. She cracked open the door, but it was still chained.

"I can see the sign, lass. Where is Deirdre?"

"Who are you?"

"I'm a close friend of the family. Deirdre was a bridesmaid at my sister Morgan's wedding." He showed her his press pass.

The girl's eyes lit up. "Morgan, yes, I met her." She opened the door. "I'm Yvonne, the store clerk."

Collin shook her hand. A striking lass. "Where is Deirdre?"

"I don't know, sir. Why do you want to know?"

"I need to talk to her about Morgan. Why are you closed?"

"Deirdre said there were not enough customers to keep the grocery open while the war is still going, so she asked me to keep it clean while she's gone."

"Where did she go, and when did she leave? I must speak with her."

"I don't know where she went, but she left three days after that terrible burning of the Custom House on the river."

"Can I talk to Derek, then?"

"He went with her."

"Did he, now?"

"Yes, sir."

Collin thanked the girl and went around to the Temple Bar pub for a drink. He wondered where Deirdre and Derek had gone. It wasn't like her to leave her business, especially in the hands of such a young woman. He sat in a familiar cubby nursing his B&C stout, thoughts running around in his head. It was early in July, and he was stuck in Dublin. Healy wanted him there. The work that he and Maureen had done with their Castle operatives showed that the war was going to reach a truce, at least, and quickly. The political initiatives seemed to be coming to a head. Even Robertson in Toronto was happy to have him back in the southern Irish capital and submitting positive news for the *Tely. I've got to find a way to get back to Meenmore, collect our family treasure, and convince Morgan to come home with me. I've run out of time.*

Collin reported that from July 4th until Friday the 8th, the southern Unionists and the Sinn Féin were meeting at the Mansion House, seat of the Dáil Éireann in Dublin, to discuss a possible peace agreement. The press was not permitted into the meetings or even to wait on Dawson Street outside the stately gray government edifice just two doors south of the Royal Irish Academy.

On the 8th, Maureen showed up in front of the Shelbourne in a gleaming new 1921 Packard Single Six roadster and honked her horn at the appointed hour of nine o'clock. Collin was waiting in the lobby. He rushed out to meet his colleague with her new toy. He had read about this snazzy American motor company and wondered how this fine example of their craftsmanship had made it across the pond to Dublin.

He hopped onto the upholstered brown leather passenger seat of the luxury vehicle and closed the door. "My, my. Aren't we the cat's meow?"

"Hello to you, too." She cocked her head quizzically. "The *what?*"

"The cat's meow. It's an American expression going around this year. It means something outstanding." He changed tack. "Maureen. How are you this fine sunny July day, and where did this marvelous driving machine come from?"

Maureen purred a response. "I'm perfectly fine. My dad owns this beast, and he lent it to me for today."

"Do tell. And where are we going since we can't get into Mansion House?"

"Don't get too comfortable. We're only going around the corner onto Dawson Street."

Collin was confused. "We could have walked there in two minutes."

"But we wouldn't get into the Royal Irish Automobile and Aero Club just across the street from Mansion House. My dad's a member. They have a wonderful restaurant overlooking Dawson Street with a commanding view of Mansion House. We can be the first reporters on the scene when the representatives pour out of the building."

Collin smiled like a Cheshire cat. "You amaze me, lass."

"I know. I'm to die for."

Collin's smile evaporated as Maureen pulled out into traffic. "I wish you hadn't put it like that."

After the automobile was parked in the club's parking lot amidst *oohs* and *ahs* from the members, they spent most of the day lounging in the splendor of the club's hallowed halls. Collin learned that the RIAAC earned the 'royal' prefix in recognition of the humanitarian work carried out by its members during the Great War. They used their own automobiles as ambulances to transport the wounded.

Maureen went on and on about the Packard. Turned out she had a grease-monkey background growing up with her father's Automobile Sales Company. The roadster had a mammoth fifty-two horsepower engine, a big authoritative machine that was surprisingly nimble for its size and weight. Its raked windscreen and tall cowl with wood spike wheels gave it an appealing racing appearance.

With time to kill, Collin and Maureen inspected the racing photographs on the corridor wall going back as far as the club's inception in 1909. Quite prestigious as the authorized Motorsport Ireland affiliate of the Fédération Internationale del/Automobile. He found it odd that the members in attendance, who appeared affluent, were acting as if there was no war going on in the city. Based upon their conversations in the restaurant, they were oblivious to the monumental negotiations going on to determine the fate of the Irish people, all occurring just across the street in Mansion House. Clearly there was a caste system at work here in Dublin. Those who were well-off had turned a blind eye to the plight of the common man. This would be an article for the *Tely*.

Collin looked at his watch—two o'clock. They'd had lunch with meaningless chit-chat. He was impatient. But that was the life of a newspaper reporter. Always waiting for, never creating, the news.

"I don't expect the government meeting to wrap up for hours yet. I'm going to visit an acquaintance at the RIA, Maureen. It's just a few doors down. Care to join me?"

Maureen decided to stay and talk about automobiles with the other patrons.

Collin was greeted with enthusiasm by the woman staffing the front desk of the RIA. Fortunately for Collin, the revered Professor Lawlor was in residence. She fetched him.

He came down the circular stairs, dressed in a hounds-tooth cardigan, wearing his pince-nez, the epitome of an absentminded professor. "O'Donnell. To what do I owe this honor? I expected you to be on the hunt for some Moroccan pirate."

In a sense, he was. He had a hunch. "No, Sir. I wondered if I could speak to that student of yours who helped us translate the crazy journal."

"That's right. Fazaar. Good chap. Unfortunately, he was unexpectedly called away for a family emergency, I understand."

"I am sorry. That's too bad, Sir. When did that happen?"

"Just a couple of days after you were here last, lad. Can I help you?"

Collin's suspicions were raised. "No. That's all right. I just had one more Arabic word for him to translate."

"Sorry, I can't help you there."

Deirdre, Derek, and now Fazaar, all disappeared. What did it mean, if anything? Possibly a coincidence. His reporter's antennae were up. He really needed to get back to Donegal. Collin thanked the professor for the information and took his leave to return to the Automobile Club.

At four o'clock, over tea, while they watched through the front window, members of the Dáil Éireann streamed out of the front door of Mansion House. Most of them didn't look happy.

"C'mon, let's go, Maureen. This is what we've been waiting for."

They mingled with the closed-mouthed Southern Ireland ministers but got nowhere, even with their press passes. Just as a Dublin Metropolitan policeman started toward them, the President of the Irish Republic, Éamon de Valera himself, stepped out of the building. He was busy reading a paper and ran right into Maureen, knocking her down.

"Excuse me, madam! My apologies," he exclaimed as he offered her his hand to help her up.

Collin saw his opportunity. "Excuse us, sir. We are with *The Times*. Is there anything you could share with Mr. Healy?"

De Valera looked over his pince-nez. Maureen was up and still holding onto his hand. The policeman would be on them in a second.

The president thought for a moment. The policeman took hold of Collin's arm to move him away, and de Valera put up his hand to stop him. "Leave them be, sergeant. That will be all."

After the policeman left, de Valera checked the reporters' credentials. "I've read some of your reports," he said to Collin. "I'm surprised that Healy has allowed them to be published. You have been very fair and accurate about our objectives and initiatives to free Ireland."

"I try to be impartial, sir."

"Indeed. As for you, young lady, your reports are more along party lines for your paper."

What could Maureen say? He was right.

Turning back to Collin, he said, "We have reached a consensus today. It is time to announce it to your boss, but you must promise that you won't publish it until I make a formal announcement."

This is going to be my scoop for Healy, Collin thought. "You have my word, Sir."

Unable to get the words out, Maureen nodded her head.

"All right, then. We have decided to meet with Lloyd George to discuss peace on our terms."

This was monumental. Then, out of the blue, he handed Collin the paper he had been reading, saying, "This is the letter I intend to send the British Prime Minister later this evening. You can contact my office later. Once the letter goes out by telegraph, you will be free to publish it in your paper." De Valera took the copy of Collin's press card and stuck it in the inside pocket of his tweed waistcoat. "Now, if you will excuse me." Without further ado, the tall man was off down Dawson Street toward St. Stephen's Green in pursuit of some of his ministers.

Back in the restaurant of the Automobile Club, their tea at the table by the window was stone cold. That didn't matter. Collin and Morgan were ecstatic. There before them on the table was the coup of their careers to date. Collin read the letter in subdued tones that only Maureen could hear.

Mansion House, Dublin
July 8, 1921.

The Right Honorable
David Lloyd George
10 Downing Street
London

Sir:

>*The desire you express on the part of the British Government to end the centuries of conflict between the peoples of these two islands and to establish relations of neighbourly harmony is the genuine desire*

*of the people of Ireland. I have consulted with my colleagues and
secured views of representatives of the minority of our nation in regard
to the invitation you have sent me. In reply, I desire to say that I am
ready to meet and discuss with you on what basis such a conference as
that proposed can reasonably hope to achieve the object desired.*

I, am, Sir, faithfully yours
Éamon de Valera.

Healy was pleased with his reporters' work. *The Times* published the
letter in the early morning edition, just after it was delivered to Number
Ten Downing Street. The Irish paper scooped its British counterparts. The
Tely was the first to report this first step forward in Canada that Saturday
afternoon.

From there, things moved fast. Lloyd George issued a positive response.

*In accordance with the prime minister's offer and Mr. de Valera's reply,
arrangements are being made for hostilities to cease from Monday July 11
at noon.*
10 Downing Street, July 8, 1921.

De Valera sent out orders on Saturday to all divisions of Volunteers
throughout the country to cease hostilities.

Healy got word that things were about to erupt in the north. The
Unionists were not happy with the British position. He called in his troops
on Saturday afternoon. "Maureen, I want you and Collin up in Belfast. I
think all hell is going to break loose there."

Collin set his teacup down. He needed a Jameson, but none was
offered. "When, Sir?"

"Immediately!"

They took the Great Northern Railway train to the Belfast Great
Victoria Street Station in downtown Belfast. It was not recommended to
travel in Belfast by personal automobile.

When they emerged from the railway station at ten o'clock in the
gathering dusk, they found the populace scattering. Was it because of
curfew or fear? An Ulster Special Constabulary USP policeman dressed
smartly in his all-black uniform and peaked cap walked by. "Excuse me,
sir," Collin asked. "Can you tell me what is going on?"

The policeman reached for his holstered weapon, but then Collin flashed his press card. "Canadian, eh?"

"Yes, Sir."

"You'd best be careful, the both of you. I think that all hell is going to break loose soon." The same words that Healy had used. "Today, an RIC group was making the rounds to preserve the peace, and they were attacked on Raglan Avenue by Catholic louts. One officer, poor Conlon, is dead, and two are wounded. I think this will incite violence, so it will. I would avoid that area tonight for you and your young lady." The officer headed north on Great Victoria Street toward the trouble.

Collin thought about that recommendation. He remembered the night that Cork City erupted in flames. He would have died if it were not for Tadgh's valor in killing the enemy. There was no advantage in taunting the devil again. The war was almost over. They had found the treasure, and Collin believed he could convince Morgan to move to Canada with him. "I agree with the policeman, Maureen. We should find a suitable place to lay our heads for the night. It will be safer to assess the situation tomorrow."

Maureen stared at her colleague before answering. "I appreciate your attempt to protect me, Collin, but I'm a married woman capable of looking after myself. There may be important developments overnight."

"I don't advise roaming around in the dark, lass. I was in the middle of mob violence in Cork City at night. Things could get very dangerous, and you've got a family to think of, as have I."

Maureen's eyes twinkled. "I thought you were the intrepid reporter."

"Trust me, Maureen. I've been shot at enough recently."

"Oh yes. The Custom House."

"You don't know the half of it, lass."

Maureen looked up at her colleague, and her eyes opened wide. When Collin didn't say anything, she urged him to cough up more information by gesturing with her arms.

Collin hesitated and then said, "Off the record, as I already told you, I was in the middle of mayhem with bullets flying during the Burning of Cork last Fall. Earlier this year, we were attacked when the British forces burnt my sister's home to the ground with us in it." He didn't bother to relay the Pettigo escape situation.

Maureen looked around. "Wow, you have been a busy boy, haven't you? All right then. There was no time to plan for this trip. We've the shirts on our backs and no hotel reservations. What do you suggest?"

"Stay here, Maureen. I'll be right back." Collin ducked into the train station rotunda and emerged with a city map which he consulted, pointing. "We're here, and the trouble is between Falls and Shankill Roads to the northwest. I suggest we head east in the city."

Four blocks away, they came upon the Hastings Grand Central Hotel. This five-story stone edifice spanned a complete city block on Bedford Street. Collin looked at the stream of people going in and out of the front entrance. "This hotel must have two hundred rooms. Surely, they can put us up." Unfortunately, he was mistaken. The front desk manager told them that the hotel was full-up due to the angst of the citizenry. They expected fighting to break out at any moment, and those who were affluent enough had sought shelter away from the danger. The manager had other bad news. The other hotels in the area were also filled.

Collin took out his wallet and removed some pound notes. "I'm sure there is something you can do, Sir."

The manager took the money and consulted his room list. "Oh, I see now. There is one cancellation here, Sir. It's a small turret room."

Collin said, "You mean two rooms, don't you?"

"No, I'm sorry, sir. It's one room or nothing."

Maureen's eyes twinkled again. She grasped Collin's arm and leaned into him. "One room will be fine, won't it, dear."

Collin felt her breast brush against his forearm and remembered its softness from Tralee. That night he had resisted her charms. "I suppose it will have to do." He took the key, and they headed for the restaurant. It had just closed at eleven o'clock. They hadn't seen any other eating establishments along the way. His stomach rumbled since they had only shared a half-stale sandwich on the train. He turned toward the bar. "They say that Guinness is a meal in itself, lass. Fancy one?"

"If that's all that's available, yes."

They took their liquid supper up to their room. When the manager had said, "Small turret room," he wasn't exaggerating. There was only a single bed and no chair. And the washroom was at the other end of the hall. At least they were on the top floor with a window facing west. They would have some fresh air. Collin was dismayed. This was a far cry from his accommodation at the Shelbourne. Was Maureen trying to signal him with that arm squeeze? She'd done it before. And now she was giggling at the sight of this tiny room.

He popped open his Guinness and said, "You take the bed, and I'll take the, uh . . . floor."

Maureen put her bottle on the single nightstand and checked the small armoire. "Aha, here's a spare blanket. Will this help, gallant Sir?"

"That'll be grand, so it will, lass."

"Come sit on the bed with me, Collin, while we have our drink. Let's discuss our plan for tomorrow."

Collin thought of Kathy and the kids. She'd be livid if she knew about these sleeping arrangements, even though Maureen was her cousin. He should telegraph his family. What would he tell them?

"I remember Tralee, Maureen."

"So do I, Collin. And I'm married now, as you know. Times have changed. Come sit by me." She took his hand and pulled him to the bed. "Sit here beside me. I've met your fine wife, but you've been gone how long, now?"

"Over six months."

Maureen shifted her weight against his side. "You must miss her terribly for a lot of reasons."

Collin took a swig from his bottle. "I do, lass. I expect I'll be headed home now that the truce is going into force."

"You know, you could lie down with me on the bed to sleep, Collin. We've our clothes on, and I won't bite. You need your rest before tomorrow, and that wood floor looks mighty hard, lad."

Collin missed the intimacy of lying with Kathy in their conjugal bed, ached for it. He had been alone for over half a year. Maureen's offer to lie together clothed in close proximity sorely tempted him. She was a very beautiful young woman. It would be such a welcome relief. He emptied his bottle of Guinness in one last swallow and stood up, away from the warmth of her body. "I shouldn't, lass, nor should you. How old are your children?"

Maureen turned her mouth down in a pout but didn't try to change his mind. "Suit yourself, Collin. I don't really fancy this Guinness if you want it. I'll be right back after I freshen up."

With that, she was gone down the hall. Collin didn't get it. Maureen was presumably happily married with a husband to go to at night, flirting with a married man who hadn't seen his family for a long time. When she came back, Collin passed her in the hallway on his way to the bathroom without saying a word. When he returned, the light was off, and Maureen was in bed. He was happy to leave it at that as he rolled up his coat for a pillow and spread the blanket over himself on the floor under the window.

Sleep wouldn't come. The hard planks creaked under him as he tried to get comfortable. His biggest problem was the family. How could he ensure that Morgan wouldn't choose Aidan, Biddy, and Peader over her own brother and his family? How could she choose to live in war-ravaged Ireland instead of pristine Canada with an opportunity to be a doctor?

He decided that Jack was the key. He had seen how Morgan was warming to him, especially since he had stood up for her at Meenmore. And how he had thrown his body in front of her to save her from bullets during their escape from Pettigo. Not to mention that he had given her another chance to live since those dying moments of the *Lusitania*. He had to convince Jack to move to Canada with Morgan. Having determined a course of action, he relaxed and dropped off to sleep.

Some hours later, the gun battle erupted. Collin uncoiled from the floor with a start. His watch said it was six o'clock. Maureen was gone. He went to the bathroom and splashed water on his face. He was starving and headed down to the ground floor.

There she was, sitting relaxed and collected in the sunshine at the east window of the Seahorse restaurant. Maureen didn't look as if she had slept in her clothes, but then, he hadn't seen her get into bed, had he.

"Hello there," Maureen called out, waving when he entered the restaurant. "I couldn't wait for you, sleepyhead. I was famished."

Collin couldn't believe what a chameleon she was. There was no talk of the night before, and she definitely had a spring in her step. She had consumed most of her full Irish breakfast already.

"My, what a bright light you are this morning. You must have slept well, Maureen."

"Yes, thanks to you. You look the worse for wear, though."

Collin wasn't sure if her thanks referred to him relinquishing the bed or sarcastically leaving her alone to sleep. Either way, it didn't warrant a response. The waitress took his order for steak and eggs. As usual, Maureen was engrossed in her notes, her pen flying over the page.

When his meal came, he said, "I'm sure you heard the gunfire a few minutes ago, Maureen. We need to map out our strategy for today."

Maureen pulled out a map. It looked familiar, quite like his own. He checked his pockets and came up empty. She must have taken it from his pants pocket while he was sleeping.

"I've already thought it through." She spread it out in front of her as the waitress cleared away her dishes. "We'll take the tram to an observation point, here." She circled an item on the map with her pen.

Collin looked up over his steak at the inked spot on the map. It was the Royal Victoria Hospital, one-mile due west on the south side of Falls Road, in the Catholic quarter.

She said, "I heard from the bellman the Catholic nationalists on Falls Road and the Protestant unionists on Shankill Road are fighting it out in the one-mile-wide, No Man's Land between the two. It's a residential area. They should be receiving casualties at the hospital. We should get good information from them."

Collin realized that Maureen had the situation well in hand—a location out of the line of fire. Kathy would approve. "Good work, girl. I'll be finished in a minute."

"Fine," she said, folding up the map and putting it in her handbag. "I'll just use the ladies' room before we leave and meet you in the lobby."

With that, she was gone, leaving Collin to pay the bill. Was she miffed about last night? If so, she wasn't going to say it.

At the front desk, the manager apologized to him for the spartan conditions of their accommodations and announced that he had two regular rooms for that evening if Collin wanted them. After what had happened the night before, Collin booked them.

He could hear the rifle shots reverberating off the downtown buildings as they arrived at the hospital on foot at eight o'clock. The tram hadn't come. Frequent short staccato bursts of machine gun fire broke the calm. A tram on its way east to downtown came racing up Falls Road, bells ringing. The conductor ground it to a halt opposite the hospital and hopped out. He cupped a hand around his mouth and yelled, "We've been shot at! I have wounded inside."

Collin could see the bullet holes in the windows. Some had penetrated the glass from the north side and had broken the south side windows. Orderlies with stretchers raced out just as riders clambered down out of the tram. Collin elbowed against the tide in time to see three patrons sprawled on the blood-spattered seats. He snapped a No. 2 Autographic Brownie picture for the paper and cleared the way for the orderlies. Where was Maureen? He entered the hospital and found her checking with the triage nursing station.

She looked up toward him. "This nurse says that the police, mostly USP, have been driving around the Falls area in armored cars firing on the houses and citizens."

"They're probably the ones that attacked the tram then, Maureen."

The orderlies continued wheeling in the wounded. One man was near death with a bullet wound in the neck.

Maureen was shaking. "This is terrible, Collin. Innocent bystanders."

"Does this remind you of something?"

"Yes, the Rising. Here we go again, this time in a northern city."

"With the Protestants attacking the Catholics, Maureen."

"Precisely. The Republicans will fight back."

Collin took a picture of the triage room activity. "Mark my words. This is the start of a terrible situation here in the north. The Catholics are trapped with an unruly citizenry."

Boom! The north windows of the hospital rattled. Some broke.

"What was that?" Maureen gasped; her eyes wide.

Collin remembered that sound from the attack at Creagh. "Mills bomb." This explosion was followed by a percussion of similar crashes that shook the building.

Maureen raced into Collin's unsuspecting arms, burying her head in his chest. "Make it stop," she cried.

Collin pried her away and sat her down on a bench in the triage corridor. "We'll be safe in here, Maureen, to be sure."

Maureen was still shaking but no longer panicked as she stared into Collin's understanding eyes. "You promise?"

"Yes. Stay here for a minute. I'll be right back." Collin went to the door in time to see billows of smoke rising to the northwest. This was getting worse by the minute. He wondered about her reaction as he walked back to her. Sitting down beside her, he asked, "Where were you during the Rising?"

"Trapped in our offices for three days. And terrified the entire time."

That explained it. Collin wanted to go out into the war zone, but he knew how foolhardy that would have been. He decided to wait it out at the hospital and then take pictures of the damage. He turned to Maureen and asked. "Are you happy to stay here at the moment?"

"Yes, if you stay with me."

They waited most of Sunday for word of the battle while the wounded and dying were brought in. They interviewed several of the least injured and found out that the Protestants had initiated the attack. They'd fired gunshots from windows, rooftops, and street corners. The Catholic Republicans had retaliated. At one point, mid-morning, a twelve-year-old Catholic girl, Mary McGowan, was brought in and declared dead on arrival. Her mother was distraught. She lamented that a USC in an armored car had indiscriminately shot at their house, bullets piercing the exterior walls and windows, killing her daughter.

Mid-afternoon, Collin got word from a fireman bringing in a woman who had been shot in the neck. She said that a mob of thousands of Protestants had stormed south from Shankill with petrol and torches intent on burning out the Catholics.

That evening, the hospital administrator announced over a loudspeaker that the commander of the IRA's Belfast Brigade, Roger McCorley, had finally talked to a senior RIC official. They agreed on a ceasefire. For the moment, the gunfire subsided, with only sporadic shots being heard after that.

Collin got the tally of the damages from the hospital staff. A total of sixteen people had died, of which eleven were Catholics. Many more were wounded. Collin found out from the police that at least two hundred homes were destroyed, with at least three-quarters of them Catholic. Their fires burned into the night.

The two reporters stayed overnight on Sunday at the Hastings, uneventfully in separate rooms, and headed back to Dublin by train the next morning. On the way back, Collin wrote an article for the *Tely* called, 'The Bloody Sunday Battle for Belfast.' He started it with,

> *As a harbinger of things to come, and perhaps because their opportunity for mayhem was closing, a riot broke out in Belfast on bloody Sunday, July 10, to be precise. Protestant Unionists condemned the truce as a sellout to the Catholic Republicans. This will be a new form of oppression for those Catholics unfortunate enough to live in Northern Ireland . . .*

Maureen's article for *The Irish Times* was more slanted to the Unionists being in the right to protect what little of Ireland they had left after the Home Rule segregated the country. She thought it was a statement to motivate their British masters to hold the line with the Catholics in their upcoming negotiations. She failed to mention that the mob that had headed south from Shankhill had burned down the Catholic portion of the city. De Valera cautioned citizens in a written communiqué that Monday to adhere to the truce but be wary in case the upcoming negotiations fell through and the British resumed hostilities.

Chapter Sixteen
Ceasefire

Monday, July 11, 1921
The Irish Times Office, Dublin, Ireland

Collin met with Maureen and Mr. Healy when they returned from Belfast just after the truce went into effect at noon. Healy puffed on his pipe, as usual, while he read the handwritten copy Maureen had given him. "I'm pleased with this report, Maureen. Well, Collin, what does yours say?"

"It's a slightly different slant on the problem, Sir. I think that splitting Ireland will be a major problem in the north. The Catholics will be trapped. We saw the escalation of the conflict yesterday."

Healy was skeptical of Collin's view. "This initiative by de Valera and Lloyd George looks like an honest attempt on both sides to reach a settlement, but it will take several months before we know the outcome of deliberations. It is time for you to go home, Collin. Perhaps Mr. Robertson will send you back here when the negotiations are nearing completion."

"I am eager to go home, sir. I fear it is getting tense on the home front."

"That's what I wanted to talk to you about. Your boss got an emphatic letter from your wife to send you home. He arranged passage on the 22nd on the *Aquitania* out of Queenstown. You'd best not miss the ship, Collin."

"Did he, now?" Collin's eyes narrowed. "I need to return to see my sister in Donegal before I leave. I am hoping to convince her to move to Canada with me."

Maureen winked at Collin. "Do you think you could convince Mr. Robertson to pay for passage for both of them, Sir?"

"Good thinking. Despite some of your contrary opinions, Collin, you have done an exceptional job of helping us report on this despicable war. Leave the telephone number where we can get in touch with you. I'll let you know."

Collin silently mouthed *thank you* to Maureen, who stayed with her boss when the Canadian reporter left. He would need to quickly get to Meenmore to unearth his family inheritance and convince Morgan to emigrate. With or without Jack.

♣ ♣ ♣ ♣

The next day, Collin called the tailor shop with the good news that he was going home soon. He would be coming to Meenmore on Saturday to pick up Morgan after he closed out his business in Dublin. Biddy announced Collin's plan at supper when she returned.

This prompted Jack into action. That night after supper, he asked Morgan if she would like to sit outside on the garden swing. Biddy's flowers, cultivated lovingly as war therapy, were spectacular in their bright pinks and violet hues, and the fragrance was divine. The night air was fresh at twilight as it buffeted the dragonflies throughout the garden.

Morgan loved the tiny lily of the valley, while Jack preferred the bright-hued asters. He stooped down to pick a small bouquet of the white flowers for Morgan before they both sat down.

"It's such a relief that the war is over, or at least suspended, Morgan."

"A hiatus, I think. But that's not why you asked me out here, Jack, is it?"

"No, it's not, my love."

"I've been keeping you at arm's length, Jack, but I want you to know—"

Jack put his hand gently over her mouth. "Before you say anything more, I'd like to speak. All right?"

"Certainly."

"Good. I have been patient because of the memory of Tadgh and how hard that is for you. I know that Collin is coming here to convince you to go to Canada with him and that he will be going home immediately. But I must now speak my piece before it is too late."

"What makes you think that I would agree to go to Canada, Jack?"

"To get away from the dangers over here, your past, and to further your medical career."

Morgan rolled her eyes. "You don't give yourself much credit, do you."

"That's why I need to speak." He knelt on the ground below the swing. "I love you, Morgan, and have loved you since we met on the *Lusitania* that fateful day. We could have a wonderful family life here in Ireland, your homeland, with your Irish family. I know that Aidan, Biddy, and Peader would agree. We could live here in Donegal in one of those cottages you love so much." He reached into a coat pocket for the box with the small diamond ring, his mother's ring that he had kept safe all this time, just in case. *Is now the time? I'm on my knees. Is she ready?* Jack decided no. He couldn't take the rejection.

Morgan stood up from the swing and took Jack's hands, then focused on his eyes as she faced him. "What about Deirdre?"

"I haven't told her yet, Morgan. That should be done in person. I still care for her, but you are the love of my life."

Morgan sat back down on the swing bench and pushed the ground with her feet to start a rocking motion. "Would you go with me to Canada, Jack?"

"I want to stay in our homeland, my love. I've been to Canada on Cunard, to Montreal and Quebec City, and it is too cold for me there in the winter. I think we would be happier here."

"I need time to think over what you've said, Jack, at least until Collin comes back."

"Just remember that Aidan and your relatives, your family roots, are here."

"I know. It's a consideration."

Jack put his arm around Morgan, stopping the swing, and said, "Know that I will support you whatever your decision will be."

He pressed against her side, feeling softness through her clothing.

Morgan allowed his hand to rest on her thigh. She felt an immediate electric response as he pulled her into him, kissing her, not stopping. She leaned in, hungry for him. Just like the kiss at the lough, she took in the love he had for her, and it was good. His strong arms enveloped her body, and she sank into him.

From the kitchen window, Biddy saw the embrace and chuckled, thinking, *well, it's about time, so it is.*

Five days later, on Saturday morning, July 16th, Morgan was expecting her brother to arrive. Instead, she was surprised when Deirdre came walking up the path in the rain carrying a valise. She rushed out to meet the grocery owner and greeted her, gesturing toward the open doorway. "What are you doing here, dearie? How did you ever find us?" Once inside, she took the valise from Deirdre and set it down, dripping on the floor.

"I'm full of surprises, Morgan, just like when I showed up the morning of your wedding."

"I remember. My last-minute, bodacious bridesmaid."

"Bodacious?"

"Bold and audacious, Deirdre." But really, how—?"

"Jack called me a while back from your aunt's tailor shop." Deirdre shook her coat off and hung it on the coat rack. "Where is that man?"

"Lying down this morning, resting to get his strength back."

"Strength back? Has he been sick?"

"In a manner of speaking, yes. He was injured in an automobile accident recently. It's been a bit hectic up here. He's on the mend, to be sure. But who's handling your grocery? Derek?"

Deirdre shook her head. "I closed it temporarily because business was slow with the war raging, especially after the Custom House attack and burning. Can I see Jack?"

Morgan took her friend to the sitting room where Jack was napping on the chesterfield.

Deirdre went to him, gave him a peck on the cheek, and gently rocked his shoulder. "Jack, my dear. I'm here, love."

Jack, bewildered at being roused out of his sleep, eyes shut and groggy, said, "I'm right here, Morgan."

"No, it's me, darling, your Deirdre. I've missed you, my love."

Now Jack's eyes shot open, and he sat up quickly, then winced. "Deirdre, how did you get here?"

"By train, silly, just to see you. You've had a run-in with an automobile, I understand."

"A bullet through the windscreen when we drove through those bastard Auxies in Pettigo."

Deirdre stared at Morgan.

In turn, Morgan stood in the middle of the room with her mouth catching flies. All she could think of saying was, "Jack most likely saved my life, Deirdre."

"Did he, now? Dear Jack, I understand you are going to live."

"Apparently, but you'll have to ask my nurse." He smiled at Morgan and gave a thumbs-up sign.

"She said you'll be fine with a little more rest." Deirdre sat on the edge of the chesterfield and tried to hold his hand. "I need you to come back with me to the grocery. I'm going to open it now that the skirmishes have ended." Her eyes glistened. "I've been lonely for you."

Jack looked at Morgan for help, but she wouldn't bail him out.

"I . . . I am not quite myself, Deirdre. Not the man you remember."

"You look your same handsome self to me, my love."

Jack was trying to get his bearings. His brain wasn't fully awake yet. "Well, some things have changed."

"What things, pray tell?"

"Things."

Morgan could see that he was having trouble telling her. "How about some tea, Deirdre, and biscuits? You must be famished. Let's let Jack have his rest for another hour."

In the kitchen, Morgan put the kettle on. Busying herself gave her time to think. She could see that Deirdre's arrival was now a catalyst for her own decision-making. If she supported Deirdre and let Jack down easy, she would be free to go to Canada and would know that Jack would be well cared for. If she herself wanted Jack, now was the time to fight for him.

When the kettle started whistling, Morgan poured the hot water into the rosehip in the teapot, put on the cozy, and brought it to the table. Deirdre, perched on the edge of her chair, pulled the saucer and teacup nearer.

Morgan cleared her throat and said, "Jack will have to tell you himself, but he and I have been seeing much of each other since we left you in Dublin. He's a grand fellow, you know."

"Oh yes, I know that. Intimately, in fact. And you?"

"We're not intimate friends, Deirdre, if that's your question. Not yet, anyway." Morgan felt her face flush.

Deirdre's hand touched her abdomen, and she felt movement below the table. *Oh, we've been intimate, all right!* Jack's child inside her belly kicked. She wasn't going to let these two know that she was pregnant with Jack's baby, not unless she needed to. Fortunately, with loose clothing, she didn't show. She hadn't even shared the news of that bundle of joy with Derek. It had been almost five months since Jack left with Morgan after they had heard about Tadgh's capture. Deirdre never thought she would want children when she was managing the pub. But now, his child growing within her, she desperately wanted Jack and a family of her own.

She had thought things through on her way to Donegal.

If I tell Jack about the baby, he will do the right thing. But if he loves Morgan more, he will resent me for the rest of our lives. No, I must find out if he chooses me, not because of our baby. If he chooses me, then Morgan would likely go to Canada, except for the incentive I've arranged. That might not be enough because of her opportunity to become a doctor there and with a price on her head here in Ireland.

She and Collin are the bloodline. Now that the path forward has been uncovered by them, it is exposed. I must follow it to protect the Word. They are the conduit and cannot both leave. My Da died for our Templar cause. I promised him on his deathbed, and I must put that first and my happiness second if it comes to that!

Deirdre had debated whether to bring Morgan, Jack, and Collin into the Templar fold. That would solve the problem. She thought Jack and Morgan could be trusted, but not Collin. She'd seen the way he had watched her, questioning her during the discovery process. Any attempts to get close to him had been rebuffed. Lawlor thought him a bad risk. Her instincts were not to trust him. As a result, Morgan shouldn't be told. And Jack was close to them both and too free with his words.

She had decided.

The first objective is to see where Jack stands, then convince him of our love. When he chooses me, we'll see what happens with the incentive. If it is not enough, then I may have to tell Morgan about my Templar responsibilities and convince her not to share our mission with her brother. I'd hate to do it, but Morgan can be silenced if absolutely necessary. Jack can be won over. If Jack chooses Morgan, they must stay here in Ireland to continue the search.

Deirdre was cornered. The worst case would be for Jack to choose Morgan and have them both move to Canada. She couldn't let that happen. Every decision would inflict pain somewhere. She wished she'd never been involved in the Templar crusade and that she'd never let the McCarthys search for that damned Temple chest. But she was, and she did.

Deirdre was shocked that Morgan's relationship with Jack had developed to this stage. Her pride was hurt since she thought that Jack loved her passionately. Heavens, Morgan was just recently widowed.

"Deirdre, did you hear me?" Morgan asked, standing beside her with the teapot in her hand.

"What? Sorry, Morgan, I guess my thoughts were elsewhere."

"Would you like tea now?"

"Yes." Deirdre pushed her cup under the spout, and Morgan poured.

"Two lumps, right?"

"Thanks. Where's Collin? Surely he'll be going home to Canada now that the war is ended."

"He's expected here today. I thought it was him on the walk when you arrived. Didn't you see him at the station or on the train?"

"Ah, no. Maybe he took another train since he's not here."

It wasn't like him to miss a train, Morgan thought, her eyes turning dark. "He is planning to go home soon."

Deirdre needed to know Morgan's plans. "Not much time left, then."

"Time for what?"

"For you to decide whether to go with him."

"I haven't decided. There are advantages, you know. But Jack wants to stay here."

"I would always stay in my homeland, Morgan, but that's just me. And you're from America, aren't you?"

"No, I was born right here in Donegal Town, Deirdre. I thought you knew that."

Deirdre knew she had made her point.

She selected a shortbread biscuit perched on the offered plate and snapped it in half. Her nostrils flared. "I love Jack, Morgan, and I know he loves me. We talked about owning the grocery together. I need a man about the place."

Morgan's green eyes narrowed and flashed anger as she picked up the milk bottle. She held it over Deirdre's cup, and she couldn't stop her hand from shaking. "Milk?"

"Thanks."

"I thought you had Derek, that you two could run the operation yourselves."

Deirdre held her cup out while Morgan dripped some in her cup. "Derek's a fine friend and employee. But that's as far as it goes. Jack's a wonder, and absence makes the heart grow fonder, as they say."

Morgan left her tea untouched. Marrying Jack now was more than a possibility, crystallized in her mind for the first time. Maybe it was just jealousy, but she didn't think so. She'd lost Tadgh. She had lost Byron, and now Jack was left, the man who saved her on the sinking deck of that torpedoed ship. Saved her before Tadgh saved her. Morgan took the plunge, inhaled deeply, and let the words tumble out, "Jack expressed his love for me recently, Deirdre."

"Did he now? And how do you feel about that, Morgan?"

"It's been less than five months since my poor Tadgh was murdered. I still miss him terribly. But Jack is a wonderful fellow—kind, strong— but you know all that."

"Yes, I do. That's why I love him." Deirdre paused for effect. "But you didn't answer my question."

Morgan fidgeted with her cup, thinking of her discussion with Aunt Biddy about Jack. "I have recently come to realize that I may be falling in love with him, too."

"Falling? You loved your Tadgh, too, just a few months ago. Are you certain of the feelings you have now?"

Morgan wasn't about to tell the woman that she loved Jack before she had revealed it to him herself. It had become more apparent to her while she was talking to Deirdre. "It's a developing affection, Deirdre."

"We will see about that. I need to talk to Jack, alone."

Morgan took a sip, and her hand shook, holding the cup. She set it down a little too hard, cracking it. Dark tea pooled out into the saucer. "I admire you, Deirdre. You've been my friend and bridesmaid, but you're not going to do that. We'll talk to him together."

Deirdre got up from the table, hands on hips. "This may not be my house, but you are not the boss of me."

Biddy strode into the kitchen from weeding the vegetable garden. "Deirdre, right? From Morgan's wedding. Pink Dress. What is all the fuss, girls?"

Morgan threw down her napkin. "Deirdre's come for Jack. Says she loves him."

Deirdre spat back, "Of course I love him, and I'm certain of his love for me."

"I never understand you young'uns. Good luck to the three of ya. You'll have to stay, young lady, until you sort this out."

Morgan turned on her aunt, eyes glaring. *Is she siding with my rival?* "I need you to stay out of my business, Biddy."

Biddy reacted. "There, there, Morgan. It's not as bad as all that, surely."

Morgan continued to stare; arms crossed on her chest.

Deirdre smiled. "Thank you, Biddy. I was hoping to stay a few days if that's all right."

"The more, the merrier. Got me in a good mood that you can't break, Morgan. The deadly war has stopped for the minute, and I expect Peader and Aidan will be home soon. Do stay, dear."

Morgan shook her head and then stabbed her finger in the air. She needed Jack. Wanted him. Bridesmaid be damned. "Stay if you must, Deirdre, but Jack will choose me. And remember, we will be speaking to him together."

Deirdre turned on her heel. "Biddy, can you show me where I may unpack my valise, please?" She flounced over to the older woman.

Biddy led Deirdre out of the kitchen, leaving Morgan fuming alone.

On their way to the front door to pick up her bag, they passed by the sitting room. Deirdre glanced in. Jack was sleeping.

Biddy asked, "Have you heard from my nephew Collin?"

"Not recently, Biddy," Deirdre answered. "I've been, well, away."

"In the war? Where?"

"Here and there. But I'm here, now."

"Let me show you to the guest room. You can get settled. How did you get here, by the way?"

"I was dropped off by a friend."

Collin called the tailor shop at four in the afternoon, arranging to be picked up by Morgan at the Donegal Town railway station. After checking on Jack and giving him his afternoon tea in the garden, Morgan went inside to change before taking the shop's lorry to get her brother. The rain had stopped, and the sun was basking the purple heather fields in its afternoon splendor. As she got ready, Morgan reflected on her tense conversation with Deirdre. Jack would have to decide. She was very fond of the man and could see herself having a loving family life with him. It all seemed idyllic compared to her recent violent memories. Jack was not a warmonger and had a strong, almost noble character. He understood her perhaps better than Tadgh ever had. She felt guilty about taking him away from Deirdre, but it was Jack, after all, who had taken the initiative. Deirdre would have to accept that she would be giving him up.

Deirdre had finished setting the dining room table for supper and noticed Jack in the garden. Biddy was busy in the kitchen.

She had no intention of waiting for Morgan to talk with Jack. She needed to find out where he stood. She found him sitting on the bench swing in the secluded portion of the garden finishing his tea. She could smell honeysuckle in the air. "We haven't been alone together in a long time, and I miss you, Jack." She sat down beside him and placed her hand on his thigh. He didn't move it away. Then she pushed off with her shoes, and the bench started swinging.

"I miss you, too, Deirdre, really, I do. But a lot has happened—Tadgh's death, for instance. You remember I was always sweet on Morgan. Now she is receptive to me. I didn't mean for us to fall in love, but it happened."

She slipped her hand through the buttons on his tunic and felt his bare skin. "What about our lovemaking?" She leaned over and kissed him on the lips.

"You are a vixen, Deirdre, and always will be."

"Well, then?" She put her other hand in his lap and left it there.

Jack could feel himself slipping under her spell again, and he tried to focus on the beautiful image of Morgan's face, her mesmerizing green eyes. "There's more to life than making love."

"What about us? Our plans for you to own the grocery with me and grow our business together?"

"You tempt me, my dear. There's stability with you, but Morgan—"

"Did you know Collin is trying to get her to move back to Canada with him?"

"He tried that before she married Tadgh, and he wasn't successful."

"He's offering her the opportunity to become a doctor, a choice for women that only exists in Canada right now."

"But I want to stay in Ireland. It's my home."

"And you can, my love. With me. Remember our wonderful times in Dublin." Deirdre looked around to ensure they were alone and stopped the swing with her foot. Then she knelt before him, opening his trousers.

Jack put his hand in front of his crotch. "No, Deirdre. I can't let you do that right now. You must understand."

She tried to pry his hand away gently. "Just let me satisfy you, my love. Let's go somewhere more private. It has been such a long time—"

Morgan came out of the house to get in the lorry. Her path led her past a small gap in the hedge where a bush was dying. She saw Deirdre kneeling in front of the swing with Jack's trousers open. She jumped back and hid behind the hedge to avoid detection. *Damn that Deirdre—she didn't wait, and she wasn't doing much talking.* She debated whether to interrupt them and have it out right there in the open. No. She had to meet Collin and deal with his side of the problem. With this new development, she needed time to think. She watched the scene unfold.

Jack leaned forward and lifted Deirdre's head with one hand and stroked her closely cropped blond hair with the other. "I do love you, Deirdre. You have given me a new lease on life. I value your friendship and love helping you with the grocery. But Morgan has been my unattainable love from long before I met you until now. Can't you see?"

Deirdre pressed into his trousers, wanting to feel that familiar rising from him and whispered, "Are you sure you haven't just magnified your image of Morgan because of your trauma after the *Lusitania*? It's natural, Jack. Patients do that with their nurses all the time. It doesn't last. It's not real." Her warm breath blew on him. And yes, she felt movement.

"It's not like that, Deirdre." His voice grew husky.

"Are you sure, my love? Touch me. You know that I am real." She took his hand and rested it on her open blouse, pressed against him.

"I know that."

Jack didn't reach for her like before. His hand was still. Deirdre realized she was losing the battle. She knew where Jack's heart resided at the moment. Only for the moment. She could sway him; she was sure of it. "I understand what you're telling me, my love. I will always be here for you when you are ready."

Jack thought with a jolt. *That's what I told Morgan.*

After rebuttoning his fly, slowly, luxuriously, she left Jack resting on the bench seat and thought to bring him an alcoholic drink. She would touch him again when she returned. He just needed some time.

After she left, Jack felt relief flood over him but realized that he had just rejected one love of his life without knowing if the other one would have him. He hoped he hadn't been too harsh, but at least he had finally been honest.

Morgan picked up Collin at the Donegal Town train station, and they started back toward Dungloe. She asked, "Did you see Deirdre on your way here, on the train, I mean?"

"No. Why? She wasn't at the grocery when I went by there a few days ago."

"Well, she showed up today and said she came by train."

"From Dublin?"

"She didn't say."

"Why did she come, Morgan?"

"To claim Jack. We got into a spat about it."

Collin wondered about the timing of that. He didn't wish ill on his sister, but this could be a good turn of events for his plans. He rationalized it was for his sister's own good.

Collin said, "It should be safe enough for us to go to Lough Derg tomorrow and finally claim our inheritance. I heard from my source at the Castle that they are granting amnesty to some freedom fighters whom they no longer consider a threat as a sign of goodwill for the upcoming truce negotiations. Especially those who are permanently incapacitated."

"I don't want to risk ending up in that dungeon again, Brother." She shuddered.

"I'll make sure that doesn't happen."

Morgan navigated through the Diamond, out past the Church of Ireland, and a few miles toward Dungloe. "Everybody is arriving at once, Collin. Auntie says Peader and Aidan will come down out of the hills soon."

"That's what Tadgh and Jack promised."

Collin had to know. "What does Jack want?"

"I thought he wanted me. I just saw them together in a romantic position. Now I'm not sure about Jack at all. She's a charmer."

"But you're more beautiful with more substance, Sis."

"G'wan with ya, as auntie would say."

Collin decided this might be his last chance to convince her. "Did you ever discuss your coming to Canada and becoming a doctor with Jack?"

"I mentioned it. He wants to stay here in Donegal."

"Why Donegal?" Collin knew the reason but asked anyway. He wanted to hear her say it. Why hadn't he thought of this angle before?

"If I stay with him, we need to be away from Cork and Dublin."

It was harsh, but he had to say it. "You mean, you need to stay away from there because you're a wanted killer and supposedly his sister."

Morgan clutched the wheel hard and slowed the vehicle. Her face grew hot.

"Do you think you would be safe from prosecution here in Donegal?"

"If there is a new Irish Government." Her head started to pound.

"Think about it, Sis. The guards you and Aidan killed were not military adversaries. They were civil servants."

Collin's words reopened that mental wound. "Oh, Collin, it was to save Tadgh. I hate having become one of them."

"Them?"

"Killers. I just wanted to save lives. I'm going to go to Hell when I die."

Morgan was shaking so much that Collin asked her to pull over to the side of the road. When she did, he reached over and held her hand tight. "You told me you had to shoot that warder to save Aidan's life. A split-second reaction," he said.

"Maybe he wouldn't have shot Aidan."

"You know he would have, Sis, then shot you, too. Then Tadgh would have died. You can make a case for self-defense with God when the time comes, but, unfortunately, not with the police here on earth since you had no witnesses."

Morgan appreciated her brother's honest words, but she couldn't stop the tears. This discussion had opened all the wounds.

Collin saw his opening, "With poor Tadgh gone and the current war hopefully over, I thought you would be free to come to Toronto with me and become a doctor. I thought you'd love it, and that would give you a brand-new start. You would not be a fugitive there."

"I don't know how safe it would be there, either Brother, what with Ma's murder and Kathy's attempted rape."

"That was a long time ago, and because of one evil weasel in New York, that scoundrel Enrico."

Morgan shivered. "My whole life has been here since the accident, Collin. Aidan's here, Jack, Aunt Biddy, and Peader. We've been through everything together." She realized she was repeating herself. "We've talked about this before, Brother."

"You could convince Jack to come with you if that's what you want. I've been ordered home. I leave on the 22nd from Queenstown. I think the newspapers will pay for your passage and mine, maybe even Jack's. I can't stay any longer. Please come, Sis. You may not see it now, but I know it is what's best for you."

Morgan pulled back. "What, next Friday, in five days? What about the treasure? I've been worried and waiting until you are back. We must go for it tomorrow!"

"I'm sure it's safe, lass, but we'll go now that the British army is standing down."

"What about the epistle? There's still that mystery."

"Our Clans Pact was to find the family treasures and use them for the revolution. We've done that. Whatever the British, Barbary pirates, and Knights Templar were after back in the 1600s doesn't concern us. We've already risked our lives enough."

"Aren't you curious, Brother? It was, after all, our ancestor who wanted to protect *whatever it is,* as you put it."

"I have already risked my marriage again with what we have done. I promised—"

"I know. Good point. But I really shouldn't go with you, Collin. Aidan and the memory of Tadgh, what he stood for. I can't let them down now, can I." Morgan started to cry again. She wiped her eyes with the back of her hand.

Collin handed her his handkerchief. "Do you want me to drive?"

"I'll be fine."

"I know the memory of Tadgh is important, but he's gone, and we have to face that reality. He'll always be in your heart."

"I know. I am, and he will. And now, Jack has become essential to me. But Deirdre is trying to lure him away."

"That's why you may need to get away and start fresh, Sis. Up until now, since Creagh, you have been hosted by Maurice and now Aunt Biddy. But that can't go on forever. You will need to stand on your own two feet. You're a strong woman, Sis, and can chart a new course in medicine in Canada. And while you are in university, you can live with Kathy and me. I get a good salary."

"I have the last of the jewels that we brought from home, Collin. There hasn't been the time or opportunity to pawn them. I have no idea what they are worth."

Collin knew that they would fetch a pretty penny. "We can take care of that in Toronto."

"You and Jack are just pushing too hard, Brother. I need time to think." She started the car and drove on.

Collin and Morgan went silent, each with their own thoughts, until Morgan turned on Meenmore Road. She said, "I need to see what Jack wants to do." Just saying his name made her smile.

"I'm sure he will come if he truly loves you, Morgan."

"Remember five years ago? You said the same of Tadgh. And what was my response?"

"I don't remember."

Morgan looked with devilish eyes at her brother. "You remember everything, Collin. I said I would not force him to leave his country and make him unhappy because it would ruin our relationship."

"Surely Jack doesn't have the same passionate commitment to a cause here, Morgan."

"I don't know. But perhaps for *his* country. I'll have to ask him, and then there is Aidan to consider."

The meal late that evening should have been a joyous reunion. The cease-fire was in place, for the most part. Word came from the baker that Peader and Aidan would be home the next day and that Head Constable Duffy was recalled to Dublin. But the mood was tense, and the banal conversation stalled.

Jack was uncharacteristically quiet while the talk centered on Collin's upcoming trip home. Jack, for his part, had two lovers who now glared at each other like cagey jackals silently circling their prey—*him*! They looked at him again as if they were in a market stall, evaluating the wares. Deirdre had been with him in the garden, and she did arouse him. That was certain. It got him thinking about a life with a vixen like that with undeniable charms. And he already knew her in the Biblical sense, and she knew exactly how to please him. His mind filled with memories of her and her ways. But then Morgan, the unattainable, drove him to frustration with her emerald eyes and raven hair.

Collin announced to the family that the liner would leave Queenstown on the 22nd.

Morgan opened up, her eyes glistening, and turned her sultry voice on Jack, asking him if he would reconsider moving to Canada.

The table was silent, waiting, all eyes on Jack, who fidgeted with his serviette. He suspected this was coming and was nervous. Who was pushing now? He cleared his throat. "As I've told you, Morgan, I went to Montreal and Quebec City several times on Cunard liners. Before the war, of course. It seemed quite interesting but damned cold in the winter. I haven't changed my view. I much prefer Ireland's weather. Warmer because of the Gulf Stream and the North Atlantic Drift, I think. Did you know it was discovered by Ponce de Leon?" He rattled on, talking around the issue.

All Morgan heard was, *I don't want to go to Canada. I want to stay right here.*

Deirdre smiled and asked for more potatoes. "You have a lovely home here, Mrs. O'Donnell."

"I try, dear. We're just lucky that it didn't get burned to the ground like so many others."

Collin took a slug of his stout. "I heard your spunk kept that from happening, Auntie."

Biddy brandished her table knife in the air. "I've always been good with a frying pan, in and out of the kitchen."

Morgan added, in a triumphant tone, that Jack had stood up against the British intrusion on one occasion and paid the price for it.

The tapers flickered in the candelabra on the table as a gust of wind came through the open window. Then several candles blew out at once. The house power went off, leaving the room in semi-darkness.

Collin got up and went to the window. The rain started blowing in from the sea as he closed the casements. Through the rain, he saw that the neighboring house was also dark. Heading to the sideboard, he asked, "Auntie, where are the matches?"

"Right there in the second drawer down. Should we check the fuse box?" Pointing at the window, Collin answered, "No, it looks like a general power outage, Auntie."

Biddy exclaimed, "Damn these new-fangled electric lights!"

Collin relit the candles at the table, casting an eerie glow on the family and surroundings.

Morgan took the outage as a sign that it was time for a decision. She stood up and went to the window. Out of the blackness, with rain pelting off the rattling panes, lightning flashed, almost blinding her and instantaneously lighting up the room. At that moment, she thought she could see Sir Owain's arm and lance thrust into the sky. Then he was gone. She rubbed her eyes and stared again. Nothing. Was she imagining it? She shivered. Change and answers were coming. Now was the time to have Jack choose right here with Deirdre, Collin, and the others present. It would be easier under the cloak of darkness. Returning to her seat, she took a large gulp of wine and coughed. "Sit down, Collin. I need to know something important from Jack, and we're running out of time."

She turned to Jack now, and he seemed to tense up in the chair, his shoulders hunched up a little. "You told me once I motivated you to recover from the *Lusitania* disaster. You also told me that you loved me. You've been a wonderful friend to me after Tadgh died. I have grown to love you, too. There, I've said it. I know that Deirdre is here to win you over. Do you love me enough to come with me to Canada if I decide to go with Collin?"

Again, quiet at the table.

Deirdre listened to Morgan try to lure the man in like a prize fish. *Fight for Jack or fight for her Templar responsibility? Which would it be?* She wondered whether Jack had already made that decision for her. She needed time to think, but there was no time. Morgan had made sure of that. She had to act.

Before Jack could speak, Deirdre stood up and walked to his chair, resting her hand gently on his shoulder. Her fingers caressed his neck. She turned his face towards her with her other hand, saying, "Since Morgan has forced the issue, I will say my piece. It is true that I came here to profess my love for you, Jack. I miss you terribly since you've been away. I want what's best for you, my dear, and I know you want to stay here in Ireland. Where I will be."

Jack squirmed in his chair, his arm rubbing the small of his back to relieve the pain that had suddenly erupted there. He tried to think. He hadn't expected Morgan to confront him with this in public and certainly not with Deirdre present. He hated the cold and spoke the truth. "I do want to stay here in Ireland. This is my home."

Collin saw his chances evaporating unless Jack would choose Deirdre. He interjected. "I have your best interests in mind, Morgan, when I say that you, and Jack, if he can be persuaded to, should come to Canada with me, as we discussed. This war in Ireland may be at a lull now, but it's not over, that's certain. You are a healer. Your future as a doctor awaits in Toronto."

Morgan didn't like the way Deirdre was draped all over Jack. "I could stay here with you in Ireland, Jack, if necessary," she said from across the table, in a whisper, almost pleading.

Biddy shook her head, and everyone at the table turned back to the ex-Cunard manager for his decision.

Jack suddenly realized the conundrum he was in. It had come to a head. The woman he loved most needed to go to Canada, and he wasn't prepared to leave his homeland. He finally said, "I can't keep you from your career path, Morgan. If you stay here, you would be persecuted even up here in Donegal. I can't have that."

Faced with entreaties of love from both of his women and in public, Jack was confused. He was being bombarded from all sides. Both women had advantages. Morgan had constraints. Deirdre, lust. He stood up, gently moved Deirdre aside, and paced around the table before saying, "I have been dreading this confrontation. I admit I love both of you, though Morgan, for longer. The circumstances are complicated." Looking at Morgan, he said, "I know you are still in mourning, lass. War makes us hurried bedfellows. Damn, I shouldn't have said that!"

His hands shook. "I meant the ravages of war remind us that life is fleeting, that we must reach out and seize the most important things before it is too late. I don't want to disappoint either of you, and I want to protect you both. I need time to think."

Morgan got up and held Jack's hand before she spoke. The two women stood almost nose to nose. "When I had to make my decision right here on this very table, almost five years ago, I asked my two champions, one of whom is here tonight, to let me think about it overnight. I answered in the morning with a piece of paper with Tadgh's name on it, rest his soul. Collin needs an immediate answer, as he did once before. I suggest we leave you to make your own decision overnight, my love, and come back in the morning with a piece of paper either saying, Morgan or Deirdre. Can you do that, Jack?"

"Yes. I guess I must. I feel bad. But it's only fair to both of you."

Collin spoke up. "Does that mean that you will come to Canada with me, Morgan?"

"If Jack chooses Deirdre, yes. If he chooses me, then it will depend on what he finally wants to do."

Biddy stood up and brought the fruit and custard to the table. "Good. You're handling this better than I thought. No catfights yet. Anyone for dessert?"

No one wanted any. They had lost their appetites.

Deirdre and Jack agonized overnight in separate bedrooms. Sleep wouldn't come. If Jack hadn't been bunking in a room with Collin, she would have gone to him. As it was, Deirdre was relegated to a room with Morgan. Not a word passed between the two women after they left the supper table. Deirdre left her clothes on. Just before dawn, Deirdre realized that she had to tell Morgan about the baby, especially after what she had told her brother last night.

In the morning, the two women lingered upstairs and waited to go down to breakfast. As she was combing her hair, Deirdre said, "We need to talk before we hear what Jack has to say." She sat on the bed. "Sit here with me, Morgan."

Morgan looked at her with suspicious eyes and sat down.

Deirdre stared at her adversary. "Whether Jack chooses you or me, we need to have a conversation afterward before you decide about moving to Canada with your brother. Will you agree to that?"

"Jack is going to choose me, Deirdre. I'm certain of that. What conversation?"

"I'll tell you after."

"No. I won't agree to anything like that."

Deirdre had no choice. "About the fact that you need to stay here in Ireland for Jack's sake."

"Other than his concern about the cold, why?"

"How do you view your role with Aidan, Morgan? He's a consideration, don't you think?"

"What's Aidan got to do with it?"

"Humor me."

"Aidan has grown into a capable man, Deirdre. I still would like to guide him away from the violence. There is some motherly instinct there, but he could now fend for himself if need be."

Deirdre uncharacteristically lowered her eyes before speaking again. "Well, I have a motherly instinct too, Morgan."

Morgan's eyes grew wide as saucers. "What do you mean?"

"I think you know what I mean if you look closely." She put Morgan's hand gently on her tummy. "There, did you feel the kick?"

"It's Jack's?"

"What do you think? Five months ago, I knew it to the very night among many nights."

Morgan winced at the thought of him with Deirdre, and then a flashback to Tadgh's miscarried child who never had a chance to become a rebel.

Deirdre had just played her ace card, and she knew it.

"That's why you are wearing that loose dress. And that is why you are here, isn't it? Have you told him?"

"No, not yet. He needs to decide about us first. I don't want him just doing the right thing. He would hate me later, especially if he wanted you. But he needs to know. If he chooses you, then I won't stand in your way, but he will need to stay close to be a part of our child's upbringing. He will be a father and close to us. Do you understand, Morgan?"

"What if he chooses you, then?"

"Then he'll be happy with the news, won't he."

"Then why would we need to have a conversation about my moving to Canada?"

"I'll leave that for later when he makes the right decision."

Morgan turned and pretended to be straightening the covers on the bed. She was reeling from the news. Perhaps she should allow Deirdre to have Jack. Collin would be happy to show Morgan a new life in Canada. That way, Jack would bring up his own child. But she loved him and wanted a family life with him. *This was so unfair.*

"Will you agree to let me tell Jack after he makes his decision?"

Morgan pulled on her skirt and adjusted the waistband. "I don't like keeping secrets, but I will agree to that, yes. It's your news to share, not mine."

"If he chooses to be with you, then will you stay in Ireland for his and my child's sakes?"

"I see your point, but I will have to think about it, Deirdre, when he does choose me."

"That's all I ask. Let's go down and see what Jack has decided."

Biddy was making breakfast when the women joined her in the kitchen.

"Sleep well, lasses?" their hostess asked with a sly grin.

"Not a wink, Auntie," Morgan said, heading for the stove where the teapot had steeped.

"I slept like a baby," Deirdre lied. "Have you seen Jack?"

Sensing her meaning, Morgan winced before turning away to the cupboard.

Biddy pointed out the window. "He's out there thrashing about, I expect."

"And my brother?" Morgan asked, taking a cup from the sideboard.

"He just went out to talk to Jack, girls. Said he'd be back momentarily with the lad, so he did."

A few minutes later, Morgan and Deirdre sat on opposite sides of the table, staring down into their teacups, and not saying a word.

The silence was interrupted when they heard a motorcycle drive up outside.

Morgan rushed to the door on instinct, hoping, maybe . . . but no, of course not. She had to stop having these flashbacks. It was Peader, with Aidan on the back. They jumped off the vehicle and Aidan bounded into Morgan's arms. They had driven on the main road, something they couldn't have done without severe risk just days before.

Biddy was overjoyed and set two more places for breakfast while Morgan explained the situation with Jack.

Collin was meeting with Jack in the garden. The smell of bacon wafted through the window. "How did you sleep, lad?"

"Not at all." He turned to face the newspaperman. "Collin, have you ever been at a point where you knew your decision would be pivotal to your whole life, and you didn't know what to do?"

Collin thought for a moment. "Yes, a couple of times. Once, when I was a young thug and caught in a warehouse fire, I decided to cut someone free from bondage. It was Sam. He saved my life. That act of mercy led to many wonderful things in my life, including finding my wife and family and discovering my long-lost sister."

"What made you decide to do the right thing at that moment?"

"My internal belief in good versus evil, right versus wrong, love versus hate. Something that, until that moment, I didn't know I had within me. I guess each of us must face such a decision at least once, and our inner voice will come through."

"But some people make the wrong decision."

"There is that possibility. But look on the bright side. We're all still alive, unlike poor Tadgh. I'm not going to try to influence your decision, Jack. You've heard my speech already. Make your decision and then come inside and face the women. I know you'll do the right thing."

As he slapped Jack on the shoulder and turned toward the kitchen door, leaving him pacing, Collin thought, *Heaven help me, I'm sounding just like Sam.*

Collin was happy to see Aidan and Peader safely home. Peader announced that the Brigades' orders were to stand down but not disband. There was an element of uncertainty as to the future.

"What will happen if the outcome of negotiations is the continuation of partition, Peader?"

"That's the key question, Collin, isn't it? It would be hard for me to accept that solution when so many have died for the cause of freedom for all of Ireland. What would happen to the Catholics now trapped within the six counties of Northern Ireland?"

Collin sat down at the kitchen table. "I was there a few days ago, in Belfast. There will be hell to pay, I can tell you." Collin continued, "Where would you stand?"

Peader slammed his fist on the table, rattling the teacups and spilling the salt. "After all we've been through, I would stand on the side of freedom for all, Collin." He righted the saltshaker, then swept up the spilled crystals and threw them over his left shoulder."

"Bravo!" Aidan cried. "I would stand with you."

"God, no," Biddy wailed. "Jesus, help us if it comes to that." She plopped plates of egg and toast in front of the men.

Morgan caught Deirdre's gaze and then addressed the group. "Haven't you men had enough of this killing?"

Aidan took a rasher of bacon from the plate in the center of the table. "I wouldn't be able to live with myself if I let Tadgh down, could I now." He took his teacup and raised it high. "To my wonderful brother, Tadgh. May he rest in peace."

They all stood and raised their cups in salute to their fallen hero.

Jack picked that moment to come in from the garden. Everyone sat down in silence. "Who are we saluting?"

Morgan looked up at the gathering. "My beloved Tadgh, of course." Her chin lifted proudly, and her eyes blazed.

They all drank and set glasses down with a thud.

'Of course. How stupid of me." He picked up an empty glass, raised it high, then set it back down. "Any breakfast left?"

Morgan couldn't meet anyone's eyes after she drank, staring off into the distance.

Biddy got up and went to the sideboard to fix Jack a plate.

Morgan and Deirdre sat forward in their seats and waited as Jack sat down at the end of the table between them.

"I can see that everyone is waiting. God help me, I have decided, and I hope you can all forgive me. Hardest thing I've ever had to do." He put the piece of folded paper on the table in front of him and sat back.

At that moment, they heard a full-throated motorcycle rumble outside. Peader got up to see who could be tampering with his machine. He went to the vestibule and opened the front door, expecting to yell at a vandal.

Instead, Peader stood there, transfixed, with his mouth open.

At the door stood a bedraggled Irishman with a patch over one eye, leaning on his crutch. Where his lower right leg should have been, a peg was strapped below the knee. Though his body appeared tattered and worn, he had a fire in his warm amber eye.

"Who is it, Peader?" Morgan yelled from the kitchen.

The answer didn't come from Peader.

"It is I, aroon, the Clan Chieftain of your heart, Tadgh McCarthy!"

Ceasefire

THE END of Book Six
Book Seven, titled *Asunder,* is coming soon!

CAST OF CHARACTERS

North America—Historical

Dorothy Finlay—Sam and Lil's Younger Daughter

Elizabeth Finlay (Lil)—Sam's Wife

Ernest Finlay—Sam and Lil's Elder Son

Norah Finlay—Sam and Lil's Elder Daughter

Samuel Stevenson Finlay—Artist & Director of Art at Riverdale High School, Toronto

Stephen Finlay—Sam and Lil's Newborn Son

John Ross Robertson—Publisher and Editor-in-Chief, Toronto Evening Telegram (Tely)

North America—Fictional

Jim Fletcher—*Toronto Evening Telegram*, News Director, Collin's Boss

Collin O'Donnell—Young Irishman from Toronto

Kathleen O'Donnell (Kathy)—Young Irish Woman in Toronto, Collin's Wife. (née O'Sullivan)

Liam O'Donnell—Kathy and Collin's Son

Claire O'Donnell—Kathy and Collin's Elder Daughter

Shaina O'Donnell—Kathy and Collin's Newborn Daughter

Fiona O'Sullivan—Kathleen's Mother

Ryan O'Sullivan—Kathleen's Father

Europe—Historical

Don Juan del Aguila—Military Leader, Spanish Forces at Kinsale Ireland 1601-2

Tom Barry—O/C 3rd Cork West Flying Column, IRA

Pope Benedict XV—Born Giacomo Paolo Giovanni Battista della Chiesa, Letter helped bring an End to Irish War of Independence

Harry Boland—Michael Collins' 2ⁿᵈ I/C

Richard Boyle—Lord Cork, Lismore Castle, British Leader Confederate War, 1640s

Lord Broghill—Roger Boyle, Richard's Son, Laid Siege to Blarney Castle in 1646

Cathal Brugha—Chief of Staff, Irish Republican Army (IRA), War of Independence

Sir George Carew—British Lord Totnes, President of Munster in 1601

Frank Carney—C/O, 1st Northern Division, IRA during the War of Independence

Sir Neville Chamberlain—Chief Inspector, Royal Irish Constabulary (RIC) Ireland

Michael Collins—Adjutant General, Irish Volunteers, Director of Intelligence (IRA)

Robert Crosbie—Editor, *The Cork Examiner* Newspaper during the War of Independence

St. Dabheog—Built the First Monastery on Saints Island, Lough Derg, in 400s CE

Robert Devereux—Earl of Essex, Queen Elizabeth I Favorite, Led Irish Campaign, 1599

Sir Henry Docwra—Governor of Derry after crushing the O'Donnell Irish Clan in 1602

Alan Ellis—Newspaper Reporter, *The Cork Examiner* - during the Burning of Cork

Tom Ennis—2nd Battalion Dublin Brigade, IRA Lead, Customs House Burning

James FitzThomas Fitz Gerald—Sugán Earl of Desmond, Maurice's Ancestor, Captured and Jailed before the Battle of Kinsale

Thomas Fitzmaurice—18th Lord Kerry and Baron Lixnaw, Ally of Red Hugh O'Donnell

King George V—King of Great Britain during the War of Independence

David Lloyd George—Prime Minister, Great Britain during the War of Independence

Thomas Gilmartin—Roman Cath. Archbishop of Tuam.IRA Excommunication Letter

Molly Gleeson—Proprietress, an Stad Hotel and Pub, Dublin

Arthur Griffith—Founder of Sinn Fein Party and Leader in de Valera's Absence

Con Healy—IRA Marksman, Tralee who Killed Major Mackinnon

John Edward Healy—Publisher, *The Irish Times*

Denis Polastron de la Hilliere—Knights of St. John Courier from Grand Master Antoine de Paule

Superintendent Huston—Head of Cork Fire Brigade during the Burning of Cork

Jan Janszoon von Haarlem—Murat Reis the Younger, Grand Admiral Republic of Salé

Dean Patrick Keown—Prior, Lough Derg Monastery during the War of Independence

Owen Latimer—Lieutenant Col, K Company Auxiliaries Commander, Burned Cork

Reverend J.H. Lawlor—Professor of Ecclesiastical Studies, Dublin University Researcher of Ancient Gaelic Documents Including *an Cathach of St. Columba*

Lewis Lord of Kinalmeaky—British Commander, Destroyed Kilbrittain Castle in 1642 Richard Boyle's Son, Delivered *Book of Lismore* to his father

Florence MacCarthaigh—Clan Chieftain until 1601, Arrested by George Carew before Battle of Kinsale in January 1602

MacCarthaigh Raibhaigh—Lord Finghin, Recipient of the *Book of MacCarthaigh Reagh* at Kilbrittain, written in the late 1400s

Tomas Mac Curtain—Head of IRB for Cork, Tadgh's Commanding Officer, Lord Mayor of Cork, Murdered by British

Major Mackinnon —Vicious Auxiliaries Leader, 'Scourge of Tralee'

Constance Markiewicz—Countess, Deputy Commandant Battalion #2, St. Stephen's Green

McCarthy Mor—Muscry Chieftain, Blarney, Leader Confederate War Rebellion, 1640s

Jacques de Molay—Last Head of the Knights Templar, Burned at the Stake in 1314

Sean O'Casey—Irish Playwright, Tadgh's Literary Mentor

Brigid O'Donnell—"Biddy," Peader's Mother in Dungloe, Tailor

James O'Donnell—Peader's Father, Seasonal Worker in Scotland

Peader O'Donnell—College Student, Later to be a Revolutionary Leader, "Peadar", O/C No. 2 Brigade, Donegal IRA during the War of Independence

Niall Garve O'Donnell—Cousin of Red Hugh O'Donnell, Irish Traitor

Red Hugh O'Donnell—Last Free Chieftain O'Donnell Clan until 1602, Battle of Kinsale

Rory O'Donnell—1st Earl of Tyrconnell, Red Hugh's Younger Brother Led Flight of the Earls to Europe in 1607

Seán O'Donoghue—IRA Captain, Leader of Dillon Cross Attack, Cork

Sam O'Flaherty—O/C No. 4 Brigade, Donegal South-West IRA

Sean O'Hegarty—O/C No. 1 Brigade, Cork IRA

Hugh O'Neill—Clan Chieftain, Northeast Ireland. Compatriot of Red Hugh O'Donnell at the Battle of Kinsale, 1602

Sir Owain—Twelfth Century European Knight, Endured Entrance to Purgatory then Returned to Temple Castle, Now Ghost for Lost Souls there

Charlotte Perceval—Matron of Temple House, Ballymote Ireland

King Phillip III—Catholic King of Spain in 1601, Provided Army to Irish Clans

John Joe Sheehy—Commander, Tralee IRA, War of Independence

Daniel Shields—Traitor to the IRA, Led British to Clonmult Ambush

Joseph Sweeney—O/C No. 1 Donegal Brigade, IRA during the War of Independence, Later O/C 1st Northern Division, IRA

Johnathan Swift—Lawyer, Friend of John Temple

Abigail Swift—Johnathan Swift's Wife

Johnathan Swift—Abigail's Son, Satirical Essayist (Gulliver's Travels), Dean, St. Patrick's Cathedral, Dublin

Martha Temple—William Temple's Wife

William Temple—4th Provost, Trinity College, Devereux Supporter

John Temple—William Temple's Son – Master of the Rolls, Ireland

Sir William Temple—John Temple's Son, Baronet, British Ambassador

Wolfe Tone—Father of Irish Republicanism and Leader of 1798 Rebellion

Eamon de Valera—President of Dáil Éireann (Sinn Fein Party)

Fra Alof de Wignacort—Grand Master, Knights Hospitaller, 1601-1622

Lord Wimborne—Ivor Churchill Guest, British Lord Lieutenant for Ireland

Europe—Fictional

Captain Maurice Collis—Fishing Captain, Fenit, Ireland, Descendant of the Fitzmaurice Clan, Supporter of Tadgh

Martha Collis—Wife of Maurice Collis

Deirdre—Owner and Barkeeper of the Temple Bar Pub, Dublin, Ireland, Owner and Shopkeeper of Gilroy's Grocery, Temple Bar, Dublin

Tony Fuller—Historian, Artfert Cathedral

Captain Haig—Captain of the Troop Ship *Aquitania*

Henry Hollingsworth—Graduate Student, Working for Professor Lawlor at RIA

Abbad al-Khattabi—Nephew of Abd el-Krion RIF Military Commander, Descendant of Jan Janszoon and Member British Israeli Association

Fazaar Al-Khattabi—Abbad's Brother, Lawlor Student

Floren Janszoon von Haarlem—Brother of Jan Janszoon von Haarlem, Murat Reis the Younger

Jack Jordan—Third Bosun's Mate, HMS *Lusitania*, Manager Cunard Operations, Queenstown, Ireland, Manager Gilroy's Grocery for Deirdre, Deirdre's Lover

Brian MacSweeney—Red Hugh O'Donnell, Warrior Leader Sent to Liberate Fitzmaurice

Aidan McCarthy—Tadgh's Younger Brother, Irish Volunteer

Tadgh McCarthy—Young Irish Revolutionary, Member of Cork IRB, Communications, and Transportation Specialist

Morgan McCarthy—Irish Woman Rescued by Tadgh McCarthy, Tadgh's Wife, (née Claire O'Donnell)

Molly McGuire—Member, Cumann na mBan, Supporter of Tom Barry, Member British Israeli Association, Lover of Abbad

Martin Murphy—Captain of Supply Ships for Beamish & Crawford (B&C) Brewery

Finian O'Donnell—Collin's Father, Murdered in Donegal

Shaina O'Donnell—Collin's Mother, Murdered in Toronto

Maureen O'Sullivan—Journalist for *The Irish Times* Newspaper, Dublin, Ireland, Kathy's cousin

Derek Slocum—Deirdre's Cook and Bodyguard, Ex-Marine

George Thompson—Cunard Manager

Jeffrey Wiggins—Transportation Leader, Beamish & Crawford (B&C) Brewery, Cork City, Ireland, and Tadgh's Colleague at B&C

William—Cunard Longshoreman, Tries to Steal the Munitions at Queenstown.

HISTORICAL BACKGROUND

The purpose of this historical background is to illuminate the historical facts embedded in Book Six: Fortunes, particularly those associated with the Clans Pact Adventurers.

The Irish War of Independence was waged very differently from the Easter Rising Rebellion where the Irish patriots occupied key locations mainly in Dublin and waited for the British to attack them in the open. As we have already discussed, this was a heroic act of martyrdom intended to inflame the Irish people against the occupying British.

Primarily due to the inspired leadership of Michael Collins, the War of Independence was fought using the military methodology that had made the Clans so successful before the pitched battle of Kinsale in 1601, namely hit-and-run guerrilla warfare tactics.

As a result, there were many local skirmishes that confounded and enraged the British authorities. I have chosen several important battles and events which intertwine with my Adventurers storyline. Of course, there are also fictitious adventures that interact with the British.

Therefore, I have included a brief overview of the Irish War of Independence, and separately a list of the historical events that are embedded in my novel in this background section.

Ref.	Subject	Location
1	Irish War of Independence Summary	Author's Note
2	War of Independence Historical Events in Novel Six: *Fortunes*	Ch. 3, pg 42
3	*Book of Ballymote* (*Leabhar Bhaile an Mhóta*)	Ch. 1, pg 11
4	Order of Solomon's Temple, (Knights Templar)	Ch. 2, pg 20
5	Knights of the Hospital of Saint John the Baptist in Jerusalem, (Knights Hospitaller)	Ch. 1, pg 14
6	Barbary Pirates	Ch. 2, pg 27

1. The Irish War of Independence - Summary *

This summary is a concise overview of the history of the war that is repeated here, with some additions for a more complete background.

The Irish War of Independence (Irish: Cogadh na Saoirse) or Anglo-Irish War was a guerrilla war fought in Ireland from 1919 to 1921 between the Irish Republican Army (IRA, the army of the Irish Republic) and British forces: the British Army, along with the quasi-military Royal Irish Constabulary (RIC) and its paramilitary forces the Auxiliaries and Ulster Special Constabulary (USC). It was an escalation of the Irish revolutionary period into warfare.

In April 1916, Irish republicans launched the Easter Rising against British rule and proclaimed an Irish Republic. Although it was crushed after a week of fighting, the Easter Rising and the British response led to greater popular support for Irish independence.

Eamon de Valera, who commanded the battalion at Boland's Bakery during the Easter Rising, was uniquely spared execution because of his American birth. He became the political leader of the revolution along with Arthur Griffith, who had started the Sinn Fein political movement.

Michael Collins, who had served as aide-de-camp to Joseph Plunkett, one of the Easter Rising organizers at the Dublin General Post Office, emerged as the military leader of the War of Independence. Michael organized the guerrilla hit-and-run flying columns of the military Irish Republican Army (IRA) and employed an elite intelligence gathering and assassination team to confound the British forces in Ireland.

In the December 1918 election, the republican party Sinn Féin won a landslide victory in Ireland. On 21 January 1919, they formed a breakaway government (Dáil Éireann) and declared Irish independence. That day, two RIC officers were shot dead in the Soloheadbeg ambush by IRA volunteers acting on their own initiative. The conflict developed gradually. For much of 1919, IRA activity involved capturing weaponry and freeing republican prisoners, while the Dáil set about building a state.

In September, the British government outlawed the Dáil and Sinn Féin, and the conflict intensified. The IRA began ambushing RIC and British Army patrols, attacking their barracks and forcing isolated barracks to be abandoned. The British government bolstered the RIC with recruits from Britain—the Black and Tans and Auxiliaries, many of whom had survived the deadly trenches of WWI—They became notorious for ill-discipline and reprisal attacks on civilians, some of which were authorized by the British government. Thus, the conflict is sometimes called the Black and Tan War.

The conflict also involved civil disobedience, notably the refusal of Irish railway men to transport British forces or military supplies, the refusal to obey the courts, and a disruption of roads and communications systems.

In mid-1920, republicans won control of most county councils, and British authority collapsed in most of the south and west, forcing the British government to introduce emergency powers. About three hundred people had been killed by late 1920.

The conflict escalated in November. On Bloody Sunday in Dublin, 21 November 1920, fourteen British intelligence operatives were assassinated in the morning; then, in the afternoon, the RIC opened fire on a crowd at a Gaelic football match, killing fourteen civilians and wounding sixty-five. A week later, seventeen Auxiliaries were killed by the IRA in the Kilmichael Ambush in County Cork.

The British government declared martial law in much of southern Ireland. The center of Cork city was burnt out by British forces in December 1920. Violence continued to escalate over the next seven months when 1,000 people were killed, and 4,500 republicans were interned. Much of the fighting took place in Munster (particularly County Cork), Dublin, and Belfast, which together saw over 75 percent of the conflict deaths.

The conflict in northeast Ulster had a sectarian aspect. While the Catholic minority there mostly backed Irish independence, the Protestant majority were mostly unionist/loyalist. A Special Constabulary was formed, comprised mostly of Protestants, and loyalist paramilitaries were active. They attacked Catholics in reprisal for IRA actions, and in Belfast, a sectarian conflict raged in which almost five hundred were killed, most of them Catholics.

In May 1921, Ireland was partitioned under British law by the Government of Ireland Act, which created Northern Ireland. Both sides agreed to a ceasefire (or 'truce') on 11 July 1921.

Michael Collins and Arthur Griffiths led the Irish delegation at these talks. Recognizing the British determination to retain its northern industrial center at all costs, with Winston Churchill threatening to destroy Ireland if this was not agreed, the Irish delegation accepted the split of Ireland between the six northern counties to stay in Great Britain and the remaining 26 southern counties to form the new Republic of Ireland country. These post-ceasefire talks led to the signing of the Anglo-Irish Treaty on 6 December, 1921, ending British rule in the Republic.

The Irish Free State awarded 62,868 medals for service during the War of Independence, of which 15,224 were issued to IRA fighters of the flying columns.

After a ten-month transitional period overseen by a provisional government, the Irish Free State was created as a self-governing Dominion on 6 December, 1922, with British forces withdrawing from the new Republic of Ireland. Northern Ireland remained within the United Kingdom.

Revolution: Book Five covered the period from 1916, after the Easter Rising, until the period occurring after the Bloody Sunday events in Dublin, November 1920. *Fortunes: Book Six* continues the saga throughout the end of the War of Independence until the ceasefire in July 1921.

Eamon de Valera and many followers did not agree that the country should be split in this way. Still the political revolutionary leader, he rallied republican supporters who fought against the Irish Free State military in 1922-23 in the Irish Civil War. But that is the subject of the last two novels in the Irish Clans series: *Asunder* and *Revelation*.

* Reference: https://en.wikipedia.org/wiki/Dáil_Éireann_(Irish Republic)

2. Historical Events in Novel Six: Fortunes—After Bloody Sunday, Dublin

November 28, 1920
>Kilmichael Ambush—West Cork IRA Tom Barry, 17 Auxiliaries killed. Reprisal, 3 IRA killed.

December 10, 1920
>Martial Law in Cork, Kerry, Tipperary, and Limerick.

December 1920
>Eamon de Valera returns to Ireland, Dublin, from America.

December 11. 1920
>Burning of Cork, Reprisal for Kilmichael Ambush.

December 23, 1920
>Government of Ireland Act. Separate North and South.

January 21, 1921
>Peader O'Donnell made head of the No. 2 Donegal Flying Column.

February 9, 1921
>Occupation of Skibbereen by the IRA.

February 20, 1921
>Clonmult Ambush near Midleton 12 IRA killed surrounded in a house. Informer Dan Shields—(Tadgh captured).

February 22, 1921
>First Donegal burnings.

February 28, 1921
>6 IRA Prisoners executed at Cork Gaol—(Tadgh among them).

March 11, 1921
>Dail Eireann declares war on British.

Mar 19, 1921
>Crossberry Ambush by Tom Barry IRA.

March 21, 1921

Donegal IRA column attacks RIC in Falcarragh under Peader O'Donnell.

April 15, 1921

Major McKinnon, brutal auxiliary officer killed at Tralee Golf Course.

May 10, 1921

Peader O'Donnell attacked and wounded in the arm and hand.

May 25, 1921

Dublin IRA occupy and burn the Custom House in Dublin. 5 IRA killed and 80 captured. Eamon deValera orders and Collins opposes.

May 1921

Pope Benedict XV encourages Ireland and Great Britain to come to an agreement.

June 6, 1921

British call off burning reprisals.

June 13, 1921

1st Northern Division O/C Joe Sweeney attacked in South-West Donegal and chased for several days by Auxies near Lough Derg.

June 22, 1921

King George V pushes to stop hostilities.

June 24, 1921

British Cabinet proposes talks with Sinn Fein before they would stop Martial Law.

July 10, 1921

Belfast Bloody Sunday—161 houses destroyed, 16 civilians killed.

July 11, 1921

War of Independence ceasefire, but sporadic fighting continues.

3. *Book of Ballymote (Leabhar Bhaile an Mhŏta)* *

I include this background section again for the convenience of the reader. The Book of Ballymote is a compendium of older works and valuable documents handed down from ancient times, similar to the Book of Lismore. It was created in about 1390 at the Castle of Ballymote, Sligo, for Tonnaltagh McDonagh, who occupied the castle at that time. Manus O'Duigan was the primary scribe for most of this tome.

In 1522 this manuscript was purchased by Aeg Óg O'Donnell, prince of Tir Conaill, for the price of 140 milch cows. We can only imagine why the O'Donnell clan wanted this ancient collection of documents. It was in Red Hugh O'Donnell's possession during his reign as Chieftain, leading up to the Battle of Kinsale.

It remained in the hands of Rory O'Donnell until the Flight of the Earls in 1607. After that, its whereabouts is not known until it was acquired by Trinity College. It stayed at Trinity until 1767. One can only assume that William Temple, 4th Provost of Trinity College from 1609 until his sudden death in 1627, would have had a hand in its acquisition. A Trinity scribe copied elements of the document in 1622.

In 1719 it was lent by the college library to Anthony Raymond, vicar of Trim, and thence to other scholars. In 1785 the manuscript was presented by Chevalier Thomas O'Gorman to the newly formed Royal Irish Academy as its first acquisition for safekeeping. Apparently, O'Gorman acquired it from a millwright's widow in Drogheda for £20.

The Irish writing is in two columns with decorated capital letters of interwoven designs in red, black, green, vermilion, and chrome. It is bound in leather with oak boards. The 251 vellum folios are 15.75 x 10.25 inches in size.

The table of contents that had been scribbled down by Reverend Hugh Jackson Lawlor and passed over to Tadgh and Peader is provided below:

Book of Ballymote
Leabhar Bhaile an Mhŏta)
Table of Contents

1. Drawing of Noah's Ark

2. History of the Lost Israelites—Migration from Israel into Europe to become Gaels and Anglo-Saxons

3. The Life of Saint Patrick

4. *Lebor Gabála Erenn* (*The Book of Invasions*) Six civilizations, including Tuatha Dé Danann and Milesians

5. Instructions of King Cormac mac Airt

6. Triads of Ireland Including Customs, Law, and Behavior

7. Stories of Fionn MacCumhail (Finn MacCool) and Brian Borumh (Brian Boru).

8. Genealogies of Clans and Kings of Ulster, Leinster, Connaught, and Munster

9. Irish Versification

10. *Auraicept na n-Éces* (scholar's primer) Including In Lebor Ogaim, a rare treatise on the Ogham language

11. The *Lebor na gCeart* (Book of Rights)

12. Various Greek and Latin fragments on the fall of Troy—including part of the *Aeneid*

* last leaf is a faded vellum fragment.

Book of Ballymote
Folio Example
Courtesy Royal Irish Academy

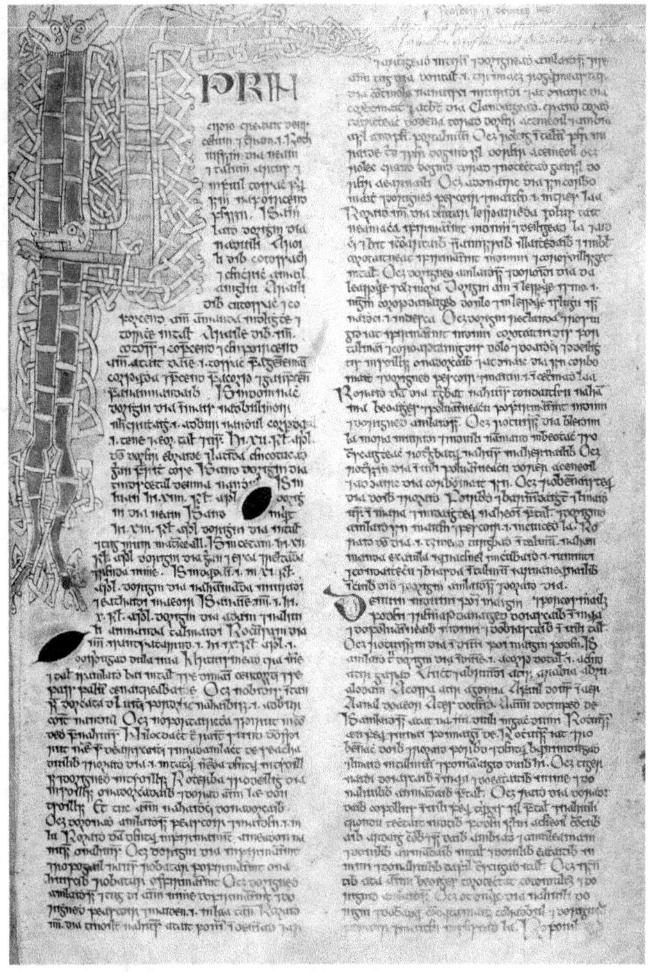

4. Order of Solomon's Temple (Knights Templar)

The Knights Templar, or Order of Solomon's Temple, was a Catholic military order founded in 1119 with vows of poverty by six knights from France at first and then from all over Christendom. Their mission was to protect pilgrims traveling to and from the Holy Land, principally Jerusalem. They were initially headquartered on Temple Mount, thought to be the site of Solomon's Temple.

At the Council of Pisa in 1135, Pope Innocent II initiated the first papal monetary donation to the Order. Another significant benefit came in 1139 when Innocent II's papal bull Omne Datum Optimum exempted the Order from obedience to local laws. This ruling meant that the Templars could pass freely through all borders, were not required to pay any taxes, and were exempt from all authority except that of the Pope.

The Order grew in size and reputation. And with these attributes came resources. Knights joining the Order would place all their assets under Templar control while serving the cause. Templars were often the advance shock troops in key battles of the Crusades against the Muslims, as the heavily armored knights on their warhorses would set out to charge at the enemy, ahead of the main army bodies, in an attempt to break opposition lines. One of their most famous victories was in 1177 during the Battle of Montgisard, where some 500 Templar knights helped several thousand infantry to defeat Saladin's army of more than 26,000 soldiers.

They were astute at finance, applying the spoils of war to their organization. In fact, ninety percent of their members did not fight but operated powerful banking and logistics systems with almost one thousand commanderies and fortifications from Europe to the Holy Land by the late twelfth century.

They acquired large tracts of land, both in Europe and the Middle East; they bought and managed farms and vineyards; they built massive stone cathedrals and castles; they were involved in manufacturing, import and export; they had their own fleet of ships; and at one point they even owned the entire island of Cyprus.

Templar power started to erode after they were involved in several unsuccessful campaigns, including the pivotal Battle of Hattin. The Templars were forced to relocate their headquarters out of Jerusalem. Mysteries abound about what Jewish treasures and relics they may have uncovered and covertly taken with them. They moved to the seaport of Acre, which they held for the next century. It was lost in 1291. Their headquarters then moved to Limassol on the island of Cyprus. In 1303, however, the Templars lost the island to the Egyptian Mamluk Sultanate in the siege of Arwad. With the island gone, the Crusaders lost their last foothold in the Holy Land.

What remained was the vast wealth of land and coinage of the realm. So financially powerful were they that Kings gave their wealth to the Order for safekeeping.

Pope Clements V called a meeting in early 1307 in France with the Grand Masters of the Templars and its sister organization for the nursing of pilgrims, the Order of the Knights of the Hospital at Saint John of Jerusalem, or Knights Hospitaller, in an attempt to integrate the organizations. Both leaders rejected the idea.

King Phillip IV of France, who was deeply in debt to the Templars at that time, wanted a way out of his predicament. He used or created rumors about the Templars' secret initiation ceremonies being immoral to pressure Pope Clement V to have many of the Order's members in France arrested at dawn on Friday, October 13, 1307, including Grand Master Jacques de Molay and many of his knights in Paris. Their lands and other assets were seized, many granted to the Knights Hospitallers by the Pope.

As legend has it, hearing of these arrests that fateful Friday, Roger Bellechance (Jolly Roger), admiral of the Templar fleet, set sail from the Templar port of La Rochelle with nearly a dozen ships carrying Templar treasures and knights, potentially heading for a temporary safe haven with the Sinclairs in Scotland. He sailed under the skull and crossbones flag for the first time. This was a prescient symbol of the fate to come for Templar leaders in Paris.

Relenting to Phillip's demands, Pope Clement then issued the papal bull Pastoralis praeeminentiae on 22 November 1307, which instructed all Christian monarchs in Europe to arrest all Templars and seize their assets. Pope Clement called for papal hearings to determine the Templars' guilt or innocence.

The captive templars were tortured into giving false confessions, and some were burned at the stake. Under further pressure, Pope Clement V disbanded the Order in 1312. Finally, on 18 March 1314, the last Grand Master, Jacques de Molay recanted his confessions and was burned at the stake facing Notre Dame cathedral. According to legend, he called out from the flames that both Pope Clement and King Philip would soon meet him before God. Pope Clement died only a month later, and King Philip died while hunting within the same year.

In Ireland, the templars were arrested on charges of heresy, and their properties seized on February 2, 1308. They were held in Dublin Castle for two years without torture and convicted in 1310. Instead of being burned at the stake, they were allowed to enter monastic life in Ireland.

Templars fled to the few safe locations left, Scotland being one of them. There are stories that one route they took was north along the west coast of Ireland, far from the English influence in Dublin. They were supported by the Knights Hospitallers, who now owned the monasteries at Ardfert near Tralee and Ballymote in Sligo near an earlier Templar castle. There was great sympathy for the Templar cause in West Ireland at the time, with many feeling that the charges of heresy were trumped up by the King of France and the Pope.

The whereabouts of the treasures that were spirited away by Jolly Roger, including the mysteries of what the Templars may have found in the holy city, potentially under Solomon's Temple in its catacombs, remains a secret to this day. There are stories of Henry Sinclair of Rosslyn of Scotland sailing to Newfoundland and burying a treasure under the sands of Oak Island off Nova Scotia. But many claim that it is part of the mythology built around the Templar stories.

5. Knights of the Hospital of Saint John the Baptist in Jerusalem (Knights Hospitaller)

The Knights Hospitaller order preceded the Knights Templar in Jerusalem. Merchants from Amalfi, Italy, founded a hospital in the Muristan district of Jerusalem dedicated to John the Baptist to care for sick, poor, or injured pilgrims to the Holy Land. Blessed Gerard became its head in 1080. After the conquest of Jerusalem in 1099 during the First Crusade, a group of Crusaders formed a religious order to support the hospital.

After the fall of Jerusalem, the Knights Hospitaller moved to Accra with their counterpart Knights Templar. Eventually, they settled on the Island of Rhodes in 1310, when the Templars were being arrested, and many of their assets were turned over to the Hospitallers by the Pope. By this time, they were a strong Papal force in the Mediterranean and elsewhere.

On Rhodes, the Hospitallers were forced to become a more militarized force, fighting especially with the Barbary pirates, also known as Ottoman corsairs. They withstood two invasions in the 15th century, one by the Sultan of Egypt in 1444 and another by the Ottoman Sultan Mehmed the Conqueror in 1480, who, after capturing Constantinople and defeating the Byzantine Empire in 1453, made the Knights a priority target.

In 1522, an entirely new sort of force arrived: 400 ships under the command of Sultan Suleiman the Magnificent delivered somewhere between 100,000 and 200,000 men to the island. Against this force, the Knights, under Grand Master Philippe Villiers de L'Isle-Adam, had about 7,000 men-at-arms and their fortifications. The siege lasted six months, at the end of which the surviving defeated Hospitallers were allowed to withdraw to Sicily.

In 1530, after seven years of moving from place to place in Europe, Pope Clement VII – himself a Knight – reached an agreement with Charles V, Holy Roman Emperor, also King of Spain and Sicily, to provide the knights permanent quarters at Birgu on Malta.

In 1565 the greatly outnumbered Hospitallers survived the long, grand siege of Suleiman to permanently retain their home in Malta. They built a new, highly fortified city Valetta on the south shore of the island. There they flourished for two centuries through the architectural and cultural golden age of Malta until Napoleon invaded and expelled the Order for a time.

6. Barbary Pirates

The Barbary pirates, Barbary corsairs, or Ottoman corsairs, were Muslin pirates and privateers who operated from Norh Africa, based primarily in the ports of Salé. Rabat, Algiers, Tunis, and Tripoli. This area was known in Eurpoe as the Barbary Coast, in reference to the Berbers. They operated active ships during the Crusades but became a formidable marauding force starting in the fifteenth century. Some of their ruthless leaders were of European Christian origin, such as John Wars and Zymen Danseker, converting to the Muslin fath. Notorious carsairs Hayreddin Barbarossa and Oruç Reis, Turkish Barbarossa brothers, took control of Algiers on behalf of the Ottomans in the early 16th century.

The Barbary corsairs were seafaring pirates who used hit-and-run tactics on merchant shipping and coastal Christian towns in Southern Europe, eventually expanding to northern islands in the Atlantic Ocean. They plundered treasures and took slaves. It is said that between 1530 and 1780, they captured over a million slaves, many men chained to the oars of their fighting ships, and many women becoming concubines for the Ottoman leaders' harems or sold for profit. Wealthy families could sometimes repatriate their loved ones with money. Like the Templars, the Barbary pirates became very wealthy.

The European pirates brought advanced sailing and shipbuilding techniques to the Barbary Coast around 1600, which enabled the corsairs to extend their activities into the Atlantic Ocean.

It is said that some of the outcast and hunted Templars took up with their former adversaries along the Barbary Coast in retaliation for their treatment by their Secular and Papal overlords. The skull and crossbones flag became a symbol of pirates throughout the Mediterranean and New World and everywhere in between.

Jan Janszoon von Haarlem, known as Reis Murat the Younger, was a Dutchman who converted to Islam after being captured in 1618. He founded the Republic of Salé, serving as its first President and Commander. His Salé Rover fleet numbered eighteen.

In 1627 Murat Reis captured the island of Lundy in the Bristol Channel, holding it as his northern base until 1632.

In 1631 he led a raid on Iceland to acquire slaves. On his way back, he stopped at Baltimore, West Cork, on June 20th, the only Barbary pirate attack on Ireland. There he seized little property but captured 108 English slaves, leaving the terrified Irish inhabitants behind.

In 1635, near the Tunisian coast, Murat Reis was surprised and captured by the Knights Hospitaller of Malta. He was imprisoned and tortured in the notorious dark dungeons. He escaped during a massive Corsair attack on Malta in 1640, a broken and ill man.

The effects of the Barbary raids peaked in the early-to-mid-17th century.

In 1785, pirates from Algiers captured two American merchant ships and held twenty-one men aboard for ransom, demanding about $60,000. Americans refused, and negotiations dragged on for more than ten years. President Jefferson brought the standoff to an end by dispatching American warships to Tripoli to engage the Ottoman Empire. In the First and Second Tripolian Wars (1801 – 1805), America was victorious, the prisoners were freed, and the Barbary pirates never again took American ships hostage for ransom.

There is a great affinity between the peoples and governments of the United States of America and the Republic of Ireland. Both countries suffered under the yoke of British authority, and both needed a bloody revolution to break free of their oppressor.

In both cases, the revolution was fueled by a world war. World War 1, 1914-1918 was really the second world war on planet earth. The Seven Years War 1753-1963, which pitted Britain with Prussia against France with Spain in a struggle for global dominance, was the first.

Interestingly, this world war had roots in colonial America in conflicts between Great Britain and France in 1754, when the British sought to expand into territory (Canada) claimed by the French in North America. The war came to be known as the French and Indian War, with both the British and the French and their respective Native American allies fighting for control of territory.

Hostilities were heightened when a joint British and native Mingo force led by a 22-year-old Lieutenant Colonel, George Washington, and Chief Tanacharison, ambushed a small French force at the Battle of Jumoville Glen on 28 May 1754. The conflict exploded across the colonial boundaries and extended to Britain's seizure of hundreds of French merchant ships at sea, with Horace Walpole describing his contemporary Washington's role therein as "the volley fired by a young Virginian in the backwoods of America that set the world on fire."

Although fighting on the side of Britain at the time, this ignited a young Washington to eventually lead the fight for freedom of the thirteen colonies of America when Britain turned the thumb screws of taxation on its American territory.

The British finally won this war for Canada with their victory over the French on the Plains of Abraham, Quebec, in 1759.

When the time came after the 1767 punitive Townshend Tax Act leading to the Boston Massacre of 1770 by the British, and the Tea Act leading to the Boston Tea Party and the retaliatory British Intolerable Acts, the fuse was lit for revolution. Washington was the architect. The French were the patriots' allies.

A hundred and forty years later in Ireland, World War I was a catalyst for revolution. This time it was Germany as an ally who afforded the opportunity for a successful campaign, while the British were focused on the terrible war on the continent. For over three hundred years after the defeat of the Gaelic Irish Clans and their Spanish supporters at the Battle of Kinsale in 1602, the Irish were in rebellion against their oppressive overlords. Taxation was only a small part of their problem. The British had attempted to annihilate all vestiges of the Irish way of life, religion, legal Brehon system, and its populace.

In this case, the rebellion that "set Ireland on fire" was the Easter Rising in 1916. Interestingly it was financially bankrolled and overseen by affluent Irish patriots in the United States, organized in a group called the Clan na Gael. A young Irish rebel, Michael Collins, was the aide-de-camp for Joseph Plunkett, one of the main organizers, as they hunkered down in the rebel headquarters, the Dublin General Post Office, during that fateful week.

Michael knew that this method of attempting to overthrow the British by occupying buildings and hoping they would not be bombed by their oppressor was militarily fatal and martyrdom at best. He survived in captivity to plot a different kind of revolution, [1] one that returned to the ways of his Gaelic clansmen, guerilla warfare. These were the hit-and-run tactics to disrupt society and business, the British way of life. They would destroy the police garda stations and men, disrupt the postal, telephone, and railway systems, blockade the roads, and do anything to bring the nation to a halt. Beyond that, Michael knew that the British had an effective spy system, particularly out of the British stronghold Castle. He would develop his own spy and assassination system to ferret out and eliminate the British spies to keep his military actions secret and secure.

Washington is the pioneer in seventeenth-century America and Collins in twentieth-century Ireland—two inspirational champions who led their patriots to overthrow the brutal British.

Yet there are crucial differences. There were thirteen fledgling colonies in an untamed country spread out down the Atlantic seaboard in 1775. Conflict erupted in Massachusetts, the furthest north colony, and spread southward. The British forces in America were an ocean away from King George III and his government, with military supply lines tenuous at best. Here, pitched battles could be successful, like the battle of Saratoga.

Ireland in the twentieth century was a well-developed industrialized country, totally under the thumb of Britain. Military supply lines were immediately available, with England one hundred and thirty-five miles away. The Irish rebels did not have the military technology and weaponry of the British. There was no way to defeat the British by force.

Yet the patriots of both republics were successful in breaking free from Britain's tyranny.

Another difference is how quickly civil war came to both countries after the split from British rule was over—eighty-four years in the case of the United States of America—and zero years in the case of the Republic of Ireland, for entirely distinct reasons.

Happy reading!
Stephen Finlay Archer

ACKNOWLEDGMENTS

Once again, the author is indebted to Manzanita Writers Press of San Andreas, California, for its tireless support in editing and production of these novels. Of note are its founding director and creative editor Monika Rose, as well as book designer Joyce Dedini who took me under their wings to wrestle my manuscripts into shape. Thank you, ladies!

There are a number of readers who have given me constructive feedback for *Book Six Fortunes*, including Bob Kolakowski, Kathy Archer, and Joy Roberts. Thank you all.

The image of one folio from the magnificent *Book Ballymote*, which is presented in the historical background section 3, is reproduced by permission of the Royal Irish Academy. Thank you.

I wish to acknowledge once again the painting of the Customs House on Fire, which was so brilliantly painted by Mr. Norman Teeling, the visual illustrative chronicler of the Irish struggle for freedom in the twentieth century.

Northern Ireland's famous artist Sir John Lavery was best known for portraits and wartime depictions. He was tangentially involved in the War of Independence and the Irish Civil War by giving Michael Collins and his compatriots the use of his London home during the prolonged negotiations leading to the Anglo-Irish Treaty of December 1921. He painted "Penitential Beds," which sounds like it should be hard prison bunk beds, but it is a beautiful landscape of the ancient Celtic monk's beehive dwelling ruins on Station Island, Lough Derg, Donegal where pilgrims have come from all over Europe to walk these penitential bed circles since the dawn of Christianity in Ireland. Thank you, Prior La Flynn, for the use of this delightful painting, the images of the Betelius and Carve maps and the photograph of St. Patrick's Cross, all contained in your informative booklet titled St. Patrick's Purgatory (1987).

The Map #4 Lough Derg Pilgrim's Path was expertly created by East West Mapping found at (www.eastwestmapping.ei). Thank you for its important use to help tell my story.

Most of all, I wish to express my undying love and appreciation to the woman who, for more than thirty years, has been the wind beneath my wings, my darling wife, Kathy. She has wholeheartedly supported this new journey in our lives, even though it was not in our plans when we retired from the aerospace business almost two decades ago. It is she who wisely recommends that I finish writing the entire saga of the Irish Clans series of novels first, rather than focusing on marketing along the journey. I love you Grandly and Forever!

Stephen Finlay Archer

The author writes Irish historical fiction. His latest eight-novel series, *The Irish Clans*, covers the Irish revolutionary period from 1915 to 1923. This Irish family saga, full of swashbuckling characters and page-turning action, tells the true story of Ireland's conflict with England. It is also a personal portrayal since the fictitious story involves his own ancestral family as they are drawn into the conflict of their Irish homeland, while residing in his birthplace of Toronto, Canada.

Archer lives in Northern California with his wife Kathy. He is a member of Writers Unlimited in California Goldrush Country and the North American Historical Novel Society. Before his retirement, he was an Aerospace Manager directing large-scale, delivery-in orbit, satellite systems for the U.S. Navy and NASA/NOAA.

Stephen Finlay Archer's books are available on Amazon.com and directly from the author, publisher, and Ingram distribution.

Stephen can be reached at:

Email: stephenfinlayarcher@gmail.com
Website: www.stephenfinlayarcher.com
LinkedIn: (Stephen Finlay Archer)
Twitter: @StephenFinlayArcher
Facebook: StephenFinlayArcher
Blog: www.stephenfinlayarcher.com/blog

TESTIMONIALS

***Midwest Book Review of The Irish Clans Series by Stephen Finlay Archer by* Diane Donovan, Editor**

I was pleased to read your fine books and to recommend them to others: I hope your efforts generate many sales for you!

Searchers: The Irish Clans: Book One
ISBN 9780990801931

Searchers is the first book in a series of novels about the Irish revolutionary wars between clans. It's especially recommended for historical novel readers who want an in-depth touch of the military, social, cultural, and religious history of Ireland's clans, politics, and Celtic heritage.

It's a fictitious epic that presents the premise of a secret Clans Pact that hides wealth from the British, crafting an engaging series of clashes and scenarios from real-world experiences.

In this opening story, a death in 1915 Ireland fuels the flames of revolution while concurrently, in America, Irish immigrants who remain connected to the Old Country become immersed in the conflict. Three very different characters are drawn into this fray: Claire, an Irish girl who has amnesia after surviving the Torpedo sinking of the Lusitania ocean liner and is renamed Morgan by Tadgh. She has connections to the past that could influence future choices; Tadgh, a rebel sea captain who becomes embroiled in a decision that will lead to his validity as a Clan Chieftain; and Collin, a Canadian husband faced with an impossible choice.

This story operates on many levels as it outlines a search for identity, wealth, redemption, and validity which captures disparate personal transformations.

Irish peoples around the world became embroiled in the revolutionary clashes that emerged between 1915 and 1923. *Searchers* displays an attention to detail that captures these events as they evolve on more than the home soil of Ireland.

From growing commitments to the cause displayed by Morgan and others to relics, secrets, and emerging political battles with the British, Stephen Finlay Archer crafts a story replete in the special interests, that's both personal and political, centered on and reflected by characters who stand up to each other to support their ideals of the Irish identity.

Dialogue between these characters neatly sum up and outlines many of these dilemmas: "Don't ya be throwing Denis McCarthy's words back at me, Sean," Tadgh protested. "Parnell tried the pen, and the British bastards spoke with forked tongue. Look what's happening to the Home Rule Bill to finally integrate our homeland. These demons are allowing for the buildup of arms for the Ulster Volunteers to stop the bill by force if necessary."

Readers might think they need prior familiarity with Irish history in order to appreciate the evolving scenario in *Searchers*, but the only prerequisite is an interest in Irish culture and affairs.

Archer takes care of the rest, personalizing the simmering politics of the nation and times by creating a host of characters who display special interests and values. These take on new meaning under the changing, volatile political environment that affects the world.

The result is a fine introduction to the series that successfully crafts a series of encounters and scenarios to set the stage for future stories of each individual and Ireland as a whole. Historical fiction collections and any interested in Irish heritage will welcome the detailed survey introduced in *Searchers: The Irish Clans.*

Entente: The Irish Clans: Book Two
ISBN 9780990801955

The ancient clans' pact and influence that was outlined and developed in *Searchers* expands in *Entente: The Irish Clans: Book Two* of the series.

Here, Irish revolutionaries involve Germany in their cause as World War I emerges, challenging Irish Republican Tadgh McCarthy and his lover Morgan to continue their battle for Irish freedom, albeit under the cloak of a wider-ranging war.

As these events take place, Irish Canadian Collin continues to agonize over his vanished sister Claire's fate and his own failing marriage.

The interplays between politics and personal lives and family clans and world events, that began in *Searchers* broadens and continues in Entente, where the overlay of war changes everything in a blend of fact and fiction that keeps readers involved not just in politics, but personal lives.

Stephen Finlay Archer's ability to weave history into a gripping, action-packed story line that captures disparate characters' special interests and dilemmas keeps his series absorbing even for readers who may harbor little initial interest in the historical fiction genre.

Morgan and Tadgh's relationship and concerns were introduced in *Searchers,* but here the two really blossom as world events expand to encompass and challenge their beliefs and objectives.

From blockades and risky confrontations to preparations for a Rising that operate within the confines of bigger conflicts, Archer creates another thoroughly engrossing story that contrasts Irish interests and perspectives with events going on in the rest of the world.

His ability to keep these developments moving swiftly on both a personal and political level makes Entente a powerful story. It builds on its predecessor's events, but also stands nicely alone as it weaves a tale of Irish forces continuing their struggles under the atmosphere and outside conflicts of other nations during World War I.

Readers who like historical fiction infused with the lives of ordinary people turned revolutionaries will find *Entente's* ability to craft believable characters and scenarios based on historical truth spiced with fictional events makes for riveting reading that, once again, is hard to put down.

Rising: The Irish Clans: Book Three
ISBN 9780998691008

Book 3 of The Irish Clans, Rising, continues the evolving story of Irish rebels Tadgh and Morgan, and Irish Canadian Collin, whose sister is still missing. Here, Tadgh and Morgan participate in the Dublin Easter Rising while Collin makes the decision to leave his wife and newborn son to continue his search for his missing sister in Ireland.

As the Clan continues to look for the Clans Pact treasures and faces many opponents, the tides of war rise. The 1916 era is brought to life by Stephen Finlay Archer's attention to not just historical detail, but interpersonal relationships.

As events move from Canada to Ireland and characters move beyond their comfort zones to tackle new problems and possibilities, readers gain a vivid sense of the times, its influences, and the conundrums faced by all as the world changes: "This is only the beginning, Sean. You mind me. We will exterminate the British here in Ireland." O'Casey pretended not to hear.

From a battle on the Irish Sea at Dublin, Ireland to terrible situations experienced by those devoted to the Cause in that city, and clues provided in the Clans Pact, readers receive a combination of treasure hunt, evolving social and political challenges, and changing hearts and minds. Each character is charged with operating outside of their experience and expectations, growing from their decisions and world influences alike.

Between dangers on the waters to intrigue on shore, Archer juxtaposes disparate journeys of life and death and brings tension to a riveting new level as each character searches for answers, lives through atrocities, and uncovers answers to their personal and political conundrums.

It's hard to say what is more compelling: the intrigue and plots evolved by rebels Tadgh and Morgan as they struggle to uncover the Clans Pact secrets, or Collin's desperate attempts to find his missing sister against all odds.

Sometimes, the love for one's life and country clash. Sometimes the characters despair of any kind of resolution that will allow them to live in freedom, health, and happiness.

The intrigue and questions keep Rising fast paced as Archer highlights the ideas and actions that lend to an inevitable clash, personalizing Irish and world politics in a manner that will keep even readers without a ground in Irish affairs engrossed and wondering what will happen next.

That's because each character's individual perspective, efforts, and convictions shine in a story replete with action, unexpected twists, and ongoing challenges.

Historical fiction and Irish readers are in for a treat.

McCarthy Gold: The Irish Clans: Book Four
ISBN 9780998691046

Book 4 of the Irish Clans series takes place after the Easter Uprising chronicled in the third story and follows The Clans' search for the McCarthy gold treasure and the ongoing efforts of Collins to find his sister.

Containing more of a treasure hunt atmosphere than the previous books, *McCarthy Gold* will engage readers with a different tone and flavor that retains the historical backdrop while moving into puzzles and problem-solving scenarios to intrigue those interested in hidden treasures and suspense.

Each character continues to develop as new dilemmas affect their choices. Will Collin permanently abandon his wife and their newborn child in Canada to pursue the truth about his sister's whereabouts? Can Tadgh and Morgan keep their activities secret from the Protestant Times and other forces like rogue policeman Boyle that would interfere with their mission?

From the historical religious significance of the O'Donnell Clan to Boyle's hunt for treasures (now likely in possession of the McCarthy Clans Pact), Stephen Finlay Archer provides a story that entwines politics, passion, and intrigue with an edict to fulfill forefathers' noble plans: "We are the generation chosen by God and destiny to recover the treasures of our Clans so that they can be used to fuel our glorious revolution."

Once again, history and mystery entwine with cultural revelations that probe the foundations of social and historical change in Ireland.

Because the Clans and their stories and books are interwoven and build upon a foundation established in Book 1, it's highly recommended that readers adopt a sequential pursuit of this series. The rich development of characters, perspectives, and missions of transformation and discovery could not be gained from reading just one of these books, while the progressive action and adventures that build upon one another to further the story are nicely constructed.

McCarthy Gold introduces new considerations about the effects of heritage, wealth, and the attitudes of traitors and believers on events that unfold here.

Its development further intrigue and suspense keeps the action vivid as the historical backdrop expands, making for a fine series addition that continues to grow its characters and purposes against a historically accurate, rich backdrop of action.

All these books should be standard acquisitions for any library interested in Irish history and culture.

Revolution: The Irish Clans: Book Five
ISBN 9781952314001

While it may seem that revolution already fuels the atmosphere in the first four books in the Irish Clans series, Book 5 takes a closer look at the unfolding events that opened the series in 1915 and moves towards a civil war in 1922–1923.

Once again, the lasting legacy and rekindled growth of the McCarthy and O'Donnell Clans add fuel to the fire of anti-British forces and internal debates that threaten to tear Ireland apart.

Hidden treasure and new possibilities again play a major role in the uprising as individuals pursue both personal goals and wider-ranging ideals. But the heart of *Revolution* lies in its ability to depict connections between historical events, the 1900s challenges that affect Morgan and Tadgh's lives, and the forces that bring them to the brink of drowning.

From puzzles and their connections to quaffing drinks in pubs that foster the plans and rudiments of war, Morgan and Tadgh navigate an increasingly dangerous atmosphere that's on the brink of exploding. Readers are introduced to Irish culture and sentiments in a manner that brings these times and perspectives to life.

As Archer builds his series, it's evident that its foundation of solid historical facts (reviewed in the back of each book, to provide history buffs with detailed information) lends to the evolving story.

It's easy to absorb medieval Irish history, myths, and culture when these elements are presented through the eyes, hearts, and experiences of memorable characters whose individual concerns and pursuits become embroiled in Irish politics.

Revolution both enhances the series and, once again, concludes in a cliffhanger designed to set the stage for the next addition to the series.

Archer's ability to build intrigue, incorporate a secret pact and treasure hunt into Ireland's evolving struggles, and present all events through the eyes of characters who each hold personal strengths and ambitions creates a story that is engrossing, hard to put down, and another strong compliment to the series as a whole.

Collections strong in historical fiction, treasure hunt intrigue, and Irish culture and history will find each book in this series a sterling example of the ability of historical fiction to educate in a lively, compelling manner.

Historical Fiction Company

Editorial Review of *Revolution: The Irish Clans, Book Five*
By Stephen Finlay Archer - Book release in December 2021

'He counseled Michael Collins to act as if the Republic was a fact. He would often say, "We defeat the British by ignoring them. As the American John Adams once said, 'Revolution starts in the hearts and the minds of the people.'"'

This immersive and jam-packed story begins with the Irish revolution in 1915 and extends to the civil war ending in 1922 to 1923. To say this is epic is putting it mildly, and to just simply note that there are mythological elements which bind the past and the present would not do the book justice.

The author brings to the reader an incredible history of the McCarthy and O'Donnell Clans, and while history tells of their defeat in ancient times, they are by no means extinct. Linked by blood and a medieval pact across the ocean, Ireland and America, the lives of the characters entwine in a quest to support the revolution headed by none other than the infamous Michael Collins. While one part of the family, Collin, and Kathy O'Donnell, seek to begin a new life, settling in a home and raising children, in Toronto Canada, another part of the same family, Tadgh and Morgan McCarthy, fight on the front lines to bring freedom to Ireland, fighting alongside Michael and a host of other revolutionaries.

The connection begins with the Black Tom explosion near Ellis Island which damages the Statue of Liberty, a fireball which nearly kills Collin and Kathy... and links Germany to the Irish Clan na Gael who is trying to use the German war to their advantage—that is, to find a way to export guns from America to Ireland for their cause while hiding the shipment under pretense that the guns are going to Britain for the war effort. Enter Tadgh McCarthy.

Tadgh uses his contacts in America while staying with his wife's brother, Collin, to put the deal in motion. All is set and all goes well, at least for a time. Without giving away any spoilers, the author does a remarkable job in revealing the actual history of the time period, the passion and the patriotism fueled in the fiery hearts of Ireland's Gaelic heritage—not just during WWI but tracing the roots into the far past where religious myths and divine intervention, where 'luck' plays a role in unearthing a vast Clan treasure, one which funds the revolution.

In one quote from the author, he states that 'readers who are interested in Ireland's struggles for freedom and its storied but often mystical history will enjoy The Irish Clans series. Readers who enjoyed The Da Vinci Code, National Treasure, or Outlander will be enthralled by my stories.' I have to concur with his statement, for the essence of all three of those books resonates in just this one book alone, and now I am intrigued to start with book one and read them all.

At the heart of the story is real people who simply want a better life for themselves and their families, and Mr. Archer does a remarkable job at offering us well-rounded, passionate characters in extraordinary circumstances. This book is alive with action and lush detail, giving the reader an Irish history lesson wrapped in an intense and captivating story.

This is drama to the ultimate level. It has it all – history, adventure, intrigue, war, passion, love, escape, betrayal, sorrow, pain – all the elements which connect us all as humans. This engrossing book is a voice speaking from the past and linking history to the possibilities of myths and the promises of the future.

I began this review with the poignant quote stated to Michael Collins, the quote by John Adams of revolution beginning in the hearts and minds of the people. This vibrant story captures this in every detail – the lengths a person, a country, will go to find freedom from oppression. Every society has its story of freedom. This is Ireland's story, and the implications echo across generations and across oceans. 'Man's inhumanity to man' screams loud in this book, the sacrifice, the blood, the bravery, and desperation for justice.

From a reader's standpoint, the prose was easy to follow, and very engaging, providing just enough history to infuse knowledge while not diverting from the storyline. Mr. Archer is quite the original storyteller, taking elements from all the aforementioned books and crafting a well-told story; however, my one side point is that about halfway through, I felt I was reading two different books. When the storyline veered from Bloody Sunday to the search for the ancient lost medieval treasure, I felt as if I switched books... not so much in engagement and interest (as the story still intrigues) but just in the flow. I understood why the switch was necessary as Archer introduced the mystical Celtic vein, but I did feel like I went from reading "Rob Roy" to "National Treasure." Overall, though, even with the switch, I was always immersed in the story and the development of what happens to the characters and their fight for freedom.

Some of my favorite passages from the book:

The side trip taken by Collin O'Donnell to Independence Hall in Philadelphia when he sees the Liberty Bell - "The impact of liberty, the concept of freedom, resonated. There was damage, that crack, but he took comfort in the fact that history on the side of righteousness had prevailed. Perhaps this would be a model for Ireland."

The brutality and oppression experienced by the revolutionaries—"The IRA had just killed three soldiers in Dublin, the first such deaths in that city since the battles in the Easter Rising. As a result, Churchill authorized the Black and Tans to begin burning towns and killing civilians. This reminded Griffiths of the slash and burn tactics employed by Cromwell's monsters during the Confederate wars of the sixteen hundreds. Something drastic had to be done."

"God in heaven, this is a tragic day for Ireland."—the presentation of Bloody Sunday is heartbreaking. Michael Collins 'disappears like a ghost into the fog' after Tadgh and Morgan survive the episode at the stadium, and Tadgh vows to him to find a way to continue to help the cause. Thus, he and his wife, Morgan, delve further into their family history in search of the treasure and secrets hidden in the Book of Ballymote.

I am left on the edge of what is to come, and I look forward to continuing the saga with Tadgh and Morgan McCarthy.

Revolution: The Irish Clans, Book Five is awarded five stars by The Historical Fiction Company